HAZEL MCHAFF~~IE~~ trained ... Sciences, and became a Research Fellow ... in the field ha~~s~~ led ... has published almost a hundred art... the last of which, *Crucial Decisions at* British Medical Association Book of the ... most prestigious awards in medical publishing. Her novel ... represented a culmination of her far-reaching medical knowledge and her literary talent.

Praise for Hazel McHaffie's medical novels

There are very few novels which deal with the issues of contemporary medical ethics in the lively and intensely readable way which Hazel McHaffie's books do. She uses her undoubted skill as a storyteller to weave tales of moral quandary, showing us with subtlety and sympathy how we might tackle some of the ethical issues which modern medicine has thrown up. She has demonstrated that hard cases make good reading. ALEXANDER MCCALL SMITH

McHaffie accomplishes something of great value for the reader – something deep within the ethical and far away from the bio-ethical. She exposes the potential for authenticity within intimate human relationships. THE LANCET

From Tolstoy to Cronin, writers have raided medicine in search of the raw material of literature. How appropriate that Hazel McHaffie should be repaying the compliment by using fiction to help us grapple with the ethical dilemmas so often and so effortlessly conjured up by modern medicine. GEOFF WATTS, WRITER, JOURNALIST AND BBC PRESENTER ON SCIENTIFIC AND MEDICAL TOPICS

McHaffie's books are skillfully written to bring out the complex ethical issues we as doctors, nurses, patients, or relatives, may face in dealing with difficult issues... These books are a welcome development of what has been called the narrative turn in medical ethics. THE BRITISH MEDICAL JOURNAL

Hazel McHaffie illuminates the novel moral complexities of the modern world with dramatic insight... a great read. JAMES LE FANU, GP, WRITER AND MEDICAL COLUMNIST FOR THE DAILY TELEGRAPH

[The author] has woven and moulded her extensive knowledge of ethics, moral dilemmas and clinical concerns with great skill into real life, everyday, stories of drama and of tragedy. INFANT

Right To Die

HAZEL MCHAFFIE

Luath Press Limited

EDINBURGH

www.luath.co.uk

First published 2008

ISBN (10): 1-906307-21-0
ISBN (13): 978-1-906307-21-9

The paper used in this book is recyclable.
It is made from low-chlorine pulps produced in a low-energy,
low-emission manner from renewable forests.

The author's right to be identified as author of this book
under the Copyright, Designs and Patents Act 1988 has been asserted.

The publisher acknowledges subsidy from
Scottish
Arts Council
towards publication of this volume.

Printed and bound by CPI Mackays, Chatham

Typeset in 10.5 point Sabon and 9.5 point Frutiger Light

Acknowledgements

Degenerative illnesses strike fear into the hearts of most of us and learning about the effects of Motor Neurone Disease was a daunting experience. I am indebted to Dr William Whiteley, Sandra Wilson, Ann Callaghan, Carole Ferguson and the Motor Neurone Disease Association for their guidance and advice.

During the writing of *Right to Die* three members of my own family were fighting serious illnesses, so immersing myself in the decline of my principal character could have been overwhelming. The combined support of a wide circle of special people, too numerous to mention by name, kept me afloat and I thank them all most sincerely. They should take credit for enabling any emotional authenticity in the book.

Professor Kenneth Boyd deserves a special mention. He has managed to fit reading my manuscripts into his busy schedule for more than a decade now and I am immensely grateful for his constant encouragement and wise critique.

To the team at Luath – Gavin MacDougall and Leila Cruickshank in particular – a big thank you for believing in the product and involving me in the choices. Jennie Renton is the best editor any author could wish for. She held a kindly mirror up to my faults and then stood back while I did my own pruning. I salute you, Jennie.

Once again my two most devoted fans, Jonathan McHaffie and Rosalyn Crich, who are also my son and daughter, maintained an active interest in my writing and gave me valuable feedback. And my husband, David, tolerated my preoccupation with his usual equanimity, gave me the benefit of his meticulous eye for detail and became the invisible coffee-maker.

For Pat, who faced her own dying with such courage and faith,
but chose a very different ending.

'Murderess! Murderess! Murderess!' Already huddled into a corner of her cell, her only retreat was to close her eyes to the condemnation.

Two rough hands reached out and jerked her arms from their protective arc around her head; ten inches away a single pair of eyes glittered with hatred. Dark brown eyes. Eyes that Adam had inherited from his mother, except that his had been liquid, soft, admiring…

'Yes! Murderess! May you rot in hell. Eternally!' Mavis ground out through clenched teeth.

Sharp fingers clawed the flesh of Naomi's arms, then Mavis spat in her face and flung her daughter-in-law from her.

It was no consolation to wake from this recurring nightmare. The guilt Naomi carried during her conscious hours was no more restful than the tortures of the night. She didn't need Freud to analyse the central role Adam's mother played in every variation of her dream.

She threw back the bedclothes and let the breeze from the open window dry the trickles of sweat from her body. For a long time she lay staring at the ceiling, but in the end, as always, her eyes flicked to the bedside cabinet… to the plain white envelope. Even from her position on the far side of the bed, the typed instruction was clearly legible: *Open only after my death.*

Maybe that was why these fearful nightmares persisted. Maybe if she moved the envelope somewhere where she couldn't see it… But then she'd never open it.

With trembling fingers she inched open the sealed flap. Words lurched on the single sheet of paper before reluctantly forming an orderly queue. Naomi read the entire page without moving anything but her eyes; even her breathing seemed suspended.

Every instinct screamed at her not to obey his instructions, not to go into his study, but clutching the paper in one suddenly damp hand, she forced herself to get up and walk down the hallway.

Do it, girl.

Open the door.

Go to his desk.

Switch on his computer.

Rows of icons glared at the intrusion. Robotically her finger on the mouse button guided the cursor.

Open folder: 'Diary of a disease'.

Open file 1: 'The beginning'.

13 JUNE 2006—Today I heard my future collapsing. Not yesterday as you might expect – the day I got my diagnosis – but today. Curiously, it wasn't one spectacular explosion, but a kind of defeated crumbling in on itself. The sound of... what? Twenty, thirty, forty years, just being extinguished. The authorities know exactly who's responsible for this vile deed, but as the victim of the crime, it'll take me a bit longer to get up to speed with the villain's *modus operandi* and the consequences for the future – what's left of it, that is. And being a wordsmith by trade, I guess I want to try to capture my reactions, exactly what it feels like here and now, before other people throw disguises over the bits and pieces that survive the blast, and before I have time to adjust to the changing dimensions of my life.

Perhaps I should have been prepared to some extent at least, but I confess I wasn't. I was expecting to hear 'virus', 'stress', 'after-effects of whatever' – standard answers to a hotch-potch of symptoms. Medical-speak for 'I haven't a clue'. Presumably it takes time to unwire the brain from that sort of expectation and leave it receptive to a completely different message. In my case it took fifteen hours.

I heard the actual words at 4.15 yesterday afternoon. I don't remember driving home afterwards but I do recall a vague surprise that the house was fixed in its usual place, the washing machine had finished its cycle and the clothes lay deflated around the drum waiting to be hung out on the line as if nothing had happened. How annoying. Why hadn't Naomi pegged them out before she left for work? – in case. And I remember a feeling of betrayal that the cat wasn't intuitive enough to know that this was one occasion when I'd have appreciated the feel of her softness wrapping around my leg, one of her full-bodied purrs vibrating against a limb still sensitised to such a welcome. Instead I got a half-hearted identity check before she closed her eyes and settled back to sleep.

I felt incredibly alone.

When I surfaced at dawn this morning the doctor's words were written in capital letters across my first coherent thought. I fought the realisation, willing myself back to that daze of yesterday, when I was incapable of joined-up thinking, never mind anything remotely analytical or philosophical – or better still, to the blissful ignorance of the day before.

But today's knowledge refused to be suppressed. As the blood-orange stain from the rising sun spread higher in the sky, the reality of my predicament seeped out through my restraining sandbags. So here I am; trying to take the next logical step. One thing I do know: I can't deal with anyone else's emotions or opinions, and certainly not their platitudes – not yet. Not until I've got my own ideas into some sort of order. And that won't happen overnight. I've got to inch myself into this one.

I've always been wary of knee-jerk reactions. My phlegmatic responses infuriate Naomi at times, I know.

'Sometimes – just once in a blue moon – can't you get mad and scream against an injustice or a tragedy or just something that irritates you?' she yelled at me one day.

'Why? What good would that do?' I said.

'It'd let me see you're flesh and blood, not a stone!' She was positively spitting exasperation. I could see that, even back then when I was still pretty clueless about female behaviour.

But perhaps that very habit will stand me in good stead now. Heaven knows, I need all the help I can get. Anyway, I'm going to try to apply a bit of logic to this situation. Take it step by step. Talk myself through it.

Okay. Here goes.

Point 1. You've had what they call a life-changing experience.

Agreed.

Point 2. You've got to try to get to grips with this and work out a strategy to cope with the change and live the life.

Agreed.

Point 3. First step in the strategy.

???

....

I've been sitting here for several minutes now. Not writing anything, staring at the screen. I put the dots in just so the machine would know I was still there, still 'active'.

I never saw myself as a coward. Last week if somebody had challenged me to say what I would do in these circumstances, I'd have been pretty confident I'd be strong and practical and just get on with it. I am one of life's copers. I don't do hysterical. I don't do maudlin. I don't do ostrich.

First illusion shattered – well, maybe just cracked.

Point 4. I have to get over or around or underneath this block.

But how?

I know. I'll pretend it's a column for the rag that pays my wages. Just the usual Wednesday scribble.

First draft: *Adam's Analysis*

I've always hated that expression: today is the first day of the rest of your life. So hackneyed. But today – the day after my diagnosis – I felt the truth of it. Nothing will ever be the same again. My face has been pressed up against my mortality, its filthy stench has been forced into my nostrils, its grit has grazed the corneas of my eyes. Whichever of my senses I use, the stimuli I process will be tainted by the effects of yesterday's encounter with destiny.

Okay, I know we're all on the road to death but this is like getting into a souped-up machine with no brakes and teetering on the brink of a one-in-three gradient with no escape routes and no emergency services standing by.

How do I personally feel?

I feel as if I'm lying flat on the floor with an entire building crushing my chest. Whichever way I swivel my eyes it's pitch black. I know they say (who exactly are 'they'?) once the shock wears off, the ceiling lifts. It'll have to lift a bit if I'm not to suffocate to death this very week. But the brutal reality is, this particular ceiling isn't ever going to lift very far. Even on good days I know it'll be there, lurking like a malevolent presence. I can't go back to the illusions of babyhood; thinking that if I can't see it, it doesn't exist. Speaking of which, we had a geometry teacher, Mr Fuggins, (yep, that really was his name) who used to prove to us with step-by-step logic, that if a cactus flowered in the desert and nobody saw it, it didn't flower; that a yellow canary was actually blue; or that two and two equalled five. I never could see the flaw in his arguments and it was an ongoing insecurity in a troubled adolescence.

Anyway this thing is there and not even Fuggins, long since gone to argue philosophy with his Maker, could magic it away. Worse than that, it's actually coming towards me – in tiny increments maybe – but the general direction is always down, never up. There are no heroic firemen out there who're going to rush in and shore it up at the eleventh hour. I'm not going to be able to gather one superhuman burst of power and energy and escape from this particular collapsing building. And I don't believe in an interventionist God.

It will come down.

I will be trapped inside it.

Nobody will rescue me.

Given that inexorable fact, what am I going to do to distract my attention while this happens? And how will I spend my life – what's left of it?

You hear of people who know they have x minutes left before a bomb goes off, or a vehicle bursts into flames, or they drown. People say their whole life flashes before them. But what about when the countdown is longer – weeks or months – or even years? You can't keep flashing back. I mean, even I'd get bored with that number of replays of my quite unexceptional life up to now.

Okay, I know there are saintly souls facing death who dedicate their lives to doing something altruistic. Carrying out daring stunts. (Nothing to lose really if your days are numbered anyway, says he, cynically.) Raising stacks of money for good causes. Establishing help-lines to encourage other people going through the same tunnel. Is that the sort of thing I want for myself? I don't know. Not yet. I have no perspective on this thing yet.

But one thing I do see, even at this early stage. I'll have to measure my life in other terms now. The question is, what terms? What really matters?

A sudden leap of fluff from the floor made Naomi startle. The pale blue-grey hair slid silkily through her fingers as Noelani curled onto her lap.

'I know. I know. You can't work it out. He's gone but he's here. Me too.'

Slow tears dripped into the forgiving fur as her breath caught unevenly in her throat. It was like listening to Adam's voice again. His presence seemed to be curling out of the screen, pervading the very air in the room. His fingers were on the mouse, warm over hers.

'Oh, Noelani. What are we going to do without him?'

The wide eyes of the Persian stared back unblinkingly. The breed had been her choice, the name Adam's.

'Why on earth Noelani?' she'd asked.

'It's Hawaiian for beautiful one from heaven,' he'd grinned.

'And since when did you know Hawaiian?'

'Since yesterday. Got it out of a book of names. Nice choice though, huh?'

Noelani was certainly beautiful. With all the elegance of her pedigree but all the common sense bred out of her. More heavenly than earthly – he had a point. And she was indisputably his cat; his study was her territory, she shadowed him more assiduously than any private eye.

Naomi shivered and resolutely turned her back on the haunting emptiness. She made herself back-track through the text to mention of her own name. The incident had remained in her memory too. They'd only been together a short while then. She'd been fuming about the iniquity of a group of suburban housewives campaigning against a hostel being proposed for their street. Adam had listened to her ranting with a bemused expression on his face, and then shrugged his shoulders without comment.

'Have you been listening to a word I've said?' she'd flung at him.

'Yes.'

'And?'

'And what?'

'Well, what do you think?'

'About what?'

'These bigoted, privileged housewives, of course!'

'You've said it already.'

'But what do *you* think?'

'It's life. The not-in-my-backyard syndrome.' He'd actually flicked his hand dismissively, fuelling her rage.

'But don't you *care* about these deprived kids?' She'd glared at him.

'Yes, of course I care.'

'Well then?'

'Well what?'

'Well – why don't you *sound* like you care?'

'What does caring sound like? Screaming and shouting? What good would that do?'

'Like me, you mean?'

'Each to their own. But I don't personally go for the hysterical approach.'

It had been the last straw.

'Sometimes – just once in a blue moon – can't you get mad and scream against an injustice or a tragedy or just something that irritates you?' she'd yelled.

'Why? What good would that do?'

'It'd let me see you're flesh and blood, not a stone! That's what. Oh, you are the most maddening creature alive!'

She'd stormed out of the room and thrown washing into the machine before venting her frustration on the unsuspecting roses. The harsh pruning had actually resulted in a vigorous new growth and an abundance of flowers that summer. A happy summer. Happy because they'd committed themselves to being together for the long haul. Happy because their lives were good – fulfilled, healthy. Happy because they had plans for the future. Shared plans.

Summer was always her time of year. She was like an addict deprived of her supply in the melancholy months of winter. Even her mother had teased her that she was a foundling stolen from a tropical desert island.

It was summer now too. Its warmth stole uninvited into Adam's study, its golden light reflected off the edge of his screen. But this year it was an impertinence. How *could* the sun shine? The whole world should have remained shackled to winter.

She jerked the screen crossly to shut out the oblong glare. In the sudden opaqueness behind her fingers she had a sensation of Adam reaching out to her. He'd told her once: 'I'm the wound; you're the cry of pain.' It bound them together in the struggle. If she could only touch him now! Since he had gone

6

beyond her reach she had begun to realise how much touch had meant in their relationship – the easy incidental brushes of close proximity, the spontaneous reaching out of everyday affection, the intimate exploration of passion. Her body was his; his body was hers.

She closed her eyes, willing him to stay, wrapping her arms around herself, hugging the illusion before it faded… as it always did, leaving her free-floating, bereft.

She reached out instinctively. The reflection on the screen approached… retreated.

The cat looked up reproachfully before closing her eyes and settling back to sleep across Naomi's legs.

14 JUNE—Yesterday was another shattering-of-my-illusions day. What a pitiful output! This is me, a professional writer, for goodness' sake! Words are my currency. They've kept me in my favourite brand of port; financed the holidays; paid the mortgage since I was twenty-four. Ask me to write a column on… I don't know – *custard!* – and I can find an angle that'll have you smiling, or make you think, or just force you to dash off a response. And when you've got editors breathing down your neck every week you have to think laterally, quirkily. No mileage in telling Joe Bloggs what he sees and knows without any help from his friends.

So here goes!

I'm picturing my mind like a bag made of stretchy fabric. Sexy silver Lycra – why not! It expands to accommodate thoughts as they come in. It sags when I'm not funnelling new stuff into it. Nobody likes flab. I certainly don't – hence all those hours at the pool and the squash court. So I'm going to set myself a target.

Resolve 1: Keep the bag expanded. Don't let it deflate whatever happens to the old carcass.

Resolve 2: Keep the 'I' in MIND. The real me. The logical, rational, thinking me. The essential Adam Willoughby O'Neill. (Thirty-eight years on I'm still trying to forgive my father for my middle name.) It'll be symbolic of my mental attitude. If the bag stays nice and rounded, so will I be. As long as I retain my identity this thing hasn't beaten me.

Writing 'MIND' inches me towards my goal. Take the 'I' out of it and what have you got? MND. MND. Shorthand. For a disease. A disease which I have. I don't want it, but it's here to stay.

MND. Motor Neurone Disease.

What do I feel at this exact moment, acknowledging that?

Strange. Nothing in particular. Presumably that's because it's just so many letters. I haven't really owned it yet. I'm not really inside it.

Hmm, let's go back to when I first heard it.

Was it only two days ago? Seems like two hundred years. I was still in work mode then. Adam O'Neill, investigative journalist, columnist, would-be novelist. Researching my material. Amassing facts.

What's MND – exactly? What's the treatment? How long have I got? What will happen? What are the options? I was inside my professional armour. The facts weren't for me the man, the patient; they were for my column. Fire away. Ask the relevant questions while you have the expert captive.

And today? Yep. Sitting here consciously absorbing it, it's a totally different kettle of fish.

MND. Motor Neurone Disease.

It's a life sentence. Okay, now we're talking my language. Letters, words, sentences. A sentence. A life sentence. I could write a satirical piece on that. *(Transfer to Ideas folder later) But not now. I mustn't let work deflect me from today's goal.

In spite of the pain Naomi felt a smile twitch the corners of her mouth.

'Trust you, Adam!'

Even in the midst of his personal hell he'd clung to his habits. Free-falling through horror he'd seen the potential to turn his own agony into literary gain.

'I told you! You were never off-duty!' She wagged her finger at the screen.

How often it had happened. The notebook and pencil would suddenly appear in a restaurant where they were supposed to be enjoying an intimate dinner, or she'd find him behind a pot plant scribbling instead of mingling at an art exhibition, or she'd half-wake in the night to find him sitting up in bed committing his ideas to paper before he could go back to sleep. Writing was in his blood. His antennae were always alert for a story, an unusual take, a way in to an opinion. Even, it seemed, facing his own disintegration.

'Come back! All is forgiven. Oh Adam. Adam. How could you leave me?'

A life sentence. No reprieve. No cure. That's why it's 'life'. There's no prospect of a stay of execution hovering on the horizon, nor even just out of sight. Dr Devlin admitted as much.

Devilish Devlin. What a glorious name for this man who announces banishment to hell. It conjures up this cartoon neurologist poking his pronged fork into a cowering patient.

'But it doesn't mean you can't go on living a good life – maybe for some considerable time,' he said, rather too quickly, I thought. Better-throw-this-drowning-man-a-lifebelt sort of reaction.

Okay, let's look at that jolly little promise.

'A good life.' What's that when you unravel it and look at the components? Who knows? All things to all men, I'd say. Is my idea of a good life the same as his? What happens if I don't like this so-called good life? Will my own idea of what's good change as I start to feel the tentacles tightening? Funny how many different metaphors for this thing are coming to my brain. *(Metaphors of illness – transfer to Ideas folder).

Will I end up…?

No, I don't want to go there. Not yet. Not today. I need to pace myself.

'For some considerable time.'

Of course, I instantly asked him, 'Meaning? How long exactly?'

'We can never be exact about these things. Medicine isn't an exact science,' he said.

Literary philistine.

'Well, give me a scale. Some idea.' I wasn't going to let him sneak out of the hole he'd dug that easily. 'Average time.'

'Average? Two to five years. In Scotland something like ten per cent of patients live for five years. But of course some patients have been known to survive over thirty years.'

A second lifebelt. Thrown a second too late. Hey, hang on a minute! A lifebelt? More like a concrete block!

Which is worse: contemplating having only two years to go or knowing that if I'm 'lucky' I might spin this out for over three decades? I ask you! Imagine being slowly extinguished by this creeping disintegration for *thirty years*! No, I don't want to – I *won't* – I *refuse* to imagine any such thing. I'm in control here. It's down to me to make damn sure no such thing happens. But that's for another day. First look at the shape of the monster; then consider the weapons; *then* decide on the strategy.

So what does it look like, this new enemy? It's a bit like a piece of writing. It isn't defined by a full stop – not yet anyway. Nobody knows just how many paragraphs and pages and chapters the book might have, what they'll contain, but I mustn't start writing the end before I've worked out the plot, thought through the sequence, identified the main characters.

Today, right now, there's definitely a storyline: MND's the substance of the book; but *I'm* the principal character, *and* I'm the author – thus far, anyway. I just have to work out how the story will unravel.

Naomi leaned back in Adam's chair staring at his words, seeing instead a sudden vivid image of his face. Her eyes went instinctively to the photograph on the mantelpiece. It had been his choice for his personal sanctum; his favourite. He was standing behind her, arms lightly round her, his chin on her shoulder as they paused for his brother to capture that relaxed, informal moment. Four years ago. Before it happened.

She stared at the picture. His broad smile was so carefree, so happy. His skin was toned, bronzed, smooth over the strong muscles. He exuded health and vitality. She could feel the warmth of his firm embrace, his hand surreptitiously glancing against her breast, the whispered intimacies sweet in her ear.

The emptiness around her now was like a vacuum pumping the reason for her existence out of her body, leaving her light-headed.

Other images invaded her mind. Uncaptured. Unwelcome. Only partially buried. The 'after' images. The shadow in his dark brown eyes exaggerated by the frown drawing his eyebrows together, the right one quirked unevenly above the left. The signs of inner tension: that slightly-too-white crown on his left incisor that had broken the evenness of his smile ever since his climbing accident, clenching down on his lower lip; the restless hand suddenly combing through the wiry fair hair; the involuntary pressure of two fingers against his temple. The naked look she sometimes saw when she took him by surprise. The ragged jealousy when he'd suspected she and Brendan were…

All the doubt, the suspicion… had he recorded it? What would his diary reveal? Dare she read on? Once out, the messages could never be taken back.

She had to! She mustn't stop. Not now. Not yet. If she were ever to understand what had happened she had to really listen to him – his feelings, his thoughts. Only now, when it was too late for her to change anything, would this man allow her to see beyond the careful façade, the pragmatism, the logical arguments, the emotional control that had so infuriated her.

But could she bear it?

The persistent ache of longing settled more heavily inside her. And this was only the beginning of his story – the simple facts.

If only. If only…

I have the drawing in front of me. Devlin may be top of his esoteric tree in the medical world but he wouldn't have made the grade at art school. No doubt about that. But he managed to make the crude sketch look grotesque enough. Ugly spiky neurones looking ready to invade a planet. Pathways of nerves like a hideously complicated underground train track. The wiring system of the human body, he called it. Like a circuit for the Blackpool illuminations. Everything connected to something. Each bit essential to keep the whole thing functioning. By the time he'd finished I had hairy tarantulas crawling on my bare skin.

'This disease affects the nerves in the brain and spinal cord,' Devlin said, scribbling over various bits of his drawing. I noticed he used the definite article not the personal pronoun. Trying to keep his distance, helping me to keep mine. Just now at least. Until he'd conveyed the facts.

'The usual messages get confused.' His pen zigzagged across the pathways. 'And then lost.' A straight line severed the connection with three decisive movements.

'The muscles then start to weaken and waste away.' The bulging onions were reduced to flat, useless strips with two strokes of his pen.

It was his suggestion that I brought the drawing home, as an aid to breaking the news to my family. It's just as revolting here, in spite of – maybe because of – its amateurish execution.

The spinal cord is particularly repulsive. In his doodling while he talked, he kept tracking around the skeletal outline and it has assumed all the dominance of a serpent rearing its head to inflict a mortal blow. Speaking of cord – as in spinal – I always want to spell that 'chord'. As in co-ordination of sounds, harmony. Only now there are some discordant notes sliding in without invitation here, so perhaps 'cord' is better. As in knotted rope. Noose. Stranglehold.

In the privacy of my study, staring at that sketch, I'm suddenly aware – at a kind of visceral level – of the cruel irony of my situation. Communication has been such a core thing in my life. Words, thoughts, ideas, literature, writing, reading – the components of communication – are central to my professional as well as my personal life. But at this very second my physiological self is losing the knack of communicating effectively. Okay, maybe I'll retain the power of speech for some time – perhaps even until the end. Who knows? Depends when that end is to be and how much say I have in determining it. But one by one the switches in my internal wiring will be flipped off. It'll eventually be blackness personified in there. My only hope is to keep all the lights blazing in the upper storey.

I wanted to drag my eyes away from that slow but systematic 'weakening and wasting' of the muscles. But somehow I couldn't.

'Usually the hands and feet. But sometimes unfortunately the mouth and throat. Depending on the type.'

Before I could start to get a grip on this new nightmare scenario, Devlin was dragging me deeper into the swamp.

'If the lower motor neurones are affected, the muscles become weak and floppy.' He let his own hand hang uselessly. 'But if it's the upper neurones, the muscles become weak and stiff instead of supple. It just depends.' His fingers assumed grotesque contortions.

'And in my case?' It came out just as if I'd asked, 'And the next train, what time's that?'

'In your case, you have the most common form. We call it amyotrophic lateral sclerosis. Usually referred to as ALS.'

Common? Don't you call me common, matey!

'Which in real terms means?'

'Both upper and lower motor neurones are affected. That means stiffness and weakness. We usually see this type in older patients – the over fifty-fives. But in your case...' He shrugged. 'Well, it's just one of those things.'

I couldn't even begin to go there so I rushed off in a different direction.

'What causes it?'

'We don't really know. There's a lot of research going on, and we now know a whole lot more about the disease itself and the way motor neurones function. But very little about why it happens.'

'*Very little*. So you know something.' Do you get paid for procrastinating in your job?

'Well, in about one case in twenty, there's a family history of the disease. We presume that in these instances there's a genetic origin. And we've actually identified the gene responsible in about one in five of this small group of familial cases – there's a mutation of something called the superoxide dismutase 1 gene – known as SOD-1. Rather aptly named, I always think.' Wow! This guy's human somewhere underneath that austere façade! I like it. 'But it's not genetic in your case. And quite how many people in the non-familial group have gene mutations we simply don't know.'

'So, are you saying you have absolutely no idea what causes it in the vast majority of cases? Apart from the sodding variety.'

'I'm afraid so. Scientists, researchers around the world are searching for answers as to the possible causes. There are all sorts of theories.' Another eloquent shrug.

You'd have thought I had enough natural curiosity and personal investment here to be soaking up what he had to tell me, but he might as well have been speaking Swahili. Free radicals, excess glutamate, deficient neuronal blood supply, slow viruses. I heard a few of the words but they went no further than my eardrums.

What does it matter anyway? It doesn't change a thing. There are more important things to focus on.

'So what can you do? What's the treatment?'

'We can offer you treatment but I'm sorry to say, not a cure. We'll do everything we can to ease any symptoms and prevent unnecessary complication but it wouldn't be fair to hold out any false hope.'

Sledgehammer came to mind. What happened to softly-softly?

'There are a number of drug trials going on and I think in time we should look at some of these and see how you feel. It's probably not appropriate just now.'

He was right. My cup runneth over already; spare me a deluge on top of everything else.

Naomi frowned suddenly. She double-checked the dates. Yes. An abrupt end. Nothing for five days.

Odd.

19 JUNE—This past weekend seems to have lasted a fortnight. I don't think I've ever craved access to my computer so much as I did over these three days. It was a form of cold turkey, I guess. My brain was still feverishly working on the text, especially in the stillness of the night, my soul searching for a forgiving receptacle, something strong enough to bear the weight of my chaos. I tried scribbling down some of the thoughts but it was too inhibiting – it's the flow, the interconnectedness of words as well as ideas that I was seeking.

On previous trips I've always loved the sheer depth of the silences in that remote part of Cumbria; this time I felt as if I was being sucked through a giant pipette and lifted away from the rest of humanity for a glimpse of eternity. All that blackness. All that nothingness.

When we booked, the weekend break – pre-the-diagnosis – three nights in the Lake District, just the two of us, Naomi and me, sounded like bliss. Only a couple of hours' drive from Edinburgh, but a completely different world. Tramping in those peaks, soaking up those views, savouring each other again. Far away from deadlines, editors and emails.

As it was, my mind seemed to reconstruct even the simplest things. How long would – no, *will* I be able to tramp? How soon will my view of life really start to shrink? How long will Naomi still want me? (Heavy-weight groans here! She's just so beautiful, so utterly luscious herself.) How long can I keep my editor, or worse, *Harry!* from knowing my secret?

Will there come a time when even emails are beyond me?

Poor Naomi got a raw deal. I know she wanted me to let her inside the steel fences. She's got sharing down to a fine art. And she invented comfort! But I daren't. I haven't staked out my exclusive territory yet, haven't measured up the spaces she might be able to sidle into alongside me. Until I do, I have to keep everything padlocked. I know she's getting snagged on the barbed wire trying to find a way inside for herself, but she'll cope better with her own scratches than she would knowing I'm mortally wounded.

Sugar. Sugar. *SUGAR. SUGAR!* As she would say.

Just thinking about her and what she's facing makes me want to go out and throw myself in front of the next Virgin Voyager. Just to get it over with so she can get on with the rest of her life.

The words blurred. The rest of her life. Without Adam. It was unbearable.

Sometimes even yet she forgot. She'd wander into his study looking for him. She'd come home and call to him. The realisation when it struck knocked her off-balance all over again. Distraction, hard work, sleep – nothing erased the sheer emptiness.

He was right about the barbed wire. Well, partially right. She *had* felt the scratches but written it off as her own ineptitude. Even sensing something of his lead-lined defences she'd seen it as her responsibility to find a way to take some of the weight, not his job to hand the burden over.

The trip to the Lakes had seemed like a perfect opportunity. Away from the demands of busy lives, time to talk about this monster that had forced its way into their ordered lives; to face it together. But he'd made it perfectly plain it was no such thing. Striding up the hills, teasing her if she fell behind, quick to cut short the breaks. Keeping her laughing through dinner with ridiculous tales from work, jokes from his literary friends. At night stilling her tentative broaching with his kisses, fierce kisses that seemed to pack the longing of decades into seconds.

Through the veneer she'd glimpsed something of the brittleness, but it seemed disloyal to persist.

Naomi shrank down into herself now, recalling the sheer frustration of every speculative attempt thwarted. Why hadn't he confided all this to *her* instead of his computer? Why had he shut her out? Couldn't he see it devalued the impact of the diagnosis on her, denying her a role.

In carefully calibrated doses she replayed the video of that weekend through her head: the manic walking, the obsessive banter, the fierce loving. But this time, through his metaphors, she saw things for what they really had been. A diversion away from the land mines inside his own barricades. For her own protection. While she slept, he was returning to look deeper and deeper into that crater alone and unaided.

In the depths of his despair he had still put her interests before his own. And she had silently cursed his selfishness.

She laid her head on the desk in front of his confession and wept.

20 JUNE—Harry's reminders about his deadlines are really starting to rile me. 2.15 this morning I finished working on that cursed column this week. And boy, was I knackered. That tells me more than anything else how much I need to get some of this other baggage out of my system. When writing's a struggle something's cluttering up the space.

One thing I have decided; for the purposes of this diary of my disease, I have to forget the old literary brio and just write as I feel. It doesn't matter. There'll be no coven of critics circling out there ready to pounce on my pedestrian prose, denounce my implausible plot, dissect my uni-dimensional characters. If I just let it flow, this machine can be my counsellor, my confidante, my depository. That should take some pressure off.

And another thing I must record – now, while it's fresh. Lying in bed last night, I caught myself thinking about the world going on without me. How will Naomi remember me? I need to get this right. For afterwards. For her.

Naomi shuddered and hunched herself deeper into her jacket. The sun might be staining the walls of Adam's study golden yellow but the bleakness she felt was the colour of December.

His aloneness tore at her heart. Even now, too late, she wanted to reach out and encircle him with her love. But from the beginning he'd been standing outside her orbit, planning his solitary strategy, hiding the mental torment. Nothing new in fact. He spent most of his life working alone. She could see him yet, totally absorbed, crouched in front of the screen, not surfacing until he'd perfected each column, each sentence, each word, each punctuation mark.

'Mr Perfectionist,' she'd said when he'd let his meal go cold yet again. 'You descended through the mules not the monkeys!'

'Devil's in the detail,' he'd retorted, mechanically putting the food into his mouth, not tasting it; still with his writing.

She'd tested him once, slipping a hefty dose of horseradish sauce into his mashed potato. He'd swallowed it without so much as a puzzled look.

Oh, if she could only cook for him now there'd be no recrimination, no tricks. Several times she'd automatically laid two places at the table, warmed two plates, and she still hadn't properly adjusted the portions. Every time a knife turned in her heart, robbing her all over again of appetite and purpose.

It was a struggle to return to the screen.

21 JUNE—I've got the house to myself tonight. Naomi's out at some hen party, not due back till after midnight. A whole evening to write this diary. Better than any trick cyclist's couch any day!

Part of the problem is I haven't worked out the structure. Old Macdonald – our English teacher, not the farming legend – used to say: 'Start at the beginning, boy, start at the beginning. Hopefully before I retire you'll have got to the end.' Blooming heck, the beggar went to school with Methuselah's Dad! Way past retirement age already by the look of him. I used to have visions of him sitting swathed in that greening academic gown slowly metamorphosing into a skeleton while he waited for one of us to finish writing an essay.

Okay. The beginning.

I've never been one to dwell on my health; far too much to pack into life to get side-tracked with niggles and aches. But in retrospect, I guess, it started with a sort of clumsiness. I got pretty fed up with myself. Losing a game of squash against Fred, my timing a fraction out. Feeling I was in danger of falling over my own feet. Slopping coffee on my copy. Cutting myself shaving on the very morning I was meeting Kirsty Wark!

Once I started to notice it, of course, I took steps. Cut down on the caffeine. In my line of work you need something to keep you fired up. Five mugs in a day is nothing unusual, wine at night, the odd snifter of spirits later to keep you firing on all cylinders into the wee small hours. Goes with the territory. I cut back on that, too, even my all-time favourite, port.

It seemed to work; I was back in control. And it was about then that people started to notice my column. Quality stuff, the chief said. Worth missing the odd glass of Cabernet for that! He slipped extra assignments in my direction. Other editors tried to seduce me their way.

Naomi leaned back in the chair. What understatement. Adam had been like a man possessed. Snatching sleep when he must, he'd careered headlong through every day, spilling out sparkling columns and features apparently effortlessly, energy left over for working on his novel well into the night. He'd diverted her remonstrances with a lopsided grin, promising her 'a night to remember' or 'the luxury of your choice with the proceeds'. And he'd more than fulfilled those promises.

'The better the memories, the emptier the present,' a bereavement counsellor had written in her sympathy card. Memories didn't come better than hers.

She hadn't noticed the 'clumsiness'. Had she been too absorbed in her own career? Would it have made any difference if she had seen the warning signs?

I have to admit I knew I was getting stressed, but heck, we're all living on our nerves in the media business. You need some tension to get the adrenaline rush.

I put what happened in Nottingham down to stress. Now I suspect it was an early manifestation of trouble. I was researching a piece about some kid being denied entry to an exclusive private school. Foundation for a diatribe on injustice. Boy, what a grind! The lads in that school could do with a dose of state education in an area of multiple deprivation. The parents of the excluded kid had more attitude than personality, and the headmaster was a supercilious git, so I was pretty hacked off with the whole scenario by the end of the day. I didn't take much notice of the stairs incident.

Anyway, there I was running up the spiral staircase at the hotel after dinner. The lifts were having tantrums and I was keen to get the copy finished and forget about the morons I'd spent the day with. But half way up the second flight I was suddenly struggling. It was as if the power supply had been reduced to half. I had to lean on the banister rail and wait to recharge.

I was fine again sitting in my room typing up the story and I had an early night – well, 1 o'clock instead of 4! And I drove home in a oner next morning. Naomi left me in no doubt about the stupidity of *that* little aberration afterwards, but I needed to put distance between myself and the whole sorry pack of over-privileged whingers. By the time I got home I remember my arms felt stiff and my right wrist seemed oddly flabby but then, I'd been steering the mighty chariot for best part of nine hours, give or take a traffic jam or two.

So, given my ostrich tendencies, what was it that took me to the quack in the end? Being beaten at golf! I've always been better than Fred on the old hallowed turf. Always. Ten years now we've been slicing up the divots together on a fairly regular basis and suddenly I find myself struggling to keep up with him walking from hole to hole, and I just couldn't seem to find what it takes to whack the ball for the long drives. Now that's more than a chap's pride can tolerate.

The GP, Dr Curtis, didn't know me – I was going to say, from Adam. Huh! And I couldn't really breeze in to a perfect stranger and say, 'I want a cure for being beaten at golf!' I warbled on about weakness and clumsiness, knowing he was probably thinking, What a time waster! But he just sat there, apparently listening, and then he overhauled the old carcass, listening to the hullabaloo inside, knocking joints, assaulting reflexes, extracting blood, asking a million completely unconnected questions. Hmmming and uhh-hhuing cryptically like a veritable Dr Cameron on a dour day.

A couple of weeks later he calls me back to say bloods are all normal, etcetera, etcetera, but he'd like me to see this guy Devlin. Neurologist. Hello? What's up, Doc? I thought. Even I – king of hospital-avoiders – even I know you don't get to see one of the men on pedestals unless your local witch doctor thinks you might be in trouble. I asked, casually: 'Why?' He mumbled on about viruses and post-viral syndromes and various incomprehensible differential diagnoses for a bit, but when I tried to extract the uncoded thinking, he was as vague as the Cuillins in the middle of a downpour on Skye. 'Let's just wait and see,' seems to be the stock phrase in the medical fraternity.

I rationalised it: he didn't want to say something incautious and have me after him in the courts. They're all increasingly litigation-conscious now, aren't they? And the last person you want pursuing you through the legal system is a bloody journalist! Especially one who writes a weekly column in a national newspaper, never mind a scribbler who's getting rather well known for his perspicacious exposés!

Naomi let out a long sigh. She'd been so confident that Adam believed his theory of post-viral fatigue she'd let him go off unaccompanied to both the hospital appointments without making any effort to change his mind. Oh, she'd *offered* to go with him, but he'd dismissed the need out of hand. 'Completely unnecessary. You've got far more important things to do with your time than nursemaid me.'

He hadn't mentioned the fact that the hospital had recommended he bring someone with him for the second visit. 'They might do more tests. I'll just take a taxi. No time to fit a court case for dangerous driving into my busy schedule this month!'

So he'd been entirely on his own, hearing the diagnosis, asking the questions, returning home afterwards. She'd been at a conference that day. At the exact moment he'd heard what was wrong, she'd been indulging in a leisurely break with Kit, with nothing more serious on her mind than whether to choose a doughnut or a chocolate éclair with her coffee.

She hadn't touched a doughnut since. Come to think of it she hadn't touched food much at all. Everything tasted like cardboard.

The first visit to Dr Devlin. An odd-looking fellow. Dapper, inasmuch as he's ultra neat, every strand of hair in place, tie colour co-ordinated with his shirt, impeccable Windsor knot, shoes polished like an Army recruit's been waxing since dawn – that kind of thing. But his right eye hasn't been on speaking terms with his left for some time, I'd say. The minute one veers round to fix your attention the other casts its gaze to the ceiling. You do your best to ignore it but eventually it becomes mesmerising and I got confused about which one was really representing its owner. On top of that he has a nervous habit of jerking his shoulder as if the head of the humerus doesn't quite settle neatly into the socket, or maybe he's still recovering from carrying his golf bag over the weekend. It crossed my mind that, being a neurologist, he cultivated these eccentricities so that patients would focus on his disadvantages rather than their own problems, but I doubt it's possible.

However, he wasn't behind the door when brains were allocated. Smart cookie and no mistake. Only snag is, he's signed an oath not to divulge his mighty medical musings. Sealed with his own blood, I shouldn't wonder.

Okay, he deigned to tell me about a catalogue of tests they would do: various 'bloods', lumbar puncture, MRI scan, electromyography... but my uninitiated brain skipped about between the possible connections and failed to find any underlying logic. It seemed reasonable to ask what he was looking for.

'Oh, we just need to get a better overview of how your body is functioning. Give us a baseline. Let's wait till we get a clearer picture of everything before we start speculating about what might be wrong – if indeed there is anything really amiss.'

So bloody patronising I wanted to do something violent. But I concentrated on visualising him naked, directing traffic in Oxford Street. Seb, a journalist friend, gave me that little gem of advice when I was a raw recruit taking my first tentative steps as a reporter. Stops you taking the insults personally and possibly lowering your own standard of professional behaviour, he reckoned.

But the fact remains, his state of undress notwithstanding, I definitely didn't like Devlin's insinuation. I mean, *me* – lead-swinging? It took the combined force of Naomi and the quack to get me to agree to set foot on the medical conveyor belt in the first place.

Naomi knew he'd got under my skin and did her best to bandage the wounded pride, bless her: he didn't mean it like that, she soothed; in these cash-strapped days, in a beleaguered NHS, nobody who expected a lucrative pension would commission all these expensive tests unless they were pretty confident there was a chance they might throw up something of consequence. Well, maybe not in quite those words! But then she realised what she'd said and instantly went into reverse and smothered me in reassurances.

Of course, back then I didn't think it would be anything *serious*; and I certainly didn't know that there are no specific tests for MND (which was what this guy with X-ray eyes – even if they zapped independently – was already suspecting). I just didn't need anybody suggesting I was being a wimp and wasting medical time. I think at the time I mumbled something acerbic about it being the GP's idea to refer me to Devlin, not mine.

Anyway he's armour-plated. Years of practice warding off the barbs of shell-shocked consumers, I guess, harden the skin. So he wasn't about to succumb to any weapons in my little amateur armamentarium. My real frustration was that he couldn't see I was the kind of guy who needs to have the facts pinned on his mental noticeboard. As I loitered at the door on my way out, when I thought they were supposed to ask, 'Was there something else?' all I got was: 'Let's wait and see how we go for the next few weeks.'

'Us... we?' How I loathe this use of the first person plural. No matter how much they think they're empathising, they are not living with these symptoms and doubts. They will be miles away, swinging golf clubs or doing the salsa with gay abandon when I tumble down an escalator and send a little old lady to kingdom come because they didn't warn me of the dangers. *(For Ideas folder: *language of power in medicine*.)

During the second visit, it was the complete opposite. Just when I could have done with blurred edges, he delivered the verdict like a judge with a black cap on his head. Even his shirt was black, relieved only by the thin gold stripe in his matching tie. It has just occurred to me that those two visits were a bit like his eyes – totally unconnected. No hint of disaster in one, unequivocal devastation in the other. A spot of time in a charm school might improve his people skills!

Funny how metaphors keep flashing into my mind. In the weeks between those two consultations, an army of SAS men were assembling stealthily behind the castle wall. Not a sound could I detect, but out of sight they were all taking up their positions, forming into ranks. On the single command of the operations chief, they all sprang into action. One almighty hullabaloo and suddenly they've taken over the entire caboodle, lock, stock and two smoking barrels, lifting me out of the sea of tranquillity and whisking me away to a foreign prison with glass walls and no exits. And short of shooting myself or taking my secret cyanide capsule, I'm here for the duration. *(For Illness as metaphor file.)

Of course, in fairness, Devlin and his merrie men were actually stalking in the forest gathering evidence. Their reconnoitring over those five months of tests gave them a more accurate picture of the geography and the opposition. I concede that he might have done me a favour waiting until he was sure without hinting or surmising. I just got on with my life. It never entered my head who the real enemy was. Okay, the batteries weren't fully charged yet but eighteen-hour days and yesterday-deadlines aren't exactly conducive to speedy recoveries from exhaustion, even for the rudely healthy. I didn't expect a miracle cure. I just blotted out the inconvenience and turned up the volume.

So Devlin gave me five extra months of delusion.

If only Adam had shared these emotions with her, Naomi thought. How differently she would have reacted from the outset... wouldn't she?

It had been a particularly boring conference in a lecture theatre with no natural light and intermittent air-conditioning, and she'd come home with the beginning of a migraine headache, to find Adam juggling saucepans on the Aga. His terse, 'Tell you after dinner – just let me concentrate on getting this curry right,' didn't arouse any suspicion and she'd slipped away to have a long soak in a herbal bath.

The room was darkening fast as she sank into the armchair opposite him, curled one leg under her and said, 'Right. Now tell all. What did Dr Devlin have to say this time?'

She could see him now – etched against the dying light, sitting forward in his chair, elbows on his knees, hands lightly linked, his expression emotionless. No preamble. No prevarication.

'It's not good news, Naomi. It's Motor Neurone Disease. Progressive. No cure. Devlin says...'

She had stared at him blankly.

His speech was mechanical, robotic even.

As the enormity of the situation impinged on her brain she felt the stirrings of... what?... *resentment*. How could he catalogue the facts of his own disintegration, as if none of this would touch her? She would have to witness him falling apart before her eyes. Even as she watched his lips reciting Devlin's words, her own mental images appalled her.

This strong, handsome *young* man, this person she loved above any other in the entire world, would 'gradually lose the power of his limbs' and need 'help with the activities of daily living – eating, bathing, toileting'… *she was sitting beside his chair painstakingly spooning liquidised food into his slack mouth, one eye on the clock which persisted in ticking out normal office working hours, not the elongated seconds of an invalid's pace of living.*

He would eventually 'lose the power to walk'… *she saw herself pushing him around in a wheelchair, his emaciated body draped in an old man's rug, grotesquely distorted limbs shouting his impotence to the staring world.*

He might 'lose his ability to communicate verbally'… *she saw a quivering finger laboriously tapping out words on a keypad; heard the devastating silence of a mealtime without his crazy banter, or worse still, animal grunts spluttering through his liquidised food.*

Eventually the paralysis would 'switch off' his capacity even to breathe… *she was watching helplessly while he clutched at his throat, powerless to trade on the free abundance of air, drowning gradually in his own secretions.*

'If we let it go that far,' Adam said tonelessly.

Shocked by the extent of her own revulsion, she was suddenly galvanised into action. Throwing herself on her knees in front of him she clutched at his clasped hands.

'No, Adam! No! Tell me it isn't. Tell me this is one of your crazy jokes.'

He shook his head slowly, staring at her with a stranger's eyes.

His hands clenched suddenly on hers. She could *feel* his strength. He'd fight this. She looked down at the squared fingers twined with her thin pale ones. No, they'd work at this – *together.*

'We won't let it happen. We'll beat it. I'll help you.'

He withdrew his fingers from hers and cupped her chin, the better to focus her attention. The intensity of his scrutiny was too much for her to bear. She dropped her eyes instead to his tie, her fingers jerking along the silky fabric. The diagonal rows of black penny-farthings on the red stripes mocked in their frivolity.

'Naomi, listen to me. No, really listen.'

She dragged her eyes back to his, willing her brain to stop long enough to hear him out. The pressure of his thumbs under her jaw was almost painful.

'There is no doubt, apparently. I have this thing. Period. And it's just a question of time. I need a bit of space to work out how I'm going to handle it, so I want you to just be there and give me the space to deal with it in my own way. Okay?'

'But I want to…'

'Please. *Please*, Naomi.' Sharp. Brittle. Excluding.

Non-negotiable.

She withdrew back to her own seat, but a moment later, mumbling something about a cup of tea, escaped to the kitchen. Fighting back the panic she watched her own hands filling the kettle, selecting mugs, pouring the boiling water, carrying the steaming mugs. Her fingers metamorphosed into Adam's, creeping across the table to envelop hers, circling up her spine, caressing her body, pulling her closer still... what if...?

He took the dangerously hot liquid in hands that looked exactly like her husband's.

The detachment, the sheer lack of audible reaction was unnerving. Anger, sadness, fear, aggression even – anything would have been preferable to this impassivity. Turned in on himself, he seemed already to have left her. Even in bed that night he maintained his isolation. After shutting himself in the study with his computer for most of the evening, he tried to slip under the duvet without waking her, but she had simply been waiting for the opportunity to wrap him in her arms.

'I'm here for you, darling,' she'd whispered.

Silence.

'Please, Adam, let me in. I want to...'

'Not now. Please. Just let me sort things out for myself.' The rejection stung.

'But...'

The sudden rush of air told her he'd thrown back the covers. She saw his silhouette travel across the window and move towards the door.

'For heaven's sake, Naomi. Can't you please do as I ask? Just this once.'

She lay alone in the cooling bed, the tears falling unchecked. Anger would be preferable, would it? Huhh. Fear linked arms with the hurt. This wasn't the Adam she recognised, the unflappable, phlegmatic half of the partnership, the one who jollied *her* out of her depressions and moods. Fair enough, maybe his turn for a burst of irritation was long overdue but surely he wasn't changing already. Not before he'd even dressed in the coat of illness. Was it enough just to have it hanging on the hook waiting?

The antique clock in the hall plodded ponderously towards dawn. And still Adam did not reappear. At 3 o'clock Naomi slid fearfully into her dressing gown and went in search of him. She heard the skitter of computer keys before she saw the light under his study door. Not daring to approach too close, she whispered tentatively from the doorway.

'Adam. I'm so, so sorry. Please forgive me?'

He half-turned and held out a hand. She advanced to grasp it in both her own and carry it to her cheek.

'I'm the one who should apologise. Sorry I snapped,' he said. The words were right, the tone all wrong.

'Won't you come back to bed? You must be exhausted.'

'Soon. I'm just finishing off this feature. Harry was cursing about it yesterday morning. Didn't like the reference to fox hunting; couldn't I find a punchier opening sentence; what the hell was I trying to say; couldn't I give it more pizzazz; all that kind of guff. Well, I'll give him pizzazz. He'll be jolly well choking on the pizzazz like fizz the wrong way up his poking nose!'

'Wow! What on earth are you writing about?'

'Death!'

The explosion left a deafening silence in its wake.

'Look, Naomi, you go back to bed. Five minutes and I'll have this wrapped up, and then I'll join you. I'm all right. The better for rattling this piece off.'

'D'you want a hot chocolate? You must be exhausted.'

'Good idea. I'll be finished here by the time you've made it.'

She backed away, the unease stubbornly clinging to her mind. Sitting in bed listening for the sound of his footsteps she forced herself to dismiss the aggrieved feelings. He was the one who had the sword of Damocles suspended over his head. Where better to vent his emotions than on her? It wasn't personal. Not really.

She had drained her own mug before he joined her.

'That'll larn 'im!'

'I beg your pardon?'

'Harry. I defy him to reject *this* piece.'

'You're freezing,' she said inconsequentially, wriggling in to impart something of her own warmth.

Strong arms drew her close, his lips found hers, his fingers slid over her breast, the curve of her hip ... No, memories didn't get better than that.

Naomi dragged her mind back to the present.

Devlin isn't the touchy-feely kind, though he did nod in the direction of the emotion associated with this thing, during that tell-it-like-it-is session.

'Research shows it's best to let your feelings out rather than have frustration and guilt build up,' he said.

Research shows, does it? All very authenticating. It's scientifically determined. It's permissible to feel the odd churn here and there if it's evidence-based!

But I have to admit, in many ways the guy was in tune with where I was at – nine days ago today. Facts, please. I need to set my parameters here, fill in the wavy bits later on. I guess that's why I was such a beast to Naomi. What a swine hurting her, shutting her out. But my hold on sanity was pretty precarious; I had no reserves left to deal with her emotions.

It was incredibly therapeutic scribbling all that vitriol for my column and yelling abuse at Harry in my head. By the time I went back to bed Naomi had got the message that I didn't want to talk. Having her close, needing me – well, I guess it was therapeutic too, right then.

But about this business of letting off steam. The way I see it, you have this airbag filling up with evil smelling gas. *(For Illness as metaphor folder.) Imagine it filling up and filling up until it explodes. It taints everyone for miles around. But if you occasionally let it seep out in a controlled way at a safe height or deposit it in designated places, it might wrinkle a few noses but it doesn't do more than offend them glancingly. I'll just have to be cautious about where and when with these emotions which I think I've got safely bottled up – especially where Naomi's concerned. She'll have enough nastinesses of her own.

'Oh Adam, forgive me for blaming you,' Naomi wailed aloud at the screen.

Sad to say, I didn't exactly reward Devlin for his sympathy. I remember some suggestion about starting me on drugs. Sooner rather than later. I didn't let him past first post on that one! Body's a temple. Never dabbled in toxic substances to date; no intention of starting now. End of.

And there was some talk of referring me to some Association or other – Clinical Nurse Specialists, someone on the end of a phone… My mind just shut down. Period. There ain't no way I'm having my life taken over by anybody, no matter how qualified, no matter how well-intentioned. *I AM NOT*! To his credit, he didn't persist. My rigid upbringing made me take the proffered leaflet but not 'in case' I change my mind. No way, José!

It occurs to me that I chose the right profession – way back when I was a snotty little blighter with pretensions way beyond my abilities. When I was about to choose my subjects and thereby effectively close some career doors, Old Macdonald suddenly decided that I was 'gifted'. Told my mother so. Even made some crass comment to the assembled mass of jeering adolescents in my year. I, of course, joined in the derision about his sad life; what did he know about reality post the Flood? etc etc. But secretly, scratching away at my bestsellers with a leaky biro under the covers by torchlight, I told myself this Oxford graduate, with a distinction in both English Language and Literature, didn't distribute compliments lightly. The idea fermented and I applied myself to getting the grades for Oxford myself. Oh, I guffed about in class and to my shame I made MacDonald's life unadulterated hell along with the rest of my cruel peers. But I sailed through the exams and the Oxbridge interviews and, once freed of the schoolboy pressure, I even wrote a smarmy letter to him thanking him for his 'inspirational teaching' and support. Habits die hard though, and I confess I waited till after dark to go out to post it.

And in truth I owe that cadaverous academic a great debt. I've had the rare fortune of being free to fill my working life with my hobby. And now in this latest unexpected turn in life, the skills I've honed in the intervening years should be invaluable. Whatever happens to the outer casing, if I can get unseen readers to experience my take on the real issues in life and critics to blast my column with their customary poison, I'll still be on a level playing field. I don't want concessions.

That's partly why I need to keep this to myself for as long as I can. Once I come out, there's no going back. I'll never know if good reviews are sympathy votes or genuine signs of respect for what I've written.

I don't want to be a marked man.

There are over five thousand people in the UK in this same boat. We aren't freaks. It's not something that comes to those who are in some way deserving of punishment. This could happen to anyone. It just happens to have happened to me.

And I don't want pity.

I want to take my place alongside my peers, ordinary everyday people whose intellect, whose social standing, whose careers, match with mine. I don't want curious looks, or covert furtive glances. Or allowances to be made.

It's not much to ask, is it?

Naomi shivered. This brave analysis of his situation filled her with sadness. He asked for so little; endured so much.

Adam's job had always been more high profile than hers. She'd been content to beaver away behind the scenes, her reward the quiet satisfaction of providing secure homes for children, turning couples into families. But he had been driven. And more haunted than she had ever realised – until now.

She had taken the success as his due. The posthumous tributes from big names, critics and authors, journalists and publishers alike, had confirmed her belief: he was a gifted wordsmith. That he had seriously understated his talents, craving recognition for his skill and dreading any concession to his disease, she had not fully appreciated until today, but it explained why he had suddenly posted his various awards on the wall of his working space.

It was a worry he need not have added to his growing burden.

24 JUNE—I misjudged Dr Curtis. Apparently Devlin contacted him and filled him in on the details. Puts a different complexion on the old 'fragmented service' we lampoon so often. A senior consultant phoning a humble GP about a perfectly ordinary male patient of thirty-eight. I don't know what he said but after morning surgery, Curtis rang. I was out earning the proverbial crust, so it was evening before I picked up his message.

'Mr O'Neill, this is Dr Curtis at the surgery. I've had a call from Dr Devlin this morning and he's filled me in on your situation. I think it would be good if you and I could meet for a bit of a chat. If you're home this evening, would you like to ring the surgery and we'll arrange a date. Thanks. Sorry to miss you this morning.'

A lifetime of obedience to authority figures drove me to ring immediately. Shock number two, the receptionist put me through to the organ grinder himself.

I was flicking through my diary looking for the first glint of slack to sneak out of the office and disport my anatomy in the witch doctor's wigwam when he suddenly said, 'I could call in tonight after evening surgery, if you're not too busy?' What's a few thousand words overdue when you get that kind of offer? And the sheer deference of the thing – 'if I wasn't too busy'. I mean! Since when did the mighty MB ChBs of this world care a stuff about the priorities of us other mortals? I know from my journalistic explorations of the real world – though not from personal experience, I confess – it's nothing to wait four hours in a clinic just so you're in pole position when the demi-god elects to put in an appearance. And it's not unknown to have him rush out to an emergency two patients before your turn, never to be seen again. The longer I had to think about why Curtis would be breaking all the moulds today, the more intrigued I became.

He arrived at 8 tonight and was still here at 9.20. This is a bit of a steep learning curve for him apparently. First case of MND he's had in fifteen years of general practice. To his credit he was pretty clued up. Armed to the teeth with professional literature and stuff off the Net. At first he concentrated on the facts and I must admit it was helpful talking about things, at an ordinary level, getting a different angle – the humble local quack not being as awe-inspiring at the ivory tower guy. So we dittered on about this and that and imperceptibly things seemed to change. It was weird. On his own territory he's very much the guy on the clothed end, holding the stethoscope and the pharmacopaeia. Here, in my sitting room, he dissolved into a chap not too much older than me, sick to his stomach about not having a magic potion, genuinely wanting to 'share the journey' with me; 'ease the burden' in any way he could.

He's a stolid kind of a fellow. Gives you the feeling he's stumbled into country practice because he's copying his dad – not that I have a clue what his father did. You get this sense that he likes a slow pace, time to reflect on life. It's good, actually. He's not looking at how many patients skim over his linoleum; more concerned with what state they're in when they leave.

Not only did he undertake to call in himself periodically, but in between, he says, don't hesitate to get in touch. Gave me his mobile number even! Devlin's going to see me regularly but Curtis is the local ringmaster. He's drafting in a physio and says he'll line up speech therapists and nursing assistance, as and when. But when he got to feeding tubes and stair lifts, I freaked out. No way!

Fortunately for me Naomi got home at that precise moment and she provided the perfect cover for tea instead of TLC. While she clattered the

Royal Doulton (yeah, right!) I steered the Doc into talking about himself and he took the bait. I guess it wasn't his fault that he'd strayed beyond my tolerances. He doesn't know about my blessed imagination; great for writing purposes, not so handy when you're visualising your own disintegration. So I'd already gone into the kind of thinking where drugs lead to oblivion, suicide to permanent escape. Unknown to her, Naomi rescued me.

This bloke is pretty good in the listening stakes. He seemed genuinely interested in what Naomi does, placing kids for fostering or adoption, and they were soon floundering around in the mire of departmental politics like two uninhibited pigs in mud (although to liken my dainty, not to mention fragrant, wife to a pig is absurdity taken to its extremity!) The iniquities of the system led on to the inadequacies of parents and truth being stranger than fiction and bingo! we hit common ground. The guy reads medical thrillers. The three of us did a fair few rounds of literary assassinations and away he goes with my copy of *A Slow Burning*, a perfect sanitised excuse for him to come back and tell me what he thought.

A level playing field.

28 JUNE—Has the NHS won the entire lottery? Has a rich maiden aunt died? I've seen the physio already! I can't believe the ninety-nine people on the rungs above me fell off the ladder within two days of Curtis contacting her.

They arranged an appointment for me at lunchtime so I could pop out 'without anyone at work questioning me' – they obviously think we work regular office hours! Chance'd be a fine thing. But nine out of ten for trying.

Anyway, enter a cross between Denzel Washington, David Attenborough and Martina Navratilova! Lydia. Lydia Lovelock. All breathless intimacy and butch muscularity. She's of Jamaican extraction and, as she tells you with disarming candour, built for comfort rather than speed. Ample, in anyone's vocabulary. Her tight cropped curls are greying uniformly, but her skin has that polished ebony lustre you see on the cheekbones and shoulders of models. Her black eyes disappear into the folds of her face when she laughs and judging by the depth and number of the creases, she laughs a lot. She's nearer six foot than five and she seems to have been poured into her uniform, which moves like a second skin when she gets down to what she's paid for. I'm no skinny weakling – well, not yet – but she can manhandle my body as if I were a well-oiled Action Man. And she has a trick of turning things into a joke against herself that takes the sting out of your subordination.

Her voice comes from the depths of some acoustic cave and the rich Jamaican pronunciations, with their rolling rs and sharpened ths, abbreviated endings and extended vowels, have a music of their own.

'Ah've always had a tin about feet. Beautiful, man. Beautiful. Jus you put da left foot in ma sweaty palm, honey. Beautiful. Jus testin you know da left fram da rrrrright. Me? Wouldn know da difference! Left, rrrrright – all da same ta me. *Six goes* it took, *six goes*, ta fool da drivin examina! Okay, now, ma hand's da pedal a da Formula One rrrrrracer... rrrrev her up, man! More! More! Let da clutch go now, man. Beautiful. Feel da trob a dat engine! Okay. Okay. Okay. Now da rrrrright one. Cool, man. Cool. Feel da strengt in dat foot. Ah sure could do wid you chauffeurin me about da place. Get me outta trouble in two shakes a da fly's tail. Know da left fram da rrrright *an'* got da powwa ta wrench da machine t'rough hundred eighty degrrrree ta rrrrrace away fram da cops. An me, Ah sure get mysel inta some pretty pickles at times. People jus don' understand some a da tins Ah do.'

I could believe it.

I can't hope to capture the melody of her accent and spending time in the effort would be counter-productive to the purpose of my recording everything about my illness. A loose approximation must suffice.

Her long firm fingers slid over my torso twisting and experimenting occasionally, pausing momentarily to repeat the tests that were part of her secret search for weakness, her disengaged banter distracting my mind from the potential invasion in spite of my resolve.

'Now, there's a body! One careful owner. Okay, you're gonna tell me you're a black-belt Judo champ. One minute I'm on my feet, next I'm staring up your nostrils, my spinal cord snapped in two. Right, man? Okay, okay. Try something gentler for a start, yeah? Give me a sporting chance, yeah?'

Only when she had the full measure of my range did she drop the false accent and revert to her normal way of talking. I was annoyed with myself for being taken in at all. But I guess the technique worked. She'd grabbed my attention. And she'd made it easy to talk about my problems without circumlocution.

'D'you take regular exercise, Adam?'

'Yep. Golf. Squash. When I can. Swimming, three, sometimes four times a week. I guess that's my only really disciplined *regular* exercise nowadays.'

'Good. Wise choice. How long at a session?'

'As many lengths as I can until I'm exhausted. Varies these days.'

'Best not to overdo it. Stop before you get exhausted.'

'But I want to keep as fit as I can for as long as I can.'

'Yeah, I understand that, honey. But with MND, you won't actually build up your muscles. It's the nerves supplying the muscles that are damaged. Excessive exercise will just tire you out. Best to regulate your activity carefully and make sure you have the energy for the things you *really* want to do.'

She winked broadly as she emphasised the word and gave a throaty suggestive gurgle that made her whole body wobble.

With anyone but Lydia I think I'd have baulked at the cautions, but she exuded a motherly wisdom that put her emphatically in my camp.

'We'll keep an eye on things, eh? We'll watch how you go and maybe adjust the exercise to suit where you are at any given time.'

That's professional-speak for downgrade as you deteriorate. But she made it seem like the fine-tuning of a sports coach. And in her hands the plural pronoun held a genuine sense of teamwork.

'Okay, you know already I'm phobic about driving tests and all things motorised. Guess you drive, eh?'

'Yep. But hey, Lydia, I'm not in the running for driving getaway cars for maverick physios.'

Again that full-bellied bass chuckle erupted from her deepest reaches.

'Sure thing. I fired all your predecessors anyway. Not a long-term career move, honey.' She patted my arm, for all the world as if consoling a disappointed applicant. 'But the old DVLA might be after you as well as me if you try to slip by unnoticed.'

'Meaning?'

'Well, honey, these guys are a tad niggardly when it comes to things like MND. They kick up a bit of a fuss if you don't notify them. They just need to *know* at this stage – they aren't scheming to take away your license or anything mean like that.'

In spite of her reassuring tone, my mind froze. I'd have to declare it. To officialdom. It was a form of coming out.

'And then?'

'Well, you know bureaucrats. Always struggling to let everyone know they're earning a living keeping Britain the imperial stronghold it always was. In triplicate. They'll pull down their mouths and look official. They'll put on their uniforms, and check their warrant cards, and yank their peaked hats further down over their sweating foreheads, and they'll puff out their puny pigeon chests, and they'll say: "Huhh. This bloke 'ere, O'Neill, Mr Adam W. Strike me, but the guy's got a licence as clean as a baby's bum! Nary a driving offence to his Irish-sounding name. Stap me, it's a mortal sin to curb 'is style. Let 'im set an example on 'er Majesty's 'ighways. 'Is GP can keep a weather eye open for us. If 'e says the guy's kosher, that's okay by us." And there you are. Licence renewed. Just a wee codicil saying it's for a certain length of time. And a wee box saying you'll agree to regular checks from your GP, just sitting there waiting for your autograph.'

Lydia rocked back in her seat with an expression of smug satisfaction as if she'd single-handedly abolished inheritance tax.

'You aren't smuggling disability badges in by the back door here are you, Lydia?' I said.

'*Moi*? Smuggling? Not my style, honey. Scouts' honour. Wait till you want to sneak in to Debenhams on Christmas Eve to get that seductive black nightdress for the little lady. *That's* when you pull out the old badge, park on the double yellows and sprint up to the old lingerie department!'

'And?' I was waiting for the sugar to dissolve so that I could taste the bitterness of the pill she was hiding, but she looked genuinely mystified.

'Look, I know I'm not going to be sprinting up the steps to anywhere for ever. I appreciate the humour – and I might put you in touch with my editor – you could earn a pound or two writing a satirical piece about your take on officialdom! But can we cut the flannel and get to the reality for a sec? What happens when the old Doc spills the beans about me staggering round on sticks?'

'Receiving you loud and clear, honey. No, Doc Curtis and I – we're legit. Our aim is to keep you mobile and independent as long as poss. And we have a shed-full of aids sitting there ready to wheel out if you need them.'

'Even in these days of postcode lotteries and dwindling resources?'

'Our friendly neighbourhood Doc? He's an on-the-ball kind of a guy. Already been to see you, huhh? Got you here to see me pronto, yeah? He's on your side. He's no film star I grant you, but underneath that crumpled shirt there's a big heart beating. And I'm on your side too, in case you haven't yet twigged. And I've been around a while, know a few useful contacts who'll go the extra mile for me if I need a favour. So, you need a specially adjustable seat? You got it! You need an adaptation on the Porsche? You got it, man!'

The sudden ringing of the phone gave me space. Lydia's brisk replies to her caller seemed oddly at variance with her earlier volubility.

'Yep?… Okey-dokey… Yeah… Gimme five… You're kidding… Thanks.'

She turned back to me with an apologetic shrug.

'Sorry to interrupt our little *tête-à-tête*, honey, but her downstairs is cracking the whip. Says my clients are starting to pile up, in danger of going a couple rounds with each other to weaken the opposition. Guess I'd better reduce the surplus population down there pronto. No point in 'em coming in for exercises and going out with broken bones!'

'Indeed. But thanks, Lydia. You're a breath of fresh air.'

'Same goes for you, honey. You look after that body for me now, right? I've got designs on it!'

'I'll do my best!'

'See you!'

There was indeed bedlam downstairs in the waiting room but I had no doubt one glance at Lydia's imposing presence in the doorway would reduce the entire battalion to the docility of lambs.

29 JUNE—Lydia has injected something into my veins with those strong manipulating hands, I do declare. Power by osmosis!

I have this new energy. The exercises she introduced me to aren't exactly ferocious but they do seem to suit my needs because I'm feeling much more relaxed and supple. Maybe it's her sheer dynamism. Whatever her elixir, I like it!

30 JUNE—I was sitting in the conservatory today, reading. The words just wouldn't penetrate the hailstorm of thoughts hammering inside my skull, and I found my eyes repeatedly straying outside. That's a dangerous activity when the lawn needs mowing, and the borders need weeding, and the lobelia are crying out for transplanting.

But the real focus of my straying eyes was Naomi.

Bugger, bugger, *bugger*!

Just looking at her brought such tightness to my throat – knowing what's ahead.

She was sitting in the pergola sewing. Snatching every ounce of sun. I've teased her often about coming out of hibernation in the summer months, but behind the teasing there's a real worry. Skin cancer. Okay, she's read all the literature and she's got the right factor for every situation and I have to say her skin is pure golden brown, not a mark, not a blotch. She's like these models you see in clothes magazines with an even tan everywhere, or those famous women who ooze pampered and purchased health after two weeks in an exclusive treatment centre, only hers comes from genetic inheritance and simple lotions and a balanced diet. And it's an all-over perfection of tone and texture and colour. I say this as something of an authority. Between us we've examined every inch of it. On a pretty regular basis.

When I got to this point, I felt this sick lurch in my stomach. How long before there's nobody to check the bits she can't examine for herself? Curses! I will *NOT* cry!

She insists on making samplers for all her nieces and godchildren (three so far, a fourth on the way) and it's always a race against time to get them ready for the due date – or as soon thereafter as name and date and gender are available. It's something to do with demonstrating the joy of their arrivals compared with all the kids she places in foster homes and adoptive families, I think. Anyway, she's determined to get the border of this one finished this week. So she was absorbed in her work and didn't know I was watching her instead of reading the ghastly report some unknown hack, hyped as 'our political editor', had produced on a fracas in Westminster.

I want to capture that vision. Imprint her on my brain. The summer version. Her thick dark hair is glinting in the sun, a smooth drape from crown to nape. I secretly wish she'd let it grow long, as she had it when we met. I loved to feel it running through my fingers, watch her brushing it like a rich skein of silk. But she insists it's an unruly thatch with a mind of its own that just doesn't square with her busy life, so she keeps it cropped.

Occasionally she stretches and arches her back, stiff from her concentration on the fine stitches. The movement is almost feline. Her slim figure is supple in the close-fitting cropped top and chinos. Out of the blue I'm choked with regret for her childlessness. I will never watch that slender body expand to accommodate an unseen but growing fetus. I will never mop her exhausted brow as she labours to deliver my daughter. I will never watch her thin arms cradle my son, the small breasts swell to feed his voracious appetite.

Damn, damn, *damn!*

I see her wave through a sudden haze. The tears are for her loss as well as mine, a deprivation we've only skimmed so far. With the complete assurance of the naïve young, we had mapped out the template for our future: careers, children (next year), pensions. We bargained without paying premature respects to death.

As if she feels my melancholy, Naomi drops her needlework on the seat and skips across the grass towards me. Cassandra, the mongrel cat who adopted us the week after we moved here, flies out from under her seat and, like a black bullet, vanishes into the shrubbery. I watch the ease of Naomi's movements, the unthinking grace...

I can't bear to think I must leave all this behind.

The text swam before Naomi's eyes. How she had hated every step of the way as inch by inch the paralysis had robbed him of his mobility, eaten away at his muscles, encroached on his very ability to stay alive.

The heat of shame scalded her face. Had he known that sometimes the thought had slipped unbidden into her mind: would she one day find someone else to take his place? Someone else to father the children she wouldn't have with him? She'd stamped on the thoughts instantly. She must not, would not, erase him.

Had he been aware that she hadn't properly recognised his sense of loss? Had he suspected, discovered even, her terrible secret?

She dragged her mind away from the possibility.

'One thing that this changes, Naomi, is having children,' he'd said. His tone was matter-of-fact, his face expressionless.

'Yes?'

'We'll need to talk about it at least.'

She'd not been able to think of a thing to say to bridge the gap.

'Apparently I'll still be *able* to – physically I mean, but we have to think of the future. For you. For the kid.'

The tears had come in spite of her best efforts.

'We have to be practical, love,' he'd soothed. 'I'm going to be pretty useless about the house myself in a bit; it'll put pressure on you. Nobody wants that less than me but I don't have much choice here. Hopefully Curtis and Lydia and their little army will bring in enough muscle and equipment to spare you the heaviest work, but whichever way you look at it, more of the burden will fall on you. If you were pregnant, or had a baby to take care of, it'd be even worse, wouldn't it? I mean, you can't be humping my thirteen-stone carcass around the place in that state. Although I guess we could rig up a train system with a pram attached to a wheelchair. How'd you fancy wearing a peaked cap, blowing a whistle? But we'd need somebody else to do the opposite shifts. Nah! Wouldn't work. Besides you're skinny enough already – can't have you fading away from the sheer daily grind now, can we? You'd be invisible!'

He'd lightly moved on and the subject hadn't been raised again for weeks. But there had been no hint of his pain. And she hadn't delved to find it. Her own disappointment had been overwhelming. She was already thirty-five. Was he in effect closing the door on motherhood for good? Even if – and it was a big if – she did eventually move on to a new relationship, it would probably be years before she was ready to have a child with anyone.

Maybe then she should…

Now, remembering her rebellious thoughts, she whispered, 'Forgive me. Forgive me.'

1 JULY — For some inexplicable reason today, walking along the road to buy a collection of newspapers to see how the enemy reported yesterday's fiasco in parliament, I had a sudden terrifying vision of falling and breaking both arms. The horror of relying on others for the intimacies of life was as real as if it had happened. I flopped down on the first available seat and found I was physically shaking. The picture was so vivid: strangers doing… no, it's too gross to solidify in written prose.

3 JULY — Devlin told me the progression of MND is very much an individual thing. They can't exactly give you a map and tell you, you're here, and this is what you'll find around the next corner.

However he did hand me one pearl of great price. When you have something like this, he said, you'll probably assume everything that misfires is attributable to the MND. But some symptoms may well be due to run-of-the-mill ailments we all get from time to time.

I see the logic. Best to be on guard against this tendency. No merit in dragging the point of no return forwards.

Plato springs to mind: attention to health can be a major hindrance in life.

Harry's breathing fire and brimstone, so I mustn't linger here on the therapeutic writing. From his foul mood I guess 'them upstairs' must be leaning on him. Sales figures showed a bit of a drop recently, I know, and everybody's a bit twitchy after the recent bad publicity for the media – a couple of rogue reporters being economical with the truth, a ding-dong battle with a minister over implications of fraudulent activities, gossip about the deputy chief's expense account. They say a week's a long time in politics; I say a day's a long time in journalism. One dodgy sentence, one infelicitous word, and you're hung out to dry.

22 JULY—I'm appalled to see how long it is since I scribbled this diary. But things have gone from bad to worse at work. Harry nitpicks endlessly and gives us hell for everything from late submissions to split infinitives. The atmosphere's hardly conducive to creative flow, so I'm working more and more at home. But that has a spin off – the working day doesn't have any end point and to stay ahead of the game (in case) I'm working half the night too.

I know I need to keep sorting out what I think and feel about this illness but I'm so preoccupied with keeping Harry off my back (somehow I don't seem to have the thick skin for his sarcasm I used to have) that all my energy is going on staying focused on the current topic for my column and searching for a new angle on anything that comes up this week. Hmmm. Somewhere under the surface I've acknowledged that I can't afford to thumb my nose at the awkward squad. If I lose my position with this paper, who else would take me on?

Maybe this absorption with work is a good thing. Perhaps it means I'm getting some perspective on my situation. I'm knackered at the end of the day, that's for sure, and I'm more unconscious than asleep at night, so I don't lie awake obsessing about the future. Lydia would do her huge ebony nut if she knew how exhausted I'm getting keeping up this punishing pace, but I've had to miss my last two appointments with her so she hasn't had the chance to castigate me.

Naomi let her mind roam back to that summer. Adam's output had been prodigious. He'd seemed so much less stressed working at home, so much more jubilantly productive. And she'd capitalised on his availability, soon coming to rely on him to get the washing in when it rained, to take delivery of parcels, to put a casserole in the oven, to take Cassandra to the vet. The merging of their roles seemed to bind them closer.

There had been no hint of anxiety about future earning potential.

She let out a long sigh. Why had he clung so stubbornly to his self-appointed role as protector and provider? Was it her fault? Had he seen her as too weak to stand alongside him in this ferocious battle?

What if this was all to come in his diary? Could she bear his disappointment as well as the dragging senselessness of every day without him? Now, when it was too late to change anything. Not tonight anyway. Not without Stella around to give her therapeutic counselling.

She hammered down on the sleep button and dragged herself to bed. There was to be no respite from the surging thoughts, and she awoke bathed in sweat after a recurrence of the nightmare. The sound of her mother-in-law's accusations refused to be obliterated and she eventually slunk downstairs to the kitchen. She smiled ruefully. How do you explain chopping vegetables for a hotpot at 4 in the morning?

But there was no one waiting for an explanation. The emptiness of the house reproached her in its silence.

The hours ground by on leaden feet until she could dial the number.

'Stella Lucas speaking.'

Naomi let out her breath slowly.

'I'm a condemned woman all over again.'

31 JULY—I told Harry today. My conscience (I blame my mother!) forced me to in the end. I couldn't keep missing appointments with Lydia, not when Curtis has gone out of his way to get help from the beginning. I told him I needed to take time out occasionally but I'd make up for it in the evenings and my output wouldn't suffer. He stared at me in that superior way he has.

'Just make sure it doesn't. There's no room in this outfit for slackers,' was all he said.

'I'd be grateful if you'd keep this to yourself meantime.'

I've no idea if he will or not but I'd nothing to lose by asking.

3 AUGUST—The more Naomi tries – oh so subtly! – to do things 'to spare me', the more I rebel. I know her intentions are exemplary but...

Well, I have this stubborn streak inherited from my maternal progenitors: you tell me I can't; I'll prove to you I can. That particular trait drove my poor old mum to distraction. They say that parents dislike most in their children those characteristics they possess themselves. After more than one titanic confrontation my mother ground out, 'What you need, young man, is a sound thrashing!' Spare the rod and spoil the child, she maintained, and society would be a better place if it took a bit more heed of Scripture and a bit less notice of the reformers and namby-pamby sociologists.

But there was another very potent reason why she could never bring herself to administer that physical corrective.

I was only a kid at the time but I swear I smelled the 'mood' the second the back door opened each evening. Neither of us ever mentioned it but, looking back, I think my mum did too. It might have been something about the heaviness of the footsteps. Or the time my father took to hang up his coat. Or the speed of his approach. I never analysed it, I just experienced it. But I can remember watching her with fearful eyes and noticing the clench of her hands or her retreat behind a chair.

Eventually he was forced to get treatment. His manager just wouldn't accept his 'attitude'. But no work meant no money coming in. There could be no sick-line without a doctor's appointment. He was a proud man as well as a stubborn one (I get it from both sides); he held out until he was sectioned.

Severe depression was what my mum called it. At least, doped up, my father was more docile but it crushed his spirit and I don't believe he ever recovered from what he saw as the stigma. Mum never really recovered from what she saw as the shame of his suicide two years later. Unless you've been dragged through this particular mire, it's probably impossible to comprehend the complexity of emotion that hangs about, not daring to name itself.

I know there's unfinished business there still for me too. But hey, this is no time to go unpacking baggage from my schooldays. I only mention it here because this week I've had a sneak preview of what it feels like to stand on the edge of that particular murky swamp with no visible stepping stones. From the slurping tongue at the edge to the deep black treachery of the middle, it's just waiting to suck you under. My rational self tells me it's legitimate to feel low; my emotional self berates me for giving the devil a foothold.

Devlin said depression was common; but back then I assigned that particular bogey to other people. It wasn't in my lexicon.

Now I'm torn. Whose genes win out here?

Moving swiftly on...

Later An absolute belter of an evening writing about our local mp's latest gaffe in the House has restored me to my customary (??) ebullient mood. His classic spoonerisms just shriek out for caricature. This time even his own party cronies guffawed at his expense.

4 AUGUST—I could see Harry was impressed by the speed of production of this piece (not that he'd ever actually express any positive emotion).

Since I told him about the MND I've had a distinct feeling he's been watching for slippage. In a perverse kind of way, knowing he's on the lookout for weakness makes me all the more determined to show my productivity is up there with the best of them. Hence the crazy hours, the personal, completely unrealistic deadlines.

I may (possibly) be fooling Harry but sadly, I can't (definitely) disguise the problem from myself. I tried. Hadn't Devlin warned me about attributing every symptom to the disease? It was just normal tiredness from my punishing lifestyle. But that little fantasy is pretty frayed and threadbare now. The strength is definitely going in my legs. Although Lydia hasn't spelled it out, I'm pretty sure I detect an adjustment in the way she badgers me into easing off. I'm finding ways to compensate but my mind is rebelling like crazy over this.

And although I keep telling myself it's frustration not depression niggling away at my temper, I honestly can't tell where one ends and the other begins.

So. This thing is already clamping down on my lower limbs. Next it will be my hands (for real this time). Wall-to-wall Velcro and elasticated waists, here we come! They'll need to drag me kicking and screaming into that little nightmare.

Can I bear it?

Hands are so essential to independence. I don't know if I'm making things worse with all this keyboard stuff but it's my life-line, my salvation, so there's no way I'm even asking the question.

How much am I prepared to tolerate? How much am I prepared to compromise?

Looking at her own hand unthinkingly stroking the ball of fur on her lap, Naomi saw instead Adam's fingers splayed against the arm of his wheelchair, stiff, unresponsive... the clenched jaw... the despair in his eyes.

A groan escaped her. She was the one who'd denied him his way out. If the positions had been reversed would she have wanted to linger through a nightmare?

If only... If only...

She got up so suddenly from his chair that Noelani, finding herself without a foothold, yowled in protest and stalked frostily from the room, her tail signalling her disapproval. Adam would have been gentler, she seemed to say. He knew how to treat a lady.

Indeed. Comparisons flooded unbidden into her mind. He had accepted her flashes of irritation with equanimity, never retaliating. He'd teased her sulks away. He'd given her a sanitised view of his suffering. He'd kept so much from her, until it was too late for her to share his pain. He'd denied himself to give her a future.

Blindly, she lurched into the kitchen. The clock indicated that it was time to eat; the bitterness in her mouth denied her appetite. Instead she went upstairs and lay on the bed, her face buried in the plain black jumper that still held his scent; her heart, her eyes, too leaden for tears.

13 AUGUST—Cassandra caused a sensation today, bless her. Somehow she crawled inside the tumble-drier and must have nestled in amongst the damp towels awaiting their evening spin. The first we knew of it was when Naomi flicked the switch as she went by, glancing idly at the load beginning its revolution.

I was in the conservatory when I heard her shriek and by the time I got to the utility room she'd switched off the power and was just staring at this splayed blackness across the porthole as the drum gradually slowed to a halt. As soon as I released the door one very bedraggled bundle of spiked fur bolted out into the garden. I eventually found her cringing under the shed. She spat and snarled at both of us to start with but gradually I coaxed her out and, once she'd deigned to forgive us, she sat on my lap being stroked for the rest of the evening, although I swear she didn't stop quivering for at least two hours.

Why do I recount this here? Because at the end of the day I realised that being preoccupied with her fear and relaxing her, I'd unwound myself for the first time in weeks. I was getting on with some reading at the same time, but it was therapeutic just having her close, stroking her rhythmically. I've heard about pets being taken in to nursing homes but hadn't really made an association for myself. Cassandra could indeed become a help to me.

We chose the name Cassandra because it means helper of men. She'd begun her time with us as Moggy. I was never a great animal lover and our way of life just isn't pet-friendly. But fresh from a brutal encounter with an articulated lorry down at the crossroads, the scrawny creature that fawned against us five years ago couldn't even help herself never mind mankind.

I staunchly resisted Naomi's appeals to take her in at first; we would nurse her back to health and feed her up, yes, anything less would be inhumane; but then she'd have to go. I'd bargained without those wide, yellow eyes, that sinewy body snaking silently around my legs, her erect tail stroking my skin in silent appeal. I'd growled at the persistent lurker that if she dared to insinuate herself more permanently she'd have to earn her keep and make sure there were no furry invaders coming into the house from the field on the other side of our fence. Our little arrangement got off to a dodgy start during which she demonstrated her growing affection with half-dead offerings laid at the altar of our bed; but the strategic use of inducements and barriers gradually persuaded her to adapt to the mysterious standards of *homo sapiens* and we formed a workable pact. Today she repaid her debt to us.

18 AUGUST—Glorious, wonderful, liberating freedom. Two whole weeks away from Harry! I'm buzzing with anticipation. There are cases to pack, books to select, last-minute emails to send, the garden to leave in a state for my mother to take care of in our absence – oh, a multitude of things to do, but I need to record the sheer buoyancy of my feelings.

Tomorrow morning we fly off, hundreds of miles away from the carping poison of my line manager's vendetta. We go with Curtis's approval and Lydia's blessing. I got a distinct impression that they were both thinking, Go while you have the chance; this time next year you might not be able to. Probably my paranoia. I'm determined not to let anything spoil Naomi's break from life's thwarted and inadequate parents and traumatised children.

Bavaria, here we come!

4 SEPTEMBER—Bavaria was fabulous. Wall-to-wall sunshine, loads to explore (so we could vary the activity levels), hotel our best choice yet, food fantastic. I fell in love with Naomi all over again.

Makes returning to a world with Harry in it all the more unattractive. But two weeks and he's off himself. Maybe he'll enjoy Tibet so much he'll lose himself somewhere in the mountains. Or be seduced by the teaching of the monks and come back a new man. I'm allowed to dream.

5 SEPTEMBER—I'm spitting blood today. I am not going gently into this dark night. And I am not needing any do-gooders to count my cussed blessings!

Naomi read this entry twice. What had happened to upset him? Something so big its presence was too real to need recording. Curious. This was an Adam she didn't recognise. What else had he suppressed?

8 SEPTEMBER—Today marks a defining moment in the trajectory of this disease. I fear I upset Naomi by rushing to my machine too soon after our meal tonight, but I have to get this down. I don't want to tell her yet, but I'm struggling to stay focused on anything else, so she'll soon get suspicious.

We had an editorial meeting from 1 to 3 this afternoon. Roy Travis was banging on about wanting to cover HRH's visit to the new marine centre and write some dotty article about the royals being up to speed on environmental issues – yeah, right! What an oleaginous creep that guy is! I was, I admit, regretting a soporific lunch with the new kid on the block, Jerry Lloyd. (Thought it might be nice to fill him in on the vagaries of the team so he didn't commit any *faux pas* detrimental to his continuation in the outfit.) *Merlans en piperade* followed by *gâteau mousse au chocolat* (liberally laced with cognac) not to mention a rather fine Bordeaux might have slipped down the alimentary track unnoticed by the brain cells ten years ago, but these days anything more than an egg sandwich midday seems to turn me into a veritable narcoleptic. But I was still in touch with the general tenor of the discussion… or so I thought. Until I was jerked rather rudely out of my pleasant little reverie by The Editor himself.

'Adam. What do you think?'

The minute I began to answer there was a sudden silence. Then the guys sniggered. What had begun life in my head as a one-line denunciation of the whole monarchic system, emerged from my mouth as the somnolent drone of a heavily-sedated patient up at the local mental hospital. I managed to cover it up with a second rather more articulate contribution, but things inside my head were whirring and ticking like the mechanism of a time bomb. Okay, from the outside it looked like the drowsy mumblings of an over-fed slacker.

But I was on the inside.

After that blinding flash another curtain came down. Is this the end of the second act?

9 SEPTEMBER—I'm still struggling with yesterday's revelation. Devlin's caution has been circling in my brain trying to get a foothold but…

Let's see. 1) Naomi hasn't noticed any problem with my speech. 2) Yesterday's little display could have been more alcohol-induced than I'm prepared to admit. Jerry was fine apparently and he matched my intake, calorie for calorie, unit for unit. Of course, he is about a decade younger! 3) Maybe I'm just sleep-deprived. 4) We all know that early afternoon is a time when the circadian rhythms slump; maybe mine are just slumping lower than they used to ten years ago.

One part of me is begging to hang on to these possibilities. Another bit of me is insisting, Don't delude yourself, face the reality and deal with it pragmatically. This diary is no place for delusion. Whatever the cause, my tongue wasn't in possession of my faculties at that crucial moment.

I need time on this one. An experiment or two might prove the point.

12 SEPTEMBER—Today I contemplated a swift exit from this nightmare. There's a surprising bounty of DIY advice available on the Internet. But Naomi makes it difficult to think straight. That look in her eyes, the softness of her skin, the feel of her body… it kills me to think of throwing all that away.

What will it do to her? I can't talk to her about it – the 'when' – not yet anyway. I have to sort this out myself. If it weren't for her I'd seriously think about ending it now. A nice little parachute accident perhaps. A fall from a bridge. A fast drive over a steep cliff. A long swim out into the ocean. How hard does it have to be? A good active, sporting kind of death would be thumbing my nose at the creeping paralysis.

Naomi closed down the computer and sat for a long time staring at the blank screen. Here he was, only three months on from the diagnosis, already looking for an escape.

Had he blamed her? *Was* it her fault?

She rose abruptly and went outside to water the garden.

Would it be better to remain in ignorance? Just because he'd left his diary didn't mean she had to read it. He wouldn't know. Or she could just defer it. Everybody said the rawness would heal. One day. But they didn't know...

If she discovered beyond doubt that he blamed her... Maybe she'd never find absolution. Except in death.

13 SEPTEMBER—Because of Naomi I have to think about my strategy. If I do feel compelled by her to hang around, how will I deal with the consequences?

This lurking anxiety about my speech has reinforced one important bonus. I'm in the right profession. No matter how much my body crumbles, I can still retain my dexterity with the written word and people not in the know need have no suspicion that in real life I'm a bumbling incoherent. Hmmm. That sounds almost positive.

I'm confused now. Is life more precious today for some other reason? Am I, in fact, in this for the long haul? I devoutly hope not.

15 SEPTEMBER—Forget positive. Forget life being precious. My mother is driving me in the direction of the loony bin rather than the homely gas oven.

Okay, I know I owe her a debt I can never repay. She brought me into the world. She scrimped and saved to give me more than the bare essentials. She was a human shield for my cowering body when my father was in one of his 'moods'. A single mum, she protected us boys from the world during the hard, condemnatory years after his suicide. She took all the flak from relations and acquaintances and every other righteously indignant body. But for a woman who knows the cutting potential of other people's counsel, she's unbelievably insensitive to my needs now, and wrapping her criticisms up in biblical authority simply compounds her iniquity as far as I'm concerned.

I didn't tell her about my diagnosis for a couple of months. It wasn't just a natural wish to protect her, more that her reaction to bad news so often jars with mine and I didn't have the stamina to hear that 'God helps those who help themselves' or that 'these things are sent to try us' or that 'everything happens for a reason.' When I did tell her, all her usual coping strategies deserted her. 'Oh dear' escaped before she could edit it, and the pain was written in her eyes. She asked genuine questions, I gave her truthful answers. I felt rather than heard her devastation. And when she left she whispered a crumpled, 'Whom the Lord loveth He chasteneth,' softly in my ear before rushing off without a backward glance.

She has been silent on the subject since. Until yesterday.

In an unguarded moment I made glancing reference to a way out of my nightmare. The torrent I unleashed took me completely by surprise. I wasn't even thinking of my father until all the religious objections known to man, every negative argument ever propounded, came tumbling out. In short, I would be consigning myself to eternal damnation if I ever usurped God's supremacy over my mortal flesh. He gave life, it was His alone to take away when He saw fit. Only she tangled it all up in her desperation.

At first I simply sat and stared at her. I had no idea she could expound on any subject for that long, and with such eloquence. But when the words themselves started impinging on my consciousness, I shrank in horror. My intellectual self told me to go easy because she'd carried 'the cross of shame' before, and if she really believed the stuff that she was disgorging now, then indeed, it was shame of the highest order lined with fear of the most primeval variety. But my emotional self recoiled from her prejudice and ignorance.

Fortunately for her, I couldn't get a word in edgewise for ten minutes. By then I'd realised I'd be wasting precious energy if I attempted to counter these views. Mere rational argument doesn't begin to dent armour that thick. All I said was, 'I didn't know you felt that strongly about it,' and shrugged my shoulders as if it were neither here nor there to me.

But as I watched her walking down the path to return to her solitary home, my overwhelming emotion was one of pity. What kind of religion holds a person in a straitjacket that unyielding? Who needs a God so lacking in compassion and understanding? Unless He's big enough to bear my anger and my questioning, I can't believe He's the being that made the world and mankind with such infinite variety, so many paradoxes, so much inconsistency. (I've just noticed I've perpetuated my childhood practice of using capital Hs for God; our Sunday School teachers taught us it was wicked to be too familiar with Him.)

Do I really know the woman who gave me life? I'd no idea she was harbouring these fanatical obsessions. But then again, suicide was a taboo subject in our house. Mention of Dad was too. Maybe it was impossible for her to detach one from the other.

I couldn't believe it when she returned to the attack again today, and at a time when she knew Naomi would definitely be out and I would be working at home.

It was a bad day for her to strike. I woke this morning with a killer of a headache. The medication I was forced to take engulfed my brain in cotton wool.

My column this week is about the human face of the police force; I was trying to make a case for a return of the bobby on the beat, essentially. A local Asian shop owner gave me a superb interview. He'd apprehended a yob stealing from his shop only to be overpowered and put in hospital during the twenty-five minute wait for the boys in blue. Though still swathed in plaster he'd given me some brilliant sound bites in a colourful if eccentric dialect reflecting his opinions on the subject of law and order which would make the Chief Constable pale, and the anonymous letters flood in 'to The Editor'.

The thoughts came reasonably easily and I soon had a framework, but I couldn't find the fluency to make the prose sparkle. After several abortive attempts I put it on one side and turned to my novel.

Until now Naomi is the only one who knows about the book. She hasn't seen it: I'm not ready yet for objective comment. Everyman and his aunty seem to think they have a novel in them, but in reality most people haven't a clue about what's involved or where to start. Even I, a writer by profession, don't know yet if I've got what it takes. But I do know time is running out for me to test the hypothesis.

This kind of creative writing is a therapy in itself. Once I'm inside my characters, leading their lives, thinking their thoughts, speaking their lines, I'm no longer Adam O'Neill, harassed by deadlines, frustrated by a headache, carrying a fatal disease. It's a glorious escape.

Anyway, today the fingers were obedient, the words flowed, and I lost all track of time. I was still in this other world when my mother arrived. I've never told anybody that I'm vulnerable in that state but Naomi knows intuitively not to invade my creative working space.

My mother, however, barging into my physical working area as well as my mental no-go zone, mistook my abstraction for signs of further deterioration, and started fussing around doing things to make me 'more comfortable'. I know I was grouchy but I can't help it. With her fidgeting, her chatter, her non-verbals, she was like a persistent wasp.

'Please, Mother, I've had a difficult week and a hellish morning. Let's go and have a cup of tea.' Pretty mild and reasonable, considering.

She started to pick up the papers strewn around in the room from my earlier research on modern policing.

'No, don't,' I said through gritted teeth. I took a long slow breath and let every word fall singly and in slow motion. 'Please. Don't. Touch.

Anything. I need to know where each article is. It may look untidy but it's ordered. I haven't finished with this lot yet.'

'It's just not fair on Naomi,' she said suddenly, sliding the ones she still held onto the edge of my desk as if testing my boundaries.

'She understands. This is my workspace. I'll clear it all up when I've finished writing that piece.'

'That's not what I mean.'

She was bending down picking up a pen that had slid from my desk. She placed it with careful deliberation directly on top of the nearest pile of papers as if to prove her point.

'Do you ever think about what *she's* going through?' It was the turn of the curtains to be brought into line.

'Mother, I have no idea what you're on about.'

'I know it's not my place to say anything, not now you're all grown up and you've left home and everything, but Naomi is far too sweet a girl to tell you.'

'Tell me what?'

'She's just getting on with it. She's not sitting around thinking of ways out, is she? She's just getting on with her job *and* running this house *and* picking up after you.'

She lifted a book and put it edge to edge with another one on the table.

'Mother...' It came out more jagged than I intended. I mentally returned the book to its proper place on the floor.

She plunged her restless hands into the pockets of her jacket.

'I'm sorry, but this is my working space, Mum. It has to be... like this or I just can't function. Look, why don't we go into the sitting room? Let me get you a cup of tea.'

'A cup of tea won't sort this out.' She dumped herself stubbornly onto the window-seat against the light, leaving her face in shadow. 'And I'm sorry to go on about this, Adam, but somebody has to before it's too late.'

I didn't trust myself to speak.

'You have to think what it would do to Naomi if you did... you know... take the law into your own hands. I *know* what it feels like. It just isn't fair.'

Ahhhh, that again.

'It's the people who care about you – they're the ones left to pick up the pieces. *You* won't know anything about it, but *they* will. They'll have the looks and the comments and the nastiness of the police suggesting things and the church people hinting things and everything.'

At that precise moment Naomi got home and put her head round the door.

'Hiya. I'm home. Cup of tea, everyone?'

'Hi, Naomi. No! *You* sit down, *I'll* get the tea. I was just about to anyway now Mother's here.'

Normally I don't leave anyone alone in my study but I was out of there faster than an Olympic athlete in peak condition.

Without recourse to strategy or subterfuge, Naomi succeeded in taking my mother into the sitting room within five minutes of my departure, and they were soon exchanging tips about gardening, the price of fish and the quickest route to the new supermarket. I took as long as I conceivably could to brew that pot of tea and by the time I wheeled it in (I've started to use a trolley in case my wrists suddenly lose power), the worst of my irritation had dissipated.

Naomi stretched her neck and rolled her head, letting the vicarious tension ease from her shoulders. It was news to her that Mavis had harried Adam in this way. So *that's* why he'd asked her those questions suddenly without preamble after Mavis had gone.

'Naomi, am I difficult to live with?'

'No more than usual,' she'd teased.

'Do my habits annoy you?'

'Apart from your slovenly dress, and your obsession about leaving the newspaper just so, and when you "forget" to bring the gardening tools in and they go rusty in the rain, you mean?'

'No, seriously…'

'You think I'm not serious?' she cried in mock indignation.

'But am I a real pain in the house?' he persisted, and now something in his tone made her shoot him a sharp look.

'Not especially, no. What brought this on?'

'Tell me. Go on. I want to know.'

'Well, everybody has their little ways. And everybody gets irritated sometimes. I'm sure you get sick of my habits too. But you're not a bad old stick. I can cope with the odd foible. The pluses still outweigh the minuses.' She grinned at him. 'Why the sudden navel-gazing?'

'Just a little reality check. Don't want to outstay my welcome,' he said lightly, not looking at her.

Cold fingers clutched at her heart.

'Adam… You're not thinking of …'

'Of?' She remembered how his dark eyes had held hers unblinkingly.

'Of… leaving me.' It came out as a fearful whisper.

'Not at the moment, but Naomi… if the going gets too tough, would it be so terrible for the tough to get going?'

She flung herself at him and burst into tears. He held her close for a long time in silence, stroking her hair.

'We have to think about you too,' he said eventually, his voice thick with emotion, 'What this thing is doing to you. I can't bear the thought of wrecking your life. Maybe too soon's better than too late.'

'You aren't... wrecking my life,' she sobbed. 'You'd wreck it... if you left me.'

'But we know it's coming, sweetheart. We have to be realistic. You're still young. I want you to go on and enjoy life again.'

'But I want to enjoy life *with you* for as long as we possibly can.'

He'd said no more but a strange unease hung in the house.

She'd got as far as phoning the Scottish Motor Neurone Disease Association for advice but it had felt too deceitful, going behind his back. She hadn't followed it up.

The memories robbed her of what little solace she'd salvaged from the knowledge that his suffering was over.

26 SEPTEMBER—I've been on a real roll with the novel. It's started to take on an autobiographical slant – not intentional but perhaps to be expected, given the dominance of what's happening to me.

My main character is a bloke called Aidan. He's six foot four (wishful thinking) with a colourful past (poetic licence) and a promising future (if only!). This week he's heard disturbing news about his health and he's trying to get to grips with the implications. I've been getting up in the night with the scenes, conversations, descriptions, just pouring out of my subconscious. What an adrenaline rush!

I'm buzzing with energy. Life feels good. Very good.

30 SEPTEMBER—Yep, delusions have been shattered; no amount of smooth talking will expunge the facts or reinvent them in a more acceptable guise. No matter how hard I concentrate, no matter how determinedly I fight them, the muscles of my mouth and throat and tongue and lips seem periodically to gang up against me. It's not always a problem but the occasional times it is, boy, is it frustrating!

I've always had an absolute passion for clear diction and the melody of speech. It's part of conveying the logic of one's thinking processes. Now some insensitive thief has stolen my fencing rapier and replaced it with a pantomime sword.

Certain consonants are particularly difficult, I find: p, b, t, d, k, g. It's unbelievably painful hearing the imprecision. It hurts my sensibilities more than the bodily clumsiness. Language is my forte. And now more than ever I have to show them that my brain is still very much alive, no matter the disintegration of my physical shell.

It's becoming a daily challenge, to say things once and be instantly understood. That sudden heavy silence, the pitying look, the too-gentle request for me to repeat myself – it's harder to deal with than anything else so far in this whole ghastly business.

Something clenched its fingers hard around Naomi's heart at this. It had been months after this entry before she had noticed anything. The realisation was brutal.

It had been disconcerting, the way he stared at her sometimes before he spoke. Was he disgusted by what she'd said? Had he momentarily forgotten who she was?

He seemed to be slipping away from her in a myriad of little deaths. To lose her communication link with him would be the cruellest punishment of all. She'd kept her fears locked out of his sight for weeks but one day he'd found her lying on the bed sobbing. He refused to leave until she'd confided in him. His explanation was slow but precise.

'It's not you, you duffer, it's me. I have to concentrate so hard on my speech, I can't even think about my non-verbals. But because I realise there's such a potential for my gestures to be inappropriate, I have to work all the harder to express myself verbally. It's a vicious circle.'

In her relief she failed to appreciate the enormity of this latest development for Adam himself. She even laughed sometimes when his unguarded words fell out in a muddle. If she had only known how it hurt him!

13 OCTOBER—I am a pigmy. I am a drain on the community. I am a leech, a philistine, a parasite. If she'd slung any of these insults at me, I think I'd have felt more robust than the quiet disappointment Lydia actually betrayed.

I'd been rehearsing excuses as to why I'd cancelled my last two appointments with her, trying to make them sound plausible but I was counting on her generous nature. I was so much looking forward to seeing this gloriously different woman who manages to roll physio, entertainer, counsellor and friend into one massively embracing person, and I was all set for a good laugh with her. She's the sort of person whose essence I want to capture in one of my characters – Lydia herself permitting.

Sure enough, she greeted me with her usual ebullience, the rich Caribbean vibrations reverberating around me as she circled and approached in her inimitable way.

'Why, if it ain't my favourite Adam O'Neill. And there was me beginning to think you'd abandoned me for a skinnier model.'

'Abandon you, Lydia? Never!'

'Well, have you been slinking in here in a Trojan horse, man? Cos I sure ain't seen you in here with my own two eyes.'

'I'm sorry. I'm sorry. *Mea culpa*. But I've just been so busy. No reflection on you. You're as wonderful as ever,' I grovelled.

'Flattery won't get you back in my good books, Mister O. No, sirree! Nor yet excuses about any nose to any grindstone. I sure do recall telling you exercise in moderation, work in moderation, everything involving muscles in moderation, but nothing to excess.'

'You did, Lydia, but it's my boss you need to tell, not me. He doesn't understand moderation. He doesn't understand rest and recreation.'

'And would that same boss know about the delicate state of your neurones, Mister O?'

'Theoretically, yes. In reality, no.'

'Meaning?'

'I've told him. But he thinks it's a form of rust due to laziness.'

'And you have tried explaining the damage from running this finely tuned vehicle with a flat tyre, yeah?'

'Well, not exactly...'

By this time she had me on the couch, on my back. Gripping alternate legs in her big black hands she moved them through angles and inclines that induced involuntary winces and sharp intakes of breath from me and brought a strangely set look to her face.

'No indeedy. No, sirree! And this tyre? Flat like a pancake. Flat so's to scrape the rim of the wheel on the ground! And the gears, they're protesting when we try to speed up,' she said, shaking her head mournfully. 'Ah, Mister O, man. You ain't taking this thing seriously. That's why.'

She stopped her movements suddenly and leaned against the couch with her ample tummy soft and squidgy against my elbow, her own arms akimbo.

'Now.' She was suddenly seriously British again. 'How many people have you told about your MND?'

'Immediate family. My line manager – else I can't get away for your pummelling. One pal at the office.'

'Full stop?'

'Full stop.'

'And just how bad have you been since I saw you last? The truth now.'

'Well...' I closed my eyes and took big breaths. The words just point blank refused to come out.

'Legs letting you down, honey?' she asked gently.

'Yep.'

'Hands not gripping like they did?'

'Yep.'

'Speech fuzzy?'

'Yep, occasionally.' I kept my eyes screwed shut.

'And you're pushing yourself to compensate and cover up, yeah?'

I nodded.

'Honey, you're *running* towards a wheelchair the way you're going right now.'

My eyes flew open and took their time focusing on the round black face.

'I'm sorry.' I heard the wobble in my voice myself, so I'm sure the perspicacious woman towering over me did too. I swear she can bore into my thoughts; reading my body language would be child's play to her.

It was the Jamaican mamma who responded to my token apology.

'Never mind sorry after the event. What you gonna do about it now? No point me swinging on the trapeze exercising these here legs of yours if you ain't gonna do your share of this double act. The old NHS ain't gonna like it. Dr Curtis ain't gonna like it. And I daresay the little lady back at home ain't gonna like it neither, huh?'

I couldn't meet her gaze.

To my astonishment she suddenly patted my hand and said gruffly, 'Hey, you're still my favourite Adam O'Neill. I can see you're done in. And for what it's worth, I guess I'd run from it too, as long as I could hide. But... hey... it does hurt me inside to see you rushing into being an invalid ahead of your time. How about we do a deal, huh? I lay off the lecturing; you take better care of that beautiful body till I'm ready for it? I mean, you do know I'm saving myself for you now, right?' She held out her big hand. 'Deal?'

I gripped it hard to let her know I was grateful.

'Now then, up you get, and just you take a gentle stroll on the old treadmill. Nothing I like better than shapely calves in black Lycra twinkling on the road to nowhere.'

As soon as I was safely established she mumbled something about needing to get a fresh supply of exercise sheets from downstairs and there I was, on my own, my feet slowly treading the rubber road, my brain struggling to regain control of my wayward emotions.

By the time she returned I was composed again and we kept up our customary banter as she took me through my paces. And in amongst the frivolity she spelled out the limits she wanted to impose.

Lydia has forced me to acknowledge that the slide is relentless. Whatever my facility in deluding myself, she wasn't deceived for a moment. But it was her vivid picture of racing towards immobility that grabbed me by the throat.

My swim this evening was more worthy of a maiden aunt with a dodgy heart than my usual thrash. And when I got in I cancelled Saturday's round of golf with Fred.

18 OCTOBER—I wasn't surprised to see Dr Curtis today. Calling in on the off-chance, he said. Sent by Lydia, I filled in.

He took his time getting round to my health and mobility. How was I getting on with work and everything? Was I maybe needing a letter to explain things to my bosses? Time off?

I went along with the fiction. No, I was coping all right at the moment, thanks.

He'd brought a couple of research papers with him that reported new work on a promising drug regime. He wondered if, being a journalist, I might be interested to know the latest thinking. By some circuitous route he led into asking how I was sleeping. I told him the only thing keeping me awake was my novel and off he went on a discussion of how far I'd got, if I had an agent, recent bestsellers and the latest reviews.

I was caught off guard when he suddenly asked if I had noticed any change in my mood, depression, anxiety... I found myself sharing the dark moments. Before I had properly taken stock I was telling him about my father.

Whoever trained Curtis, trained him well, though I suspect you've got the knack or you haven't. He has it, and then some. He makes you think he's heard it all before, nothing shocks him and he pretty much knew that's how you felt anyway, he just wanted you to tell him so yourself. Lots of people hearing about my father would look at me differently; not Curtis. He somehow gave me permission to handle things in my own way, just shout if he could be of any help.

When he'd gone I put the research papers in my desk drawer without so much as a glance. He'd given me the reassurance I needed: my reactions were perfectly normal. At some future date I might try to analyse just how this guy operates, but for now I'm content just to savour the effect of his administrations. And hope Curtis outlives me!

Naomi smiled softly. Dr Curtis had indeed outlived his patient. And he'd been a true friend. He'd understood Adam's need to preserve his identity, to be more than his illness, to make his own choices. And in that final act of friendship...

No, she mustn't let her own knowledge of the ending distort Adam's experience.

20 OCTOBER — Between them Curtis and Lydia – and Cassandra! – seem to have worked some kind of magic. I'm sleeping so much better. Somehow, just knowing they know, and having them on my side, is a real source of comfort. Help! I must watch that sentimentality doesn't sneak out of the diary and spill over into real life.

Lydia assures me it's not a crime to just 'let it all hang loose'. So, I've decided, any sign of problems... nip the negative reactions in the bud and cue the relaxation techniques. My favourite so far is a tape of deep ocean sounds. Plus Cassandra.

Who knows? I might yet be persuaded down the yoga path. Imagine Harry's face were he to find me meditating, or better still levitating, instead of gulping down the sixth draught of caffeine. It'd be worth the ritual humiliation from my colleagues just for that priceless vision.

29 OCTOBER—Thirty-nine today. An unexpectedly exciting day thanks to the digital camera Naomi gave me. I can see this might be my new obsession.

Obsession it had been at first. She'd felt a surge of relief watching Adam enthusiastically exploring the range and scope of his new toy, actively seeking new subjects, animated in discussion with his brother-in-law about pixels and lenses. Surely he wouldn't be amassing skills and a large file of photos if he planned an imminent escape.

She glanced over at the poster-sized picture he'd taken of her in bed, bare shoulders, bare legs, brown against the white sheet draped discreetly over her body. Her expression said it all. She turned away. The bed, the nights… everything… it was all just so empty.

15 NOVEMBER—The novel is racing along. And my stash of photographs is mounting.

That chat with Lydia made me think again about telling folk and this week I felt robust enough to grasp the nettle.

It's been a mixed blessing. Curiously, analysing people's reactions has been interesting. I might even write something on that. *(Reactions – for Ideas folder) At work, I've run the gamut of everything from the instant tears of Wanda on Reception to a gruff, 'Sorry, mate, shout if we can help,' from the blokes in marketing.

Harry, of course, knew already. If the medical people get his body after death, I think they'll find his heart is made out of meccano, and his brain surrounded by a semi-permeable membrane that keeps all human feeling out. The blighter is just waiting to pounce on any sign of weakness. If he can't immediately see a fault in my work he'll hark back to earlier causes for complaint (well, as he sees them) and project warnings for the future. It wouldn't surprise me if he hasn't got some young sycophant groomed to replace me before my seat is cold. (It has just occurred to me, though, that he must have respected my request that he keep the information to himself. I don't believe all these folk were acting. A point in his favour. Whatever his motive.)

Fortunately the powers on high have been decent about it. Digby Arkwright, the chief, is a bumbling grandfatherly figure and comes in for a fair bit of ridicule among the troops, but when the chips are down he's a fair-minded guy and believes in running a happy ship. Newspapers are in his blood – he's the third generation with printers' ink in his veins. He made kind noises about my track record which amounted to something along the lines of, you've more than proved yourself, we're lucky to have someone of your calibre on board and if you need a bit of slack now, take it, there's a job here as long as you want it. Stick that, Harry!

Outside of work I've had all kinds of responses too: from a kind of withdrawing as if I've got something contagious, through patronising pity, to a rush to do things to 'spare me'. I feel like hanging a placard round my neck saying, I'm not deranged, I'm not incapable, I'm not infectious, I just need you to treat me normally. I'm only telling you so you'll understand slight peculiarities in my gait or my speech or whatever.

And because Lydia recommended I did. I must remember to tell her why someone like me should not rush out of the closet.

3 DECEMBER—It was Naomi's birthday yesterday. Thirty-six. And she still looks twenty-six. I couldn't help wishing I could stop her biological clock. How long will it be before she meets someone else who's fit and healthy and can give her a baby or two?

Naomi shuddered. She stared at the entry for a long moment before abruptly closing down Adam's computer and going in search of comfort in the kitchen.

The nightmare was even more intense that night. This time she was in the well of a court of law. Serried ranks of lawyers were shaking their fists, baying for a return of the death penalty. But for once her mother-in-law was silent. Her smug expression said it all; the legal world was pronouncing verdict and sentence for her.

It was another two days before Naomi could face returning to Adam's thoughts.

12 DECEMBER—I was supposed to see Devlin on Monday for my six-month check, but somebody from the hospital rang to say he was off sick and could I make another appointment for January. She said he specially wanted to see me himself. I'm not so self-deluded that I believe that, but it does help to know I'll see him in person. I'm sure his henchmen are perfectly well able to put me through my paces and decide whether to give me a six-months or four-months appointment. After all, what does any of it matter to someone with a limited span like mine? But I'm vulnerable enough to think I stand the best chance seeing the top man himself.

I wonder what's wrong with Devlin.

It's hard to believe it's six months since I got the news. Reality check: I'm still in a job. I'm still walking, still talking, still doing pretty much everything I want to do. And I'm six months further into my magnum opus. Put like that it feels positive.

17 DECEMBER—While other people are writing Christmas lists, I've started to compile a glossary of things people say alongside my private responses. Outwardly, I'm afraid, I'm still locked into the hypocrisy of polite social exchanges.

'You can still lead a full life.'
Being in a wheelchair, struggling for breath, may seem full to you, pal, but I've known better and by my yardstick it stinks.

'Your attitude will make all the difference.'
Why do people put the onus on me? If I deteriorate quickly, will that be a comment on my approach to life? If it's legitimate for you to be fed up with trivia, why can't I be frustrated by this major disaster?

'Try not to worry about the future, we none of us know what it holds anyway.'
Maybe, but I know pretty much what mine looks like; you can still believe that on the law of averages you'll have a reasonable lifespan and kids and a career and a pension.

'Enjoy today. Think positively about what you can do, not what you can't do.'
I'd like the feel of that if I said it myself; I hate it when other people in perfect health slug it to me.

'Channel your energy into creating the best quality of life you can.'
Ditto.

'It's a good thing you don't have kids.'
Now that is below the belt. I'd give a king's ransom to have the assurance that something of me lived on after my death.

'At least Naomi's still young enough to start again.'
Start what? D'you think I haven't recognised the fact that she's young and attractive and desirable and ready for the next stage in her hormonal life? Do you have to tell me she'll probably have kids with some other bloke? Do you?! Damn it, I want her to be happy with *me*! Have kids with *me*!

'Live positively with MND.'
That's one of the most patronising comments to date. It conjures up those Pollyannas who are paralysed from the neck down, or whose families are wiped out by a senseless act of terrorism, who go on record as saying they're a better person for having tribulations in their lives. *Ergo*, they're glad they've had these things happen to them. Give me a break! Goodness thrust upon you can't be the same value as goodness you chose to cultivate, can it?

'I see you've kept your sense of humour – that makes all the difference.'

I'm sure it helps you, but remember it costs me. Just because I'm poking fun at my own inebriated gait or my drunken slurring doesn't mean I'm laughing on the inside. Sometimes it's just a cover to defend myself from pity, or ridicule, or too much sympathy. Or it's because if I don't laugh I'll slip below the surface and in all likelihood never come up for air again.

On a good day I can tell myself most of these things but if there's one piece of advice I'd give to everybody about dealing with folk in trouble, it's this: Never ever count their blessings for them, or exhort them to count them themselves. Contrarily I know if someone else commiserates with my plight, my instinctive response is along the lines of: Things could be a lot worse; and to focus on what I can do. But that's my prerogative, no one else's.

Naomi read the list a second time and Adam's commentary three times.

How different things looked from the other side. How well he had captured the paradoxes. She too had hated the exhortations to be positive. But she hadn't appreciated how much it had cost Adam to retain his light-hearted view of life. It had seemed simply an extension of the man she knew and loved. He had always been a raconteur, given to amusing quips, ready to see the funny side of situations and mock his own behaviour or mistakes. And even since the onset of his MND, fighting for balance, struggling for air, how often he had turned her tears to giggles, given *her* the courage to go on.

Unexpectedly, into her mind came a vivid picture of Adam on the phone. It was early on in the history of the disease. Still able-bodied, still perfectly coherent, he'd suddenly crossed his eyes and started to writhe absurdly, his limbs as well as his face grossly contorted, one quavering finger stabbing at a button on her cardigan. But to the caller he would sound perfectly lucid and reasonable, thanking them for their kind offer to be put in touch with someone who dealt in communication aids for stroke victims. But what had been going on behind that merriment?

And now that laughter had gone out of her life. She missed it every day. A sense of humour *did* make a difference. *He* had made the difference. Now the onus was on her, she couldn't seem to summon up the strength to take up his mantle and put the lightness back into her situation. What blessings were there to count now?

19 DECEMBER — Contradictions seem to be multiplying with the awesome speed of rabbits these days.

I want information but I don't want to know more than I have to. Logically I can't defend this. For goodness' sake, I'm a trained investigator; I'm a professional snoop. I'm pathologically nosey. It's instinctive as well as learned. Why am I bucking the trend now?

I tell myself to just accept what I can do today, to be grateful I'm still functioning, and to work at keeping the 'I' in MIND, but all too frequently I find myself looking back at the me I was before this disease first clenched its fingertips into my left leg. Why is my brain rebelling so against my best intentions?

I'm also bothered about how people are perceiving me now. Annoying. What does it matter what they think? It shouldn't if I'm secure in myself. But somehow it does. It reminds me of a thought I've sometimes had at the funerals of old people. To many of the mourners this person was only ever bent and slow. I want the eulogy to capture the vital character they once were. I rather like the practice of having a photograph of the young version – pretty girl, happy father, successful career woman or whatever – on the front of the order of service to remind people.

In my case, although I won't be old, there will be people at my funeral who never knew the me I was even at the beginning of this year. For some of my older acquaintances the most abiding memories will be of my incapacity. I might add something to my 'wishes for after my death' file tonight. They might make some mention of my athletic abilities, my physical achievements, as well as the mental ones.

And maybe that's a good-enough reason to hang on to my older friends and acquaintances. It's tempting to immerse myself in the world of the disabled, cut the ties that bind me so unequally to the former yardsticks for success. Only people whose own horizons are limited would understand the excitement of getting through a day without an accident, the satisfaction of being understood without repeating myself.

What a mercy she had opened that folder 'Wishes for after my death'.

The photo she'd chosen showed Adam climbing in Snowdonia, tanned and triumphant. In reality there had been no need of such a visual display of his strength. All the old friends had clung to their memories – so many cards, so many letters, so many verbal exchanges, had dwelt on the good times.

'They hadn't forgotten, Adam. You should have heard them. If they didn't talk to you about the good times, that was only because they didn't want to remind you of what you'd lost.'

Indeed their sadness was the deeper just because he belonged more to the mountains than the wheelchair.

Those friends he had accumulated in his uneasy sojourn in the world of disability reached out in genuine sympathy too, knowing the horror of so many gathering shades of death, during the long drawn out goodbye. They too had climbed their own mountains.

She'd read and re-read the messages – she'd stopped counting after two hundred – that had come to her since that terrible day when she'd opened his death instructions. Not one, not even Harry's condolences, had diminished the real Adam, the man inside the demolition site.

24 DECEMBER—Outside it's Christmas Eve. For some reason I can't analyse, this makes me feel incredibly sad.

I'll go and collect some more cones for the fire tomorrow. Christmas is one of the few times we light the big open fire in the sitting room. My mother will doubtless make a comment about the danger of sparks. Naomi's parents will glance at her but say nothing. And I'll just ignore it and throw on more for good measure.

Roll on 27 December when normality returns.

27 DECEMBER—Nobody warned me Joel was coming. I still don't know whose idea it was to keep it as a surprise or why. Everybody else knew. I'm sure they meant well, but I'm not a child who needs surprises. I'm not at death's door, anxious to say my last goodbyes.

Joel, of course, made the whole thing into a joke. When my mother arrived she just pecked me on the cheek and walked on past me, her 'Happy Christmas' trailing behind her. I was about to close the door when there was an explosion of sound and colour. The shrill of three party blowers inches from my face preceded: 'Felicitations, big brother! *Joyeux Noël. Froehliche Weihnacten. God Jul. Buon Natale. Glaedelig Jul. Boas Festas. Felix Navidad.* And whatever else this pagan festival might offer to gladden your cardiac muscles.'

Christmas instantly took on a different complexion. Joel evened up the balance of the generations and the house lit up with merriment.

In a way I think I've always envied my young brother his light-hearted approach to life. Being five years my junior, he was largely protected from the worst excesses of Dad's violence and depression, and around the time of his suicide Joel lived with our grandparents more than he lived at home. I always got the impression that Mother favoured him (although Joel's perception is of a distant neurotic figure who couldn't wait to hustle him off to her parents). I was exhorted to be the responsible one, the man of the house; he was free to indulge in childhood folly. Even after we'd grown up I felt a sense of obligation to stay near enough to help Mother with tax bills, the beech hedge, repair jobs around the house; Joel seemed to see no moral duty beyond an occasional postcard or phone call and came home only to be waited on hand and foot, and even thanked for coming. Like the biblical elder brother, I resented the prodigal's reception, but unlike him I couldn't find it in my heart to do anything but rejoice in his occasional reappearances.

When I'd phoned Joel to tell him about my MND he'd been uncharacteristically silent.

I reassured him I could still do everything I'd always done and I had no intention of letting this thing beat me, so he needn't think for one moment he'd be able to take advantage of my disability or that sudden inheritance would allow him to live a life of indolence in the near future.

'Disabled? You're disabled?' His voice had sounded odd.

'No. Not in the way you're thinking. I just wanted you to hear from me in person before other people put their own slant on things.' For other people, read Mother.

Fortunately, over Christmas, I wasn't pushing myself and I doubt whether Joel would have detected anything out of the ordinary. But I took precautions just in case. I passed the wine to him to pour, admonishing him to 'earn his keep'. I used the trolley to remove the dishes, joking about the extra load he created. When he suggested a walk after lunch, I was mockingly indignant that *he* might be free as a bird but I had responsibilities to my other guests. Ahhhh. Writing this I see I was colluding in the pretence, treating Joel as the kid to be shielded. Joel, who's almost the same age as Naomi – and what protection has *she* got?

Anyway, Naomi instantly came to my rescue here and suggested Trivial Pursuit instead. Her parents have great general knowledge, my mother hogged all the Bible and Natural History questions, so the older generation certainly gave us a run for our money. In spite of Joel's scurrilous remarks about how easy their questions were, it pleased me to see a dawning respect for his worthy opponents.

Naomi's dad is an ardent royalist. Old school. Stands to attention when he hears the National Anthem, even in his own home. So of course, The Queen was essential viewing. We used the opportunity to clear up the debris in the dining room and when we next checked, all three of the parents were dozing in their chairs to the lullaby of some perennial film.

I wasn't even thinking about my illness, so Joel's sudden reference to it caught me off guard.

'Can I give you something – you know, nerves, stem cells, whatever? Anything to stop this thing getting you.'

I stared at him blankly.

'Have I said something stupid?' he shot out quickly.

'No. You just took me by surprise. I wasn't expecting…'

'You weren't expecting your ramshackle kid brother to have the odd spark of decency in him, eh?'

'No, you know I don't mean that. I wasn't even thinking of the MND. But… thanks, Joel. That's quite something.'

'I want to help. Can I? Is there anything?'

'Short of a miracle, I think not. Good of you to offer but it isn't something that you can donate, nice as the idea is.'

'What *can* I do then?'

'At this moment, just be yourself. You've turned this Christmas around just by being here. I don't know who set it up but I'm so pleased you came.'

Naomi came back into the kitchen and added her endorsement.

'Amen to that! It's brilliant having you here, Joel. And thanks to your misspent youth, your knowledge of pop music and forbidden films gave us the edge with Trivial Pursuit.'

Levity returned and Joel made no further reference to the MND. I didn't want to let it intrude into this good time but that one remark has made me realise that I have to think of the wider family. Joel may seem like a self-centred, independent guy, but if I'm not here, will he feel more responsibility for Mother? Will he feel guilty if he thinks he hasn't done his bit for me? I must talk to him sometime.

Memories of that Christmas sparkled across Naomi's mind. It had been Joel's idea to catch his brother unawares.

For her, a bigger surprise had been the change in her madcap brother-in-law since the diagnosis. On her recommendation he'd kept up an outward show of crazy unpredictability in front of Adam; behind the scenes he'd proved an unexpectedly mature and sensitive support to her. He knew intuitively how to amuse his brother. He made it his business to learn how to work within Adam's boundaries. She found she could relax, relying on his boundless wit.

The prospect of the festive season had oppressed her. The forced conversation of ill-assorted parents, the strain of too much inactivity, her own hyper-sensitivity to any reference to the future, the risk of nostalgia – everything held peril. Joel's gaiety had transformed the whole scenario for everyone.

31 DECEMBER—I've never been one for superstitious nonsense about the New Year but tonight I have to admit to chaos in the emotional department. There's a weird sense of a chapter of my life closing. It's the end of the era of wellness.

I was about to say this is a year that will be etched in my memory for ever, but given the expected length of my life that's not much of a statement. This time last year I was a perfectly ordinary bloke, hurtling through the months with nothing much more to worry about than paying the bills on time and the slow leak in the roof over the smallest bedroom. Oh, and coping with Harry's foul moods and impossible deadlines. As 2006 draws to a close I'm more preoccupied with how long I shall be able to keep any money coming in and just when would be the right time to move to a single-storey house, or whether we should adapt the downstairs of this place. And occasionally, whether I'll hang around that long.

Naomi's the real reason for my melancholy. I've always accepted that I neglect her shamefully – what with my frequent absences and my crazy work schedule. But today I'm sick with worry about my presence. How will she cope with my disintegration? Would my permanent absence be kinder?

She's in the sitting room on her own right now, watching something mindless on the box, working on her cross-stitch. I had to make a pretence of having to scribble ideas for the novel down while they were fresh. It's like a physical pain looking at her and thinking what I'm thinking *vis-à-vis* endings. I'm too close to tears for listening to anything sentimental or loving. So I've come in here to let it out in this diary and get a grip before we toast ourselves and welcome in a New Year.

What exactly am I welcoming? It's too grim to contemplate. Maybe once we're safely into January I'll find the courage but tonight I want to just shut all the doors, secure all the windows, and ignore everything except the fact that she's here with me and I'm still able to be almost everything to and with her that we were this time last year.

I need some strong diversion therapy, so I'm going to write a bright and stimulating section of my novel: Aidan is composing a satirical piece about New Year resolutions. Hopefully the buzz from that'll get me through being alone with Naomi for the transition to next year. A year ago I'd have revelled in the prospect of the two of us snuggling up. Tonight I'm struggling. But I *will* find the right degree of enthusiasm. I *will* find the humour to deflect the sadness. I *will* metamorphose into the seductive lover. I *WILL!*

The memories of Adam's lively repartee, his normality, flooded through her mind with a poignancy that constricted her throat and brought stinging tears to her eyes now. There had been no hint of his struggle.

1 JANUARY 2007—I wish I had the words to capture how I feel about Naomi. I think I appreciated the enormous importance and strength of our relationship more last night than I've ever done. That, of course, was partly what was threatening my control.

I think – hope! – I managed to equip myself creditably in the thespian stakes. I made sure I kept control of what we talked about around midnight, steering the chat into silly territory as soon as the bells and the first kiss were out of the way. If she was disappointed that I wasn't more sloppy or sentimental, she didn't show it. And we made up for it in bed.

But I'm not going to jeopardise the precarious state of my emotions by being introspective, even in this diary in the cold light of day, so I'm off to suggest a tramp along the river – surely even Lydia would grant me that little reward for my efforts of yesterday.

3 JANUARY—Being back within the orbit of Harry's malign tongue seems particularly lowering this year. January ought to signal a new start but Harry shows no sign of change – unless it's to be even more cussed than before. He actually ripped my latest offering to shreds and tossed it back

to me – electronically – with a blistering message: 'If this is the best you can do, suggest you spend the day drafting a letter to DA.' But as I've said there ain't no way Harry is driving me to resign. So I sat right down and wrote a piece on bullying in the workplace. If he recognised himself he gave no hint of it, but like I say, the guy's made of meccano.

10 JANUARY—I've finally summoned the courage to send for a pack of information from the Motor Neurone Disease Association and it arrived today. Prompt service.

It's neatly packaged information, well-ordered and easily accessed. But instantly it's in-your-face. For a kick off it calls itself 'Your personal guide'. Hmmm. Not the tone I'm personally looking for. And then – for goodness' sake! – the fastener's stuck with Velcro! They might as well put in a voucher for money off a pack of incontinence pads. I had to force myself through the first stages of the process. I actually pencilled in 'im' in front of the lurid 'personal' sticker. Then I took the green felt monster that came free with a cereal packet and slammed it onto one side of that vile Velcro fastener. Thumbing my nose at its significance.

I skimmed over the pages that invited me to record my own details, gritting my teeth by this stage. It smelt like a primary kid's jotter! Shall I hang my apron on this peg, Miss? And please may I colour in the boxes? But then, mercifully, there was a section on information about the disease itself. Just facts. Facts any journalist trying to find out about it would want to see.

Apparently only two people in every hundred thousand get MND. Pretty uncommon by any standards. You're almost bound to ask, why me? It's like seeing one of those old sepia photos where someone is ringed because otherwise you'd never recognise them. Was I ringed from birth? If I'd dodged behind the rows of folk and poked my grinning face up somewhere else would the mantle have fallen on some other poor sod? I have this sudden picture of a giant hand whirling out of heaven selecting me: It's for You-hoo! Only this lottery isn't worth a single, solitary dime.

It seems that death by MND is faster than death by MS so there are less people with MND at any time even though the incidence of both diseases is approximately the same. I haven't decided yet if that's the short or the long straw.

It's rarely familial; only five to ten per cent of cases. I've never heard of anyone else in the family with it, and anyway I've been told mine isn't that kind. There are implications there – especially with the inherited variety – but I don't want to look at them yet.

Sufficient unto the day, as the Good Book says.

And my mother.

The thought ricocheted in her head.

'You have to be thankful it isn't the genetic type, Naomi. Imagine knowing your kids might have inherited it too.'

Naomi felt again the surge of rage she'd experienced the first time she heard those words from her cousin.

'Thankful? *Thankful?*' she'd exploded. 'Just remind me again how lucky we are that Adam's got this thing, will you?'

'I didn't mean that. You know I didn't. I'm only saying...' Dorothy stammered.

'Yeah, yeah, yeah. It could have been worse. I wish I had a pound for every blessing I've been told to count since you all knew about Adam.'

At least Dorothy had the grace to look chastened.

'I'm sorry, I didn't mean...'

Naomi sighed.

'No, nobody does. So why say it?'

Their unmeant words continued to reverberate: 'Just take one day at a time.' 'You mustn't be selfish – think of the family. This affects them too, you know.' 'With the right frame of mind you can achieve the impossible!' 'It's a personal challenge.' 'Keep smiling – think of Adam.'

For Adam the platitudes and admonitions had been a thousand times worse.

Dorothy's face merged with her mother-in-law's in her dreams that night, sneering, the taunts sibilant in their ferocity: 'Murderess! Murderess! Murderess!'

15 JANUARY—Today I had another appointment with the Big Chief Wallawalla himself. I'm going to record it in some detail because my brain won't retain all this stuff.

I am reassured that Devilish Devlin's keeping a watchful eye on me personally because he of all people surely knows how to spot deviations from the projected path and he certainly ought to be up to speed with any new therapies. On the other hand, I didn't want an expert eye to detect anything I couldn't yet see myself.

He is the expert and there's no mistaking it. But what a subject to specialise in! Hundred per cent mortality figures. Never any cures. I'm gob-smacked just thinking of breaking news like that to people time after time. What does that take out of somebody like him? And just how many poor beggars hearing the death knell want to shoot the messenger?

Devlin looked as calm and unflappable as ever. He was wearing rimless glasses. Somehow the lack of a containing frame made his eyes look even more unrestrained as they struggled alternately to peer over the plastic barriers, getting into a frenzy when the opposition won.

It was a mauve ensemble day: shirt, tie, triangle of handkerchief. I read somewhere that mauve sends out signals to male homosexuals. I looked at Devlin and tried to imagine him in the role. With those eyes? Even on a perfectly unambiguous playing field there's scope for misunderstanding. In a game where the rules are subtle and some of the players are unsure themselves which side they're batting for, he'd never get past first post. It's a jolly good thing Devlin can't scan my thoughts with his x-ray vision. At least, I devoutly hope he can't!

At this point I had to say something just to stop him seeing into my head, so I blurted out something about hoping he was better himself. I guess I shouldn't have expected for one second that he would let anything personal ooze around that rigid guard. He just thanked me and said he was fine. I knew he'd have said that even if he had three weeks to live. He instantly moved into asking me how I'd been. Like two acquaintances meeting casually on a station platform and exchanging civilities until the train arrived.

But that's where the illusion ended, because of course, though I know nothing at all about him, he knows more about me, the physical me anyway – and probably more about the psychological too – than anyone else alive. He can probe and touch and test and take incredible liberties with my person; but I am instantly feeling I've been too familiar asking a simple non-invasive question as to how he's feeling. Weird. *(Balance of power – add to Ideas folder.)*

Anyway I wasn't going to waste valuable time analysing that with the clock ticking in the good doctor's consulting room. The bumph from the MND Association had reminded me of the age thing that Devlin had mentioned at that bombshell visit. MND usually affects people over fifty, so why do I get it in my thirties? He was big enough to say they don't know. Stephen Hawking developed it in his early twenties. Why? Nobody knows.

Today he volunteered that he had been a tad suspicious when he first probed my family history, on hearing about my father dying aged thirty-seven. He admitted my GP had since filled him in on that. I mumbled something akin to an apology. He must have thought it strange that I hadn't been forthcoming but until Curtis sneaked up on me unawares, suicide wasn't something I ever really made eye contact with.

He asked a stack of questions and checked me over with his usual noncommittal noises in what seemed like a suspiciously long exploration of my repertoire. I was just starting to get that feeling of dread, when he gave a sudden smile. It was the first time I'd ever seen any evidence of real warmth in him, and I confess, it counted.

Overall he pronounced himself satisfied with my present condition; well, he wrapped it up in more professional language, but that's what it amounted to. The audit over, I expected to be instantly shepherded back out into the real world. Not so. Devlin leaned back in his chair, steepled his fingers and did his utmost to look directly at me. Was there anything I'd like to talk about? He knew, he said, that people needed to take their own time assimilating information. Where was I with this? He'd be happy to discuss any aspect of MND if it would be helpful.

I was devoutly thankful I'd read the MND Association pack from cover to cover.

'I was wondering if you could fill me in on some of the treatments,' I said. 'I made a list of the drugs and things but to be honest the jargon was pretty incomprehensible to someone as clueless as me.'

He was kind enough not to mention my refusal to listen to a word about drugs at my last appointment and conceded it was a daunting subject to contemplate. Was there anything specific I had in mind? I actually had the list with me, so I spread the scabby bit of paper out on the desk and started at the top. Even the names of the drugs were complicated.

'Riluzole or Rilutek? The report said it's had "modest results". What does that mean in real terms?'

'There's some evidence of improved survival rates with it, yes.'

Survival... ahhh! The more I hear that term, the ghastlier it gets. Seems to me, living longer with this thing isn't necessarily a positive outcome. Still, I'm not about to share that thought in this particular wigwam. Not yet.

'But... ?'

'Sorry?' He looked truly mystified.

'Do I hear a "but" in there somewhere?'

He shrugged his shoulders. 'Well, these drugs probably only slow progression by a few months at most. Not all neurologists feel they're appropriate.'

'How do drugs like that actually work, then?' I asked. Back to AO'N, journalist, on safer ground.

And I even took in the first part of what Devlin said. Apparently there's something called glutamate, which is an amino acid that acts as the main neurotransmitter in your central nervous system. People with MND have too much glutamate and that affects key parts of the brain and spinal cord and damages the nerves. This drug, Riluzole, inhibits the amount of glutamate being released into the synapses.

I have this crazy mental picture of an old man producing excess saliva. You stick a dry crust in his mouth to mop some of it up and it disguises his problem for a while, but eventually the bread is saturated and the drooling starts all over again – and this time it's mucky stuff littered with fragments of regurgitated toast. I want to put a bib on him, turn his chair to face the wall, hide the defeat in his eyes. I'm not so keen on the analogy by this time.

I don't know if Devlin picked up on my vibe but he suddenly said, 'I seem to remember you're not personally keen on taking medication. However, I should tell you that there's a newish line of enquiry into something called neurotrophic drugs, which may slow down the degenerative process. Have you come across those?'

I skimmed my list. Yep, there it was.

'These drugs are chemically similar to the proteins our bodies make normally when we're in good health, which ensure nerve cells survive and function. But the drugs are still at the testing stage. We don't really know exactly how they work and it's incredibly difficult to get them to the right spot. Basically, what we're doing at the moment is smuggling them into the body disguised as other cells such as viruses – although the nasty elements of the viruses have been removed first, of course.'

I grinned at him.

'Go in for treatment for MND and come out with HIV, huh?'

He half smiled.

'We wouldn't use viruses of that sort. What we're hoping to do is to hoodwink the immune system into believing the cells are who they appear to be. The problem is that the immune system has a nasty habit of rebelling against the intrusion of foreign cells. Other scientists have been trying to overcome this resistance by using something like fats instead of viruses to carry the genes to the nerve cells. I must be perfectly frank with you. Clever as these ideas are in theory, test results have been rather disappointing.'

'In an odd sort of way it's comforting to know that nature isn't so easily tricked, isn't it?'

'Hmmm. An unusual line of thinking but I see your point.'

'From the little I've read, I get the impression that these experimental treatments tend to be tried out on patients who are already extremely severely compromised. Yes?'

'That's certainly the case with some of the trials.'

'So they don't stand much chance of being effective anyway, do they?'

'That is one of the obstacles in work with gene therapy, for example, and it's one of the big problems when it comes to translating laboratory knowledge into clinical practice. There's a tendency to limit the risk by offering it to those who have least to lose.'

'So how does someone like me decide whether or not to try a drug or a treatment then?'

'Well, I'm not trying to fob you off with a non-answer, but it's way too complicated to explain the pros and cons of every option in a few minutes. I could give you some literature on the subject, so that you could see what's already been trialled and some of the other avenues of thought that offer promise. I don't myself really understand all the complex science behind these things but you're welcome to see what the researchers know so far and why some of the trials have been stopped and where they've tried new ideas out. I should perhaps warn you, though, that it's not a very encouraging picture so far. Most of the trials have shown no improvement. I think you ought to know that before you see this stuff.'

'Thanks. I appreciate the honesty.'

'It's not all doom and gloom though,' Devlin rushed on. 'The brightest star on the horizon at the moment is probably stem cell work. You'll have heard of stem cells?'

'I don't really understand it, except that early cells can develop into specialised cells, given the right environment. I knew someone who had leukaemia and she was given stem cells which would turn into new blood cells. Am I vaguely in the right ball park?'

'Certainly. And what the aim would be with ALS – MND, if you prefer – would be to try to create new nerve cells using stem cells, pluripotent cells, which are potentially capable of turning into any kind of cell. Basically what it involves is taking these early cells that haven't yet decided what they'll be when they grow up and giving them instructions that turn them into healthy nerve cells. Very much what we're doing with bone marrow transplants, where we're giving a patient stem cells designed to turn into various kinds of blood cells. Turning a cell into a nerve cell is obviously different, but as far as ALS goes, from a purely scientific point of view this is the most promising development on the horizon.'

'But?'

He looked at me with his head on one side.

'Sorry?'

'I feel another "but" in there somewhere.'

Devlin nodded with a resigned air.

'You're right. It's an area of work that's fraught with ethical as well as medical problems. To begin with there's a lot of resistance in a number of quarters; people questioning the wisdom or morality of this kind of tinkering with cells. Is it ethically acceptable? There are plenty of people who would say most definitely not. But in any case, stem cell work is very much in its infancy. Even its most enthusiastic supporters would say, don't expect any clinical trials for ALS for at least a couple of years, probably far more. And the trials themselves take years to do effectively. Nobody wants to rush into something this experimental when we don't know either the short-term or the long-term consequences. So we are nowhere near being in a position to offer this treatment to patients generally.'

I heard the implication loud and clear: not in your lifetime. It was a fine balancing act: hope, comfort, but not too much promise.

'Whether or not you'd personally be interested in taking part in experimental drug treatments is something perhaps we might discuss when you've had a chance to read more about the options and the risks and the ethical concerns and so on. I'm anxious not to raise any false hope.'

'I appreciate that. And as you say, I need to know a lot more about the risks.'

20 JANUARY—Devlin was right on one thing. It was hard going. And it wasn't just my resistance to taking drugs of any kind, it was dense and difficult information to understand. I gave up reading the scientific stuff after a couple of attempts, on the basis that I needed to have a better grasp of the overall picture to see these fine details in context.

So I went back to the material I'd downloaded from the Internet and some 'self-help' literature. Self-help has a whole new meaning to me these days. *(Add to Ideas file – *Self-help*.) Some stark facts leaped out at me.

'The senses remain intact.' There's a pretty cruel inventor at work here. I'll make sure you savour this thing to the full. No merciful numbing – not even of the intellect. No, you'll be aware, fully aware, of what's happening, you poor sod.

This isn't really connected but it flashed into my mind. I remember the actor, Michael J Fox, talking about the 'brutal assumption of authority' over his life that Parkinson's Disease assumed. And the phrase holds resonance for me now. It is a battle for supremacy. I need to fight to retain the areas in which I still have sovereignty. I need to hang on to the authority I have to be myself, to keep the 'I' in MIND. Consciously. Deliberately. Persistently.

And I guess that means I need periodically to take stock of where I am, what control I still have and where the defences are weakest.

'Sphincters are not usually affected.' So incontinence isn't on the list. Phew! But hey, wait a minute. If your legs won't take you to a safe place when your bladder or bowel tell you it's loo time you might as well be incontinent, mightn't you?

'Sexual needs should not be ignored.' Gee thanks, matey! Like I needed that permission. 'mND does not usually affect the ability to have an erection or to reach orgasm.' So it's a matter of being creative when the old limbs become recalcitrant, then. Naomi permitting.

'It's not contagious.' Well, maybe the degeneration of the nerves isn't, but the stigma, the fear, the anxiety, they sure as hell are.

'It's progressive and life-limiting.' This thought has stubbornly lingered in the cracks between my brain cells, I have to admit. I've come to the conclusion that slow disintegration is worse than a sudden illness that strikes you down rapidly. You have time – far too much time – to absorb the full implications of what's ahead. It's a bit like knowing your brakes are faulty and at any minute they'll fail and you'll be rushing headlong towards a precipice.

But it's not all negative. Once you've accepted your own mortality, you have this unusual opportunity to work out how you want to make your mark, a time-limited chance to repair broken relationships, leave your affairs in order, get rid of incriminating evidence. Most people will cruise through the bulk of their lives not even nodding in the direction of the Grim Reaper. When they slam into a tree at a hundred miles per hour, or board a plane with a terrorist, or go into a coma, or fall down a mineshaft, some poor grieving relative has to sort out the underpants with sagging elastic, and pay the bill for back copies of 'Naughty but Nice'. And now Cousin Billy will never have the chance to say sorry for stealing their girlfriend, and the wronged wife will never get that overdue explanation for being abandoned. Not that I have a string of wronged anythings queuing up for absolution.

Those of us ringed for the disease don't know how fast, or how long, or exactly when. They tell you that in your case it's slower or faster or whatever, as if you personally achieved this distinction. But the fact remains, you do have an unexpected opportunity to put your house in order before it's too late.

Even saying this in the privacy of this diary, it smacks of Pollyanna. I'd give it all away for the carefree unconcern of the unmarked man. I know I would. Sagging elastic notwithstanding. To hang with Cousin Billy!

'And I'd cheerfully have sorted out the chaos to have one more month, one more week, one more hour,' Naomi whispered. She looked up from the screen and her eyes wandered around his study at the things he *had* left behind. So many memories. Bitter-sweet memories.

29 JANUARY—Against my every inclination I've returned to Devlin's little scientific offerings. Although I didn't get any deeper into the jungle of technical detail, I did match up the overall findings with the simpler accounts in the other literature, so I'm getting a clearer picture of what types of arrows the big Indians have in their quivers. And it stinks.

So some drugs have 'modest benefits'. (Modest seems like an odd word to my journalistic mind. As if its hemline is below-the-knee or it's falsely self-effacing. I know what they mean, but I'd have chosen a different descriptor myself.) Why would I want extra time to watch myself staying alive against the odds? What's the point? We know there's no cure, so let's just get on with it.

Okay, the pamphlets say there's merit in relieving or managing symptoms. Maybe. But not prolonging the horror. Definitely not.

They can help you maintain your independence.

What independence?

I'm perfectly well aware that I'm feeling down and I know I'm being totally unreasonable but I'm not going to pull myself together. It's a grey, drizzly, freezing-cold almost-February day and that pesky, vindictive, nit-picking bully, called Harry Bloody Mansfield, is doing his utmost to pressure me into resigning.

I WILL NOT LET HIM BROWBEAT ME INTO SUBMISSION.

I WILL NOT LET MND BROWBEAT ME INTO SUBMISSION.

I AM IN CONTROL HERE.

And tomorrow everything will seem different.

30 JANUARY—Contemplated the pros and cons of ending it all, today. Not easy.

Like I said yesterday, maybe tomorrow will look different.

Nausea washed over her remembering that day.

She'd come home earlier than expected. The silence in the house... the order in his study... it was unnerving. Where was he?

She'd found him standing in the garage with the door closed staring at the car. Her knees had buckled beneath her, and she'd had to lean on the bonnet of the car herself.

'What... are you... doing?' she'd managed.

'Just thinking' was all he vouchsafed before putting an arm around her shoulders and leading her back into the house.

From that evening she knew a moment of fear every time she opened the front door after a day at work.

12 FEBRUARY—Those different tomorrows didn't materialise, hence the silence of the past fortnight.

I've decided that the quality of the life I have left is as much if not more important than the length of that life. And what do I want as part of that 'quality'?

I want to be as cheerful as I can be.

I want to be as free from pain and discomfort as possible.

I want to retain my abilities for as long as possible.

I want to contribute usefully to my profession for as long as I can.

I want to maintain my relationship with Naomi, as it is, for as long as I can.

I want to leave her with good memories of me.

If treatment will assist me to realise those aims, then I want to know which treatment, and when.

Okay, Devlin, I'm listening. Actually I've taken a tangible, positive step today too. I've put photos of Naomi all over the place – not so she can see them and be embarrassed (like she was when I stuck the one of her in bed on my wall), but where I'll see them and be constantly reminded – reminded that she'll soon only have memories. Do I want her to remember me as grouchy or morose or defeated? Do I want her to remember me with disappointment or shame, as Mother remembers my dad? Do I heck! Seeing her face when she found me in the garage was enough to convince me of that. It's down to me to make sure she doesn't. And this time around is for real, it's no dummy run, no rehearsal.

So when I'm feeling more robust about all this I'll get back to Devlin's papers. For her sake.

It had been a shock finding the photos everywhere – not just in the usual places like his wallet or desk drawer, but tucked inside his sock drawer, threaded into the back of his tie rack, in the pocket of his overnight bag, in folders, books, CD covers. She'd started to find them when he began to need practical assistance. When she'd challenged him he'd grinned at her.

'Didn't know I was so sentimental, huh?'

'You're not!' she'd shot back.

'Well, it just shows how little you know the guy you married.'

It had never occurred to her he was working so hard for her sake back then. If only... If only...

She looked across at the photograph of him and shook her head.

'Oh Adam! Why didn't you tell me all this?'

2 MARCH—Lydia shocked me today.

Now, I'm essentially a private person. My body is my exclusive possession – well, it used to be anyway. I realise there has to be some loosening of the reins of ownership when illness strikes but even so, I see a big difference between taking liberties with my body and exposing my mind. That's hallowed ground. But Lydia seems to creep inside my head and turn over stones even I don't look under.

'You don't need to struggle on your own, honey.'

'Struggle? I'm not struggling.'

'And you don't need to set yourself impossible goals.'

'No?'

'You and me, Mister O, we ain't in competition. We're pals. Best mates. Doing the three-legged race. Together.'

I couldn't help but smile at the picture she conjured up. No doubt about it, she'd steam down the track bearing me along with her effortlessly even if I made no contribution whatever. A dynamo to my brake.

'I love your analogy, Lydia, but you've lost me, I'm afraid. I haven't a clue what you're talking about.'

'I can feel how bad it's getting. No need to pretend with me.'

Seems Lydia knows exactly how many of my arrows are hitting the outer ring of the target, how many are missing altogether – the mental resolve as well as the physical objectives. Damn her perspicacity. I wanted her to go along with my fiction.

Who else sees behind the façade?

What else had this woman seen that she, his wife, had missed?

7 MARCH—Dr Curtis came today. His receptionist rang to check I was in and available. To tell the truth, even if I hadn't been, I think I'd have re-jigged things to be here. I'm impressed by what this man is trying to do. GPs I know have a whole host of targets to meet and they get the raw end of things with all the piffling complaints and the griping and the lead-swingers and the hypochondriacs. Seems to me they do a lot of the hard graft but get precious little of the glory. In spite of the demands on his time and energy, Curtis has made it his business to add me to his list of optional extras. Here he is dotting in for a spot of the old TLC outside of his working hours. And I know he's often in the surgery until 7, 8 at night. If he has a wife and kids, they don't see a lot of him.

He didn't even wait till I called him. He thought about me and volunteered to come – just to see how I'm 'getting on', as he put it mildly.

He'd heard from Devlin, he said, in a routine letter, that from an MND point of view I was doing quite nicely. He didn't mention Lydia, but I'm pretty sure she'd have whispered some inside info too, knowing Lydia.

'How d'you feel you're doing physically?'

'Pretty reasonable, I'd say. Nothing spectacular. Just ticking along.'

'And how are you coping?' he asked in the same friendly light tone.

'Fine.'

'I was just wondering – would you be interested in talking to someone?'

'As in?'

'A counsellor?'

'Why? D'you think I'm losing the plot? And there was I kidding myself I was one of the steel-plated variety!'

'Oh no! Don't misunderstand me. You seem to be completely on the ball and handling this really well. But what about what's underneath? This is a big thing to grapple with. I just want to be sure we're giving you all the support you need.'

'Well, I'm totally blown away by all this attention. Dr Devlin's been really helpful. Sees me himself, too. Lydia is brilliant. And I'm terrifically grateful for your visits. Way beyond what I need or deserve, I'd say. But thanks anyway.'

'But would it help to let off steam to someone who isn't part of the actual physical care-giving team?'

'I don't think I need that. I can talk to you, can't I?'

'Well, yes, of course. That, too. But you could have dedicated time to talk about how you're feeling to somebody whose job it is to listen. And who isn't distracted by all the other things.'

'But you listen. I guess it'd be different if it was just a rushed two minute appointment down at the surgery. I'd be a bit cagey about taking up your time if there were twenty really sick people outside in your waiting room. But with you dropping in like this... I'm sure you have a million other more important things to do tonight but you make me feel like this is important. I appreciate that.'

'It is important.'

'I'm sure not all GPs operate like you.'

'Some of my colleagues are hotter on the technical stuff. Some of them specialise and get right into the research and latest advances and everything. I'm one of the low-key brigade. A stage-hand not a film star! Don't have the drive, I guess. As my primary school teacher said in my report, "Hugo is a plodder but he gets there in the end." I was always rather in the shadow of my older sister, I'm afraid.'

'Comparisons are odious, to quote a dreadful cliché.' I grimaced.

'Indeed. I thought so at the time anyway. Now? Well, I'm comfortable doing what I do and we don't move in the same circles professionally, so people don't know I'm the also-ran!'

'What does your sister do? Is she in medicine too?'

'No. She's some big noise in nuclear physics. Part of the international scene. All way beyond me.'

'But... well, take it from me, you do make a difference. Where it counts. People like me need people like you who have time to care, to share the struggle. Not that I think you're an also-ran, I hasten to add. I mean you can't be any intellectual slouch yourself. Seems to me you GPs need just as much skill to know about tons of illnesses as a consultant needs to stay abreast of a tiny bit of medicine. Don't you?'

'In a way. But I know my limitations and one thing I do believe in is drafting in experts when we need them. Dr Devlin will keep an eye on your MND and suggest treatments and so on. Lydia will take care of the physio side of things and keep you as mobile as possible. We'll call in the MND Nurse, the Speech and Language Therapist, as and when you need them. I'll help with any minor things that might crop up along the way.

But a professional listener might just be the ticket for helping you deal with the psychological side of this. That's all I was thinking.'

'I have to say, I think you're under-selling yourself. You've been incredibly kind and to be honest, you've surprised me. As you know, I haven't had much experience of illness, so I haven't dabbled in the NHS before. But you take the time to listen and you understand.'

'Well, thanks for that,' he said with an embarrassed air.

'No, I really mean it. It makes a difference having you folk on my side, I can tell you. You. Lydia. You don't treat me like just another patient, all in a day's work. You really seem to care how I feel and go that extra mile.'

'Lydia's a one-off! I'm glad you like her. She's a great person to have on your team.'

'I count myself very fortunate.'

Long after Curtis had gone I thought about this. It could make a useful reflective feature I think. *(Add to Ideas folder: *kindness an optional extra*.)

'Kind' seems too loose a term for what I'm trying to get at. It's more a disposition thing – when somebody is disposed to do one good, to be generous in the giving, to be friendly about it, to do it because they care about you and really want to do something for you. It comes from within, stems from inherent qualities of goodness. If it's genuine anyway.

On the face of it you'd think that anyone wanting to enter the caring professions must be naturally kind, wouldn't you? But watching the staff in hospital I'm not so sure. One of the doctors I saw when I went for tests (Dr FG Smith-Franklin, Senior Registrar, if his badge was to be believed), well, you wouldn't mistake him for kind. Technically proficient, probably. Professionally detached, yeah. But I got the distinct impression he'd had kindness trained out of him – if he ever had it in the first place. Would it take up too much valuable time to be kind as well as professional? Would it make him too vulnerable to show his natural emotion? Would it risk him identifying too much with my plight? Would it leave him too empty and drained to be a person outside of his white coat? I might explore this with some of the medics I come across from here on in.

For now though, do I want a counsellor? I told Curtis I'd think about it. A counsellor would set boundaries around her time, around her remit. I don't want a listening ear at 3PM on a Friday afternoon, I want it when I want it. I need it when I need it. And how long would it take me to feel safe with a professional listener? Especially somebody who doesn't see what's really happening to me, who only sees my scrubbed-up self. My hunch is I'd feel more comfortable sharing my thoughts with a trusted friend, somebody who sees for himself what I'm battling with, who shares the bad patches, who sees me as I am, who cares through it all. Who goes on caring, not just for the regulation fifty-five minutes. Someone like Curtis.

And it needn't take more than five minutes sometimes – just to receive that little touch of kindness in with the prescription. It's as much an attitude as anything else that I'm looking for.

I don't want to lay bare the mental, emotional, psychological aspects for scrutiny and dissection. I don't want someone trying to winkle out that bit more of my inner self. I don't want to divorce the emotions from the whole beastly thing and offer them naked to somebody who has permission to ignore the context and probe my childhood or my marriage or my fear of dying – or any other stupid red herring the psychobabble lists as a legitimate target for somebody paid by the hour to analyse my chance comments and show me how maladjusted I am to a terminal condition.

No, I think Curtis is exactly the man I need. I really believe I could tell him how bad it is and he'd take it quite calmly and help me through without sending for the straitjackets. He's already shown he's a bespoke man, not limited to off-the-peg. He knows there are no-go areas – like PEG tubes and ventilation. I told him loud and clear, I'll not be here for that bit.

But more importantly, there's a big question coming up that I need to talk about and I need to know it's in safe hands when I share it.

Naomi did a double take. Nineteen days without a single entry. After the apparent luxury of a lengthy discourse on kindness it was odd.

26 MARCH — I've found another outlet for my tensions, another diversion. Hence the long silence.

It comes in the shape of Hester Ramonides! She's bounced into my novel and she's my current preoccupation. She's helped me through several sleepless nights and I find her irresistible.

Hester has synaesthesia – along with six per cent of the population in the UK, apparently, although I've only recently come across it. There's a joining up of sensations – words with colours, for example. In the normal brain there's a division; in the synaesthete it's missing. I'm intrigued. Imagine tasting or smelling music, or feeling the texture of words, or seeing language in technicolour. My character Hester is a fellow patient of Aidan's, and she sees words and letters in 3-D and colour.

I know you can't produce these effects artificially and I don't suppose it's a joking matter for those people who live with synaesthesia in real life, but in order to get a feel for Hester's sensations I've been practising with my own thoughts. It seems there are several well-known writers who do have this extraordinary perception of words and if I can find one of them

I might get them to check the description in my book for authenticity – although no two people experience this curious phenomenon in exactly the same way so that allows me some latitude.

For Hester, MOTOR begins as glossy black, iridescent sparks on the circles with the final letter fading to a blur of pale grey with frills of smoky blue inside the loop of the R. There's a hint of olive green down one side of the T which fades in and out with the changing light. NEURONE is an all-over oceanic greenish-grey with spiky letters at the beginning but the O and N start to roll out more smoothly and have opalescent halos around them with hints of fuchsia pink and dark turquoise underlining the bottom edge of the letters.

I wanted to make DISEASE spectral white with a bilious yellow shadowing each letter, but I realise that's too stereotypical. Instead it's horizontally banded with the colour and bloom of black grapes at the top going through a spiteful mustard to a sort of murky pink with little bumps like the suction pads of a non-slip bathmat here and there anchoring it to the line. And there are waving navy-blue tentacles coming out of the last E.

Like I say, I'm having great fun with Hester Ramonides!

28 MARCH—Lydia should have become a spin doctor. She's a natural!

'Why Mister O, this is a golden opportunity you are missing!' she said with one of her throaty laughs, manhandling my legs in her powerful black hands, Caribbean drums thrumming through her vowels.

'Oh?'

'Well, you are getting tired, yes?'

'With you putting my poor old body through the mill, is it any wonder?' I retorted. 'Ever thought of becoming an interrogator of spies? You wouldn't need training for the torture techniques!'

'Not *now*, I don't mean. I mean tired day by day, after just normal, everyday lolloping through life. Yes?' Somehow she didn't miss a beat with her exercises in spite of her tongue running off at a tangent.

'Oh, I see. Well yes, I get tired.'

'And what should you do when you get tired, huh?'

'Sleep?'

'Yeeeeeees. And?'

'Rest?'

'Sure thing, honey! Lots of luuuuvvaly rest. In bed.' She threw me a broad grin and a wink.

'So?'

'Sakes alive! And you a writer and all! Big imagination. Not like us lesser mortals.'

I stared at her feeling somehow mentally deficient but seeing no clues.

'Well, you sure are not the most compliant of my customers when it comes to taking things easy. That I must say.'

'Sorry.'

'Sorry is not the point. What you need is incentive, honey. Innnn-ceeen-tive.'

'And the incentive you're offering is?'

'I am not offering! No, sirree! A person can get struck off in my business for propositioning a customer. No. It's the little lady who will do the offering.'

Enlightenment hit me at last.

'Lydia! I'm not at all sure that you wouldn't already be struck off for exceeding your brief!'

'It is not exceeding my brief to get you to relax more, Mister O. Only you have not been listening to my pearls of wisdom up till now. You and me, we got to find some way to make you ease up. And I am just thinking sidey-ways. You need rest. You need bed. But you do seem allergic to bed. So! We need to find a way to make bed more exciting. Pop the little lady in it. You get my drift?'

'I most certainly do get your drift, Lydia. I'm only amazed that I didn't get it earlier. I guess I didn't expect an indecent proposal from my physio!'

'There aint nothing indecent about lying down and hugging the Missus when you are struggling to get about on the old pins. No, sirree! Decent enough for the Methodist minister, as my granny would say.'

I had to laugh. I felt the vibration of her own enjoyment through the ample flesh pressed against my arm, although she managed somehow to preserve a solemn expression.

'And a little bit of loving is just the thing when you are feeling a mite down.'

'You'll be writing me a prescription in a minute!'

'Maybe it's the little lady who needs the prescription, too.' She kept her eyes on her hands kneading and working rhythmically.

Silence fell. Like I say, this amazing mountain of a woman has a way of wriggling through small spaces and seeing what you think you've hidden – in this case, what I hadn't even noticed. In all my anxiety for Naomi I hadn't really thought beyond being cheerful and positive so she'd remember me kindly.

I need to think this through. At this precise moment I have a nasty suspicion that when we make love I'll see Lydia's approving smile lurking somewhere above us!

Naomi sat back slowly in Adam's chair. So it had been Lydia's suggestion. Would she have complied with such alacrity if she'd known?

She smiled now, remembering. Special memories. The new closeness had certainly eased her own heartache. They couldn't know what lay ahead – indeed it was merciful not knowing for sure – but while they could share this depth of happiness and intimacy, life was still good. Very good.

'I could die happy this very minute,' Adam had said sleepily on one particularly memorable occasion.

It was just a figure of speech, said without thinking, but she had involuntarily tightened her hold, shivering in spite of the warmth around them.

'Sorry.' He'd instantly understood. 'Sorry. I wasn't thinking of… I didn't mean to spoil the moment.'

'I know.'

They hadn't talked then but the thoughts had squeezed into their bed nevertheless and would not be evicted.

It was she who broached the subject – tentatively – a few days later, lying in his arms, the semi-darkness protecting her emotions.

'Adam.'

'Uhhhm?'

'This last few weeks – being close again – it's made me wonder.'

'Mmmhhmm?'

'Are you awake?' she asked suspiciously.

'Mmhhmm.'

'No, are you? Really awake?' She propped herself up on one elbow and peered closer.

'Yeah. I'm awake. And listening. Go for it, girl, before I think of something else to occupy my mind.'

'Be serious.'

'Oh, I'm serious. Deadly serious. Shall I show you just how serious I am?'

'Pleeeeeeeease. I mean it. I want to say something important.'

'Okay. I'm listening.'

'I'm not stupid, I know this can't last for ever. But because it's so good right now, d'you think… could we re-consider… having a baby?'

'What?!'

She could see – and feel – he was wide awake now.

'You heard.'

'But we agreed… now… it wouldn't be sensible.'

'That was right at the beginning. When we could only think about things getting worse. But here we are nearly a year on and…'

'But it's all still to come. I'm already getting weaker.'

'Yes, but you can still do almost everything like before.'

'At the moment. But nine months on, who knows? A year. Two years. We have to be realistic, sweetheart. How would you feel if I'm not able to look after myself, and you're struggling with a baby and a home and me? And no job to keep you sane.'

'But I'd have something of you…' She couldn't say it.

'On one level I see that might be a comfort. But when I'm gone, when you start to make new relationships, having someone else's baby might not be such an attractive proposition as just you on your ownio.'

'Don't. Please, don't.' The tears threatened to choke her.

'I must. Don't you see? We have to think of afterwards. I have to think for you then too. Of course, if I'm being totally selfish, I want you to have my baby. We planned it. That's what we both wanted. But now – no, it wouldn't be fair on you. It wouldn't.'

'Not even if I'm prepared to take the risk? My mum and dad would help. My sister too. We could get help in. And you'd be able to enjoy it – the baby, I mean. Even if you can't get about like now. And it'd give you something to keep going for.'

'Have you been talking to my mother?' His voice was tight.

'Your mother? Why would I talk to your mother about this? I wouldn't talk to anybody else about something so... personal. This is between you and me. Nobody else.'

At the time she hadn't made the connection. She hadn't read his diary.

'That's exactly right,' he'd said with a hardness of tone that hurt every bit as much as his words. 'You and me. Together. And if I'm not going to be here to help with that responsibility then I don't think it's right to go down that road.'

Desolation robbed her of the power to speak.

After what felt like an eternity of silence he'd whispered more softly, 'I'm sorry. I'm so, so sorry.'

'Won't you at least think about it?'

'Okay, I'll think about it.'

They'd said no more then. But the idea had taken root in her mind.

Remembering now, the pain was as raw as if it had just been said.

'Oh, Adam! Why didn't you just say yes? Why? Why?' The words were wrenched from the depths of her guilt. 'If only you'd said yes. None of this would have happened.'

If only...

29 MARCH—Naomi's returned to the baby thing. If she only knew how tempting her suggestion is! But I *have* to be strong. I have to! For her sake.

I hope it doesn't spoil things. Lydia's solution to my tiredness is great but there's a huge difference between sex for our relaxation, for pleasure, for our relationship, and sex to make babies.

It shook me, I must admit. I hadn't realised how much she still hankers for a child. If she even suspected how much I want to give her one, I think she might get herself pregnant – 'by mistake' – just to take the decision on herself. But on top of worrying about her I'd be anxious about the genetic thing. They say this isn't the inherited kind but what if they got it wrong? Imagine deliberately having a child and passing that pretty little gene on. It'd be a million times worse knowing you'd inflicted something like this on your *child*. Even inadvertently.

This has given me a twist to the plot of my novel. Aidan knows he was responsible for getting an ex-girlfriend, Moira, pregnant. She left and he didn't know what happened to her or even if she kept the baby. When he gets MND and he's told it's the inherited kind he starts thinking about his kid – should he seek Moira out, tell her, warn her? Or are they better all living in ignorance? That'll keep a bit of dramatic tension going during the critical middle section. The old will-he-won't-he question.

At least I've no skeletons like that to come clanking out of the closet when someone opens the door by mistake, but I certainly have to watch this predisposition to father a child.

Life sucks sometimes. Just when I was thinking it was pretty good too. I can't believe how much Naomi means to me. And all this quality time together, all the closeness, it's put a whole new gloss on life. I've been feeling positive and energised. The ceiling has lifted – noticeably. Everything seems possible again. But now I'm going to be suspicious she's all the time thinking 'baby'.

Naomi closed her eyes. Maybe she should just stop reading right now. Knowing more about Adam's hopes could put her therapy back months.

Should she phone Stella? What would she advise?

No. She couldn't go through the rest of her life relying on counselling.

Tomorrow. Tomorrow in the clarity of another day she'd make the decision herself: to read or not to read on.

She scraped Adam's chair back, flicked the screen off and dragged herself to bed. She clutched the pillow he'd slept on close to her chest. She rocked it, low moans muffled in its softness. Not until dawn was breaking did she finally drift into exhausted sleep.

31 MARCH—Joel's been up. That lad should carry a government health warning: Seriously good for your health! He's better than any tonic. With him I can truly be myself. And when he's here I have neither time nor inclination for the diary.

1 APRIL—How I wish this was just an April fool! Just when I was feeling relatively sanguine about where I am with this disease, and congratulating myself on having things pretty much in perspective, along comes a blunderbuss in the shape of my mother.

She was forever telling us when we were kids that children must obey and respect their parents. The Good Book says so. But the said fount of all wisdom (the Bible not my mother, I hasten to clarify!) also says that fathers should not provoke their children to wrath – and it's a fair assumption that 'fathers' would include 'mothers' in today's parlance, given that we've moved a street away from the totally patriarchal system of biblical times. Wrath? It's worse than a good clean burst of anger. The rigid rules of my childhood years still prevent me from saying what I really want to say, so the irritation gets to explosion point but is denied any natural spontaneous outlet.

And because I don't fight back, she assumes she hasn't got through to me. I feel rather like the Pharaoh in Egypt during the time of Moses. Just get rid of one pesky plague and another one comes bombing through the doorposts. You wouldn't believe how many guises fear for my eternal welfare can come in!

She is desperate for me to make my peace with God, return to the church. Before it's too late. But a second-hand faith is no faith at all. It has to be mine and I'm not there yet.

My more charitable self tells me there's more to her persistence than religious fear. I suspect there's also an element of superstition in there somewhere: obey and you'll be rewarded. Experience tells me it doesn't work like that yet I shouldn't deny her a crutch if she needs one – after all she's enduring exactly what I don't want for my own child.

Why do I find it so hard to be tolerant with her? Why is it that those closest to us get the worst as well as the best from us? Naomi excepted, in my case. If we were together for forty years, maybe things would change. But we won't be. And it ought to be easier to keep things like they are now, given that we know it's not for long.

On the other hand, my increasing frustration and dependence might impose stresses that tip us over into that state of getting on each other's nerves that you see in so many long-term relationships. And suppressed annoyance with my mother might spill out towards Naomi – simply because she's here. I must watch for this.

It was bitter-sweet reading. She reached out to touch the words.

'Thank you,' she whispered. 'Thank you for loving me... like that. Thank you for being you.'

He had taken such a personal responsibility for keeping their relationship strong. As if her contribution was constant and certain.

The betrayal when... if... it hit him must have been the more devastating. But if Stella was right, better to know the truth in this instance than to create her own nightmares.

Nightmares. The very word made her shudder.

The pictures had been especially vivid of late. And Mavis's face grew more distorted as time went on, her condemnation streaked through with implacable hatred.

3 APRIL—I came across a very apposite quote today. 'You can never remember to forget all the time.' That sums up my position now, while the symptoms are not too intrusive. A lot of the time I'm not even thinking of my predicament, but when I'm least expecting it, up it pops waving its Jolly Roger flag. A nasty way of spoiling an otherwise tranquil moment.

6 APRIL—I'm so engrossed in the novel I haven't got space for much scribbling in this diary but one thing I have added to my equation is the thought that now, when I have the ability to kill myself, I haven't the desire to do so; when I have the desire, maybe I won't have the ability.

This could present problems. I don't want to involve other people if I can help it; I'm determined they shouldn't be penalised for my decisions. How will I know when I've reached that midpoint on the seesaw before it tips down against me and I'm no longer able to do the job effectively myself? Maybe I'll have a casual chat with Curtis. On behalf of Aidan.

11 APRIL—As they say, some days you're the pigeon, some days you're the statue! Splat on for weeks by the office bully, Harry, but today it was my turn to let the filth fly.

I couldn't believe anyone could be so blatant in deceit! Jerry Bloody Lloyd, the very Jerry I buddied when he first arrived, has only taken my rough draft for the Saturday supplement and written a column for the local rag. Oh, the language is different, of course. In the secrecy of this confessional I can honestly say I wouldn't touch his pedestrian prose with a barge pole. But the sentiments, the logic of my argument – they're there. Three days ahead of my piece coming out, too. Three days! Too late to do anything about it. Too early for it not to look like plagiarism. Mine, damn it!

I saw red. I was so mad I suspect I even sounded like Harry – a level I do not want to sink to. I'm particularly aggrieved because the piece is about families and what kind of a world we might be bringing children into – well, those fortunate fertile folk who are in a position to reproduce their genes. It stemmed from thinking about Naomi and having kids, and I planned to leave it for her to read. So it's personal. I only showed it to Jerry because we were talking about the latest atrocities in the Middle East and I was commenting on how we hacks can turn all these events into ideas for articles or features. He swears he thought I was telling him to use this, giving him a leg up. Leg up! Think your own thoughts, you creep, make your own connections. I'm not your wet nurse.

Well, he'll not repeat that mistake again. That's for sure!

15 APRIL—Thinking about Harry and Jerry and my mother and Joel and Naomi and Curtis and Devlin and Lydia, and all the other assorted

shapes and sizes that cross my path, makes me wonder just what mark I'll really have made on life. The very reflection makes me feel totally infinitesimal and irrelevant. 'What is man that Thou art mindful of him?' They will all carry on their lives perfectly satisfactorily without me. Harry will find some other poor sod to victimise. Devlin will focus his roving eyes on some other disintegrating collection of neurones. Lydia will flirt outrageously with some other supine man. Mother and Naomi will fill their lives.

My memory will fade.

So why am I still suppressing my own instincts and caring about other people's feelings? I remember my great-grandmother saying when she was ninety, she no longer had to worry about anyone else's opinions, she could say just what she wanted to say. The when-I-am-old-I-shall-wear-purple syndrome. So why can't I leave my own inhibitions behind?

Is it just that the habits of a lifetime die hard? I'm not entirely sure. I think I personally need to be at peace with myself before I take that last step into the unknown.

Not because I fear my mother's hell fire.

Not because I think Reverend Castlemaine will point out all my deficiencies during his eulogy.

Not because I think God will call me to account for every idle word I utter (a threat my mother flung at us if we ever let slip a naughty word in her hearing).

No, I think it's as simple as that I just want them all (well, all except Harry) to think well of me now, and to remember me fondly or at least kindly later.

I don't like the idea of unresolved conflict or unpaid debt.

Is there more to it? I don't know.

I've been standing back and looking at my chief tormentors in life and wondering a) why they rile me so and b) how I can let their barbs glance off me so I don't waste effort getting fired up. Lydia is forever telling me to conserve my energy for the good things in life.

My mother is probably the hardest one to box in, because of the complexity of emotion and history. I have to remind myself that she loves me – in her own way; and she only wants me to live for ever. And maybe I shouldn't deny her the satisfaction of at least trying to save me. I suspect it must be immensely satisfying, attacking people from the safety of a religious position. All the vicious thrill of striking a blow for truth, with none of the guilt of being the proponent of these ideas. So I'm trying to look beyond her and see the vanity of what she's reproducing. Dismissing something detached from her is less upsetting.

It'll probably take some practice, but I'll give it a go.

Harry is my other *bête noire*. I've given up trying to look for ways of improving our relationship. But when he's being particularly obnoxious I'm thinking of holding up a fork and imagining him in jail. Can anyone complain officially about a dying man having a fork about his person and occasionally putting it up to one eye? I could always plead insanity. And the speed of court procedure being what it is nowadays, I'll be long dead before the case ever gets near a real lawyer or psychiatrist.

Hmmm. I can't actually think of anyone else who's consistently annoying. A thought has just struck me: maybe Mother's cross with God, not me!

17 APRIL—I mentioned the real possibility of suicide to Naomi last night.

Wished I hadn't.

It was such a brief entry. She read it again slowly.

No mention of her anger: it wasn't just *his* illness! Not even a reproach about her selfishness, thinking of the life she would have after he'd gone.

But back then… how desperately she'd clung to every precious second. The mere thought of deliberately curtailing that time appalled her. Besides, there was a new reason now to want him alive.

She'd lashed out. And his silence thereafter had served merely to fuel her wrath. How *could* he?

Oh, it was all too cruel.

If she'd only told him then…

If only…

20 APRIL—This time last year I was living life in the fast lane. Now I'm going to bed by midnight, I've turned down two assignments abroad, I've talked to Arkwright about more local work to reduce the travelling. I'm working from home as much as possible to maximise productivity. All to conserve my energy. How old does that sound!

I've given up golf with Fred altogether.

And on top of all my personal problems, I'm worried about Naomi. She's had a bad dose of D & V this week. Says it's an occupational hazard, working with kids. I know she's always had a delicate digestive system, but she seems really peaky with it. Probably run down already from the hours she puts in, on top of the anxiety about me. Worrying about her affects me, so it's a vicious circle.

We probably need a holiday.

The thrice-blessed Lydia keeps checking. I respect her judgment and I value her support, so I do take her advice seriously – much as I kid her on that she's simply a pugilist who lost her way. She's so much more than an exercise guru. She's a fount of wisdom with this wonderful knack of never drawing attention to her own role in these insights, she just drops the idea and leaves you to think about it, almost as if it just suddenly came into your head.

It was through talking to her that I realised that I've been more frustrated than depressed. Frustrated by the need to curb my activities. Frustrated by the uncertainty: will I be able to get from A to B, or carry something, or fulfil an engagement. Not knowing if or when. Hanging back from commitment in case my fears are realised. For some reason I haven't quite fathomed, frustration is an easier enemy than depression. (Probably something to do with my dad.)

Lydia's helping me set staged goals, focus on my present abilities rather than future inabilities. And all that with her gentle brand of teasing that takes the sting out of advice.

I've still to ask her if she minds being immortalised in my *magnum opus*.

'Now, Mister O,' she said today, as she stood ready to catch me while I put various parts of my anatomy through extraordinary contortions under her tutelage, 'this here beautiful body is giving me a glow of pure delight. All this resting and loving and respect for its needs is exactly what it was craving.'

'Careful, Lydia, praise to the face is open disgrace, you know.'

'Praise, honey? Who said anything about praise? I'm just sharing with you my own emotion watching that wheelchair going backwards into the future.'

'Thanks largely to you and your magic touch.'

'Well now, speaking of touch, I was wondering – just wondering mind, nothing more – how you might fancy a different kind of touch. Maybe not right now. Maybe something to think about for later on.'

'Mmhhhmm?'

'Well, there's a whole lot of other things outside conventional medicine, that they do say as help.'

'Witch doctors and black magic and things that go bump in the night, you mean?'

'Well, honey, whatever turns you on. Whatever turns you on. Just a bit farther back... goooood, goooood, perfect. Now let the muscles relax slowly, slowly, slowly. Beautiful. Okay, okay, just you lie there and think of England while you catch your breath. No, I was thinking more along the lines of complementary medicine.'

'You mean acupuncture, aromatherapy, reflexology, that kind of thing?'

'Exactly so. Can you see yourself lying back inhaling essence of magnolia and tea-tree fumes? Having pins stuck in your ear lobes? Yeeees. Mind you, honey, I have my own personal reservation about a skinny blonde massaging these luuuuuvvaly legs I've been admiring all these months.'

'Ahhhh, have no fear, Lydia, no skinny blonde could ever compete with your charms.'

'We have to think of the feelings of the little lady back at home.'

'And don't you think she's jealous of you, then?'

'Me? Oh, *I'm* on her side. Just you make sure she know that, Mister O. I'm just here making sure this beautiful body is in as best a shape as I can for her delight.'

'I'll tell her that.'

'You do that, honey.'

'Complementary medicine isn't something I've considered, I have to say, although now I come to think of it, an hour or so in the lotus position might be just the thing to clear the brain and free it up for fresh ideas. As well as give the office something to talk about.'

Lydia's eyes disappeared inside the wrinkles of her smile.

'Sure thing! I read somewhere that yoga was found to reduce fatigue in patients with multiple sclerosis.' She'd lapsed back into her normal professional voice.

'Seriously? So does it follow it's beneficial for mnd too?'

'Well, I haven't seen any *studies* on it – not for MND, I mean. It was just an idea.'

'But would you personally recommend becoming a pin-cushion with my lungs full of bitter aloe, and a nubile pagan priestess sending exciting messages to unexpected places through the soles of my feet?'

'*Recommend?* No, actually I wouldn't put it that strongly. But it's something you might like to ponder.'

'Have you ever tried it yourself?'

'I did once have my hands massaged. Oh, and my head and neck.'

'And?'

'I think I must be too thick-skinned. It didn't do a lot for me.'

'Too sceptical maybe?'

'Possibly.' She grinned at me.

'And the needles?'

She shuddered theatrically. 'Too chicken by half, me!'

'Not much of an advert, are you?'

'None whatever. And of course, it's entirely up to you. But if you are interested I could get you some literature.'

'Thanks, Lydia. I'll keep it in mind.'

'Right then, enough of this slacking. Back to business.'

22 APRIL—I could have done without this. On the very evening before I go to see Devlin for my four-months check! I want him to see what good

shape I'm in, encourage him to revise his predictions. What I did not want was to be frazzled by someone else's anxiety.

I guess illness – and the fear of it – can bring out the worst as well as the best in people.

It must be four months at least since I even heard from my cousin, Milly. She lives on the Isle of Man and we've little in common except our maternal relations: her mother is my mother's sister. The two sisters stay in touch by phone and send things at Christmas and on birthdays, but I maintain only a token link with both my aunt and Milly. We don't even write that extra message in the Christmas cards. My mother keeps them up to speed with family news and I'm certain that neither of them has even sent me a card since hearing about my MND. So getting Milly's phone call caught me off guard.

No point in trying to record the actual conversation. I was, and still am, so gob-smacked by her insensitivity I'd probably distort it wholesale anyway. But it went roughly along these lines:

Milly: Her mother had told her I was seeing the consultant neurologist this week, could I get him to check again to see if my MND was the kind that runs in families.
Me: (mildly) They've already checked that. It isn't.
Milly: Well, just to be sure, could I get him to do the test again.
Me: Why?
Milly: She needed to know. For her own peace of mind.
Her peace of mind!
Me: And why the sudden interest? (I suspect my sarcasm showed, but stuff that, why should I care?)
Milly: She was sure she had it too.
Me: (instantly contrite – and my mind now in overdrive) Oh no! Tell me about it.
Milly: Lots of almost incoherent thoughts about how scared she was, how awful it would be, what would her children do, etc. etc.
Me: Lots of soothing noises but trying to coax her past the 'too scared to say' stage.
Milly: She'd been getting bad cramps, lately. Waking in the night with them. Having to get up and stand on the cold tiles in the downstairs loo.
Me: And?
Milly: (wailing) Last night in the middle of this trek to the tiles she'd stubbed her toe on the step into the loo and was convinced that was the first sign of loss of sensation. She just *knew* she had MND. (More wailing and gnashing of teeth.)
Me: (working to keep my voice even) Had she seen her own GP?

Milly: She was too afraid to have it confirmed. But if my consultant said yes, it was the inherited kind, she'd *have* to go then. She owed it to her children. (Lots of wailing about their bleak and hopeless futures.)

Me: I'd check, but if Devlin assured me there was no mistake then she'd just have to accept it.

Milly: She just knew he'd got it wrong. She just knew it.

In the whole of this exchange there had been no smidgeon of sensitivity to my reality, only her surmise. I said all sorts of reassuring things – *falsely* reassuring coming from my position of ignorance, of course, but it seemed like the right thing to do in the circumstances. By the time I put the phone down I felt shattered.

'And thanks for asking, I'm fine – or I was until you rang!' I spat out at the innocent handset.

I inwardly cursed my mother for passing on information to these self-centred people with whom I share ancestry but precious little else. Did they ever express any sympathy for my 'bleak and hopeless future', I wondered?

This was one experience Adam had shared. It had been a good feeling, being the one to absorb his anger and contempt, to stand proxy for all those who let him down. To be his safety vent, feel his trust.

23 APRIL — Wow! Devlin was a positive vision in yellow today. Now, I'm not a yellow man myself, but I must admit he has this colour co-ordination thing down to a fine art. The exact shade of shirt-lemon was echoed in his bow tie, his handkerchief and… yep, in his socks!

I sneaked a look when he crossed his legs. He had little bees up the outer edges of his otherwise black ankles that matched perfectly. I wouldn't be at all surprised if his underpants weren't chosen to complete the ensemble!

But there was nothing in the least waspish about his response to my – or rather Milly's – impertinence.

'It's a natural reaction,' he said, without rancour. 'Relatives do wonder, will it be me next? I can't, of course, say categorically, not having seen the lady in question, although it sounds unlikely from what you've told me. But she's nothing to lose by going along to see her own doctor. If he knows there's ALS in the family, it might make him view her symptoms with some sympathy.'

So even he suspected hysteria. And he hadn't heard Milly!

But I had other fish to fry.

'Can you tell me more about the inherited aspect? Am I right in thinking that it's down to a faulty gene?'

'Well, as you know, only a small minority of cases are familial to start with. There are at least half-a-dozen, if not a dozen, different genetic variations of the disease, but a mutation of one specific gene has been associated with a small proportion. So this particular anomaly accounts for no more than two per cent of all cases of MND. That's a very small number. Tiny, in fact.'

I looked at him with some respect. Being able to trot out figures when he didn't know the question was coming is impressive. Me, I'm a words man. Numbers just don't stick. I have difficulty even remembering my car registration number. The unworthy thought popped into my mind that he might be making the entire thing up. I wouldn't know.

'When this discovery was made in 1993 it was hailed as a breakthrough, because at last scientists had identified a cause of MND. However, their optimism was rather deflated when they found something like ninety or a hundred different mutations of this gene around the world – they're still finding new ones – and all these mutations had resulted in MND.'

'So if someone has the non-familial kind, is it possible that their genes might mutate and they could pass on a faulty gene?'

'I have to admit that's not something I've ever really thought about. I suppose it's technically possible, since we don't know what causes the gene to mutate. But I don't think we have any evidence of it and I should think the statistical probability is billions to one.'

So if you ignore Sod's Law that's not something I need to worry about for my children… always supposing…

'In point of fact, a lot of people waste a lot of precious time worrying about things that'll never happen,' Devlin was saying. 'Inheritance is always something of a lottery. And any of us could develop a whole raft of illnesses or die from accidents or infection, even if our parents give us the full complement of healthy genes.'

He actually smiled as he said it although I can't be a hundred per cent sure he was looking at me as he did so.

I quit while I was ahead and didn't ask him any more questions. He professed himself well pleased with my 'progress'. What does progress mean in this context? I decided not to spoil the moment by probing that one.

We parted on mutually satisfied terms, for 'another four months'. Then, just as I was about to leave the room, he suddenly asked, 'Mr O'Neill, I was wondering if you would consider being a patient for the next round of clinicals here. I know you're a very busy man but your case is interesting and I think would be a good one for the students.'

'How much time would it involve?' I had to be cautious. Harry wouldn't give a toss if life was interesting for already privileged medical wannabes.

'As long as you can free up. We'd arrange things around your commitments. If you feel you could give us a little time.'

'Can I think about it and get back to you?'

'By all means. Just ring my secretary if you feel it's something you might be able to fit in. And don't worry, if you can't manage it – for any reason. You're under no obligation.'

I was, but I knew what he meant and I appreciated the sentiment. He'd still give me the VIP treatment.

30 APRIL — In spite of her protestations to the contrary I don't think Naomi's properly recovered from that D & V bug yet. She felt too nauseous to have breakfast this morning but assured me she tucked in once she got to the office. Admittedly she did finish the salad I made for dinner – a change from picking at things. She's skinny enough without skipping meals.

Devlin's secretary was gushingly grateful when I rang to say add my name to the list of patients willing to expose their anatomies to inexpert fumblings. I felt as if I'd bequeathed my body to medical science. Now there's a possibility I haven't considered. Should I? Save Naomi the expense and trauma of a funeral. Could I – or she – cope with the knowledge that my shell in all its nakedness and deformity will be/is being gawped at and mauled by pimply youths and brainy young women?

Adam had never mentioned this possibility so she hadn't even had to think about it. Naomi leaned back in his chair staring at his words. Would it have been acceptable to her? The response was instant and visceral: No! Irrational though it might be, she needed to know he was at peace, his body beyond further humiliation, the secrets of his tissues safe from further revelations.

Her eyes went to the photograph. That unclouded smile made her heart lurch. Hopes and dreams intact. Unaware of the impending destruction. Strange to think that if he'd been killed suddenly about that time then they would never have known of the defect he carried – that hideous stalker that had become bolder with the passing weeks, cruelly robbing him of so much he held dear.

No, nature had wrought havoc enough in his life. He deserved to be unmolested after death.

1 MAY — It was probably knowing about my hospital appointment that prompted Curtis to come calling today. This time he said he was doing a house call nearby and had just dropped by on the off-chance, and since it was 11 in the morning, it was indeed an off-chance.

Perfect timing. I was at home working on a big feature, avoiding interruptions. Naomi was away, visiting one of her adoptive families. The birth mother had asked to see the boy she'd given up and all parties needed Naomi there to make sure everybody stuck to the rules, so I knew she wouldn't suddenly appear. Ideally I'd have liked enough warning to prepare my questions but otherwise Curtis was a welcome distraction.

The good doctor was in his shirt-sleeves with his tweed jacket slung by one finger over his shoulder, looking more like a country squire than usual. I used the opportunity to suggest coffee in the garden and he slumped onto the wooden bench with a sigh. I could see him leaning back with his eyes closed while I brewed up, looking older in repose than when animated in conversation.

'This is more like it. Your garden's looking glorious.'

'Thanks to Naomi. She's the green-fingered one in the family. And the inspiration. I just do as I'm told.'

He inhaled expansively.

'Mmmm. Those azaleas smell fantastic. I only wish my patch looked half as good.'

'I can't imagine gardening figures very high on your agenda.'

'It ought to but, sad to say, it doesn't,' he admitted with a rueful half-smile.

We roamed casually over hobbies and energy levels and onto mine in particular. Then I plunged.

'Can I ask you something a bit off the wall?'

'By all means.'

'In confidence?'

'Of course.'

'I realise I've been lucky so far, still getting about and doing most things in spite of the increasing weakness. But I know it can't last and I've been giving some thought to decisions for later.'

'Uhhuh.'

'First off, I don't want anyone else getting into hot water because of me, okay?'

'Okay.' He was guarded.

'I know about Diane Pretty and Annie Lindsell and Reginald Crew and all those cases, and I know the family or the doctor can be left with a mess on their hands. I definitely don't want that.'

'Riiiight,' He extended the word over several spaces, as if hesitant to commit himself to even hearing what I'd said.

'Well, I suppose my question is, how will I know when it's the right time to say enough is enough?'

'I'm not quite sure…'

'I don't want to drag out the last bit and end up totally dependent and unable to do anything about it. But for Naomi's sake I don't want to quit too prematurely. My question is, will I know when it's the optimal point in between? Would you be allowed to tell me when that time had come if I asked you to? Just *tell* me I mean, not actually *do* anything. I'm afraid that I'll keep hanging on and maybe lose the opportunity to take things into my own hands.' It fell out in a rush.

There was a long pause during which I was painfully aware of my ragged breathing. Was he? When he did eventually speak, his voice was calm but devoid of expression.

'We're talking suicide here, are we?'

'In a nutshell, yes.'

'The optimal moment? That's a tough one. I don't know. The thing is, the perspective changes when you have something drawn out but progressive like this. What feels like an intolerable burden today might not seem so terrible when you get there.'

'Exactly. That's what I'm afraid of. I don't want to put Naomi through a ghastly disintegration.'

'Have you talked to her about how she feels?'

'I tried. Once. She just got too upset. Wants to hang on to me for as long as poss. So I want to make the decision and just get on with it to make it easier on her.'

'You could make an advanced directive.'

'That's not quite what I was meaning. It's relevant too, I guess, but before we talk about that, say I want to go before we get to that point, could you just tip me the wink and say, "This is as good as it gets, best to do it now, you mightn't be able to next week." Or words to that effect?'

'I'm not sure I could, actually. I see your point but it's a very subjective thing. And the goal posts tend to move. You might say to me today, "Tell me when I'm on the brink of not being able to hold a gun steady" – let's say. But supposing in x months time I say to you, "I doubt you'll be able to hold a gun next week," you might by then realise that actually not being able to hold a gun isn't terribly significant because life is still precious. You can still enjoy good music, a beautiful garden, the company of your wife, a good book. You can still write and you haven't finished your novel. So you want to hang on to accomplish certain things. So you say, "Tell me when I won't be able to slip a poly-bag over my head, Doc." And at that next stage you say, "I'm still enjoying my music, my garden, my wife, my writing, tell me when I'll be past swallowing ninety pills, Doc." You see what I mean?'

'Yes, but that route takes me to the very position that I want to avoid. An impasse where I can't, and nobody else should or will.'

'It could do, I agree.'

'So if I decide now that I'll go to a fixed point – let's say for argument's sake, until I'm on the brink of not being able to attend to my own personal needs – could you make sure I do it at that point?'

'I guess I could physically say you've arrived at that point, but I wouldn't choose to say, "Do it now."' He spoke slowly in a bland and unemotional tone but I could feel the tension in the air.

'Well, you wouldn't need to say that, would you? But just out of interest, why wouldn't you want to?'

'Because I'd have a problem with suggesting you end your life. My aim is to help you have as good a quality of life as we can possibly manage. To help you live the life you have with as much dignity and enjoyment as possible.'

'But if I decide this is the point at which life becomes intolerable?'

'Forgive me for sounding rather patronising but experience tells me that point changes.'

'So what's your suggestion?'

'That we monitor your progress. Best not to make an arbitrary decision based on how you feel now. Let's wait and see how things go. We can try anything that will help to prevent or at least alleviate the things that you find distressing. And if that isn't possible then we can look at the various options for treatment, and you can say which you will consider and which you want to refuse. Because, of course, you're perfectly entitled to refuse treatment at any stage. That's a different thing from saying, "I want to actively hasten my death." But you know that. You've already declined drugs.'

'Ahh, we're in the realm of the difference between allowing to die and actively killing. The medical argument.'

'Is it a medical argument? Of course, it's doctors who tend to get asked to help people out of these sorts of predicaments. And they know that it feels different. Maybe that's why it seems like a doctors' cop out.'

'To you too – it feels different?'

'Undoubtedly.'

'So even if it was legal, and there wouldn't be repercussions, you wouldn't be willing to bump me off?'

'No, I wouldn't want to.'

'Not even if it was my expressed and sustained wish?'

'I still wouldn't want to, no. But that's not to say I don't have sympathy with the request. And if it was a case of unrelieved pain or distress I would be willing to give a patient a large dose of drugs to ease the suffering even if those drugs would actually hasten death. That wouldn't trouble my conscience. My aim is to help patients die, as well as live, with dignity and in peace.'

'It's a fine line between that and killing, though, it seems to me.'

'I agree. It can be.'

'So, you'll take into account my wishes?'

'Most certainly. Within the boundaries of the law and my professional obligations.'

'That's good to hear. Not that it surprises me. I must say I've been tremendously grateful for your support with this thing.'

Curtis shrugged dismissively.

'And thanks for listening. I can't talk to Naomi about this, so I'd be grateful if you could let me bounce ideas off you occasionally. Before the window of opportunity closes.'

'I think we're a long way from that point, but by all means. If I can help in any way – well, that's what I'm here for. By the same token, if talking to me isn't enough, don't forget there are counsellors who're trained in this sort of thing.'

'Okay, thanks. Point taken. So these advance directives. As I understand it, they're just a precaution in case you're unable to state your wishes yourself.'

'That's one use. Recording things is also a way of demonstrating that your wish is a sustained one, you've discussed it with other people and they know that it really is what you want.'

'In case somebody tries to argue that my current wish to die is a knee-jerk reaction to my present situation?'

'That kind of thing.'

'And if it's in writing, it's legally binding?'

'If it's drawn up under the required conditions, yes.'

'Which are?'

'You were mentally competent at the time it was made. You were not under the influence of someone else at the time. You were fully aware of the relevant risks and complications. And that you intended the directive to apply in the circumstances in which you now find yourself.'

'And can I get just anybody to witness my signature?'

'Well, they're supposed to be independent. In other words, not stand to gain from your death. So if you have a secret lover with a love-child and she stands to inherit a million pounds and your estate in France, then she's not a good choice of witness!'

Curtis's sudden excursion into humour took me by surprise.

'Point taken. Keep the string of paramours hidden! Although to be politically correct, Doctor, you should have said if I have a secret lover and she or he stands to inherit!'

'Ah, but please note the subtle introduction of a love-child.'

'You've been studying too many creative writing manuals!'

He grinned back at me.

'If I didn't have a directive and there was a sudden emergency, would they take your word for it, or Naomi's, that I don't want to be resuscitated?'

'They might – or might not. Rather depends on the circumstances of the emergency. They might already have revived you before either of us are even on the scene.'

'So I should have an instruction tattooed on my chest or on a bracelet or something, huh?'

'We could talk about exactly how best to notify your intentions.'

'And if Naomi objected?'

'Ahhh. That's a tricky one.'

'I don't want her to be caught up in some legal nightmare. At the moment I'm pretty sure her resistance is because she's struggling with the idea of my death. I think that when she sees more of the deterioration she'll appreciate where I'm coming from. So it's just about what would happen before we get to that point. If she objects, it could undermine my decision?'

'There are doctors who'd attach a fair amount of weight to her opinion, yes. Legally the role of the relative is to reflect the patient's wishes, not make proxy decisions. But doctors are uneasy about flying in the face of a wife's stated wishes in cases like this.'

'So if you had my advance directive and could wheel it out duly signed and sealed that would help.'

'In the end, yes – well, it might. But there could well be delays while people looked into exactly why there were conflicting messages here and I'm afraid some doctors would err on the side of caution, not wanting to be sued by a distraught family.'

'So I guess I must talk to Naomi. Get her on my side.'

'It would be best if she was fully in the picture and willing to represent your view, yes.' He paused for a long moment before adding quietly. 'Just give it time, Adam.'

I nodded.

The shrill of his mobile phone broke the peace of the garden and he slipped quietly out of earshot to listen attentively, only his occasional staccato questions punctuating the silences. He returned full of apologies for having to attend an emergency. My thanks were somehow lost in his parting promises to return to continue the conversation. I believed him too.

Naomi forced herself to stay with it. If she were ever to get any sleep tonight, she must read on to other topics.

It hurt acutely – seeing it in black and white. She had been part of the problem. Now, more than when he was alive, she craved his humour, his light-hearted take on the world. All this serious debate weighed the heavier for his absence.

3 MAY—My spirits are low tonight. It's not frustration this time; it's depression. And I know its cause.

I saw this afternoon how much Naomi is pining for a baby. And the knowledge is much more troubling than it was before, when I thought I had all the arguments buttoned up. Her sister's two did it. Anabelle is four and Courtney is two and they really are stunners. Golden curls, wide blue eyes, dinky little noses and perfect skin (naturally tanned-looking, just like Naomi's). They're such affectionate little creatures and Naomi and I are firm favourites. The feel of their little arms wrapped around your neck, the softness of their lips kissing your cheek, their spontaneous gravitation towards you – well, it stirs something very profound. So I sympathise with where Naomi's coming from.

Anabelle is at that stage where she can hold a serious conversation and she has no inhibitions. Tells it just like it is.

'Aunty Namey?'

'Uhhmm?'

'Can I come and stay in your house these nights when it's holidays?' – holding up all ten fingers and thumbs.

'*Please may* I,' came the instant automatic correction from Sally.

Anabelle tossed her mother an exasperated look.

'Please *may* I?' she repeated in a tone of resignation, letting us know it was a formality and the question still stood.

'We'll have to see.'

'And can I play with your dressing-up box?'

'Please *may* I.'

'Please may I play with your dressing-up box?'

'You may, certainly, if you are very, very good,' Naomi smiled.

'I will be good. Gooder than this.' She stretched her arms out as wide as they would go.

'Wow! That's a very big good!'

The child skipped over to lean on the arm of my chair.

'And will you throw me up in the air, Uncle Adam? Like you used to when I was ever so tiny? Like on the video?'

The silence held its breath.

'Pleeeeeeease *may* you?' she wheedled.

Brittle laughter broke the spell.

'We'll see,' was all I dared.

I saw Naomi's face a split second before she stooped to pick up Courtney and waltzed off with her, a superficial 'Right, young lady, time to get you cleaned up for tea,' trailing behind her.

'Me, too!' Anabelle shot after her, leaving Sally and me stuck in the footsteps of innocence.

'I am superfluous to requirements when you two are around,' she offered.

'Novelty value, that's all it is.'

By the time Naomi returned with the children we were all back into the pretence of normality. But under cover of the noise and excitement I noticed the softened expression, the lingering touch. I saw the way the girls chose Naomi to sit beside them, to read the stories, to wash their hands. I saw her face. What right have I to deny her her natural fulfillment? It might be too late when the opportunity comes again.

Sitting here now I'm aware of my own yearning. I have an overwhelming desire to create with her the child she longs for.

Maybe...

Naomi shrank into her jacket, wrapping her arms around her body, staring at his inner thoughts.

He had completely misread her expression that day. Anabelle's innocent request to be thrown up and caught had brought the reality of Adam's deterioration surging into her consciousness. She would not have wanted him to take such a risk.

Her every instinct was to clutch the children closer, guard them from the unseen danger. How, then, could she have *his* baby, only to have it snatched away for its own safety, its own father part of the lurking hazards she would shield it from?

And that thought had made her shrink from him that night, from his teasing, 'Now, as to baby-making...', from his tempting touch. Pleading exhaustion. Needing time to unravel her turbulent emotions.

The cruelty hit her foursquare. Just when she was steeling herself to accept the inevitable, he was preparing to bow to her instinctive need.

Maybe Stella was wrong. Maybe it would be better not to know what he had thought, what he'd felt. She could cling to her own comforts.

She buried her face in Noelani's pulsating fur, torn by her own grief. Then with dragging steps she left the room, emptiness echoing everywhere in her mind. She made herself a mug of hot chocolate. Slowly. Mindlessly. She let the cat out. Waited till she returned.

Maybe she should read one more entry. If she could just conjure up other pictures in her head...

4 MAY — Well, my first efforts to provide an heir(ess) met with conspicuous failure! Good thing my self-confidence in that department is fairly robust or it could have marked the beginning of deep psychological hang-ups and sexual dysfunction.

Naomi closed the file abruptly, switched off the computer and left the room.

The pain was physical. She wouldn't read any more.

Stella didn't understand.

But at least she wasn't asleep long enough to be haunted by the dreaded nightmare.

7 MAY—One hell of a day. Harry spitting blood. Working until 3 AM re-writing a piece just because he was beyond listening to my rationale for focusing on world pollution.

It was eight days since she'd resolved not to read any more of Adam's diary. At first she'd known relief, but a growing compulsion had undermined her determination. She would proceed with caution. Limit her dose. Maybe skim in places. Perhaps even omit any entries that looked as if they'd be too harrowing.
Harry was safe ground.

8 MAY—Naomi was away before I even surfaced this morning. And out at some office do until midnight. Her absence meant I could lose myself in Aidan's life until I fell asleep on the desk. Another three chapters written. Brilliant therapy, as ever.

9 MAY—Poor old Naomi. She's always had a more dodgy digestion than me but she sure was vomiting her heart up this morning. Reckons it's down to the prawn soup she had yesterday, on a stomach already weakened by that blessed D & V bug. She dragged herself off to work looking wan enough to be sent straight back again by anyone other than a Harry look-alike; but she says she perked up again by coffee time.
Her indisposition, minor though it is, made me think again of my coming dependence on her.
What if she really was ill?
How would I feel about anybody else invading my privacy? The honest truth? Sick to my stomach. I don't even like to think of Naomi doing the basics – for different reasons, of course.
So am I going to let myself get to that stage?
Which bits of personal care are beyond my tolerance zone?
Is that when I say goodbye?
And if she were to become ill, do I say farewell sooner? Leaving her ill and bereaved?
Hello?! Reality check.
Am I all kinds of a self-centred git or am I really thinking of her in all of this? Seems to me, she and I are intertwined and you can't actually see just where her interests end or mine begin.
So the next question is, how does she feel about looking after a cripple?
A cripple.
In a way that word sounds too sanitised. It conjures up somebody with gammy legs; it doesn't encompass this global disintegration. But I've seen MND called a crippling disease. And these past few weeks I've been feeling the aptness of that descriptor for where I'm at at this moment in

the trajectory of my incapacity. My feet seem to be hinged too loosely at the ankles. And I've succumbed to the temptation to hang onto things as I get about… in case. I've fallen with a fair whack several times and Naomi says if I end up in Casualty she'll have a hard time proving my bruises aren't down to her. I've told her I'll be fine in a home for battered women, all those needy females looking after me.

Lydia thinks splints might help. If my ankles are supported, my feet won't drop and I shan't be so likely to fall over them.

Of course, being Lydia she wrapped it all up in her mock Caribbean drawl and her exaggerated gestures, and managed to conjure up this graphic picture of a new, turbo-assisted me, powering along in the fast lane again. But I confess I was struggling to see the humour this time around.

Splints represent the triangular wedge that prises open the gates of hell. My very first real aid to normal living. It's symbolic. Therefore to be resisted.

I stalled.

Lydia dropped to her gentle tones, 'Just give it some thought, honey.'

I thought all right.

'Get thee behind me, Satan,' I roared in the privacy of the bedroom standing looking at my reflected ankles, thinking.

Speaking to my stalker, my Nemesis, is a tactic I've adopted recently. Telling it just what I think and how I absolutely refuse to let it get a grip on the essential me, is part of this resolve to remain in control. It gives me a punch-bag.

I must talk to Naomi about her limits.

Naomi frowned. She had no recollection of such a conversation.

11 MAY — Naomi has taped down the edges of all our rugs. No discussion. No explanation. It's a *fait accompli*. My feelings have shocked me to the core.

A few weeks ago I really believed we were rock solid. Nothing could shake our closeness. Knowing we were destined soon to part for ever would keep me from hasty words or petty annoyance.

Today I feel a powerful urge to lash out, retaliate in some way.

How *could* she join in the conspiracy?

The very fact that she did it while I was out highlights the underhand nature of the crime. Treating me like a child. For my own protection, no doubt. Not wanting to upset me. Assuming control. Not asking for my opinion. Like a mother.

SHE IS NOT MY MOTHER.

I need time with this.

Wow!

12 MAY—Seeking some perspective on this seething resentment, I tried to concentrate on bigger issues last night. In some twisted way it was easier to think about it feeling mad with Naomi. Maybe she won't be as distraught to be rid of a drag of a dependent husband as she might have been to lose a beloved equal partner.

A way out. Is this what I want?

I have quite a collection of snippets from the papers now on euthanasia. The Dutch scene. The Swiss situation. Oregon's. Australia's skirmish with it.

My thoughts are muddled. Depends on my mood. Today I just need to let my mind dot around in all of this.

First then, Dignitas. The death-deliverers. They're filling a void for some people. But what a hassle flying over to Switzerland to die. I'd need to go alone while I still could; I couldn't ask Naomi to deal with that cheapskate death room, or the solo return flight, or getting my body back.

I was shocked to read about the people with perfectly treatable conditions – physical as well as mental and psychological – who've gone down this route. I get this vivid picture of a crocodile of folk, withered and hunched and disabled, wending their way along the road to this house of death, weighed down by the burden of self-denigration, feeling worthless, a drain on resources; just wanting the doubts to be stilled. You can see why they call it a slippery slope!

Next up, sanctity of life. I hate the very expression, because my mother always churns this one out. But in a perverse kind of way, I envy her the certainty. So much in this area is confusing and grey; a moral maze indeed. I like the idea of an absolute, immutable, fixed point of reference such as she has, something to take bearings from when the arguments are drawing you into troubled waters. But I just can't swallow it.

Is suffering good for the soul? The further down my own track I go, especially since this business with Naomi – the baby *and* the rugs – the more I think you have to consider spiritual and existential and psychological suffering, not just physical. And I don't feel any of them are doing me good. If it's so good why does everyone strive to avoid it?

Actually, Curtis has given me a lot of food for thought, and as far as I'm concerned, because he's in there with his sleeves rolled up, getting his hands dirty in life's real messes, his opinion carries a lot of weight – certainly more than my mother's!

I guess it's a completely different issue for philosophers to advocate euthanasia and propound the academic arguments to back up their opinions – they won't be required to implement it. That's presumably why they call it 'philosophical killing'. So I have to take Curtis's reservations seriously, even though he might not wow the courts with his scholarship or literary eloquence. His real-life understanding certainly counts for more in my book.

I had a look on the Net for relevant cases and two in particular have settled in my consciousness and made me think. Both of them happened around the same time. Both were young women, forty-three years of age. Older than me but still young to die.

One was Ms B, a quadriplegic, completely paralysed, so totally dependent – unlike me (so far). She'd had a bleed into her spinal column. Knowing there was no hope of improvement in her physical condition, she was battling to be allowed to die.

Now, I'd have thought that was a cert. She's refusing treatment. You're allowed to refuse treatment. Doctors aren't supposed to treat you against your will if you're a mentally competent adult – as she was. But the Trust was arguing that she couldn't decide until she'd tried rehabilitation in a specialist unit. She, however, bless her cotton socks, stuck to her guns and must have put up a pretty eloquent defence of her position because the judge, Dame Elizabeth Butler Sloss, went on public record as saying how impressed she was by Ms B's logical and sustained wish and arguments. The newspaper report included these sketches of a group of 'my learned friends' gathered around the hospital bed, straining their outraged ears to hear what the woman was telling them. In my mind's eye I see them clutching their robes around their legs to avoid the creeping MRSA, consciously trying to obliterate the steady bleep and blip and hiss and squoosh of the monitors and machines ticking towards infinity. But I reckon any judge who's prepared to abandon the sanitised court surroundings and step firmly into the real environs of intensive care is well on the way to forming a good judgment. And this M'Lady in particular sounds like a thoroughly good egg, with compassion running through her veins alongside the legal precedents and articles and arguments. In spite of being the front-line legal eagle, constrained by all the strait-jackets and inflexibilities of law, the said Dame felt for this poor captive woman and ruled in favour of her right to have the ventilator switched off. Quite right too.

Ahhhhah! I have an idea for my own death – my choice but wrapped up in legitimate legal paper, tied up securely with the string of medical obligation, and franked by society. Yes!

Diane Pretty – same gender, same age, same wish to die – got a completely different verdict. In spite of being so far advanced in her disease that she couldn't even speak without a machine, she spent precious weeks struggling in her wheelchair to various courtrooms to plead for the right to have her husband help her to commit suicide without risking legal punishment. She (with her husband) persisted right through to the European Court of Human Rights but she was denied that right. It's a criminal offence to assist suicide, full stop, these bewigged and befrocked and benighted mighty ones decreed.

And Diane Pretty had MND. She died the death she had feared. In a place, at a stage, in a way, at a time, not of her choosing.

So. Does this answer my queries? I guess writing it down helps me feel more sure about what I do not want.

1. There's no apparent reason why I shouldn't remain perfectly mentally competent.
2. I might get to a stage where I can no longer express my wishes.
3. I might reach a point where I am unable to take my own life without assistance.
4. I have a legal right to refuse treatment even if it means I will die.
5. If the doctor caring for me objects he must hand over my care to another doctor.
6. Ending my life in any other way holds perils and potential pitfalls for me and for anyone else involved.

Hmmm.

Conclusion – suicide earlier or refusal of treatment later. If the latter, my wishes need to be explicit, but it might be ages before there's any significant treatment to refuse.

Naomi shrank back from the screen. Here it was in black and white; tangible evidence of the closed door which had kept her out.

After his first attempt to take his future into his own hands, she'd broken down in front of Dr Curtis. Why had Adam excluded her from his intentions? How could he be so thoughtless as to what this meant to her, she'd sobbed. She'd clung to his reassurances: Adam was only trying to protect her, spare her the burden of his agonising. But why couldn't he see how hurtful it was to be shut out like this?

Dr Curtis had let her weep. Then gently, as if thinking aloud, he'd suggested she tell Adam what it felt like from her perspective.

'But I don't want to make him feel worse,' she'd wailed.

'A good cry together is just what you need,' he'd told her firmly. 'You've been protecting each other for too long. You need to reach out to each other, both of you share what you're going through. And make it soon.'

Don't leave it till it's too late to communicate freely, her inner voice had supplied. Or until a crisis forces a precipitate decision. Or until he's been successful in his suicide attempt.

'It doesn't need to be confrontational. Just talk about what he's thinking, what it feels like to you. And start off gently. Maybe re-visit the issues every now and then. Emotions fluctuate a lot in these circumstances. How he feels today won't necessarily be the same as what he thinks in two months' time. And it might help you both to voice your emotions.'

Her blotched face when she'd gone back to sit beside Adam had been enough to open up the questions. He'd held her tight, promised to share more in the future, they'd talk properly when he got home.

But that had been later. Much later.

She dragged her mind back to the spring when he'd written this entry.

Here it was again. She was part of the problem. She'd made him resent her. She'd forced him to bottle up all his uncertainty. She'd denied him his choices.

'I'm so, so sorry,' she whispered.

20 MAY — The muscle cramps and spasms are definitely worse. Just as I'm starting to relax in bed at night it's as if Nemesis says, 'Hey, big guy, don't forget, I'm still here.'

Naomi is brilliant and even when the cramp stops play, she seems to be unfazed by it. I'm the one who feels tetchy.

Last night's episode was particularly frustrating and I stomped up and down in the shower room, glowering at my reflection and slapping the tiles at each end as I paced. All the flapping about made my dressing gown slip open: shades of Belsen and Ethiopia! I think it's fair to say I've never been inclined to narcissism but I was sick to my stomach in that unguarded moment. Where my muscles once bulged they now suck in like a partially-deflated balloon.

When did this start?

Who else has noticed?

Or is it a trick of the subdued lighting, casting shadows where the full beam would give me flesh and health once more? I didn't switch on the main light. Instead I crept back to bed and burrowed underneath the duvet, nursing an ache worse than cramp.

I read yesterday that three people a day die of MND in the UK. I don't know if that should actually read three people *with* MND or if it really is the disease itself killing them. There's a small but significant difference wrapped up in that innocent little preposition.

The article also said that the average survival from onset to death is twenty-five months. If you're younger you tend to live longer. As in Stephen Hawking, diagnosed at twenty-one, who's now in his sixties. Forty years of this!

I'm obviously going to be somewhere in between, but more towards the geriatric end if the medical fraternity are right in my case. And if I get my way.

21 MAY—Curtis has confirmed; it's not a feature of my paranoia. So it's official. My muscles are definitely weakening. Result? Too little horse-power plus real fatigue.

So, today I've added a veritable armamentarium to the medicine cabinet (to encourage Naomi too, to be honest. She's still looking peaky ever since those dodgy prawns, though she won't admit to anything other than tiredness). Well, 'medicine cabinet' is poetic licence for a shelf in the kitchen! À la the advertisements there's zinc, cod liver oil capsules, folic acid, vitamin B complex, Vit B12, Vit C, Vit E – an assortment of minerals and supplements that should boost my depleted reserves, and some multivitamins to bring the sparkle back into Naomi.

And, heaven preserve us, I'm starting to think gadgets, devices, gizmos; aids to daily living!

Naomi and Lydia are singing from the same hymn sheet: let people help you with the mundane things, save your energy for more interesting activity. Only it's Lydia who injects a wicked laugh into her suggestive advice. I guess it's the old mothering, nurturing thing. But me? Nope. Maybe it's male pride but I find it easier to deal with using a gadget to enable me to retain my independence, rather than accepting help from others that just underlines my growing dependence. And at least for the time being, I'm the choir-master.

12 JUNE—It's Nemesis's anniversary today. One whole year I've been doing battle with it.

One article I read said the average time from diagnosis to death was fourteen months – although Devlin says diagnosis is too variable a marker to be useful. On that basis, though, if I'm your average ordinary Joe Bloggs, in two months' time I should be dead.

When I stopped to reflect on that little pearl of wisdom I asked myself: Do I feel nearly at the end?

Answer: No.

Is life so intolerable that I wish I had only two months left to go?

Answer: No. Not yet.

Naomi let her breath out slowly. Maybe it was worth the pain to glean these precious fragments of reassurance.

Hmmm. As a newspaper hack I've long been tuned in to the opportunities of anniversaries, and old habits do indeed die hard because today my own personal anniversary started me off on a feature on sport. I wrapped the autobiographical elements up in an impenetrable disguise, of course, but I waffled on about athletes preparing for sports and developing muscles and having goals, etc etc. It occurred to me that Rev.

Castlemaine might build a sermon along those very lines. You know, preparing for the race of life. Shades of the Apostle Paul in his letters to the young churches. Heavens! My mother would start to get glimmerings of hope for my eternal welfare if she could see how much I've retained of my childhood legacy!

At 4.15 PM I had this weird experience. I was watching the second hand tick towards blast off and I distinctly heard last year's news dropping with a resounding hollow ring into a deep hole somewhere inside my head. The echoes were still reverberating inside me when it registered: the protective numbness has gone but the sound is less harsh now. It's as if the year has muted the stridency, or perhaps I have become desensitised to the discordance.

Given the significance of the date, I thought I'd pop in and see Lydia but when I rang the surgery to arrange it, the receptionist said, stiffly I thought, Lydia was off sick. My subtle enquiries were effectively stonewalled. There it is again. I am the wrong side of an unbreachable wall. My carers may know everything there is to be known about me; they may take unspeakable liberties with my body; they may seek to invade even my mind, but I may know nothing whatsoever about them outside of their professional roles. The gatekeeper made me an appointment with the locum person. But even before I met her I knew she couldn't fill Lydia's shoes.

Not today, anyway. Perhaps not ever.

Véronique. She says it with a French roll of the tongue but in all other respects she sounds like a thoroughbred Sloane. Véronique is every inch the model physio: trim athletic figure; impeccably groomed; efficient but kindly; a ruthless time-keeper; bracingly encouraging. In every way she appears to outstrip Lydia in the objective tick boxes. Furthermore, she did her job blamelessly, putting me through Lydia's programme, consulting Lydia's notes, deferring to Lydia's expert knowledge of my case. But she isn't Lydia.

I came away unusually low in spirits. I pray Lydia's indisposition is brief and chide myself for missing her cheerful flirtation, for being this dependent on her support. I am weakened by her absence on this day of all days. I feel naked, vulnerable. Afraid.

28 JUNE—Another bombshell dropped today. I was telling Naomi about Harry's latest iniquities when she suddenly said, 'Why are you putting on that daft voice? Does he talk like that?'

I stared at her.

'What daft voice?'

'Talking through your nose like that.'

She knew from my face it wasn't part of my nonsensical repertoire and she instantly started to back-track. But the door had clanged shut.

The manual says it happens when the soft palate weakens and air escapes through the nose when you're speaking. So on top of all the other changes to the original model, I now have a nasal voice. In itself I don't see that as major major league. But what it does tell me is scary. Big time. Mega.

The paralysis is creeping higher. It's inching towards the centre of my existence. My communication skills. It's a boa constrictor wrapping its massive body round its prey, inch by inch, until it has gained complete mastery, when it will pause momentarily to enjoy the sense of power, before crushing the very life out of its prey.

But then… nobody at work has mentioned my speech. Not even Harry. Maybe it's a subconscious thing. Maybe I read about this early on and some recess in my brain has thrown up this idea and my body is just trying it on for size. When I'm relaxed at home. Devlin's warning rings in my ears for the umpteenth time.

Maybe the strike hadn't been fatal. But the look of naked… what? disbelief? dislike? rejection? whatever… had made her physically recoil.

Even today, Naomi could vividly recall her anguish at that particular change.

It was one of the things she had loved about him when they'd met, in those early days when, in her ears, the timbre of his voice eclipsed the best of Beethoven, Handel, Schubert, Bach, Mozart and Grieg, all rolled into one. When he became part of her everyday life, his speech continued to hold for her the beauty and eloquence of music. He managed somehow to pack volumes into a change of inflection, a softening of his vowels, a change of speed.

The gradual but inexorable loss of colour and cadence had been like an audible expression of his slow dying. The monotonous tone, the hoarseness, the short sentences, the frequent pauses to take a breath, to clear saliva, the deliberate exaggerated enunciation; how much more agonising they must have been for him.

'Inside my head there's the old fluent repartee; my brain is still like a river in spate, surging up to the drainage channels again and again and again, swirling away unreleased because those passageways are blocked, permanently out of commission, littered with dead and dying neurones,' he'd written.

And he was living that metaphor.

She'd heard people make a joke of his impediment to his face; she'd seen people back away thinking he was drunk; she'd caught the look of pity in the eyes of friends. She'd rushed to distract his attention, but she dared not diminish him further by fighting these demons for him. She had to respect his autonomy.

What hypocrisy!

Her eyes went reluctantly back to the computer screen. '28 June' the entry said. Had he guessed? Had he known just how far she'd gone in overriding his autonomy?

She steeled herself to read on.

29 JUNE—Give me Pharaoh's flies, frogs and locusts any day rather than the sheer relentlessness of my mother. Getting mad with an Egyptian potentate would be less personally draining than skirting round the sensitivities of one's sole surviving progenitor.

She's taken to calling unannounced during the day when she must know Naomi is out. She brings her apron, for goodness' sake! And a bucket-load – literally – of cloths and cleaners and tools of the trade. And if it's not every crevice and whorl of the banisters that she scours, it's the tops of the doors and pictures, or she empties shelves and cleans *underneath* everything! I mean to say, who *cares*?

I've tried rationally and calmly defending my territory, explaining how I need peace and solitude to work, but try telling the Niagara Falls to stream upwards; try commanding snowflakes to crystallise in rhomboidal formations; try coaxing a tigress to leave her cub to the vultures.

Oh no!

She 'won't disturb me', I can 'get on'. Naomi 'needs support', she hasn't got time for 'all the little extras' now she's got me to 'take care of'.

And the daytime's the only time she can come; when Naomi's out. She doesn't want her daughter-in-law to feel 'substandard'. This way she needn't even know anyone has been... hello!! She can just think that things aren't getting as dirty as they used to. As if Naomi would even *think* about the tops of doors, never mind measure the accumulated dust particles! As if she could fail to detect the reek of furniture polish and disinfectant.

My revered parent might as well be sitting on my desk, obscuring my view of the computer screen, clicking a pen in and out. Ideas, concentration, creative flow, everything evaporates with the sound of her studiously muted germ-removal.

Most days I grit my teeth, muck around with emails and other pretty mindless activities till she's gone. Sometimes I slink out of the house to the garden to work there. Occasionally I even force myself to stop and have a coffee with her.

Today I absolutely needed to be here to finish a piece on Third World debt. With a deadline writ large on my screen as well as behind my eyes, my fluency was already seriously under threat, so I wandered out and suggested a quick drink 'before you go'.

The duster twirled more viciously over the cornice in the dining room. By now even the spiders must hide at the sound of that damn bucket. I tried direct appeal, told her about the pressure to produce the goods, the specifics of my work-load. All outwardly very calm, very soothing. Or so I thought anyway.

'I'll just...'

'No, Mother, you won't! That's enough. Thanks but no thanks. I know you mean well, but please – *NO MORE CLEANING!* I have a living to earn. I have deadlines to meet. And frankly I don't care a stuff if Miss Havisham herself is hiding in the accumulated filth of a century in this house. I just need to *WORK!*

'But Naomi...'

'*But Naomi* nothing. She'd much rather come home to a civilised husband festooned in cobwebs than a spankingly clean house and a steaming half-wit climbing the walls!'

Harsh, I know. But...

Coffee was a strained business. Caramel wafers were rejected with extreme politeness. When she'd gone, in a clattering of metal and high dudgeon, I felt all shades of a villain. Cassandra did her sympathetic best and an hour of fathomless oceanic sound-waves brought me down to picture-rail height, but I was woefully aware of the stilted language Harry would undoubtedly shred if I didn't inject some linguistic sparkle into the article before submission.

It was a relief when Naomi came home tired and went to bed as soon as she'd picked at a salad. Later I found most of that in the bin, too late to offer her a modicum of understanding. But my inner peace was restored by the time I joined her, ready to listen to her day. Except that she was fast asleep.

He hadn't looked very hard then. The damp pillow, the occasional remnant of a sob, her wakeful tension – nothing had seeped across to him? Maybe then...

1 JULY—Musings for a future weekly column which are relevant to my diary:

1. Decisions about life and death are not static things. They may need to be revised. Sometimes even reversed.

2. I'm acutely aware of the difference a day makes. Yesterday I was perilously close to insanity. Today I'm ruthlessly logical and in control.

3. Death itself isn't the enemy. What's so dreadful about it? Why do people fear it so? To me it would only be dreadful if it happens when I don't want it to.

4. Dying painfully – well now, that's another kettle of fish altogether. But that's more about pain than about death. And I can perfectly understand why people fear pain. *(For Ideas folder: *dying/pain*.)

2 JULY—I get a distinct impression that Naomi is avoiding me. She *says* it's nothing to do with my reaction to her comment about my nasal voice on Thursday. Or the rug business. I've tried to make amends, get her to open up about what's eating her, but she just pleads tiredness – physical and emotional, she says.

I don't like it. It doesn't feel right. It's not like her.

Okay, things may be hectic at work just now; troubling cases and all that. Heck, *most* of her cases would haunt me! But she's strong. And generous. She blows her top occasionally but she doesn't sulk or shut me out. Not usually.

I hope it's the truth. I hope it's not because she's started seeing me as an invalid, needing protection, enough troubles of my own. She's been a tower of strength so far; she doesn't deserve the edge of my frustration or the backlash of my impatience when things are getting me down. Am I turning into a selfish brute? Chronic illness can shrink one's horizons and dull the sensitivities.

I'm scratching around for clues here; looking for a way back in.

If only it had been that simple. Fear made her hands tremble but her brain compelled her to read on.

4 JULY—Huh! So much for concentrating on Naomi's needs.

Cassandra is a stressor I didn't anticipate. She spent most of Monday mewling pitifully. I held her on my lap while I worked but she just couldn't seem to get comfortable and she was sick five times. Yesterday she was asleep in her basket almost all day. But it wasn't that reassuring silent purr of contentment with life, the universe and her lot in particular. Suffice to say, it was the kind of immobility that had me checking her every few minutes. But even that degree of vigilance detected nothing tangible to indicate she needed more than a break from human interference.

Naomi's been just as concerned – her old self in fact. We've shared the anxiety.

Today Cassandra's all in a heap again so to hang with being labelled a paranoid owner, I'm taking her to the vet. Absence of specific symptoms notwithstanding, I need reassurance even if Cassandra's just doing what cats do – taking a sabbatical from feline activity. Scorn from the animal doctors has to be less stultifying than this level of anxiety. Good grief! If I'm like this with a *cat*, good thing I haven't had kids!

Evening Why do we set ourselves up for heartache? – especially the unnecessary kind, against our better judgment.

I'm mad at myself for falling into this trap. I was never an animal lover. Ever. And there's enough tragedy in the world of *homo sapiens*, without taking on the cares of other species.

What kind of a fool is seduced by the wiles of a mangy stray moggy in the first place? And even if simple compassion spurs him into saving the creature from starvation, what on earth would possess him to let it creep into his affections? Only an idiot.

Cassandra has certainly made a fool out of me! I can't believe how profoundly I'm affected by this.

6 JULY—I'm struggling to get the pictures out of my head. Writing about it might help to resolve things.

There was nothing they could do. It was too advanced. Best just to let her slip away peacefully. It would be a kindness. She wouldn't know a thing. We've heard it a thousand times: novels, soaps, films, even documentaries – everybody knows the lines. And any sane person would add, It's only a cat! But it isn't. It's Cassandra.

They didn't muck about. The vet was drawing up the injection before I had finished nodding agreement. I held her while they did the deed, I cuddled her before they took her away – all the things you're supposed to do to help you let go.

Still, putting that warm but lifeless body into the nurse's arms wrenched something at the core of my being. Walking away from the surgery felt like some giant betrayal.

There was no choice. Yet, in spite of knowing that the vet would have thought me cruel if I'd wanted Cassandra to linger, I still feel guilty.

Imagine if that had been my child. Or my mother. Or, heaven forbid, Naomi. Incurably ill. Dying. In pain. The Curtises, the Devlins, the mighty Law Lords – they'd all pass judgment.

Is this what lies ahead for Naomi?

Cassandra couldn't tell me if she'd choose a few more days. I, with no veterinary knowledge, can decide on her behalf. On the vet's say-so it's done. No reference to any higher authority. Wham – bang. See, diagnose, prognosticate, kill. All done in minutes. Start to finish. End of story. Next, please.

I don't believe he'll even remember Cassandra by the time he gets home to his cottage pie and two veg.

If it were my life on the line though…? My 'vets' just aren't allowed to help me on my way, not even if it's my 'considered and sustained' wish. Or at least, they can't give me that merciful instant oblivion Cassandra was blessed with.

Crazy, man!

Okay, if they think my outlook is hopeless they can starve me to death. They can stand on one side and watch me struggle for breath and drown in my own secretions, and not be compelled to leap in with delaying tactics. But they can't say, 'Let's cut out the nasty bit and help him to go with dignity.'

Ye gods! Humanity, compassion, common sense, where art thou?

So much for therapy in writing. The sight of those glazed eyes, the feel of that heartbeat stopping, are as vivid and painful as they were at 6pm yesterday.

The price of emotional involvement. The cost of caring.

Tears dripped onto the desk and Naomi wiped her sleeve roughly across her eyes.

7 JULY — Two thoughts out of this misery.

Maybe my mother is wiser than I thought. Maybe she's already living with my 'afterwards'. What does it do to a parent seeing their own child facing such a future, powerless to do anything to stop the ravages of the disease? She is contemplating losing the very being she's loved so unconditionally for a lifetime. It's the end of every hope and dream and promise wrapped up in that love since conception. She knows she must stand at my grave and weep. I mustn't lose sight of her nightmare.

Death is a great context against which to balance life's problems. All this business with Cassandra has drawn Naomi and me closer again. We need each other. What price anti-slip measures, what does a nasal voice count, against sudden extinction?

If he had only known how closely his own thoughts reflected her agonising! Had he discovered her secret, he could not have penned such words.

19 JULY — Extinction? I very nearly got myself extinguished a week ago last Monday.

There I was, standing minding my own business, waiting for the number 37 bus, when out of nowhere there's a flash of gleaming metal and next minute I, together with half the bus shelter, am pinned up against Greggs the Bakers' window, sandwiched between a few tons of BMW and a doubly reinforced plate glass window.

True to tradition there was a moment of unearthly quiet and then all hell broke loose: people screaming, doors slamming, metal creaking, voices arching across each other, yelling, 'Keep yer 'ead still, son!' 'Call an ambulance.' 'We need a fire engine. Has anybody called the Fire Brigade?' Blankets were handed across the road as if on a human chain. Strangers huddled in groups at a distance as if I were contagious. Newcomers stared, awed expletives peppering the gaps between the shouting.

All I could see of the BMW driver was one elbow, white shirt-sleeve curiously uncreased. Some executive type was leaning in the window talking so I presumed he was still alive, but there was no movement from the elbow. From where I stood it was all one-sided.

I discovered first-hand that paramedics really do ask banal questions – just like they do in *Casualty*:

'Can you hear me?'

'What's your name, mate?'

'You're going to be all right, Adam.'

(Does anybody believe they have the power of second sight any more?)

'Just keep perfectly still.'

'We'll soon have you out of here.'

That's a medical 'soon' then.

'Can you feel this?'

'Tell me where it hurts.'

Easier to say where it *didn't* hurt. And 'hurt' seems too bland a word for what you feel when crushed from the chest down to the shins.

Holding still while the fire crew eased the tangled metal away from me, I felt curiously disembodied. I had this vivid picture of being left in a thousand tiny shards that would crumble to the ground once the support was removed. But somehow the ambulance men held me inside my skin, fastened me into a full body splint, swung me in unison from upright to horizontal and away we went, sirens clearing the street before us like royal outriders.

A couple of days of being x-rayed from every angle, my reflexes tortured, the indignities of 'bedrest' *(For Ideas folder: *euphemisms*), at the mercy equally of burnt-out strangers in uniforms inured to the routines, and eager friends with a macabre thirst for the ghoulish, and I was begging to escape to the sanctuary we call home. Truth to tell, the taste of utter dependence was taking away my appetite for the MND future.

Messers Gordon JK Penstemon, Casualty Consultant, and OL Herbert, Consultant, Orthopaedic Department, (if they were the rightful owners of their badges), conferred like wise old wizards and decided, since I was obviously miraculously protected and, in spite of the combined efforts of fate and Malcolm Inches, one-time driver of the aforementioned BMW, somehow without major injury, I might as well show off my psychedelic bruises without cost to the NHS rather than drain depleted resources any further. No doubt the fact that I was a potentially disgruntled journalist lent power to their readiness to remove me from harm's way.

Since that misguided (from my side) decision, the greener-grass phenomenon has not infrequently made me long for that blessed bell signalling the eviction of the loved and the unwanted. Naomi looks paler and more anxious than pre-Cassandra's demise. My mother has perfected the art of patting bedclothes, interrupting sleep and finding every nerve-jangling activity to ensure my teeth remain locked into grit mode.

It occurs to me that Malcolm Inches might have done me a favour if he'd been more thorough. In one merciful and spectacular finale he could have swept me into the hereafter and taken all the forthcoming decisions completely out of my hands. Maybe an Intercity train's the answer after all.

I shared something of that regret with Dr Curtis when he called. He gave a half smile, said, 'I think that's just the medication talking', and didn't stay long. I sensed he was in no mood for anything deep and meaningful.

I know I should be grateful. It's not every man who has two women fighting for a slice of the action. Naomi's rights were, I thought, undisputed. My mother begs to differ.

When – if – I get too much for Naomi to manage, would it be better to have some impersonal 'official' assistance paid for by the hour to do the job and stay out of our emotions; or would it be easier to accept the personal invasion from the emotionally beholden? On balance I'd say we'd do well to find someone paid to carry out the tasks Naomi assigns, to Naomi's standard; someone who'll make no effort to compete with her; someone whom she has the capacity to get rid of if things don't work out; someone whom she can castigate freely without fear of infringing my sensibilities.

If I go that distance.

21 JULY—Two weeks on from the accident and I'm still pretty stiff. Because of the crash, Curtis thought it would be wise to get my carcass overhauled by the big white chief, so my appointment's been brought forward a month. By next Monday I should be mobile enough for that visit but I've had to postpone a tango with Véronique and our holiday in the Channel Islands.

Still no word of Lydia. Must be serious. But I haven't tried again to infiltrate the health professional mafia to find out exactly what's going on.

Today a judge passed down a life sentence on a father who battered his eighteen-month-old toddler to death. The pathologist reckoned the injuries were equivalent to those sustained in a road accident.

What kind of a father does that sort of thing?

Life, the reporter first off the blocks at the close of the court proceedings said, is mandatory for murder, but then immediately he started talking about what the judge will deem the appropriate time before this guy is eligible for parole.

*(For Ideas Folder: *life sentences*. Incl. mine.)

22 JULY—I'm starting to wonder if Naomi's seeing me differently now that I've begun to show unmistakable signs of my illness.

'D'you think you'd be okay if I wasn't back till late on Wednesday?' she suddenly asked me, a bit breathlessly, as she changed the sheets on our bed.

'Sure thing. Why?'

'I've got appointments. I can ask your mum to come over, if you like.'

'No, please, no!' I said, wringing my hands in exaggerated pleading, and whimpering.

She shook her head at me.

'As long as Dr Devlin gives you the go-ahead then.'

'I'll bribe him!'

'Seriously, idiot. You sure?'

'Yeah, sure thing. I'm tons better. And I'm steaming ahead with my novel right now, so you'll be back before I notice you've gone. I promise I won't do anything silly.'

'Fat chance!'

'You know what I mean. I'll be as careful as Aunt Matilda's granny.'

'There's plenty of hotpot left. Just reheat that in the microwave. You won't limp around carrying hot dishes, will you?'

'I'll be good, Nanny. Honest.'

'I mean it. I don't want to come home and find you burnt as well as crippled.' As soon as she'd said it she realised. 'I'm sorry. You know what I mean.'

'Course I do. One smash-up is enough to be going on with. I'll be careful. Promise.' I crossed my heart with a pious look. 'Where will you be?'

'Oh, just in Edinburgh.'

'One of your cases?'

'A mixture of things. I'll ring you to check.'

'Okay. But don't worry. I'm tons better. And I'll just have seen the Devil.'

'Adam!'

I rather like the idea of testing my own independence. If Naomi's here she automatically assumes certain roles. I lead a pretty pampered life, thanks to her efficiency. My female writer-colleagues bemoan the lack of a good wife; I know what they mean. I shouldn't have allowed this state of affairs to emerge in our household, but somehow I have.

Dr Tweedy Curtis called in this evening. He flexed a few joints and asked a few personal questions but I seemed to pass his mini-test, because he made some flip comment about not keeping a good man down.

He'd brought back a book I'd lent him, a brilliant medical thriller about a serial murderer who developed aplastic anaemia. I'd been impressed by the twist in the tale, and thought Curtis might appreciate its medical cleverness. The killer went on to have a bone marrow transplant from his sister. Result: when he was a suspect years later the forensic people said he couldn't be the killer because his DNA didn't match the samples from the crime scene. Naturally, the hotshot detective got hold of some distant relative and winkled out the story of the transplant and hey ho, the villain's clapped up in jail and they've thrown away the key.

Curtis had a fascinating take on some of the medical aspects and I reckon when I've written the first draft of my own bestseller, I could do worse than ask him to cast his eye over it.

If I was going to be around long enough, I'd suggest we put our heads together to devise a cunning plot for a new novel, but that's not going to happen now.

'D'you remember telling me I should talk to Naomi about the end bit?' I said.

He startled and looked at me oddly so I realised that my train of thought wasn't obvious to him.

'Sorry,' I grinned, 'The thoughts were connected in my head.'

'I do remember, yes,' he said carefully.

'Well, I know you're right, but I must admit I haven't got round to it yet. I don't know, we just seem to have lurched from one crisis to another these past few weeks. She's had a lot on her plate lately. Some pretty difficult cases on just now. And what with my accident and the cat and everything...'

'The cat?'

'Ahhh. Yes. Cassandra. A stray we adopted years ago. She managed to acquire something or other incurable and had to be put down about three weeks ago now.'

'I'm sorry. Not easy. Even with a pet.'

'Indeed.'

'Sounds like you've both had a bit of a plateful one way and another.'

'Exactly. I don't want to add to her stress.'

'Sensible. Best to leave it till she's more herself,' he offered vaguely.

'Will do.'

'How are *you* coping with all these things – on top of your MND?' He was looking at me directly now, something watchful about his concentration.

Naomi drew in her breath sharply. Had Dr Curtis given the game away? Adam was obviously picking something up from him.

It made me pause and think before replying.

'Okay, I think, thanks. A bit rough once or twice but getting there.'

'Are you still finding the physio helpful?'

'Indeed I am. Knowing *how* to do ordinary things as well as what exercises to do helps. I'm able to keep going for longer and my muscles don't ache as much. They also give me permission to rest – and I'm afraid I need permission! Even now.'

'I know what you mean,' he grinned understandingly.

'But I have to admit I miss Lydia. She's a one-off. No disrespect to Véronique but Lydia is in a league of her own. Any chance she'll be back soon?'

'She's due back on Monday, actually.'

'Ahhh. Brilliant. It'll be good to see her again.'

'You know about her, yes?'

'Know what?'

'Why she's been off for a couple of months?'

'No. They wouldn't say. Nothing serious, I hope.' I didn't like his tone.

'Her husband died suddenly. A heart attack. Only in his forties.'

'Oh no! How appalling. Poor Lydia.'

We sat in complete silence for a long moment.

'Should I... would it be acceptable to send a message?... break the ice before I see her... professionally, I mean?'

'I think she'd appreciate that.'

Long after he'd gone I sat there immobile, thinking about Lydia and the impact of her loss. I wish I'd known. It seems so heartless to have said nothing, done nothing. And if Curtis hadn't told me, I'd have gone in there all cylinders firing and trampled all over her pain.

Naomi let out her own breath slowly. Lydia to the rescue again. Unwittingly. Or was this Dr Curtis deliberately deflecting attention away from her?

23 JULY—I left loads of time to get to the clinic this time. For some inexplicable reason I didn't want Devlin to see me staggering about. Why I should crave good marks from this bloke who surrounds himself with all shades of ungainliness is beyond me, but there it is. I just do.

He was jaunty in red and navy today. But he seemed to be feeling the heat; a thin film of perspiration stood on his forehead and twice he fiddled with the fan on his desk, angling it towards his face. It didn't so much as stir the immaculately combed hair on his head, but he had to weigh down his papers with the stapler.

And his hand was shaking.

He wanted to know all about the accident, which bits I'd hurt most and so on. He listened to my unvarnished account of the increasing weakness, but declared himself impressed by what I could still do in spite of my recent collision with a BMW.

'Are we doing everything we can to help?' he asked.

'More than I ever expected,' I told him, praising Lydia and Véronique and Curtis in particular. 'And I appreciate your seeing me ahead of schedule too.'

'Let us know if you think you could do with anything else. Our aim is to keep you as mobile and independent as we can for as long as possible.'

'Well, there is one thing...'

'Yes?'

'Can I ask you a couple of questions – about later... you know... the end?'

'Certainly.' He sat back, steepling his fingertips with his usual precision.

'If I were to ask for help to die, would you respect that?' I blurted it out before I could lose my nerve.

'Well, we would certainly *respect* the wish.' He didn't so much as startle.

'But you might not do what I ask?'

'Well, we must and do, I think, respect deeply-held sincere views but we have our own medical standards and professional conscience, and that too must play a part. Patients certainly have the right to state their preferences but they cannot be allowed to dictate the moral values of medicine.'

'In my book, a miserable, protracted life is far worse than dying.'

'I can understand that. But some of the biggest advances of recent years have been in the field of palliative medicine.' He paused for effect and, almost furtively, wiped his upper lip with his finger. 'Patients are often surprised themselves at just how much better things are than they anticipated.'

'So would you *ever* give them something to help them on their way?'

'Some doctors are more comfortable with this idea than others. It would depend.'

'And that's part of the patient's dilemma, if I may say so. I mean, take my case: I'd give this life more of a whirl if I knew that when I said, "That's enough," you – or *somebody* who has the know-how – would be ready to help me go.'

He was nodding slowly. 'I quite understand where you're coming from.'

'So why doesn't modern medicine respond to that?'

'Well, we do respond, but perhaps just not in the way you're meaning.

And that's for a number of reasons, I think. One: we're trained to cure and to care, not to kill. And two: it's actually very hard to be sure a patient really, really means it when he says he'd rather be dead. And, of course, there's no going back to alter that course of management. And three: well, most of us doctors aren't wildly enthusiastic about spending years going through nasty court proceedings.'

He smiled rather apologetically.

'I can understand why you might not want this enshrined in law,' I said, 'but surely doctors should have a degree of discretion.'

'Many doctors would agree with you. But maybe it's something best done quietly and unobtrusively.'

Was he offering me hope? Who could tell?

'Actually, when I was in hospital after the accident, it occurred to me – the doctors might have looked at my notes, and thought, no point in pulling out the stops for this one, best let him go now.'

'Well, I doubt any doctor would make that call in your case at this moment in time.' He gave a rueful smile and somehow one of his eyes stayed in one place long enough to convey a sort of twinkling warmth with the statement.

'But say something like that were to happen when I'm further down the line. They might think, It's futile to treat this one, best let him go.'

'Well, it's possible. But for what it's worth, if, on the basis of his technical and medical expertise and experience, a doctor judges treatment to be futile, it's a *medical* decision. The patient's views and preferences are irrelevant.'

'Really? But the doctor might be allowing his own value judgments to influence that decision.'

'Indeed.'

'And the family's values might be different from his.'

'Indeed they might, and that's partly why most of us prefer to work with patients and their relatives and weigh up the pros and cons together.'

'Hmmmmm.'

'But to go back a step, if I may, saying that a doctor doesn't have an obligation to treat implies it may be permissible for him to do so, or not. That's not the same as saying he has a duty not to treat. Then it's not permissible.'

'Fair comment.'

He shrugged but offered nothing further. I saw one of his eyes glance at the clock and took the hint.

He gave me the usual invitation – four months, but contact us if you need to see us sooner. It appears on the surface to be bowing to the dictates of consumer-centred care but I suspect it's actually a cloak for 'if you deteriorate more quickly...'

All the way home I was mulling over this business of assisted death. Maybe he's right. Maybe it's best left to the discretion of the medical team rather than lawyers. Maybe attempting to regulate things would just drive the practice underground – or maybe just mean different things being covered up.

Maybe you can be too transparent. It's a bit like protecting precious artefacts, shielding them from the full glare of natural light. Shine a dim, artificial substitute on them and their contours, their detail, may be softened but they're preserved intact.

And Devlin's definitely right on one thing: doctors aren't vending machines, churning out what patients request. He's watched hundreds of patients with MND die. I've only watched one, part-way. So his clinical judgment and ethical wisdom count, as well as his technical expertise. I suspect I've been too defensive and too shackled by my own preconceived ideas to be receptive to all his cues up till now.

Naomi read this entry a second time. Slowly. And again. It was amazing how clearly and objectively he could think through something so emotionally laden. Was it this that had sustained him for so long? Or was it a form of emotional denial that had also rendered him impervious to her private agony? It seemed incredible that he had not suspected, not pressed her more for an explanation.

25 JULY—Another idea's been squashed at birth. Seems even the fully functioning bits of my anatomy are no use for transplant purposes. I ceremonially shredded my donor card yesterday. Damn. Another door closed.

Curiously enough it was pesky Harry who prompted me to investigate that question. I was proposing a feature on our local liver transplant unit – based around the anniversary of the first transplant ever carried out – and Harry dropped in a suggestion that we give it a donor angle. A quick tramp to see the transplant co-ordinator, and there I am joining the ranks of the outright rejected. Beryl, one of our copy editors, was turned down by the blood transfusion people after fifteen years of valiant service on the grounds of heart arrhythmia and they counselled her to death to bolster her self esteem. But then, nobody knew I was taking this journalistic strike personally.

Hey ho. There are no perks-for-heroes in my little battle.

Anyway, organ donation's out. So it's just a question of, do I want the whole wreck that currently houses my mind, body and soul to be excavated in the line of medical research? The brain and spinal cord would apparently be of particular interest – not because *I'm* the donor and happen to have a reasonable endowment in the upper storey, but just because they're looking for cause and effect.

I must admit Naomi's feelings on this are a big stumbling block. She's the one who'd have to live with the knowledge. I don't want her to suffer unnecessarily.

I desperately want to talk to her about the whole business of how much she can tolerate but I can't seem to find a way in that feels safe. There's something intangible around her at the moment that tells me she's vulnerable; close to tears but gritting her teeth. And now we seem to be steering back into calmer waters, she and I, I don't want to risk rocking the boat. I've tried being direct but she says she's fine; just tired. And if I'm brutally honest, I daren't probe too deeply. I don't want to hear that she's already near the end of her tether with me.

Ahhhhh. So that was why.

A quick exit from life before I need extra care seemed like a good solution on first inspection but I worry that she'll feel eternally guilty. Or worse, think I didn't value life with her. I guess I could write an explanation for her posthumous comfort. But my mother's hang-ups show me just how the stench can linger.

On the other hand, I hate the idea of Naomi having to deal with the physical side of things, of our home being tainted for her, pervaded by the aura of death and decay.

I could, I suppose, elect to go into a hospital, or a hospice. But my big worry there is that with all those experts on tap doing all manner of aggressive things, I'd linger till long after my sell-by date and Naomi's ordeal would just be protracted. Okay, I know they've got it down to a fine art, this balancing of the emotional, physical and spiritual, but I don't *want* to be so successfully cared for that the dying is strung out way past the point of common sense. And I'm not convinced I'd have the strength to fight the whole bang shoot of them with all the logical right they've got on their side.

I forgot to record, the other day, one point of fact. Curtis says I'm most unlikely to choke or drown to death. That's the fate everybody fears with this particular form of dying (as he confirmed), me included. So it helps, knowing. Best not to hang your entire strategy around an inexactitude.

The ideal? Slipping away peacefully in my sleep. How do I contrive the equivalent?

Naomi read this extract four times. Carefully. No, there was still no hint of suspicion.

But the memories uppermost in her own mind contributed to a particularly virulent variation of her nightmare. Mavis's hands around her neck were relentless, her face distorted with the sheer force of her effort as she hissed, 'Those who live by the sword shall die by the sword. A life for a life. You murder my flesh and blood, I'll murder you.'

Naomi woke with her heart pounding. She dared not close her eyes again but lay unmoving, dreading the morrow.

25 JULY—Naomi was away all day and I'm delighted to report I didn't spill anything, trip over anything or otherwise disgrace myself. One of her colleagues ran her back in the evening, but whoever it was didn't come in.

Naomi seemed pretty washed out so I made her a hot chocolate and packed her off to bed. She didn't protest.

Unusual.

This girl works too hard, gives too much of herself to other people. She needs more TLC.

Naomi cowered away from the screen, her eyes wide and staring, her reflection lurking like a pale ghost in the background.

A furtive glance was enough to show that there was no entry at all for the following day. It was as if those dreadful hours had been erased.

She closed down the computer and dragged herself into the kitchen in search of comfort. A full glass of Madeira went down without pause for breath. A second was equally tasteless.

Perhaps she should skip the rest of the entries for July. Why not? She wanted to leave the 25th out of her own calendar for ever.

The familiar pervasive sense of sorrow tightened its grip on her chest.

'Oh, Adam, Adam, Adam. Why did it have to be this way?'

29 JULY—Usually Sunday's a good day in our house. It's the one day of the week we can lie in or have a leisurely breakfast or spend quality time together before the pressures of workaday deadlines push us back into the stampede.

But today was the exception. Naomi was up and about with the lark for some reason. She mumbled something about feeling restless, not wanting to disturb my sleep. But her head was inside the cupboard under the stairs at the time so I didn't get the full story.

It occurs to me my mother may have been giving her a conscience. Why else would she suddenly need to clear out cupboards on a Sunday morning, for goodness' sake? Unless…?

Is it…? Could she be…?

When she'd finished she suddenly announced that she was off for a tramp in the woods. I looked hard at her but, I don't think it was my imagination, she didn't hold my gaze.

'I just need to clear my head,' was all she said.

'Of cobwebs?'

The smile only twisted her mouth, didn't reach her eyes.

'Or secrets?' I said lightly, watching her.

She bent down to lace up her walking shoes.

'D'you want to come with me? It's okay if you've got things you want to do.' A trifle too quick with the dis-invitation, I thought. But I know what it feels like to need your own space.

'No, off you go. Enjoy your hike. You'll cover twice the ground without me stumbling along behind you. But don't forget I'm here if you want to off-load.'

She gave me a quick kiss and was off. I watched her solitary figure until it was lost in the trees and a mist of tears. A symbolic moment. Her future. Without me.

While she was gone I tackled the Sunday papers. There are some depressingly good writers amongst the competition. But Kingsley wasn't a name I'd seen before. The Most Reverend Wilberforce JJ Kingsley. Sounds a bit reinforced. But anyway, he's produced this intriguing little thought-for-the-day on a subject I have a sort of love-hate relationship with.

Sanctity of life. My mother's bosom pal. Some automatic shutter closes as soon as her needle hits that particular groove. But the Most Reverend Wilberforce JJ Kingsley adds a new dimension to her entrenched position.

The sanctity and the value standpoints are radically different, he maintains. Sanctity or sacredness means the person is set apart, consecrated: *ergo*, life itself is not yours to meddle with. Be it long or short it's just down to you to be a faithful steward of the time you're given.

Value, by contrast, refers to inherent worth. What is this life worth? Things like the relief of suffering or wanting eternal life with God may have more value at a certain point than the present life. Furthermore, if you believe that the life to come is infinitely more wonderful than this present mortal lot then it's crazy to revere it above the future one and cling to it indecently. Well, yes, I paraphrase!

But the corollary to this, it seems to me, is that if you don't believe in an afterlife you might want to hang on to this present life, just because it is all there is; precious in its finiteness. That's what I'm afraid of: hanging on too long.

30 JULY—I sent a basket of flowers to the surgery for Lydia with a little message. Her first day back. Facing all those people who know she's been

away for weeks. But I don't want to be another person picking away at her scabs. Best to get the soppy things said.

I'd have sent them to her home but I've no idea where she lives.

I hope it's not a liberty too far.

Naomi still seems... subdued?... pensive?... withdrawn? I'm not exactly sure. I tried to get her to talk this evening, but she kept it superficial and soon hid behind the chatter of the news on the radio while she did the ironing. If she is pregnant, she's not exactly blooming yet!

31 JULY—I made a complete twerp of myself today and I can only hope the precise detail doesn't come back to Naomi.

Some woman phoned at lunchtime wanting to speak to 'Mrs O'Neill'.

'May I ask who's calling?' I said, being of a mean and suspicious disposition.

'Ummmm... Stella.'

'Stella from the Social Work Department, Stella from the Women's Institute, Stella from the KGB, or Stella from the underworld?' I let my voice sink to a conspiratorial whisper on the last word.

Suspended silence.

'I take it Mrs O'Neill isn't there?' Whoever she was she was not amused.

'If you're planning a robbery or wanting to use this house for meetings of the Ku Klux Klan, not only is she here but she's armed to the teeth, and so are her seventeen burly security men and yours truly, who, incidentally, has a black belt in Karate to boot. If you need to speak to her bodyguard, press button 1. If you're needing a can-rattler for your pet charity or you're after her cells for cloning a super-race press button 2.' I don't suppose it actually sounded remotely like a recorded message either.

Silence again.

'Hello?' I ventured after a decent interval.

'Is that Mr O'Neill?'

'Who wants to know?'

'St...' She obviously saw the pitfall instantly.

In a blinding flash it occurred to me this might be some distraught woman whose kiddie was up for adoption or some childless soul who needed a sympathetic ear.

'Look, I'm desperately sorry. Ignore my nonsense. I've been in an accident and the enforced house arrest is driving me loony. I'm afraid my wife isn't here at the moment but may I take a message?'

'Could you... would you ask her to ring Stella, please?'

'Sure thing. May I take your number?'

'She'll have it.'
'Okay. Will do.'
'Thank you.'
'No problem. And again, I'm terribly sorry.'
There was the tiniest pause before the ringing tone cut us off.

Naomi closed her eyes and took long steadying breaths. Stella had dismissed her second-hand apology lightly. But she must have wondered just what was going on in Naomi's domestic life. It didn't bear imagining what was recorded in her notes. When she'd got in from work that night, Adam had been sheepish in confession.

'Who's Stella?' he asked cautiously.
'Why?' She busied herself unpacking the shopping.
'Because she rang to speak to you today.'
'Oh, did she leave a message?'
'Just said, would you ring her.'
'Oh.'
'Is she one of your clients?'
'No. Why?'
'Thank goodness for that,' he said with a sigh of relief.
'Why?'
'Because… well, I'm afraid I… well, I went into crazy-speak.'
She turned then to look at him, waiting.
'I chuntered on as if she might be some criminal casing the joint.'
'Without even knowing who she was?' Naomi stared at him incredulously.
'I know. Lunatic. I'm terribly sorry.'
'Not just lunatic, dangerous,' she shot back.
'I know, I know. I don't know what came over me. I'm desperately sorry. Should I phone or write to apologise or something? Who is she anyway?'
'No, you'd only make it into a bigger deal than it is already. I'll explain. Tell her you're just out of the asylum. But for goodness' sake, Adam.'
He was abject in his repeated apologies but asked no more questions.
Another narrow escape.
Sagging back into his chair now, Naomi consciously worked at letting the tension out of her shoulders.

I AUGUST—Julie from three doors down called in today with a punnet of raspberries from her prolific garden. She and Naomi often exchange gardening tips and produce. But she had to make do with me tonight because Naomi was held up at work.
'Is she all right?' Julie asked.
'Yes, fine. She's just horrendously busy. Working all hours these days.'

'Oh, I just wondered. Because of her being at the hospital. I was up there on Wednesday visiting my aunt – fractured hip, you know. And I saw Naomi walking along the corridor. I called across. But she didn't hear me.'

'Wednesday? Oh, it'll just have been work. She had appointments all day. She goes to the hospital to see the new mothers whose babies are going for adoption.'

'Oh, I see. Yeah, it was the corridor that goes across to the maternity section.'

I didn't really hear the rest of her warbling. First the nesting... now going to the baby world... asleep when I go to bed, up before me in the morning...

I'm suddenly aware of holding my breath.

Naomi became aware that she was holding her own breath. She leaned forward onto her elbows the better to massage her aching neck, but that only brought Adam's suspense closer.

2 AUGUST—I'm still feeling slightly bewildered. Last night Naomi rang to say she'd be late home – had to go somewhere; salmon steaks, salad, in the fridge; not to wait for her. I was instantly thinking chemist, Mothercare...

The plain brown box she carried in from the car was unremarkable but she carried it in as if it was a Ming vase and laid it carefully on my lap.

'Consolation prize.'

I guess I was still trying to think laterally when I opened the flaps. So two wide round copper eyes staring up at me from the ball of silvery-blue fluff in one corner took me by storm.

'She's not Cassandra, I know, but she's the best I can do,' Naomi said with a kind of thickness in her voice.

I couldn't say anything for a good century. Even then I hid behind telling the creature how beautiful she was until I got a grip.

'I thought she ought to be completely different from Cassandra,' Naomi was whispering, peering over my shoulder into the box. 'She's a Blue Persian.'

'What a fabulous coat,' I said.

A fabulous hissing greeted my tentative hand.

'You'll probably be cursing those long hairs on everything before the week is out!' Her more robust tones instantly raised the mood back into my comfort zone.

'And what's the name of this little princess?'

'It's your choice. She's your cat.'

'Oh wow! Well, it'll have to be something exotic.'

I'm already up to the Ks in the book of baby names; nothing worthy of her noble ancestry and impeccable credentials so far.

3 AUGUST—The Persian Cat website confirms my sense of awe in the presence of my new playmate – well, she'll thaw eventually, I hope. She is the direct descendant of one of the oldest recognised pedigree breeds. No wonder she tolerates only minimal contact with *my* plebeian little world to date.

Our particular aristocrat is to be either Noelani (Hawaiian for beautiful one from heaven; but with an expectation of a good old British Christmas when we get better acquainted) or Rashieka (Arabic, meaning descended from royalty). She certainly hasn't allowed the common courtesies to inhibit her from instantly betraying her superiority so far. The way she minces around my study would make even my mother feel her standards were deficient.

Help! Therein lies danger!

Trying out the alternatives, I'm almost sure it'll be Noelani. If I ever get to the stage of daring to raise my voice to/for her, I fear Rashieka would be too strident a sound for everyone's sensibilities.

Suddenly, unbidden, there flashes into my mind an unworthy thought. Naomi has replaced Cassandra and I'm delighted with the new improved version. My hurt is instantly... not exactly erased, but immeasurably eased. Will Naomi replace me so easily? And with a much better model?

I feel a sudden longing for Cassandra's acceptance, for the soothing comfort of warm vibrating fur, the unquestioning devotion.

I'm staggered by the depth of my disappointment. It's like a dull nauseating malaise. And I have absolutely no right to it.

I got it all wrong. Naomi was pining not preparing. She's not pregnant. Tangible evidence.

I need time to analyse my feelings on this one. Noelani could be very helpful here but she hasn't learned to smell my moods yet.

Thank goodness I said nothing about my suspicions to Naomi.

4 AUGUST—My thinking over the last few days has made me start on my will. I need to work at it myself first; no point in paying a solicitor to translate half-baked ideas into legal-speak.

The financial bit is easy. Done and dusted. But the advance directive isn't nearly as straightforward as I thought it was before I stepped onto the slippery slope to oblivion. I've retrieved a template from the Internet but it needs tweaking to fit my bizarre circumstances.

If I'm to bequeath my tissues to medical science, speed is of the essence and everybody needs to know beforehand. Curtis found out for me; tissue is of most value during the first forty-eight hours. He also told me that the family might have to pay to move my body to a tissue bank – several hundred pounds apparently!

We can afford it but imagine what it'd do for some poor folk, altruistic and generous but financially strapped; going cap in hand to charities in the first hours of bereavement. Madness! *(For Ideas folder: *the cost of altruism.*) I've worked out an argument for anyone who tries to overrule my request, though – my sainted mother springs to mind! Respect for the living *requires* that my lesser-ranking dead tissue be used on their behalf.

Aha!

By way of light relief, I've started a 'My funeral' file. Galloped into that without a qualm. Pity I'll miss it (well, not hear and see it) with its combination of the things I'd enjoy. I've already told Naomi about it.

The echo of his laughter as he outlined crazy plans for his send-off made Naomi smile. Extravagant talk of helicopters trailing banners, party poppers and irreverent songs had taken the sting out of the subject without betraying his actual wishes. He'd even composed eight lines of doggerel about himself which he said she could read over the coffin to send him on his way with a chortle.

The actual event had been so much easier to organise because of his explicit instructions. And it was surprisingly comforting knowing it was exactly what he wanted. Dignified but not melancholy; solemn without being maudlin.

She closed her eyes against the vivid pictures: the endless walk to the front of the church – alone; the coffin; the moment when it sank out of sight…

'I can't bear it,' she whispered, her eyes swivelling to the photograph. 'I don't want to be here without you.'

6 AUGUST—Lydia is back. I was hopeless. She thanked me for the flowers; I commiserated. We got on with the exercises but you can't flirt with a new widow; you can't tease her into life. I just did as she said and neither of us attempted to fill in the spaces. I couldn't. Every topic of conversation seemed insensitive: holidays, writing novels, slurred speech. How trivial is that?

She was professional and efficient but just not the Lydia I know and love. All the colour and sparkle had gone. I came away depressed by my own inadequacy and her pain.

Is this what it'll be like for Naomi?

I only stayed a couple of hours at the office then went home to work. As if I were in mourning too.

I'm writing a piece on disabled access. It's enough to make me reach for the barbiturates. Everything from aeroplane loos right down to pavement kerbs conspires against you if you're physically disabled. And this is in an age of equality and anti-discrimination. Ha ha!

I mean, since 1995 and the jolly little enlightened Disability Discrimination Act, service providers have a duty to change the physical features of premises that make it 'unreasonably difficult' for people with disabilities to use those services, or else they have to provide an alternative way of making the service available. Unreasonably difficult? Ho ho ho! A movable feast methinks, depending on where you sit at the banquet. By golly, I even found an airline that charged disabled people for the use of a wheelchair to transfer them in the airport. *Hello?*

The Disability Rights Commission is monitoring the situation, I'm told; test cases will be brought to achieve maximum effect. By the time some of these cases get a hearing my guess is the victim will be long gone. And such is my destiny.

Maybe this will be my last foreign holiday. Ever. The finality is beginning to feel real. The last... whatever.

8 AUGUST—The mysterious Stella whoever-she-is has re-surfaced. Well, somebody purporting to be her spokesperson rang anyway. A squeaky-voiced Lottie from 'Occupational Health'. I hope the actual Stella, doubtless cringing in the background, paid her fall-guy handsomely.

Let it not be said that I am too arrogant to learn a lesson, however. I was silkily smooth, charmingly chivalrous, and politeness personified. Having established in one simple sentence that Mrs O'Neill was not currently to be located in her known residence, the innovative Lottie set out to ascertain whether or not I might be seeing the said Mrs O'Neill in the forseeable future. The temptation to trade on this open invitation to satirical riposte, I admit, was powerful but I resisted and gave a dull and predictable, yes.

Could I give her a message from Stella? I *could*. And furthermore I *would* consider doing so, I supplied in my head.

'Just say that Stella isn't able to keep her appointment next Tuesday, could Mrs O'Neill please ring to make an alternative date.'

I was mean enough to repeat the message slowly as if I were dictating to myself writing it down. I console myself with the reasonable hope that the unfortunate Lottie has never heard of Adam O'Neill, the writer, and carries pity for the poor imbecile she contacted next to her heart.

'Who's Stella?' I asked Naomi casually, after faithfully delivering the message verbatim from Lottie.

'Adam! You didn't give Lottie the lunatic treatment, did you? Please tell me you didn't!'

'Okay. I didn't.'

'What did you say?' She was glaring at me suspiciously.

'I was as smooth as Sebastian in *Brideshead Revisited* and as courteous as David Suchet's Poirot.'

She groaned.

'Everyone will think I keep a deranged idiot at home!'

'Everyone?'

'You're impossible!' And she stalked out.

Who *is* Stella?

We're off to Jersey on Saturday. Sea, sand, sun. Peace, rest, escape. Short flight, no language issues to complicate my personal impediment, lots to do without much effort. Fits the bill admirably. I'm hoping it'll bring the sparkle back into Naomi's eyes. She still seems under par.

Naomi sat back, closing her eyes, remembering. She'd left Edinburgh burdened by her heartache. The prospect of two weeks alone with Adam filled her with foreboding. She knew he was watching her, concerned about her uncharacteristic listlessness. How long could she parry his questions? How strong would her resolve be once she relaxed, when there was no work to hide behind, no bolt-hole, no Stella?

At first it had been a conscious effort, but gradually, in the concentration on his needs, she'd felt her own fear recede. She'd returned from Jersey fuelled by ultra-violet light and renewed confidence that not only was she was now unlikely to crack under pressure, but that indeed Adam's puzzlement had passed.

26 AUGUST — Jersey was terrific. Were I to be in the running for a retirement home I'd have the Channel Islands somewhere on my list. People, pace of life, climate, scenery, historical interest, all perfect for a life of leisure.

I've returned with an even prettier wife, the beginnings of a beard (Naomi's idea), and a notebook full of ideas for my writing. And if Naomi isn't pregnant it's not for want of trying. Of course, the wall-to-wall sunshine had to be a contributory factor, in her case, to this improved state of affairs; my seasonal chameleon.

A little of my personal burden lifts. Even on Jersey she didn't escape from *me*, so I'm daring to hope I'm not personally the reason for the recent melancholy.

Seeking more than assumed reassurance, I tried once asking her what had been going on.

'Oh, just all the pressures, all these families falling apart – the usual stuff.' She was touching my designer stubble at the time, watching shadow shapes forming and dissolving as her hand moved between the sun and me. I couldn't read her expression.

'On top of the worries at home,' I ventured.

'Well, yeah. Cassandra and your accident and… everything. It didn't help.'

'And worrying about the future?' I kept it brief.

'Don't let's go there. Not now. Not here. Let's just enjoy being away from all the pressures. Come on, I need to feel the sand between my toes.'

Scampering off, silhouetted against the sun, she took my spirits soaring with her and my anxiety floated out to sea. Temporarily anyway. I didn't follow her; my ungainly gait only reminds us both. Sitting in all the safety of immobility, watching her – slim, brown, lithe – I can almost believe nothing has changed.

I feel the stares wherever she and I go. Inside my head I compose a blistering reaction to the condescending receptionist who equates slurred speech to low scores on the Mensa scale; I write against my retina the thoughts of the admiring men who watch Naomi and wonder why she stays saddled to a cripple.

I lie wide-awake struggling to blot out the pictures of her future holidays, capering in the sun with someone else. In the morning I consciously adjust my blinkers, tunnelling my vision on her, my world contained in her pleasure.

Only in the illusion of normality can I forget. Naomi being her usual sunny self is part of that illusion.

31 AUGUST—It's been a hellish week. We're always under pressure during the holiday season but things are worse this year with numbers right down to the bone. I've had to touch base more. In the office Harry is spitting hydrochloric acid. Rumour has it Arkwright slated him over some editorial decision in my absence and he's looking for somewhere to dump his anger. I skidaddled home as soon as I decently could.

Noelani to the rescue! Since her brief summer 'holiday' slumming it on the commoner's turf of the local cattery, she's come to the conclusion that 14 Montgomery Crescent is possibly the nearest she'll get to a degree of civilisation that befits her genetic inheritance, and furthermore that somehow her recent banishment to a hell echoing to the cries of randy mongrel toms and feral females, was a consequence she brought entirely on herself by her spiteful behaviour.

In spite of my holiday bonhomie I'm afraid I let the owner of the said feline purgatory know exactly what I thought of her 'superior care'. Given the recognised extra needs of Persians, we had agreed over-the-odds payment in return for daily grooming, as well as gentle handling and special food. A cursory glance was enough to convince me that the imperious Noelani had received less than the attention due to a stray mongrel due for euthanasia in the morning.

But the fortnight of neglect has confirmed her allegiance. She has accepted the necessity for extra brushing of her silky fur with resignation if not exactly alacrity, and in the process sealed her territory on my lap.

The feel of her satisfaction in my hands today as I wrote my feature article soothed my agitation and gradually the staccato words coalesced and began to slide creamily from my mind.

Naomi has been instantly swallowed up in a case of fostering gone badly wrong so she's away all weekend, leaving me free to steam ahead with Aidan's story. The ideas thrown up by my subconscious in Jersey gave me a skeleton of prompts which has generated several chapters without pause. Feels good.

7 SEPTEMBER — Today I was late for the team meeting, thanks to a bar of soap. It just slithered out of my hand in the shower. Suddenly every blessed thing within reach was slippery. I flailed around for that second that stretches into infinity before crashing to the ground. Bombarded by the water still cascading over me, trapped in that column of greased whiteness, I was like a blindfolded spider in an oiled jam jar. In the end I had to inch the door open, regardless of the immediate deluge onto the floor, slide myself over the ledge and grab the radiator to haul myself out of my predicament.

Cursing my ineptitude I eventually restored the bathroom to a semblance of normality but the clock refused to show any sense of obligation and I staggered in to the meeting a good twenty minutes late. I knew my apology came out all garbled as I fell into the last available seat. Harry made some sneering aside under his breath to those nearest him. I shot a grateful glance at Celia Armstrong who silently pointed to the current item on the agenda.

Henceforth the soap is to be securely anchored by a magnetic holder, or an intrinsic rope, or a dispenser full of the liquid lather. I purchased all three on the way home. I even suppressed my pathological hatred of non-slip mats for long enough to purchase two. I have never, ever, used them in hotels – my imagination conjures up veritable armies of bugs marching towards my naked soles. But better a live journalist with verrucas than a dead one wearing plastic galoshes.

Surveying these next steps towards disability, my mind fights grim pictures of boards across the bath, a powered bath seat, a ceiling-mounted hoist, no bath at all, only a walk-in shower, big enough for three to manoeuvre inside, a discoloured seat fixed to one side, grab-rails punctuating the walls. I see a forlorn Naomi taking prospective buyers around this crippled house.

For the thousandth time, I curse my over-active imagination.

14 SEPTEMBER—I've been unaccountably low this week. Post-holiday blues? Reaction to returning to a Harry-infested world? Naomi slipping back into her old preoccupations? Familial depression?

I don't know.

I don't care.

I can't be bothered.

I can't sleep.

I don't want to eat.

I know people are making allowances for me but I hate the mental games, the conspiracy. Making allowances is for children and other people.

17 SEPTEMBER—Gaynor is my latest acquisition. She is a forty-ish lady with pale, puffy skin and an air of habitual subservience. She has pudgy hands and a large mole on the back of her neck. Her roots are grey, her ends are streaked blonde and mouse alternately as if she hesitates to leave the security of a lifetime as a nonentity.

But Gaynor wields a mean scalpel. She's in the business of turning a bed of gravel into a path of silk. I am awed by her skills. Not since I was a schoolboy have I trodden through life with such abandon.

Why anyone would ever choose to be a chiropodist is completely beyond my comprehension. I mean, when you line up a row of snotty little beggars in the classroom and ask them what they want to be when they grow up, they don't even know that feet sprout problems, do they? In their Startrite comprehensively-measured, change-every-four-months footwear, they live in constant cushioned comfort – or at least they did in my day, before fashion ruled in the comprehensives. From whence then, even awareness of chiropody?

Besides which, who in their right mind wants to handle other people's feet? I am repulsed by even my own. There is something singularly unlovely about these underpinnings that frankly turns my stomach. I was sorely tempted to keep my socks on for Gaynor. Mercifully my pedal appendages arrived in her lap freshly bathed, patted dry and liberally creamed by something delightfully fragranced to render them anonymous.

Not knowing my history she tut-tutted about my uneven weight bearing, and the iniquity of creating all sorts of pressure points ripe for corns and calluses. Learning of my diagnosis, she retracted every innuendo and manfully took all blame for every sin of omission and commission upon her own bowed shoulders. She proceeded to scrape and polish until I expected to see a mere bundle of bones rattling in the whiteness of her towel.

I left her disinfected sanctuary walking on air. Whatever they pay her, she deserves more. She is one of this gathering army of carers who can work and talk simultaneously. Already I know that she doesn't personally do domiciliary visits, but she knows a man who does.

Does one need smooth feet when MND has you in its stranglehold? My suspicion is there will be far more pressing problems (no pun intended) elsewhere.

I have the facts, in case.

18 SEPTEMBER—Today a bleak moment was transformed by one of those rare but sublime happenstances that pepper life but sparsely. My speech was particularly fractured, due I suspect in no small measure to an exhausting night wracked by cramps and spasms.

'I'm sorry... to... be such a... wreck... today,' I ground out.

'You are not a wreck,' Naomi said softly, leaning across the table to lay a hand over mine.

I nodded, knowing my despondency was writ large, unable to disguise it.

'Adam, look at me.' She waited till I did.

'Smile.' She waited patiently.

'Like you mean it.' The look in her eyes made that possible.

'Have I told you lately what that does for me?'

I shook my head slowly.

'Something inside me melts when you smile at me – like that. I feel... breathless. Wrecks don't do that for me.'

I had to laugh.

And now that look, that smile, had gone for ever. All the things that had given her that inner glow, the things they had shared, the secrets known only to the two of them. All gone. Naomi rose so quickly from Adam's chair that Noelani instinctively clenched her claws through the thin fabric of her dress before leaping straight into the wastepaper basket. The indignant expression made a laugh irresistible. Naomi stooped to sweep the cat onto her shoulder and set about smoothing both their ruffled feelings.

19 SEPTEMBER—I'm putting pressure on Naomi to get a gardener in to help with the heavy, boring stuff. She's 'thinking about it'. It makes sense.

'It would take the edge off *my* guilt,' I wheedled.

'Ahh. You're looking for an easy option, are you? Well, maybe I *like* having you beholden to me.'

'I'm going to be beholden anyway. No point in keeping that as your trump card.'

I also want her to get a cleaner in, a paid helper who comes at set hours. But she has a whacking great ace in her hand on that one. My mother's dropped the hypocrisy of secret scouring and now chunters in brazenly 'to give the place a bit of a lick'. If she minds, Naomi doesn't tell me. I *want* her to mind, too. I did give her permission to resent the interference when the pretence was first dropped, but she just shrugged and said, 'She needs a role.'

'But she should take her cue from you.'

'She could do far worse. I hate cleaning.'

I absolutely don't understand the female mind.

I've made a rather lowering discovery. Aidan's deterioration is more depressing than my own. In real life I can to a large extent ignore other people's reactions and actively work at keeping my own emotions in perspective. No such luxury in my fictional life. Walking alongside as well as inside Aidan, I am shackled to his frustration *and* too aware of everyone else's irritation.

Today I watched busy commuters dodging around him, hemmed in behind him, cursing him, as he staggered across the main concourse at Kings Cross on crutches at 5.15PM. I was one of them. Hang it, *I* was exasperated with him! What the hell is this cripple doing blocking pathways in normal working hours?

But I also gritted Aidan's teeth with the sheer effort of putting one foot in front of another, of staying vertical in the face of the surging masses all around me, of finding a spare inch to anchor the rubber toe of my sticks. *I* had a legitimate appointment too. I was a fully paid-up commuter, entitled to my space on the peak-time station.

In Hester-Ramonides-speak, my exasperation is scarlet with lightning flashes of yellow zipping across the 'sp' bit and heavy lines of metallic grey underlining the ongoing motion of the 'ion'.

My emotions at the moment, I know, are distorted by the baby issue. Still no success. Another month of fatherhood lost. Speaking of which, Naomi has started going to see Anabelle and Courtney at their house, rather than asking them here. She says the children like to have more toys and girly things around them; it makes her job of entertaining them easier. And it frees her up to talk to her sister too; she's not trying to prepare meals at the same time.

'I need the practice too,' I protest.

'Come with me,' she replies flatly.

'But you go when I'm busy.'

'That's why I go then, so you're free to get on. Undisturbed. By them and me.'

I ought to be grateful for her consideration. I'm not; I'm resentful. I don't need a proxy decision-maker. Not yet.

23 SEPTEMBER—One of the old-school Sundays. A full night's sleep without cramp. Staying in bed till 11 o'clock. With Naomi. Pancakes with maple syrup for brunch. My piece on perspectives in today's *Arts and Reviews* section looking better in reality than I remembered. The colours of the maple in our back garden stunning. A fire in the sitting room in the evening against the beginnings of autumnal chill. My own mulled wine slipping over the tongue.

Naomi's in bed already. Waiting.

Tomorrow I'll probably rebel against my diminishing standards of excellence. Today my world is the colour of autumn.

24 SEPTEMBER—One day back in the office, and I resolve to be there as little as possible. Harry may be roasting his flesh in Tanzania but his confounded memos are still flashing up with monotonous regularity. He must have primed his PA to fire them off every so many minutes.

Those still holding the fort in person seem to think I'm their personal slave. Could you just...? Will you...? When you've got a minute... Time was when I was first in the volunteer queue – little creep! Everybody's shoulder. Procrastination was anathema to me. Not nowadays. No, sir. In fact I've adopted a new slogan: Never do today what will become somebody else's responsibility tomorrow.

In my own gathering tomorrows, I'll soon be no more. Why flog myself now? There are no accolades for martyrdom in the publishing world.

Well, that's the theory. In reality, face to face with the needy, my new resolves falter. Which is why I need to work from home and selfishly husband my energy for my own deadlines.

25 SEPTEMBER—Curtis has referred me to an occupational therapist – 'in preparation', he says. Not his finest hour.

Her name is Ursula Major. Yes, honestly. Her badge confirms her parents' stupidity – or was it ignorance? For one so saddled, she's remarkably cheery. She's not an inch above five feet, ash blonde with lashes and brows so fair she looks almost albino, incongruously bulging calves and biceps, but otherwise about a size six!

Just minutes into my appointment she produced a catalogue of what she calls 'aids'. Yeah, yeah, like I really want to choose a trolley to push in front of me. Mahogany please, with inlaid marquetry, and brass wheels. Pages of the stuff – grabbers, raised seats, straps, tripods, zimmers, Closomat lavatories...

Ye gods, sock it to me straight, why don't you?

She's gushingly willing to come out to the house to see what they can do to 'adapt' things. The pages of her treasured catalogue flick assuredly to double handrails, scaffolded toilets, ramps, bath hoists, stair lifts. There's no picture of her latest acquisition but her enthusiasm makes her poetic in her endorsement. A new motorised wheelchair – well, new to *her* stable. A reject from some spinal unit in reality. One instantly wonders what dire fate befell its last occupant.

I haven't the heart to dampen her bright eagerness. By all means come if I'm on your list, have a coffee even, as long as you get the message loud and clear: I'm not ready yet to yield ownership of my castle to a bunch of carpenters. But the proffered grant form for 'necessary alterations' is the tin lid. I've suddenly got an urgent appointment with my boss.

I've become paranoid about backing up my novel. My therapy. Imagine telling my story, inch by painful inch, and then a machine failure obliterating the memory in the flick of a switch. Somebody once told me to keep copies wrapped in polythene in the freezer in case of... was it fire or gas explosion or bomb damage? Whatever.

I'm trusting the usual computer archives, and sundry backup discs. The bigger the files the more I fear over-writing today with yesterday. The more copies I make the bigger the risk.

As I say, I'm paranoid.

26 SEPTEMBER — You'd have thought I'd be pleased to receive a DVD of the 2004 Paralympics. I'm not. I can't bear to watch more than edited highlights. And since not even sports commentators will castigate a disabled loser, you can't pretend it's an extension of the cruel world of able-bodied competition. If I can't compete on equal terms, I have not the least desire to enter the race. Consolation prizes are not for me.

And I am not defined by my diagnosis nor its associated deficits.

29 SEPTEMBER — I'm beginning to suspect it was Curtis or Lydia who organised the OT consultation: sound him out; *we* know what he needs; maybe he doesn't.

Am I on the verge of derailing?

Prawns, mushroom, egg, rained onto my lap at lunch today; plopping soggily one by one to the floor. I cursed them roundly for their mutiny and slammed the denuded slices of bread I still clutched straight into the bin. Well, almost. One piece stubbornly draped itself on the edge, dripping seafood dressing the wrong side of the polythene liner.

The washing machine took care of my clothes. But even that took another annoying chunk of time out of my working day. It's ridiculous the way they reverse fasteners on waistbands so they're invisible to an observer. Who cares? And why do shirt buttons have to be so small? There's no rule says they must, is there?

For once I prayed my mother would drop by to scrub the evil smears from the carpet I couldn't reach. Perversely, of course, she stayed away. Noelani's breeding prevented her from bailing me out, even with the fishy component. Maybe I need the kind of mongrel dog that hoovers up the evidence behind its humans automatically. Forensically aware. They do exist.

Naomi substituted for my deficiency when she eventually got home. Without complaint. Or comment.

It had been a particularly lowering moment for her too. Naomi remembered now the tight look on Adam's face, her own feeling of irritation on top of the exhaustion of a draining day. The realisation that this was the future she had in store as long as he was alive. The fear that she would buckle under the demands.

Her silence as she scrubbed was a mask. Her every effort had been devoted to suppressing the protest within.

Oh, if only she could scrub carpets for him now. She'd do it gladly.

30 SEPTEMBER—I cannot be accused of lacking in initiative even in the face of my disability.

It's a combination, I suspect – autumn temperatures, decreased movement, worsening circulation to the extremities – all conspiring to chill my flesh. A quick email to a sportswear company and... Abracadabra! I'm the proud owner of some warm but light ski-wear. The label says windproof, washable at forty degrees. I look poised for a jolly little slalom down the Austrian slopes. Hmmm.

The MND leaflets advise lots of layers. Are they crazy? Do they know how long it takes to negotiate these hurdles – inwards and outwards? My only concessions to their expertise are sheepskin slippers and... would you believe it?... long johns!

Oh, I was as resistant as any bloke of my age to begin with, but when I tried them on for Naomi I stuck out one leg and adopted a model pose and a ponsy voice: 'These, daaaaling, are all the rage, don't ya kneuww.' And she, bless her, did some rather pleasant things to various parts of my anatomy. She reckons they emphasise my sexy legs. Come to think of it, Lydia always had a thing about my legs in her married days, too. And I must admit these all-encompassing underpants nicely absorb the heat from the towel rail so I start the day cosy. Bring on the check slippers and cloth cap!

Sexy legs or not, I look like an eccentric explorer in my own home.

1 OCTOBER—Ursula Major re-appeared today. Full marks for persistence; no marks for radar. A ring at lunch time; on my doorstep at 2.15.

I was remarkably patient, I thought, listening to her spiel about finding alternative ways of doing everyday tasks, conserving energy, the range of equipment available. Yawn, yawn. And to her credit, she did try to soften the edges. She can't be expected to read my distorted thought processes.

'Just give it a try – if you don't like it, or it doesn't suit you, we can return it.' Aye, right. In my book better not to order in the first place than go through all the delays and arguments of returning unwanted goods. I can see my hallway stacked high with the detritus of disability.

'You can just have these things on loan. Better than going to the unnecessary expense of buying equipment like this.' For such a limited amount of use, you mean. No point in Naomi inheriting zimmers and wheelchairs and high-back chairs with head restraints.

'Don't dismiss getting a grant. Adjusting your home is a question of safety as well as independence. No point in being more disabled than you need to be, eh?' She can laugh; I can't.

'Don't look a gift horse in the mouth. Lots of people get equipment too late to be of any use.' And this is supposed to be a comfort?

I am not hoodwinked by this bribery and corruption for a second. And I resent this intrusion. I accept I need assistance. Devlin, Curtis, Lydia – okay they're emphatically on my team. Fellow travellers. But... chiropodists, ots? Where will it all end? How many gaolers will be blocking my escape route?

Ursula Major is a straw too far. Her parting shot shows just how little she has understood me. There are places called Disabled Living Centres, she trumpets. They display and demonstrate equipment. My hostility seems to prickle through my ski-suit but the petite blonde burbles on oblivious to my reactions.

'Her name's Theresa – a lovely lady – about your age, too. She'll demonstrate things for you.'

'Look, I don't want to be rude,' I lie, 'but I have deadlines to meet for my job and a boss who's a cross between a Rottweiler and a dragon. So thanks, but no thanks. Not at the moment anyway.' I'm impressed myself by the authenticity of my hypocrisy.

She boomerangs back without missing a beat.

'Oh well, if time is an issue I can give you the name of a mail order firm and they can send you a catalogue. I expect you know how to use the Internet, yes?'

I stare at her bleakly, and nod. She rummages in her papers and gives me another leaflet. Somehow I manage to inch her to the door. I have no energy left to tackle Harry's demands.

2 OCTOBER Lydia to the rescue!

'Help!' I squealed when I shuffled into her room at the surgery. 'Save me! Rescue me! I'm teetering on the edge of committing a major crime.'

'You got a problem, Mister O?' The rhythms of the Caribbean were music to my ears.

'Sure have, Lydia. But I think you may be in a prime position to bale me out.'

'I'm listening. Just you take your time now, man. What's been happening to make you all a-fluster like this, now?'

'I'm in mortal danger of being equipmentalised to insanity.'

Not unnaturally she needed explanation. I did my best not to ridicule or denigrate her diminutive colleague, but I piled on the horrors of those infernal catalogues.

'And just what do you want from me, honey?'

'I need you to give me every tip in the book, every plan that's ever worked, anything – *anything* to keep me from sliding down the slope to rented stair lifts.'

I felt the rumble of laughter before it reached my ears.

For twenty minutes she sat beside me probing my deficiencies, suggesting solutions. Non-essentials were wrenched out of my days. Activities were prioritised on a continuum from strenuous to gentle; and then casually distributed in a beautifully balanced scatter across the twenty-four hours. Occasional hiccups of rest were slotted in as comfortably as cups of coffee. My study, the bathroom, the whole house, were suddenly rearranged, bringing important things close to hand, removing unseen booby traps. Labour-saving gadgets were dragged out of cupboards.

'Stick to the old principle, Mister O: Never stand when you can sit, never sit when you can lie...'

'...and never lie when you can tell the truth!' I finished for her.

'We can do it, honey. We can do it!' she exclaimed triumphantly, punching the air in salute.

'With you everything is possible, Lydia. I owe you, big time. Bless you.'

'Just you keep smiling, Mister O!'

Balm to my tortured soul.

Naomi thought for the hundredth time that Lydia should have inherited something from Adam's estate.

It was only after his death that she'd discovered he'd wanted to do exactly that, but Lydia had told him in no uncertain terms that to do so would, for her, spoil the pleasure of working with him. She wanted no remuneration except his enjoyment of her company and his appreciation of the limited help she could provide on his difficult journey.

The debt was, in reality, beyond monetary value.

4 OCTOBER — I'm sitting here late at night, ostensibly dealing with emails. Maintaining the illusion of a demanding professional life. I alone am awake in this crazy world.

Joel's up again this weekend. Joel. My little brother. Who can tramp in the Pentlands with Naomi, leap up and help her clear the table, look suave in designer labels. Who makes Naomi laugh again.

I have an illogical urge to bind her closer to me by means of a baby. It's not for want of trying – on my part at least! She doesn't talk about it now. I don't either. I daren't risk any suggestion of failure. And tonight the prospect seems further away than it's ever been.

Mother joined us for dinner this evening. After she'd gone, Joel, with his characteristic openness, shot out: 'What's she making of all this business, Adam?'

'You really want to know? It's not a pretty sight.'

'Bible bashing again?'

'From the sanctity-of-life soap box.'

'Ahhhh. Dad's legacy, huh?'

'Partly, yes. But… She means well. My eternal welfare is crucially important to her. In a way I envy her unshakeable convictions. They've stood her in good stead in hard times in the past. I could do with that kind of prop myself…'

'But?' Joel interrupted with a grin.

'But she's so… unscientific, irrational. I run out of noncommittal things to say.'

'Just because you can't prove things doesn't mean you should dismiss them, out of hand.'

I turned in surprise. Naomi was supposed to be safely outside with Noelani.

'I feel sorry for her. She's genuinely worried you'll do something silly,' she said defensively.

'She's talked to you about it?' I asked, staring at her in amazement.

'Yes, of course she has. She needs somebody to be there for her, too.'

'But I haven't talked to you – about *that*!'

'Well, maybe you should.' Her face was impassive.

'Time for a sharp exit, methinks,' Joel said, scrambling up from the floor. 'Night all.'

Heavy silence pervaded the room. She curled herself on the floor on the other side of the hearth, her face turned towards the fire, her expression hidden from me.

'I was only trying to protect you, Naomi.'

'Maybe. But you can't. I'm living with this too, you know.'

'But you don't need to take on the burden of my uncertainties, too.'

'It's worse not knowing what you're thinking. Hearing it from your mother doesn't help. I know how you say things you don't necessarily mean to her.'

Silence.

'Are you going to do it?' There was a hollow echo below her tiptoeing words.

'I don't know. I'm thinking about it. It depends.'

'And were you going to tell me?'

'I honestly don't know. But I'm definitely not going to implicate you if I do go down that road. I told Curtis that.'

'So *he* knows?'

'Only that I'm questioning the best way forward and that's one of the options – for the future. Not yet.'

'And does he agree?'

'It's difficult to tell. He's sympathetic but basically on the side of treating symptoms, making life worthwhile.'

'But you don't think it's worth going on.' It was a flat statement. The distance of oceans lay between us.

'At the moment it is. But I don't know about later. Damn it, Naomi, what d'you think it feels like watching everything I care about slipping out of reach?' I broke off abruptly.

'Probably as lousy as watching the person you love falling apart in front of your eyes,' she began, but got no further. I saw the fire sparkling on her tears. Still she made no move towards me.

'Would it be so wrong, Naomi? Do you agree with my mother?'

'I understand where she's coming from. I don't want you… to…'

Another eternal pause. In the end I broke into it.

'It's not a cut and dried issue, is it? I mean, okay, life is special. You don't have to be a religious nut to think that; I think it is too.'

She didn't speak.

'But – well, there are grey areas. I'd have thought you'd understand that. You see it all the time with abortions. How much are those lives worth? – in this so-called civilised society! Abortions come on demand.'

She just sat there staring into the flames. I ploughed on.

'Literally thousands of sanctified little lives ended every year. For the flimsiest of pretexts – it doesn't fit a social calendar, it was a one-night stand – you know the excuses they give. But there it's the mother deciding to end *somebody else's* life. This is *my* life and *I'm* making a rational assessment of the quality of that life. And I'd rather have a shorter, good quality life than a protracted, poor quality one.'

The complete lack of response was unnerving.

'It's absurd that the law doesn't make distinctions. Surely Shipman's more morally guilty, murdering however many patients, than Curtis would be if he helped me out of my predicament compassionately.'

'And is Dr Curtis willing to help you?'

'Probably not.'

'Why?'

'Because he thinks you're worth going on for.'

She half turned.

'D'you have to make a joke of everything?' Even with the tears drying on her cheeks, her look spoke volumes.

'No, seriously. That's exactly what he said. Reckons that as time goes on, I'll still rate life better than death because of you, my writing, music, the garden. But especially you.'

'But you disagree.' She turned away again, but not before I saw the bleakness in her eyes.

'No. I don't know. Because it's not simply about what I rate for myself. It's what I rate as best for you. Having me leeching all the life out of you, isn't what I want for you.'

'But shouldn't I have a say in that? You want to decide for yourself; why can't I decide for myself?'

'Ideally you should. But I know you. Not a selfish bone in your body. I don't want you to sacrifice yourself for me. I'm going anyway. What difference does a day make?'

'You're not thinking about a *day*.'

'Literary licence.'

'Are you going to tell me... if... when...' Again the strangled words cut off in their prime. Suddenly silent sobs were wracking her body.

It took an eternity to heave myself out of the chair and get to her. Ages later I answered her question.

'It'll depend on whether you can accept my decision or not.'

This time her silence wasn't slicing through me; not with her curled up against me, all soft and yielding.

'If Curtis could promise to help me when my time's up, I'd probably keep going longer because I'd feel secure. If he won't give that undertaking, I might have to decide sooner while I still have the capacity to do it myself. Ironic really, isn't it?'

'Mmmhhmm.'

Long after she's gone to bed here I am still mulling over the things I said. Actually that bit about it not just being about me is taking my thoughts down a new route. Makes me realise that autonomy is relative; depends on the unit you're talking about. Should it be us as individuals, us as a couple, us as part of a larger family unit? Help! My mother is squeezing through the gap!

Vivid memories of that evening were etched into her brain. His version told her more. But what could she have said? Even now, with all the benefit of the lived experience, she had no easy solutions. If he had only known the double-edged sharpness of the knife he drove into her heart that night... Yes, she had shared the burden. Out of his sight.

8 OCTOBER—Scunners! Joel must wonder what on earth's going on; driving all this way for a weekend and sandwiched between two sphinxes. What did he think, leaving this time? Would he ever see me again? I must ring him.

I was lucky. Somebody had cancelled the last appointment with Curtis – well, maybe. Whatever, the receptionist said she could slot me in. Better, this time, on his turf. Better still, no one waiting in the waiting room.

Naomi just nodded when I told her where I was going. No questions.

Curtis was exactly what I needed: professional, unemotional.

'I know you must be knackered, end of a long day, all these people loading their problems onto you...' I began.

'It's my job. Don't worry about me. I've got as long as you need. I'm glad you felt you could come.'

'You've been very good, coming to see me, letting me warble on. I don't want to take advantage.'

'You're not but, hey, I could use a cup of coffee, so how about I make us both one, and then I'm all yours.'

In the end I just blurted it out: Mother, Naomi, the pressure. Reporting, not judging – I hope.

'Difficult. You can see it from their point of view too.' he said quietly.

'The more I think about it, the more I think the whole thing's *so* unfair.'

'Uhhhuhh?'

'Okay. Imagine I'm in a persistent vegetative state. I can't say what I want. One of your cronies can decide to stop feeding me and let me die.'

I paused; he nodded slowly.

'Scenario two: I'm on a life support system but I can still communicate. I ask for it to be disconnected. They'd have to do it.'

He pursed his lips at this.

'Instead of that, here I am, able to say what I want, in line for suffering much more than someone who knows nothing, but because I don't need life-sustaining treatment, nobody seems able to help me. Where's the justice? Damned if I can find it.'

He leaned back in his chair without taking his eyes from mine.

'I sympathise. But very eminent philosophers and moral theologians have maintained that a person can't consent to his own death.'

'Why not? What about Ms B? She consented to her own death.'
Trumped!

'Indeed she did. But causing death, deliberately, isn't the same as allowing to die. In Ms B's case, she was rejecting the prolongation of her life by artificial means. And the doctors were simply allowing the underlying pathology to run its natural course. They weren't slamming potassium chloride into her.'

'So if we get MND, we're penalised because our underlying pathology takes so long to kill us. We need a serious road accident, or a sudden catastrophic stroke or heart attack to rescue us.'

'I hope you're not about to ask me to push you down the stairs!' Curtis gave me a look of mock horror.

'Like I say, you read too many novels, Doc! Between us we could hatch a few original plots, don't you think?'

He grinned back at me.

'All I'm asking is to be spared that last bit. A swift painless end before I get to an advanced state where I can be starved to death or have my ventilator disconnected. Is that so unreasonable? The only viable alternative I can see is to cut my life even shorter and do the deed myself.'

'Things like slippery slopes and landslides and dominoes flash through my brain at this point.'

He softened the potential irritation with a grimace.

'Philistine!' I countered in the same vein.

'What about the rights and interests of others – including your lovely wife?'

'Which brings us full circle. If I had some reassurance about the end you could argue it would be in her interests because it would relieve the tension now. We could enjoy the present. I'd be more bearable to live with!'

We sat for a long moment in silence – not uncomfortable.

'If she knows you're contemplating suicide, she must be horrendously stressed. Would it help for me to chat to her about all this?' he offered. 'Find out more about what she knows, what she fears, what she expects. With your knowledge, of course, building on what you've told me. You could both do without this additional stress.'

'Which is exactly why I didn't tell her until she forced me to. I'm not at that stage yet.'

'But in fairness she doesn't know when you will be.'

'Point taken.'

'If you prefer, you can tell her I'm here if she'd like to talk about it. No pressure. Or talk about it yourselves and see if you'd rather both meet with me, together.'

'I'll do that. Thanks for being a listening ear.'

'You're welcome. Any time. My advice for the time being is: try not to dwell too much on the future. You're doing incredibly well. I read all your features in the papers; only wish I could express myself half as well. And I can't wait to read the novel.'

'Well, thanks for that. And while we're on the subject... I was wondering... if it's not an imposition... would you be willing to read the first draft? I'm impressed by your ability to get to the kernel of things when you critique novels. You'd be ideal. If you could find the time.'

'I'd be honoured.'

'You'd get due acknowledgement, of course.'

'No need for that.'

'And a signed copy.'

'Ahh, now you're talking. An investment for a rainy day. An O'Neill first edition!'

'Hmmm. Fat chance! And of course, even the signature presupposes I live beyond publication day.'

He's got something special, this guy. He isn't just sticking to the rules without compassion. He's agonising too. In the kindest way. I'm back to that again. *(For Ideas folder: *kindness*)

But there really is a difference. I found this during my brief stay in hospital courtesy of Malcolm Inches. It's possible to be seen promptly and politely, be correctly diagnosed and treated, without a scrap of kindness being shown. But in the midst of all the delays and mistakes and other administrative nightmares that clutter your day when you've nothing better to do than notice when the promised urinal doesn't materialise, or the chicken korma you ordered yesterday becomes kedgeree today, or your favourite visitor misses three quarters of visiting time because the staff despatch you off to x-ray five minutes into the allotted hour – well, a single act of real kindness can soften the overall dissatisfaction.

I guess natural kindness isn't taught; it comes from within. What is kindness? – warmth, sensitivity, tact, communication? Curtis. But what does it cost him? He must go home at the end of the day drained to the dregs. Look at the load I dump on him, and I'm just one of hundreds. Maybe he'd last longer if he just stuck to the purely medical, technical things, left the emotional stuff for his family and friends.

I must admit, sometimes he gets deeper into my psyche than I intend, or I daresay he bargained for. Then he has to deal with what he finds there, talk me back into a safer place. Like he did today – I realised afterwards, I came away from his surgery with the desire to hand him the novel stronger than my wish to end my life. Was that the result of his skill? Or my vacillating emotions? I hope Naomi will talk to him.

She'd elected to go alone. Dr Curtis had been kind to her, too. Listening, confidentiality safe with him.

'It's his choice in the end,' he'd said gently.

'Now I'm confused. I thought you didn't support the idea of suicide.'

'I don't. Although I have to confess, I can understand his reasoning. And from where he sits, I'm letting him down, forcing his hand.'

'So, if you won't do what he really wants, how is it his choice?'

'Because he's a competent patient able to make up his own mind. But time changes minds. Autonomy isn't a static, absolute sort of thing. It's a dynamic state. It can be affected by all sorts of things – illness being a major example. When we're ill it's not always possible to see the issues clearly, or to make the decision we'd make if we were in good health. Because of that, we doctors have to be very aware of the dangers of precipitate action.'

'So you think Adam is diminished by his illness?'

She'd stared at him in amazement.

'I'm not sure.'

'He'd have a fit if he knew you thought that! Seems to me he's ruthlessly logical. Even though I'm appalled by his conclusion, I can't see a flaw in his argument. And that's also what frightens me.'

'In Adam's case, I have to admit, he's looking into things in enormous detail and depth. It's no knee-jerk reaction. He's impressive. He's made me brush up on the legalities and ethical arguments too – which is no bad thing!'

'But you still think his power to decide is impaired? I'm sorry, but I disagree. And it's because I think he's fully capable of arguing a case for killing himself, that I'm most afraid he'll do it. Certainly I couldn't persuade him out of it any more than I could argue his mother out of her position.'

'What is her position?'

She wrapped it up carefully. It wasn't hers to tell.

'And do you see Adam as just as immovable? In my experience, religious scruple is the position most resistant to reason and persuasion.'

'Well, I certainly never win arguments when he's thoroughly thought through the issues. And on this one, I get a distinct impression that he's argued each tiny step with himself; there's no way I could find a chink in his logic. Maybe some expert philosopher might better him, I certainly can't.'

'And I suspect I couldn't either. Which is possibly why I'm guarded in what I commit to.'

His honesty was impressive. But the ideas rankled.

'At the end of the day, even if, technically, the philosophers could better him in an argument, would their case be any more defensible than his? It's his life. If he thinks the quality of his life's too awful… Well, I know what he'd say about somebody else deciding!'

'And that would be…?'

'He'd argue that only he – inside the illness looking out – is in any position to know what's best – for him.'

'So, you'll go along with whatever he wants? No questions?' He was gentle with it, more wondering aloud than removing the rug.

'Well… No, but… Oh, I don't know! It's all so confusing.'

'I know. I understand, believe me.'

'So what do we do?'

'I'm inclined to sit tight and not do anything overtly. Listen. Be there for him, let him know we sympathise and understand his dilemma. Do everything we can to make sure his quality of life is as good as we can possibly make it. My aim certainly is to walk alongside him. And I'm looking to see if his decision is indeed a sustained one. I want him to make the best choices he can make.'

'What do you think is best?'

'That's always a dodgy question to answer. Lots of patients ask that. Sometimes it's easier to blame someone else if things go wrong …'

'Oh, I'm not…'

'No, I know you're not. And nor is Adam. He's looking for an ally.'

'So, if he says life's intolerable and you think he's been saying that all along, then why…' It sounded too impertinent to ask.

'Why don't I do something about it?'

'Well, yes.'

'It could be that later down the track we do have to re-visit that scenario. But at the moment, I think Adam's just thinking through the options.'

'Do you think… might he…?'

'He's got a lot of things to live for. He's talking about events in the future. He's totally into his novel. He's looking forward to seeing it published. What he needs is options. I think the worst thing we can do right now, is force him into declaring a position his pride will make him stick to – just to show he's nobody's puppet.'

'But what if he does decide what he wants but he's physically unable to do what it takes? He'd be so frustrated. But I just don't think I *could*…'

Dr Curtis interrupted swiftly. 'One thing he's absolutely adamant about: he doesn't want you to take responsibility for that. He's made that crystal clear. I don't think that's breaching confidentiality.'

'But…'

'We'll find a way. Whatever else, it won't come to that.'

9 OCTOBER—Feeling foul. Headache making computer work impossible. Rang Joel. Tried to explain. He probably thinks I'm losing the plot.

10 OCTOBER—Fouler still. It's an infection – virulent apparently. Hope it kills me off.

16 OCTOBER—Another week wasted in my extravagantly wasteful life.

I've just dragged myself to this machine, wrapped in blankets, yards of tissues, lozenges at the ready. Naomi's gone to the shops; she'll kill me if she finds me in here, against medical advice. But I need to jot this down. Things are getting out of proportion in my sick-bed.

What if I had ended it all on Tuesday, the most hellish day in a whole row of fiendish days? I was too far gone to be even contemplating action, never mind performing it, but if I had, where would I be now?

My mother believes my soul would have winged its way to its Maker. Or no, maybe not. Hers would, mine wouldn't. Not if I committed the ultimate sin; ending my life by my own hand. Is that the unforgivable sin? I can't remember the order in her league table. I rather suspect that's the one that merits eternal torment.

Jannine, a girl at work, tells anyone who'll remain stationary long enough to listen, that if they put their trust in her God their bodies will moulder into dust, but one day a great trumpet will sound, and miraculously all those fragments of ash will assemble themselves, and a body looking the same but now gloriously immortal, will rise again and stomp the earth for all eternity. The devil in me always wants to ask: Will I still have the tiny scar on my right buttock?

The Jehovah's Witnesses who doggedly ring my doorbell once every two months to try to save me from my heathenish ways, tell me unequivocally that death's the end for me. There's no such thing as an immortal soul, they reckon. To be fair to them, when I looked it up, as per their instructions, I couldn't find a single mention of any such thing in the Bible. They also informed me, without the slightest hint of irony, that only 144,000 people out of all these generations since year zero will be saved and get to heavenly realms. And at this moment in my present unrepentant state, I am not one of them. Me, one of that miniscule elite? Hello?! So why they're wasting precious time on a Saturday morning talking to me, I can't quite fathom. Must be to get the ticks in the book of reckoning. That's totally uncalled-for I know, and I confess to a begrudging admiration for their selfless determination and courage in the face of what must be one of the most thankless tasks in the world. But here in the privacy of this journal – well, any fool can see the numbers don't add up.

Rev. Castlemaine's got a bigger picture of God. He's a universalist. Comforts everybody with the thought that we're all precious in the Creator's sight and He wants to save us all. Being omnipotent, what He wants He gets. I warm to the Reverend's version of Christianity just because it brings hope to the hopeless and makes God something I need Him to be. But I'm not persuaded he's actually right – Castlemaine, I mean, not God.

I wonder, has God got lots of compartments in the hereafter where he humours everybody and just makes sure the walls are high enough between them to preserve their illusions? If I die believing in nothing, is that what I get? If I end it all today, will I just be nothing for evermore? A void. Emptiness. Nothingness. Day after day, year after year, century after century. For ever and ever. Amen.

Would that be so bad – if I didn't know anything about it? The way I feel today I'd settle for nothingness. But normally?

Rev. Castlemaine's theory is most appealing. But it's too cosy. The opium of the people. Brainwashing about judgement during my impressionable years deprived me of that solace.

Eternal torment is bottom of my list.

Bodily resurrection? Hmmmm. Fairer in principle, but I don't care to think of Jannine strutting complacently along Queen Street with her inane smile and her squat but indestructible body, while I remain a pile of maggot droppings.

Mother's God seems too capricious, but I'd rather be judged by Him than by my mother. She'd cast me out into outer darkness and listen to the wailing and gnashing of teeth with a sort of smug self-righteousness that puts being right above other people's welfare. Well, perhaps I might be her exception. I don't know.

Enough of this. Not exactly conducive to the sleep of the righteous.

I can't believe how weak this blessed infection has left me.

17 OCTOBER — Why didn't I refuse antibiotics? I could have. An opportunity missed. Just shows that you need to work out a strategy in advance.

Why didn't I use the opportunity of an aversion to food to start starving myself to death? After just three days of not eating I was positively skeletal. Ten days on I haven't regained the pounds but I do have an appetite, I actually feel hungry. Another wasted opportunity. Would it have been so hard?

I'm shocked by the lack of muscle power after only eight days of lying around in a heap. If I'm not ready to depart this life yet, I must make sure I keep up the exercises.

18 OCTOBER — Jerry called in this afternoon, with his partner, Brenda. Said he was 'just passing'. Nobody passes Montgomery Crescent!

He gave me – would you believe it? – a bunch of green grapes in a plastic tub with the reduced sticker half peeled off and some awkward fragments of office gossip. Usual backbiting. Usual bullying. Nothing new. I appreciated his caring enough to give up the time but I was struggling to concentrate.

Naomi took Brenda outside – she was 'dying for a fag'. I couldn't help make odious comparisons, watching them walking up and down. I think the caption is: if you must seek solace in extra helpings and silicone augmentation, swear an oath not to touch stretch fabric. I'm supposed to be growing more benevolent as I put life's trivialities into the eternal perspective. Clearly I've not got to grips with the existential dimension.

Evening Watched a sickening documentary tonight, about a teenage carer, devoted to his doubly-incontinent mother who'd been left brain-damaged by some violent intruder. He did everything for her, personal stuff, the lot. You're supposed to be awed by his selflessness; I wanted to give him permission to toddle off and realise his own dreams. No point in two wrecked lives.

Naomi couldn't resist a smile. At the time he'd left her in no doubt about how much he admired her own figure but it was a surprise to see that he had committed his observations about Brenda's size to print.

He wouldn't approve today. Bony was closer to the mark, gaunt. Grief did that to people. Who was there to care now?

19 OCTOBER—Woke at 4AM again today. Lay there, just waiting for the sky to start bleeding into the morning. I read the phrase somewhere, thought I'd try it out. No, it's not me.

This post-infection weakness seems to be affecting lots of functions. Typing even a short paragraph is exhausting. My concentration's gone to pot. Holding a conversation is a battle. Naomi has taken time off to nurse me but nothing's happening in my life while I lie here recuperating, so I'm struggling to find something to say. Her world's limited to my horizons. Result: long silences. Another portent.

Do I want her to forfeit her stimulating life to look after me?
I do not.
Do I want her to be afraid to mention her active life because of my incapacity?
I do not.
Do I want to see her vigour, her potential, being stifled by my limitations?
I do not.
Do I want the noose of my disability to tighten inexorably around our relationship?
I do not.

20 OCTOBER—My worst day yet. Sheer unadulterated excrement – at the height of a food poisoning epidemic, iced with bile, with a lump of somebody else's earwax plonked on top, and the whole glorious edifice sprayed with poisonous flatus!

It took me two hours to wash and dress this morning. A colossal effort. Then Naomi handed me this thick towelling robe. 'Try this. Wrap yourself in it,' she said. 'Save your energy.'

I was touched. Then, damn it, she informs me it was the OT's idea! Practical not lovingly thoughtful. Damn, damn, *damn*! Presumably I didn't betray my disappointment because she then said, what about a long-handled brush for the extremities and unreachable parts?

'You've got those stashed away too?' I asked, feeling the bile spitting between my teeth.

'Just in case,' she admitted.

'Next you'll be telling me that pesky OT loaned them to you!'

She didn't say a thing but shot me a reproachful look.

'Better still, why don't I give in and let you wash me, instead?' I muttered.

'Why not? I'm willing. I wish you would let me help more.' And I thought my sarcasm was cruelly blatant!

Why not?... Why *not*? Ye gods!

I'm recalling my original aim: to keep the essential spark that is me alive. But what *is* the essential me? The old Adam wouldn't have vented his spleen on a hapless Naomi.

She'd tried so hard to respect his feelings. She'd purposely not told him she was learning safe ways of moving and handling; Lydia slotted sessions in in her lunch breaks.

'No point in waiting till you've damaged your back,' she'd said. 'Learn good techniques now. In preparation.'

It made sense and Lydia made it fun. Naomi had giggled as they slid each other from seat to seat on banana boards, tweaked gripper sheets from under each other's buttocks, spread their feet wide in unladylike poses to lift without bending their spines. But the seriousness of this preparation was never far from her thoughts. She had to stay strong enough to do whatever it took for as long as it took.

Nobody factored in Adam's resistance.

She dragged her eyes unwillingly back to the screen.

Ursula Major managed somehow to leave her confounded brochure here. Why I didn't consign it to the recycling bin immediately I don't know.

It's even worse than I remember. From Velcro-ed shoes I progressed to nightshirts; key rings on trouser zips took me all the way to bottom wipers... bottom wipers! Seems Velcro's the answer to everything. I can see the whole week's wash snarled up around the foul stuff.

I am in hurtling danger of failing my second aim: to stay in control.

I feel like an onion being stripped of skins. How far is too far?

21 OCTOBER—All this thinking about establishing a sustained and logical argument has forced me to imagine end-stage scenarios. Vivid pictures. Especially during these long wakeful watches in the night when hitherto I'd have been hammering out dazzling discourses on profound topics, or plotting the next chapter of my book.

However, it does help to crystallise my position.

No death-bed heroics, that's for sure. Peace and dignity, if you please. What on earth would I be coming back to anyway? Or for?

Drugs? Specific information needed: how much, how long, where from. There must be no half-baked attempts.

Starving? Unpleasant side effects: further muscle-wasting, constipation, nausea, foul mouth, stomach pains, increased weakness – all while you're still conscious. Would my resolve stand firm? Don't want to be totally humiliated as well as scrawny and evil-smelling!

Accident? Logistically doubtful given my weakness. Don't want to traumatise some poor driver or passer-by? Or, enough of an accident to need medical intervention – which I could then refuse... They'd say I was mentally incompetent to decide for myself!

Refusal of treatment? I have to need life-saving treatment without precipitating that state deliberately. I must be conscious and aware of my dying.

Killing? I know they can't. And won't.

The problem is, the medical world equates death with failure. If you seek it the balance of your mind is disturbed. You need a higher level of competence to make this choice. *Ergo,* another raft of patients are incompetent. The doctors are back in control. Sickening!

Quality of life isn't an objective measure. It draws on issues like what's intolerable, what's futile, what's important – things only I know! They have to respect my wishes, my assessment, my preferences.

We've gone full circle. Back to the essential 'I' in MIND. History isn't on my side. Those doctors didn't respect Ms B's preferences, not even when the judge ruled in her favour. They had to move her to another hospital; she had to have other doctors – strangers – to pull the plug. Dr Cox, too, he got rapped over the knuckles for respecting Mrs Boyes' preferences, and she was in a far worse mess than I am – in excruciating pain from her arthritis, only weeks to live, pleading for death.

Conclusion? If I can't find a doctor to assist me in dying, I need to be in a situation where I require life-saving treatment, attended by a doctor who subscribes to the commandment not to strive officiously to keep me alive. Bless him, satire or not, Clough knew what he was talking about.

22 OCTOBER—I was shot to pieces after the sheer effort of typing so much yesterday, but I shall go stark raving mad if I don't drag myself

out of this whirlpool of ethical conundrums. I hate being the vulnerable party in all this. *I HATE IT!*

Curtis is my best hope. I need to slice below his sturdy conscience. He needs to hear the screams of this fellow human being trapped in a blazing car. But... he mustn't be penalised.

Maybe I should decide: these are the things I want to do before I go; once I've done them, exit stage right, in whatever way comes to mind at the time.

Naomi was suddenly vividly reminded of Dr Curtis's words: 'It's hard to pack away a life.'

This morbid introspection was partly attributable to Adam's post-viral state, a product of too much idle time on his hands. In spite of his relentless worrying, in spite of the horrors ahead, life *had* been precious to him. He'd been reluctant to leave. It was some small comfort to have that fact confirmed – by Adam himself.

Noelani, with the imperiousness born of breeding, has started to pretend she doesn't hear me calling her. Here am I, struggling to conserve my energy as per instructions, and the malicious creature forces me to search for her before I lock up for the night. The comparison between her silent, quicksilver leap past me and into her basket and my shuffling gait is too painful for benevolence. I curse her roundly for her insensitivity. Her copper stare oozes disdain.

If I didn't know better I'd suspect her of colluding with everyone else who's trying to ignore me and my rights.

I must be paranoid after all!

24 OCTOBER—We've just returned from Liverpool. Naomi did all the driving; I gave in without a protest. Another first.

It was her cousin's wedding. Nobody said anything outright but I felt the sideways glances. Most of them haven't seen me since our own wedding. It must have been a shock; all the imperceptible creeping of the paralysis fast-forwarded.

Mercifully the evening reception was one of those no-skill bops. Up here you need to be free-standing and generally in possession of your faculties to get through the orderly sequences of Scottish dance creditably. I'd have had to rivet my carcass to the furthermost seat in the darkest corner and avoid all eye contact. Mindless swaying from one foot to the other on a crowded, strobing square of parquet flooring, I can manage. Hanging on to Naomi, keeping time, thumbing my nose at Nemesis. I didn't dare to ask anyone else to take a spin with me; no merit in adding a charge of groping or indecent familiarity to my catalogue of problems!

Naomi's a sensation on the dance floor: feline, sinuous. In the midst of all those glitzy outfits, dazzling hairdos, she outshone them all. She still makes my heart lurch. I'm sure there's no shortage of men queuing up to take my place, but no question: she's mine.

26 OCTOBER—I had no choice. Harry insisted I did a full day in the office today. He was a cross between a nag and a dictator all day and it was after 6 before I even left my desk. Talk about stultifying! The stuff I wrote was probably Primary 5 standard. The team meeting was spectacular in its hostility and even Jannine spat back at the unfortunate Jerry. Jannine! She who must at all times reflect the purity of her Christian thoughts.

Harry has a lot to answer for and I found myself hoping he will have to recount his sins in public at the feet of the all-seeing and wrathful Almighty, with Jannine in attendance to witness his humiliation.

As if that weren't bad enough, I arrived home to my mother in full germ-destruction mode. The place stinks of furniture polish and lavatory bleach and kitchen bug-busters – heaven knows what she's single-handedly doing to the environment. I'm hiding in my study, Noelani cringing on my lap, but the sound of her campaign is drowning out my concentration.

Why on earth my mother should be here again today, I cannot imagine. It was only yesterday that she was furiously poking things into crevices and beating the daylights out of rugs. Nor can I fathom why Naomi should tolerate such an invasion of her space on her day off – a day to 'just mooch'. She has to be the most accommodating daughter-in-law on the planet.

27 OCTOBER—I am a new man. Not in the sense of changing nappies and hanging out the Lenor-fresh underpants; but revived, restored, re-invigorated. Back in the driving seat.

Naomi's working this Saturday so I shambled off to the study at 8.45 with a coffee and modest expectations. I read the last chapter of Aidan's story and suddenly this new idea rushed at me with all the force of an express train. Next thing I knew, Noelani was scratching at my shoe with irritating persistence. I gave her a dose of her own medicine to start with but when I finally deigned to take notice, I got a real shock: it was 2.35 and the poor beast thought we were on a suicide starvation pact!

It was the new character I'm introducing into Aidan's life that did it. Hanif Khälid by name. By the time I'd described him he was there in the flesh. And as soon as he opened his mouth the sparks just flew. Ding dong battle of wills. They got stuck into everything from joining Europe to gay marriages and I just took dictation. Brilliant. When it's a complete takeover bid, that's when I know it's working.

I'm ashamed to say, I was no more mindful of Naomi's need for sustenance in spite of Noelani's reminder, and she arrived home to a cold kitchen and a remote husband. I made reparation by taking her out for an Italian meal and some quality wine. It felt like a celebration.

Today makes me realise a good day at the writing is more therapeutic than any aromatherapy I've ever smelt, any drug I've ever taken. And more confirming than any philosophical agonising. I must hang onto that thought. I may be knackered at the end of it but it's a good kind of knackered.

Moral? Forget the navel-gazing, immerse myself in fantasy. My new resolve.

Naomi smiled softly. It had been annoying to find he hadn't even turned up the Aga. She'd been tired and cold after a trying day; he'd been indoors in the warm, no outside demands, indulging in his favourite occupation. It surely wasn't too much to expect.

He was abject in his apology. Fortellani's was perfect – once Adam had slumped into his seat and hidden his sticks under the chair. His conversation was animated, his eyes sparkling. After the weeks of lethargy and preoccupation, it was doubly reassuring.

Hanif dominated the first part of the evening. Adam became Hanif and soon had her giggling over his exaggerated pronouncements and absurd gestures. But with the dessert menu came an unexpected change of direction.

'How's the redoubtable Stella?'

She swallowed the surge of fear.

'Have you been up to your old tricks?' she countered, throwing him a hard look.

'*Moi?* Tricks? Never!' The glint in his eye seemed genuine.

She shook her head at him.

'Has she forgiven me?' he persisted.

'I've no idea, but I imagine she's got much more important things to worry about than your lunacy.'

'Haven't you seen her since? Who is she anyway?'

She turned the stem of the glass in her fingers, watching the meniscus swirl this way and that.

'She's a professional colleague. A counsellor.'

'Heavens! A stuff-of-the-soul merchant, dredging up secrets from the past. She's probably psycho-analysed me and found me seriously wanting by now then!'

'Probably.'

'Don't tell me you're pouring out your inner contradictions to a counsellor! I thought you had more self-respect!'

'Should have done so light years ago before I took you on!' She kept it light. 'Stella, where were you when I needed you?'

'Then we wouldn't be sitting here, sated on pasta and alcohol, sparkling in the candlelight, communing with our inner happiness.'

'Indeed.'

'What did she say though?'

'I don't remember. Nothing much. She's trained in being non-judgmental, luckily for you.'

After a pause she glanced up to find him staring at her with a strange expression in his eyes.

'Are you getting enough help with all this, Naomi?' The gesture took in his disability.

'I'm fine. And all the better for seeing you more cheerful.'

'Sorry. I've been an old grouch lately, I know.'

'No, you haven't. But you have been low with this infectious thingy. Not your usual self.'

'Took more out of me than I realised.'

'I know.'

He reached across the table to lay a hand over hers.

'I don't want to be a drag, Nay.'

'I know. And you're not. I shall probably regret this… but… welcome back, Mr Crazy!'

28 OCTOBER—I've had a brilliant day writing. I want to keep going while I'm on a roll but Naomi's just put paid to that: she's invited Mother for a meal. I need my parent's presence tonight like I need barbed wire around my chair.

'Just you stay in here out of harm's way,' she advised, closing the door firmly on the words. 'And remember. You owe her.'

She's right. Forty years ago today at this precise hour my mother was enduring the agony of labour on my account. I guess it's not too much to ask that we remember her key role in my existence. To fortify myself for an enforced state of benevolence I shall re-visit my novel. Hanif and Aidan will hopefully blur the edges of reality for the rest of the evening.

Later (and actually tomorrow) Before I retire to join the saint who was foolish enough to marry me, I must record my state of amazed incredulity – if that's not tautological. What the heck if it is! My astonishment is double-barrelled anyway.

By the time I put a tentative toe outside my study the testing began. It went like this:

The house looks ready for prospective buyers; all evidence of my careless habits completely eradicated. There is no sign of either of the significant women in my life but fantastic olfactory stimuli are emanating from the kitchen. I have a little reconnoitre, and find them sitting primly in the sitting room swathed in soft music and subdued lighting. Gone is that offensive wrap-around apron my mother dons for her descent into chardom. Instead this elegant figure in a black fitted dress glides across to give me an unexpected kiss. I'm further baffled by a distinct scent of perfume on her.

What is going on?!

Naomi herself is in some floaty creation in a muted pink colour that makes her dissolve in my vision and I suddenly desperately wish my mother would vanish. Their splendid appearances dictate something other than my workaday garb and by the time I've fought and won the battle of cufflinks and a new silk tie my desires are heading in a more seemly direction.

Naomi has excelled herself in the culinary department as well as the floral. Delightful but not surprising. What really bowls me over is the older woman at our table. If I had met her at the home of some of our more avant-garde friends I'd have been intrigued by her air of mystery, curious about her opinions. Indeed, she is such a stranger to me tonight that I have no difficulty in slotting into this bizarre charade these women have concocted.

I hear myself spontaneously raising a glass to acknowledge the role she has played throughout my life – the dreaded cleaning of today alongside the dedicated wage-earning of the past; present courage echoing past fortitude. Naomi's smile is all the thanks I need, but my mother takes her cue and says with poignant simplicity, that that's what mothers do.

Delightful as this artificial truce feels I am adrift in a sea of speculation.

'This,' I say, spreading my hands to encompass the entire table, 'is fantastic and I'm hugely impressed. You must have slogged for days without my even noticing. But... what is it all in aid of?'

'The end of your thirties, of course,' Naomi says. 'Who better to celebrate all the antics and alarms you've survived, man and boy – than the one person who remembers them – all forty years of them!'

'Good grief! I sincerely hope you *don't*!' I shoot out.

This woman who is the doppelgänger of my mother, smiles quietly. 'Just the good things.' I can almost believe her – as much anyway as I believe anything that's taking place tonight in this setting that so closely resembles my own dining room.

My favourite brand of port and the bitter chocolate truffles we reserve for celebrations complete the meal, and we listen in silence to the hall clock strike midnight. I glance at Naomi. She is sending palpable silent messages across the table to her mother-in-law. There is a pregnant pause before my mother takes up her glass in a hand that I notice is trembling.

'Happy birthday, Adam.' Precisely forty years ago to the minute from the moment when I slithered out of her security into helpless existence. Her mouth opens to say more but she is too overcome to voice the thoughts.

This is the first genuine hug I have given her in years.

Tears filled Naomi's eyes. That night she'd slipped out of the room at that point, her own grief and loss too great to contain. Adam had construed her absence as sensitivity, she hadn't disabused him. Whatever the motive, it had been right to leave; the moment belonged to mother and son.

Her role was to reconcile, not divide.

For those few hours, on the brink of his last year, Adam had reached across a yawning divide and pulled his mother back to safety.

It was right that neither had any idea of the dark secret she harboured.

29 OCTOBER—I didn't expect any concessions. Nobody at work even knows it's my fortieth. But does Harry have to be quite so totally bloody objectionable today? Not only has he spent valuable time ranting and raving after insisting I came in this morning to rectify all the wrongs in my 'slovenly prose' and my 'slacker's timetable' and my 'self-indulgent ramblings', but he seems to be standing guard in case I slip the noose and somehow evade his domination, single-handedly robbing me of all my creative edge. Cretin!

I'm writing this at the office – a first – because I'm childish enough to resent being bullied on my birthday. I'll email it home and then erase it. Can't be too careful. Puny, eh? Anabelle's more grown up about things.

I guess I'm super-sensitive today. Not only is this the big four oh, entry to a significant phase in a person's life, but for me it's a very different milestone from the one the cards herald. Not that anyone's been moronic enough to send me a card about primes or peaks or triumphs or sliding down the banister of life. The only two cards I've had are the sentimental tributes that wives and mothers are entitled to buy. I guess most people who know me are scared to recognise this particular birthday lest they say the wrong thing and tip me over the edge into my father's depression. Strange. Nothing from Joel.

Forty years. A lot more living than many of my forbears had. Plus, I've followed a career I've loved; I live with a woman I adore; I'm still able to get about, after a fashion, independently; my brain is still functioning; I can still scribble well enough to be published regularly; I'm writing a novel which I hope will reach the bookshops. I think, so far, I've kept the 'I' in MIND. Along the way I've met some fabulous characters – Lydia, Curtis, Devlin – who, without the MND, would not otherwise have enriched my life. And I'm not finished yet.

The fact that the future is not the one I planned is maybe more a reflection on the unwarranted and naïve assumptions I made, than it is a betrayal by a superior being. Why not me? I've had decades longer than many human beings.

Here comes my *bête noire*. Back to the grindstone.

30 OCTOBER—A pity that yesterday's entry wasn't revised, but from the moment I got home last night until I fell into bed this morning, the diary was the last thing on my mind. No need for introspection or rumination, I was too busy living life in the fast lane.

I was the last person out of the office. Even Harry scarpered once he'd demanded I do one last revision to the piece on proportionate representation. 'On my desk first thing', which meant do it tonight in my case. I can't rely on crack-of-dawn starts these days. Naomi didn't seem fazed when I rang her and she assured me she'd let the restaurant know if we were going to be seriously delayed. I promised her an extra helping of dessert to compensate.

By the time I staggered up the path, home was the only place I wanted to be, but I managed to drag my sociable face out of the closet. She'd insisted. We *had* to mark my fortieth, quietly maybe, but it couldn't go by entirely unnoticed. It might not be a normal milestone birthday but… it's there between us: it's probably my last.

Naomi's good at the right touches. A collection of candles burned on the hall table, sending a mellow camouflage over my weariness. She appeared from the kitchen looking fabulous in a shade of lavender blue that turned her grey eyes mauve. Lashings more temptation to stay at home, but she bundled me upstairs and even helped in the process of transforming a crumpled writer into a respectable escort. I was too exhausted to protest so she had me ready in record time.

At the foot of the stairs she turned.

'I need to get something from the bedroom. You go in and have a drink. I'm driving. I'll be with you in a jiffy.'

I know that in films, you're never really convinced by the surprise on the face of the birthday person, but I genuinely had no suspicion Naomi was planning anything like this. I swear there wasn't a sound from the rooms where they were gathered. Everybody seemed to be there – work colleagues, local friends, family, everyone who meant anything to me – except my mother. (Naomi explained later that's why the dinner last night. Mum had been adamant: she couldn't face having to keep cheerful in public. She'd willingly help with the cleaning, and the food, and the clearing up tomorrow, just don't ask her to do the celebration bit.) When my eyes got around to Harry, even he was grinning, smugly pleased with his ruses to keep me out of the way until they were all at the house.

Hugo Curtis put in a late and short appearance, bringing his wife to disguise his trade. Lydia had been on Naomi's list but had a prior appointment; sent her apologies along with instructions to forget all her strictures on this occasion and push the boat out. Bless her. She's done more to preserve my youth than most other people who've gathered to drain my cellar and toast my health.

In the crush of humanity I could have lurched without notice, but Naomi soon had me enthroned beside the fire, an excellent Chardonnay I didn't know we owned in one hand, the other free to be wrung by the steady stream of well-wishers. Joel understudied as host with impressive grace and managed to ensure I was supplied with nourishment that could be eaten without disaster. I suspected Naomi of instructing him in advance but in the circumstances, I held no grudge. My inhibitions slid down with the wine and I stopped worrying about my public image.

There were no toasts and no speeches thanks to Naomi's sensitivity, but the fact that I was still upright and smiling at 1 o'clock this morning was testament to the success of her planning. My speech degenerated after 11 but I'm not up to speed in metabolising alcohol these days so I had a legitimate excuse for incoherence.

Harry took the prize for the biggest surprise. As he pumped my hand with a benevolence borne of too much whisky he slurred, 'For all our sakes, take tomorrow off!' There were no witnesses and I might live to regret it but I took the instruction at face value.

When the door finally closed on the rest of the world, Naomi and I were both high and buzzing. The house looked like the proverbial bombsite but for once she took no persuading to leave the clearing up till the morning and I was at last free to tell her just how much I value all she is and does – a thing I do too rarely. Actions spoke more eloquently than my contorted consonants. I've been in a pleasant glow all day.

31 OCTOBER—It was weird going into the office today. Harry was away but there were no memos, no demands left for me, not even a left-over odour of bullying. Paradoxically I found the atmosphere so bewildering I couldn't concentrate on today's subject; the rising rate of teenage pregnancies and a decline in the number of marriages. I eventually made my excuses and brought the work home.

The world seems to have closed down since my birthday. Three of the key names I needed to consult were out of their offices, two useful contacts promised to 'ring back later'. I've used the tactic myself so I recognise insincerity when I hear it. Instead I found myself through to a militant pro-lifer of terrifying passions who harangued me for a good twenty minutes.

By 3.30 I gave up the unequal struggle and turned to the mountain of letters of thanks I now have to write. The number of gifts (donations to my favourite charity – thanks to Naomi) is such that this diary might have a few blank days.

2 NOVEMBER — Since the confirmation of my birthday I've been wandering around in a euphoric state of denial. Today that bubble burst – nay, exploded! I am once again a disabled man facing a death sentence.

When I agreed to help Devlin's students I had this idealised picture of myself as the hero of the hour. The ferocious emeritus professors would be awed by my courage and altruism. The floundering students would be eternally grateful for my subtle clues and profound understanding of my disease. They would carry a sense of undying gratitude towards MND patients into their practice and the brightest would translate it into Nobel-prize-winning research. This ghastly disease would be no more.

Okay, I thought I'd be the one in the driving seat. And I supposed they'd be somewhat impressed by my fight. Reality felt quite otherwise.

Dr Nimbus was neither emeritus nor professor. He wasn't crusty or crushing or at all impressed by me. Matter-of-fact, sums him up. His thanks were standard-issue not grovelling, his questions were most decidedly directed at the students and when I attempted to add my mite, he instantly cut me off, explaining as if to a child, that it was the students who needed to learn, not me.

The twenty raw recruits laying apologetically cold and trembling hands on my anatomy turned out to be three confident, brisk professionals.

A tutorial, Dr Nimbus said; not the career-blighting major examination of clinical competence I remember from black and white films. Tutorial or not, these wannabe MBs had done their homework. They knew the anatomy of my disease, the physiology, the manifestations, the treatments, the prognosis, the latest treatments, without hesitation, deviation or repetition. The pauses weren't long enough for any patient of above-average speed to tip them the wink, never mind my sluggish self.

Their complete command of the situation reduced me to a status lower than any since I'd been crushed by Malcolm Inches' BMW. In minutes I became 'the patient'. Not 'THE' but 'the'. *Any* patient. Indistinguishable, unremarked, unremembered. I had nothing to do but assimilate their powerful knowledge. They were under no obligation to soften the horror. Not for them the euphemisms of Devilish Devlin. Their sole intent was to impress Dr Nimbus. The more they knew, the harder he pressed for detail.

After five gruelling years of packing their brains with facts, these students were too close to real salaries to hide their lights under bushels for the sake of the sensibilities of a nobody. I listened to them rattle off all the deficiencies to which I had already succumbed, all the losses which lay ahead, and all the impotence of their profession. They left with rehearsed thanks and an air of assurance, completely oblivious to the wreckage in their wake.

It was sobering to read his honest account of that day. How different from the amusement of his *Carry on Doctor* description when he returned from this encounter.

5 NOVEMBER—I've always hated fireworks. In adulthood, I've added objection to my hatred. What possible merit can there be in blowing up thousands of pounds when it might be employed to improve our social services or reduce the waiting lists or give abandoned children a future? What a middle-aged, curmudgeonly kill-joy! Forty going on ninety. But the fact remains...

I'm writing something along those lines for my column. Today's accidents will fuel my passion: three school-kids blinded in Nottingham, five teenagers trapped in a garage full of the lethal devices in Canterbury, killed by a careless match; countless minor injuries filling casualty departments the length and breadth of the country.

As I write in the safety of my study at home, Noelani is cringing under the chair, staring wildly at the flashing sky. The spit and surge of rockets peppering the silence are curiously in tune with the anger of my thoughts.

The feature finished I turn to the MND Association's Personal Guide. My bruising encounter with tomorrow's doctors sent me back to check the information. And yes, they'd summed it up accurately. Reduced to its unvarnished core it's every bit as bad as they painted it. But it was the miniscule space devoted to 'relationships' that made me phone the Association. Didn't they know that relationships are one of the most important... Who knows what I said? The woman who answered put on that soothing voice that people reserve for the unhinged, the downright dangerous and the pathetic. She fell over herself offering things, couldn't seem to grasp the fact that I was *giving* something, not wanting something. I bellowed my name, occupation and contact details to be sure she got the message loud and clear that I was somebody. I'm probably on some blacklist somewhere by now!

Naomi leaned slowly back away from Adam's computer with a deep sigh. It was all such a battle.

6 NOVEMBER—Harry has reverted to type already. I dared to challenge a comment made by one of our reporters in yesterday's lead article: something patronising about sickness rates amongst the blue-collar

brigade. The said reporter flared up and said some damning things about society being soft on malingerers and the work-shy. Once I'd caught my breath I launched into a counter-attack.

Harry, no doubt infuriated by the take-over bid at his precious team meeting, banged his paperweight on the desk and yelled at everyone to shut up in his most colourful language. In the ensuing hung silence he had the audacity to say, and I quote: 'Okay. Okay. Okay! We all know Adam just needs time to re-establish his identity as a disabled man, so let's leave it at that and move on with this bloody agenda.'

Why I didn't walk out, I do not know. Part of me just couldn't credit he said that. Part of me didn't want to give him the satisfaction of confirming his diagnosis with my current ungainly stagger. Besides which, all the teaching of my youth still inclines me to respect authority – even moronic authority like Harry's.

Afterwards, in the privacy of the coffee area, Jannine did her Christian best to sympathise. She even lowered her guard sufficiently to call Harry an 'insensitive toad'. Phhhssssh! Ten Hail Mary's worth at least. I don't want her pity.

Jerry, more robust, got it equally wrong. 'Try not to be so subjective. It's just Harry.' Idiot. Experience is subjective. What else can I be? I am living it. It's what gives me the right to a voice on the matter. I could say – if it was worth it, which it isn't – 'You're too *objective*! Just walk a mile in my moccasins, matey, and then see what you say!

I've had it with the lot of them. Maybe I should just quit the paper now, stay at home and get my novel finished.

13 NOVEMBER—I'm back on the inequalities bandwagon. Thanks to Mrs AA of Slimbridge who wrote a moving letter to *The Times*.

On this occasion my piece is about free prescriptions. I'm staggered to find that some conditions – like the endocrine things (diabetes and thyroid problems) – qualify their owners for concessions, whilst others like chronic arthritis and degenerative diseases don't. I'm beavering away to find the official explanation and the hidden agendas. Will I rattle the cages of some sleeping tigers with this, I wonder?

I'm incensed on behalf of Mrs AA.

She's apparently a martyr to arthritis and takes a chemist-shop-full of pills every day, but she's on the breadline, whereas her posh neighbour gets everything free because she falls into this other medical category. Mrs AA's delicate enough not to divulge confidential detail. I know (where she may not) that Mrs Posh has probably been piling gold into the tax coffers and subsidising the likes of Mrs AA for years; even so, I'm sympathetic to her sense of outrage and maybe a little public exposure of the issues wouldn't come amiss. As they say, you not only have to be above reproach, you need to be *seen* to be. We shall see.

Most of my time I'm steaming along with Aidan's story and life feels good in my cosy cocoon, well above Mrs AA's breadline. Should I let the redoubtable lady know that I have an incurable and progressive illness myself? She'd warm to me more. I'd be allying myself with all sufferers everywhere. No. I'd be at a strong disadvantage with my other readers and critics. I have to stay on that level playing field for the time being.

Maybe this calls for a letter to *The Times* referring to hers. From Mr AO of Edinburgh. Then I could pile on the agony.

Depends what I unearth.

15 NOVEMBER—My hypocrisy has been uncovered. There I was on Tuesday, aligning myself with the disabled, sharing their outrage, flying their flag. Here I am two days later, turning my back on those with whom I should identify most closely: my companions on the walk – no, stagger – through MND itself.

The letter came from a Lieutenant Colonel GRS Grant-Hartwood. Very parliamentarian in his style of address. He's probably got yards of influence and connections in high places. But he's not so mighty that he won't stoop to grovelling. All this rubbish about me being a local celebrity, blah blah blah. Huhh! Fair enough, he might conceivably know my name from the paper, but who the devil told him about my MND? He doesn't specify, just says he's 'heard' I have this 'unfortunate condition'.

He's chairman of the local branch of the Scottish MND Association and wonders if I would consider coming along to talk to 'his' members – worse than doctors claiming 'their' nurses. Presumably he's got where he is because he talks like an officer and a gentleman, but who gave him the right to appropriate a motley band of human beings from all walks of life as his own? Maybe he thinks he bought it.

Well, Lieutenant Colonel Grant-Hartwood, I do not intend to get sucked into your unhealthy little empire, thank you very much.

I have an aversion to self-help groups.

I do not want to hold a mirror up to my future disability.

I do not want to feel crushed by the stories of others snared in a net of the same fabric as mine. I do not want to be identified with them.

I do not want to smell their incontinence, listen to their grunting, or weep at their graves.

Sufficient unto the day my own evil.

So thanks, but no thanks.

You may think my story would be 'inspirational'; I know it is not. Underneath this façade of success there beats the miserable frightened heart of a confirmed coward. I work on the principle that if I keep shtumm (how do you spell that?), people may suspect my deficiencies; if

I open my mouth, I'll leave them in no doubt.

Furthermore, you, Lieutenant Colonel, no doubt hold a chestful of medals for valour on the killing fields of the world; I, on the other hand, am implacably opposed to the senselessness of war, so if your commandership is what I think it is, we have nothing in common but our membership of the same species, and might well come to blows on the platform of your little closed society.

I wrote him a polite but brief letter, declining on the grounds of pressure of work.

Guilt smote Naomi. It was she who'd agreed they could contact him, but only once they'd told her he'd rung the Association. She flicked back through his entries. Yes, there it was. Bonfire night. Who knew what he'd said!

19 NOVEMBER—I'm only just beginning to appreciate how much that infection dragged me down.

Aidan's story is rushing ahead like a river in spate. I fill pages for hours together; not so good for my joints and muscles because I'm immobile in my concentration, but brilliant for my mental welfare. During the night, scenes flash before my eyes with such clarity I have to get up and commit at least a few gems to the computer; to lose them in the receding dreams would be too profligate.

In spite of all this disturbed sleep, I am truly alive. The adrenaline rush of creativity is better than any stimulant I've experimented with. And I confess I'm glimpsing the truth of Curtis's wisdom: the sheer pleasure of this life is enough to weigh the balance in favour of another day. I cannot leave without telling the world what happens to Aidan. The pull of nothingness has lost its appeal.

Having committed the latest instalment of Aidan's story to my working file (*and* to a floppy disc *and* a CD *and* my zip drive *and* to the trusty archive), I have pause for reflection. Aidan's questioning merges with my own to such an extent that our parallel worlds frequently cross over these days. Deliberately standing back one pace from his path right now, I am resolved to consider my own real-life position. Dispassionately. From the high ground of my present contentment.

I suspect that depression was distorting my judgments in the past. This is probably as good as life can be for me. The time to formulate my plan for the future is now. These are the decisions which I should translate into legal-speak.

So what do I feel? – now; when I wake up glad to be me, when I fall asleep eager for another day.

I want to finish my novel, definitely. I have plans for my other writing.

I want to keep writing for the paper as long as I can reach my own standard of prose, as long as I can exercise influence for good.

I have dreams for myself and Naomi; sensitive, unspoken dreams – even I tread softly around them.

I am prepared to accept some – limited – assistance to further these aims.

At the point where this low level of augmentation is no longer sufficient, then I'd like to go swiftly, painlessly and with dignity. No heroics, no rescue missions.

How? That's still the big question.

1. Suicide? Preferably not.
Why?
a) to protect Naomi and my mother and Joel from the backlash
b) in case I botch it and irretrievably damage my relationships with these special people
c) because I don't want to repeat history.
2. How then?
In order of preference:
a) an accident – swift and clean
b) a sudden life-threatening condition at the right moment, requiring immediate treatment, which could then be withheld, no recriminations on anyone's head
c) Doc Curtis easing me out of this world – again with no hint of suspicion or blame.

The formal declaration of my Advance Directive will have to be more judiciously expressed. Is my request reasonable under the circumstances? In essence:

- I do not want to live beyond my usefulness.
- I do not want to be a burden on others.
- When I can no longer contribute to society I want to go painlessly and with dignity.

Quite reasonable.

Later Curtis called in after surgery again today, bringing me another Jonathan Kellerman medical thriller he'd enjoyed. I tried a surprise attack.

'Are your rights and responsibilities more important than mine?'
'Hmmm.' Long pause. 'No. I'd say they're equally important.'
'Well, that's the first time I ever heard you boasting, Doc!'

He grinned at me.

'See, *I'm* actually putting *my* value lower than other people's,' I said in a preening way.

'You are? How come?'

'I don't want medical technology and skill and resources to be devoted to me until the last squeak; let them go to other more needy cases.' I sketched a halo over my head and quick as a flash he crossed his fingers, making us both laugh.

'Okay, you're a self-abasing, card-carrying hero. So?' he said.

'Well, you were the bloke who found me hanging over a precipice. You strapped the harness around me, hung the safety net under me, designed the whole damn expensive package of care. Why shouldn't you be the one to cut the safety wires?'

'Because my conscience and my ethical code don't allow me to – much as I appreciate your graphic depiction of the situation!'

'But say you did do it, what effect would that have on you?'

'Huge qualms of conscience, self-reproach, criticism from colleagues, vilification from the public, crucifixion by the media, end of career; just a few little hiccups like that.'

'So I need to fall into the clutches of a touchy-feely Intensive Care guy who's been breastfed on the milk of human kindness, who'll agree with me that free-falling into death is the kindest option.'

He shrugged. 'You could always try to find such a specimen.'

'Or a hard-nosed economist who'll see that vast sums of dwindling resources should not be wasted shoring up this waste of space that used to be me.'

'You're persistent, I'll grant you that,' he conceded, smiling ruefully.

'But am I persuading you? That's the question.'

'I can see where you're coming from.'

'A glimmer of a concession... Wow! Blimey, you're hard work, Doc!

'So my wife tells me!'

'Seems to me, society has handed you sawbones a disproportionate amount of magisterial authority. I accept that you inevitably hold an impressive hand of cards here. You have all the medical knowledge; dispensing only that information you decree the patient should share. You have the power to put a spin on it to suit your purposes. You hold the keys to treatments. You can summon up legions of colleagues with expertise to support your position. Whereas I am as powerless as a newborn babe.'

'But a lot more articulate!'

'I'm under no illusions. It'd take a very astute lawyer to win my puny case.'

'Are you thinking of going down that route?' he asked mildly.

'No. No point in pitting an amoeba against a dinosaur. I don't want to spend my last days setting my dwindling reserves on a collision course with the establishment and getting nowhere. Nor do I want even more money wasted on a cause doomed from its inception.'

'Very wise.'

'Like I say, you're hard work!'

'Sorry. If it's any consolation I sympathise with everything you've said. And agree with most of it. Goodness, I'll probably regret admitting that.'

'But you still can't see your way to a nice dose of strychnine, huh?'

'Something like that.'

He's a worthy opponent and does me good just being a listening ear. I'll soon need to stop all this pondering and commit my wishes to paper with a legal seal, and expose them to the scrutiny of witnesses. I have in mind getting Curtis to check them over first.

Every time Naomi read his arguments she felt the power of his logic. Why then had it gone so wrong for him?

26 NOVEMBER — I'm amazed to realise I haven't scribbled in this diary for a whole week. In that time Aidan has graduated from a zimmer to a wheelchair.

Today I went to see Devlin for my four-monthly check. He had a pretty Italian student with him. With some inner reluctance, I gave permission for her to sit in on my consultation.

Devlin was sombre in dress (a black shirt with a dark purple tie has the effect of royal mourning) and strangely reserved in manner. I felt a curious distance between us that only served to exaggerate my clumsiness. His look sharpened as I fluffed his mini-tests and extended the examination with my slowness.

'I was typing until 11.30 last night,' I said. 'I'm not like this at home.' And in a last ditch effort to regain my position, 'Must be the effect of a young lady in attendance.'

She gave a half smile; who knows what she thought? Devlin's eyes rolled but only within their customary orbits.

When I was on the couch, he made no effort to offer her liberties with my person and she stood discreetly just outside my line of vision. As his hands did what they were expensively trained to do, his voice probed my experience looking for the outer limits of my present abilities with more persistence. His concentration by now was absolute; there was no teaching of Miss Carla Bendetti, and I knew my façade was crumbling.

The physical bit behind us, and both now vertically inclined, the inequalities were less obvious. I started to relax. It was strangely soothing, placing the absolute truth about my weakened state in his hands, although I wrapped it all up in blankets of qualification: maybe I was imagining it; I was no expert; that's just what it felt like to me, but I could be wrong.

Without prompting he reassured me on several points. A distressing death from MND is rare. Pain is unusual. Cramps, pressure problems – there are preventive as well as alleviating things they can do for most symptoms. I'm already in the hands of the experts: the GP, nurses, physios.

By this time I'd forgotten the intruder. I found myself telling him about the tiredness.

'Describe a typical day,' he said.

He listened without interruption.

'And you wonder why you're tired?' There was a wry note in his voice.

'I was hoping it's a relic of my bad spell a few weeks ago. I did get very run down.'

'The infection won't have helped but I think you have to accept a certain amount of reduced energy levels at this stage. It's a matter of prioritising. Decide which are the most important things you want to achieve, and work out a strategy that allows you to reach that goal with the minimum amount of effort. I know it's hard for someone as energetic and busy as yourself, but you may have to set more limited goals for each day. Driving yourself too hard is going to be counter-productive in the long run. Think of it like a purse full of coins, each representing so much energy. Once it's empty, no amount of shaking will extract any more. It'll just leave you more exhausted for the next day.'

I shrugged, but gave no concessions.

'It's not easy to give yourself permission to ease off, I know. Feels like self-indulgence. But you'll actually achieve more if you learn to conserve your energy.'

It's perfectly true: I do need permission not to work till I drop. It's a genetic pre-disposition.

He couldn't have been too disappointed overall, however; he gave me another four months' grace.

Now that I've written up my account of Devlin's assessment, I have this crazy picture of him as a little man in a sombrero and a striped poncho, prancing about in front of a donkey, dangling his carrots of hope in front of me. Maybe it's good medical practice, but in circumstances like mine, it has to be a much over-rated section of the doctors' guidebook.

I have nightmarish visions of things going wrong in spite of careful planning, so I'd planned to check out the rules of engagement *vis-à-vis* resuscitation ready for my advance directive, but somehow Miss Carla Bendetti's ears were too young and idealistic for the frank discussion I'd envisaged. I feel an obligation to preserve her hope too.

'If I request, and you agree, that a DNR order is appropriate and you enter it in my notes, how do we ensure it's adhered to?'

'The decision would be clearly documented and flagged up to ensure everyone knows it's not for negotiation.'

'So there would be no margin for an individual with scruples flouting it?' I have this vivid picture of my mother at my bedside when I collapse, leaping up and down, imploring them to do something. Out-of-the-loop staff might instinctively respond to her distress. Or juniors, who measure the success of their shift in terms of the same number clocked out in the morning as they inherit when they come on in the evening, might rate their own credentials more highly than my unheard request.

'Hopefully not.' Guarded. There are no guarantees.

'I do not want degrading rescue efforts. There's absolutely no point in returning for more humiliation, more suffering, more goodbyes, more tears.'

'I understand,' he said calmly.

'I don't want ventilators, or feeding tubes, or antibiotics. I want them just to let me go.' Carla Bendetti was forgotten.

'Right.'

'There wouldn't be any repercussions for anybody in this case, would there?'

'Not if your wishes are clearly recorded. And things are sufficiently advanced.'

It's some small comfort.

Adam made it all sound so logical, so reasonable. In the same situation, Naomi knew she could not have expressed herself so cogently. She'd have relied on Adam... if only!

27 NOVEMBER—The NHS seems to be tightening its purse strings. Or the folk on the sharp end are taking seamless care seriously. I had an appointment with Lydia, but Curtis sneaked in to have a quick chat while I was with her. She popped out to get some special cream or other, he popped in, like the weather heralds on Austrian clocks. Except no *lederhosen*, no *dirndls*, no *edelweiss*.

How did I get on at the hospital? he wanted to know. Full marks for registering the date. More likely his memory was jogged by seeing me arrive, or catching sight of Lydia's list, and he checked. I gave him a resumé and he listened intently. Did I need more help? Was there anything he could do? A sick line, maybe? No. No. No.

He left with the ball squarely in my court: just give the surgery a ring if you want anything.

I hate to admit to disappointment: what a prima donna! Why *shouldn't* he kill two birds with one stone? I'm there in the vicinity of his surgery; it makes sense for him to see me too. He's got a few thousand patients; probably all of them want to be top of his list. What gives me a greater claim? Until this all started, I wouldn't have even recognised him in the street.

A cautionary tale, indeed.

Lydia returned to the room on cue. Not much escapes her perspicacious eye and she instantly adopted full Jamaican disguise.

'Why, Mister O, you sure are looking weary. You been overdoing things again when my back was turned?'

'Ahhhhh, Lydia. It's a fuel injection I need, not another lecture.'

'Oh my, oh my! Things sure ain't right when you try to pick a fight with your number one admirer.'

'Forgive me. I'm sorry. I'm in disgruntled mode. I'm not looking for a fight – least of all with *you*. It's just that I'm sick and tired of people trying to clip my wings. I *know* I'm getting weaker. I *know* I haven't got the stamina of a month ago. I *know* I have to shrink my world. I *know* I'm soon going to need assistance. But does everybody have to keep rubbing it in?'

'Is that what it feels like where you're sitting, honey?' Her silky voice let the words slither round my sensitivities.

'I know everybody means well, and I know they want to help, but it's my last chance to stay in control here. Once I acknowledge defeat, I'm on a slippery slope to dependence. I'm hanging on by my fingernails.'

'I know, I know.'

'I accept it takes me for ever to get showered and dressed in the morning these days, but damn it, I can still do it. I'm like a slug in a blizzard walking from room to room, but I can still do it. Is that so wrong?'

'Not if that's your priority.'

'It is and it isn't. The bathing and the walking themselves are not. Hanging on to my dignity and my independence is. It's a symbolic thing. Once I concede, where do we go next?'

As usual she was getting on with her therapeutic tasks while her tongue ran off down different escape routes.

'And how's the little lady coping with you so churned up?'

I stared at her impenetrable expression for a long moment.

'I've no idea.' The words dragged out slowly. 'I didn't know I was.'

'These muscles are tied up in knots so tight even a lifelong sailor couldn't undo them,' she declared in her broadest accent, kneading my shoulders with fingers that missed nothing. 'But maybe that's on account of you being angry with me for some reason. Maybe you're all sweetness and light with the little lady in the privacy of your own home.'

'I'm not angry with you, Lydia; really I'm not.'

'Aaahh. Well, then, if the blame's not laid at *my* door, we need to get you relaxing mighty quick. Afore you scrunch yourself up into reeeeeeeeeeal trouble.'

I felt the vibration of elephants crossing the room through the examination couch. Next moment, a click and a whir of a CD player, and deep rolling sounds fill the space between her calm and my tension. More thudding steps. Her fingers search and knead. Not until she's successfully uncoiled my various muscles does she speak again. This time she's on a chair beside the couch, her shrewd black eyes level with my wary ones. The Jamaican has left the room; in her stead is the archetypal British professional.

Friend to friend she explores how things are at home, just what I struggle with, how much of my personal care is still within my capabilities, what I'd consider relinquishing.

'What about someone coming in occasionally?'

'I'd rather have Naomi helping – if I need help.'

'And is that okay with her?'

'I should think so. I haven't asked. But… stands to reason she wouldn't want strangers pawing me before we need it.'

'Just so long as she doesn't overdo it, too.'

I'm instantly super-alert.

'D'you mean…?'

'It'll get harder. You both need to conserve your energy. We need to make sure we don't wear her out too soon.'

Suspicion evolves into full-blown certainty.

'Does it harm a pregnancy? Lifting, I mean.'

'Ahh. Now that's a different kettle of fish. I didn't know she was pregnant.'

'But I thought… isn't that what you're talking about?'

She leaned back in her seat and looked at me quizzically.

'I think we need to rewind here. Is she pregnant or is she not?'

'Well, not as far as I know. But she might be. Maybe you know more than me.'

'No, sir! Not on this point. I know nothing.'

'Well, I seem to remember you taking an uncommon interest in my love life in the past. I just wondered if maybe you had special radar, or inside information, or something.'

'Not me. But, is that something you're hoping for?' Her gentle tone took the impertinence out of her question.

'If it happens. It's something she wants – we both want.'

'In that case, you and I need to make doubly sure she doesn't exhaust herself.'

'And just what magical potion are you going to give me this time?' I teased, feeling suddenly vulnerable.

'Meaning?'

'It was you who tipped us into bed together at all hours to make sure I got enough rest way back when.'

'Ahhhh that! The time you accused me of professional misconduct, huh?'

'The very same.'

'Weeeell. Let's see. We're looking for something that gives you maximum flexibility, with minimum effort lifting and moving. Seems to me you've got a couple of options. More equipment. Or a bit of outside help just to ease things a wee bittee for your good lady.'

I'm only half attending.

'If Naomi was – pregnant, I mean – would it be harmful? Her helping me. I don't want to put her at risk.'

'She'd need to be careful. Joints and things soften up with pregnancy. It's easier to do damage. But we could give her some special training. Minimise the risk.'

'Maybe I ought to think about professional help, then. In a little while. When I really can't manage myself.'

'Think about it. We can put things in motion fairly quickly. When you're ready.'

My thoughts are racing.

'In the meantime, just to ease the pressure on her, how about using a zimmer in the house? You could lean on that rather than her to get from the bedroom to the shower. It'll keep you independent longer.'

Suddenly it becomes a means to a greater good. I have to protect my wife, my child.

She is looking at me with a sad look in her eyes. Too late I remember her widowhood.

'Lydia, forgive me. I'm an insensitive brute.'

She's clearly bewildered.

'All this talk of... so soon after your loss. I'm terribly sorry.'

'No need for apology.'

'I should have been more careful.'

'Please don't. To be honest it does me good to think about other people's problems. It'll spoil things if I think you're watching everything you say. Besides if *you're* on your best behaviour, *I'll* have to be. And then where would we be?'

'Fair enough. But just don't let me overstep the mark. You're a tonic for me. I don't want to be a thorn in your flesh.'

'You won't be. And just you remember, man,' – the Caribbean drums are rolling again – 'you and me, we're in this for the long haul. Together. A race for three legs, yeah? And we're in it to win it!'

I leave her magical presence with a spring in my shuffle.

Back at home, my mind is replaying our conversation. I'm suspicious that they're all watching me – Lydia, Curtis, Devlin, Ursula – anticipating the next stage. Lydia, bless her, has managed somehow to reconstruct the unacceptable and change it into the desirable. Naomi and our baby take precedence over my pride.

Not easy. I shudder to think of myself naked on a bath stool with two strange women in attendance lowering me, lifting me, washing me, drying me. With Naomi I can turn the necessity into a flirtatious choice, with my words if not my actions. There's nothing unseemly in her seeing and handling my body.

But… how will she feel when the disease distorts everything? How will she cope when she's pregnant or has a young baby? When I am no longer her top priority.

Naomi shuddered. Privacy. Fatherhood. Conspiracies. On-going anxieties; hidden fears. He'd even joked about them.

'Lydia was telling me about a couple of MND patients who were dispatched to a home or a hospital because the relatives were so house-proud they couldn't deal with the sheer untidiness of it all. At least you aren't the type to sling me out because I don't match the furniture.'

'Are you by any chance casting nasturtiums on my aesthetic standards?' she'd retorted indignantly. 'I'll have you know, I've got the colour charts in already. I thought a deep ochre for the wheelchair to co-ordinate with that mustard and sage rug your mother gave you.'

'Horrors! At least choose a colour I like!'

But that had been much further down the line. Back then, when he had first given in and used a zimmer in the house, she'd have been as opposed to outside assistance as Adam had been. Caring for him was part of loving. Resentful thoughts came much later. She'd clung stubbornly to her role, filling the gaps left by the various professionals.

Adam had wanted her to be more aggressive in pursuing her right to respite, he didn't want her to kill herself caring for him; it was she who had resisted.

He'd played his trump card – pregnancy. She made the right noises, adding layers of deception to her existing guilt. She knew he had no need to protect her on that score, but it would only serve to weaken his will to live if she took away that hope.

29 NOVEMBER—Lydia has stirred up all sorts of slurry. I feel like a bottle of Shiraz clouded with sediment.

My time has to be limited. And Naomi still doesn't seem to be pregnant. It's more than likely my fault. If this muscle-rotting disease is demolishing so much of my body, chances are it's doing things to my sperm production too. Much as I hate the idea, I think I ought to go and get that checked out. Thing is, do I tell Naomi? Last thing she needs is pressure in that quarter; if I do seem to be in full working order that suggests she might not be, and she doesn't need that.

Maybe a chat with Curtis is called for.

Naomi closed the file sharply, shut down the computer and pushed the chair back with a jerk. Noelani opened her eyes reproachfully from her cocoon of cushions but made no effort to move. Naomi picked the warm cat up without a word and left the study, making no effort to sympathise with her indignation.

30 NOVEMBER—Nothing in the manual about fertility. 'Personal details' sprang out at me, but they didn't mean that personal. So much for their claim that all the information is there when you need it.

The 'personal details' section conjures up images I'd rather not visit. It suggests writing out demographic facts so that those deputed to look after us don't have to ask umpteen questions and drain our dwindling reserves by telling our story over and over. Name, address, relatives... Wow! Surely anybody invading the privacy of my home ought to know the essentials about me.

Apparently you're just supposed to hand this form to each person with whom you come into contact. Conserve your energy, they say. Relieve yourself of the strain of speaking when it's a struggle, they say. Relieve them of the strain of trying to understand me, I think! Ahhh. I concede that strangers in uniforms in A&E departments or hospital ward won't know I own a house in Edinburgh and have a beautiful wife. Or what stage I'm at with my MND.

This folder is not good for my health. I see myself slumped in a wheelchair, slavering, grunting, while pitying eyes skim my history. If I can't communicate, what am I?

2 DECEMBER—Naomi's birthday. Not my finest hour. But it has brought me face to face with new questions which require an answer. Smartish.

After a night of cramps followed by a frustrating day, I was like a tortoise in fog by the evening. Showering and dressing took forever and I was forced to accept Naomi's help – sadly, with a bad grace, birthday or no birthday. I had no surplus energy to create a façade of gratitude. Every fibre implored, 'Stay at home. You've gone beyond your limit', but

I'd said we were going; go we would. Genetic predisposition.

I'd booked a table in a new restaurant in George Street – over the phone. We were only forty-five minutes late; they were empty enough not to care. First impressions were encouraging. Good ambience, excellent menu. The tension started to ease. Good tangy paté. Venison cooked to perfection. Vegetables nicely *al dente*. Bonus points accumulating; irritation receding. A full-bodied smooth Australian red hit the spot. *Crème brûlée*. One of my favourites. Last time I had it, a sharp crack with my spoon fragmented the caramel perfectly. Try that manoeuvre with weak wrists and it's another game altogether. Naomi made a joke of it and did a subtle swap with her rum gateau, soft and altogether more manageable. I didn't ask for rum gateau. I didn't want rum gateau. I don't even like rum gateau. I wanted *crème brûlée*.

My real mistake came after coffee. 'Exhibition by local artist' the sign said, an arrow pointing to the back of the restaurant. By the time I'd negotiated the narrow spaces between tables and arrived at the second arrow: 'To the basement', there was no way I was going back without seeing those paintings. But when your two feet aren't connected to your ankle bones and your brain has severed connections with your locomotor system, a steep flight of stairs represents potential disaster. Somehow Naomi managed to prevent my tumbling headlong into oblivion on the way down. Relief all round! Then... spring loaded doors, highly polished floorboards, absurdly narrow doorways completed the conspiracy. I emerged from that badly-lit display of something vaguely approximating to art with black gremlins on both shoulders, not to mention an impossible flight of stairs between me and escape.

It was entirely my fault. I chose to go. No one made me. But all my anger was directed at the management who had compounded their architectural iniquities by hiring staff with all the sensitivity of a herd of hippopotami (or whatever the collective noun is for those artiodactyl mammals). No less than three of them grabbed various bits of my anatomy (legitimate bits, I hasten to add) and issued loud and patronising instructions on where to place my feet, how to haul myself up on the handrail, who to lean on next. I can see why they weren't busy. They won't be getting my custom again either, that's for sure.

Naomi was very quiet on the way home. I know she deserved an apology; I couldn't dredge it up. Every nerve was too raw for self-flagellation. Threaded through the whole scenario was the unspoken but pervasive realisation: this will almost certainly be her last birthday with me. If I could go back and do it again, I would. I can't.

His struggle had completely distorted the picture. It had been tricky negotiating those stairs but nothing of his anger had been directed at her.

Naomi smiled ruefully, remembering the liquid vitriol he'd released against those waiters as soon as they were safely out of earshot. His criticisms were entirely justified; they'd treated this clever, articulate man like a moron. The words he used to describe their insensitivity were probably completely outside their lexicons. In the midst of her own anguish on his behalf, she'd known a sense of awe at the richness of his vocabulary, his similes, his descriptions.

Sadness engulfed her. What must it do to an intellect like his, to be so much at the mercy of misconstruction and condescension? To tick each special event off as the last of its kind? The only wonder was that he had found the courage to take her out at all.

5 DECEMBER—I don't know if it's connected with three days of intensive writing but tonight I couldn't even get out of my chair. Admittedly I'd been in one position for several hours and got very cold. Maybe something of Aidan's incapacity is creeping into my subconscious. Whatever the cause, I had to call Naomi to help haul me up. As soon as I saw how much I was pulling on her, I made her get my zimmer and transferred my weight to that the minute I was semi-upright, but she took the strain. Lydia's advice is writ large across my vision: I've got to protect her. The time has long since passed when I should have given in and seen the specialist nurse Curtis has up his sleeve. Having said that, I'm impressed by Naomi's technique. She bends and stands just like Lydia does when she's putting me through my paces. Perversely I resent her professionalism. She's my wife! I don't want her to handle me like a patient. I want to be the one to carry *her* to bed; I want her to melt into my arms. I know I should be grateful that she's performing her role so expertly, never making me feel insecure; I'm not. I can't tell her. I'd burst into tears.

He hadn't asked her how she knew the best way to move him. Lydia's advice had been exactly right. Her understanding of Adam's point of view, her intuition, her wisdom, had saved Naomi from many a mistake.

'Resist the temptation to do things for him. It'll take ages, it'll exhaust him, but you'll be helping him more by leaving him to do things for himself rather than underlining his inability.'

'Help him to retain what control he has. He's a proud man.'

'When you feel impatient, think of other things to do or use the time to plan things mentally. Anything that'll distract your own mind while he struggles.'

Wise counsel. With so many other demands on her, Naomi had been tempted to go for efficiency; thanks to Lydia she had resisted the temptation – usually. It had been tempting to strap his head to the chair to ease the strain of holding it up. It was Lydia who gently cautioned her to let Adam decide when he would be reduced to this. He was the one who ached all over from the sheer effort of sitting.

It had been tempting to apply for benefits for his disability early on to give him as much assistance as he needed. It was Lydia who pointed out that Adam didn't see himself as disabled yet, and that in his perception these benefits were handouts to the underprivileged.

7 DECEMBER—More milestones. I left a message for Curtis: I'll see the nurse. When it's convenient. No hurry. And I rang the MND Helpline. I need information. Something I don't want to ask of those I know personally, nor risk leaking out to Naomi. Impersonal is best at this stage. It's about the fertility thing.

After all the effort of summoning up the courage, overcoming all my reservations and prejudices, articulating the issue clearly, even if slowly, I got this woolly woman who said, 'What a good question. I'm afraid I don't know the answer.'

Back to square one.

No, not even that; a point below square one.

Of course, Mrs Woolly Woman offered to find out, ring me back, but I can't take a chance on that. What if Naomi answered? We always said we'd take a relaxed approach to conception; if it happens, it happens. There's nothing to be gained by her becoming preoccupied with getting pregnant. Guaranteed to reduce her fertility. And to put a strain on our sex life.

Naomi gritted her teeth and moved swiftly on.

8 DECEMBER—Mr Last-minute-dash has come to this; Christmas shopping finished two weeks early. (Of course, Naomi does the bulk of it, so it's no great achievement.) This year it was a case of, if you can't obtain it over the ether, it's off the list. And if they send it direct, so much the better – to hang with battles over ribbons and tags or worse still, sticky tape.

Totting up the price of things for the credit card has brought my thoughts unwillingly round to our financial state – again Naomi's province. Heavens! I owe this lass, big time! Anyway, I'm still productive for the paper and working reasonably effectively – for Arkwright, at least. Stuff Harry. He set impossible deadlines even in my heyday. But given the difference from twelve months ago, I have to face reality. My earning potential is declining. I shall at some point be eligible for incapacity benefits. Incapacity – how I hate the dull treacly sludge of it. Benefit – the very spit of its brisk emerald green syllables mocks my resistance.

'The Dept of Social Security will need to be satisfied that you cannot continue to work,' the leaflet threatens. In my case that's difficult to establish. Physically, I can do pretty much everything that my job requires; it just takes longer. I minimise inefficiency by working from home, but the sheer exhaustion of living can easily leave neither mental space nor emotional energy for thinking outside the box.

At some point I'll probably give up the journalistic stuff and concentrate on the fiction. From a mental health point of view this option would be therapeutic. When I'm in tandem with a character, thinking their thoughts, accompanying them through assorted experiences, I'm energised and gloriously free from the shackles of my disease. But would this count as being able to work?

While I'm still capable of combining the novel with the bread-and-butter work, I'm loath to forfeit my regular salary. The royalties won't be realised for some time – perhaps not even in my lifetime. And when you work out how long it takes from conception to publication, they wouldn't equate to a decent salary.

Filling in these triplicated forms, my instinct is to state what I can do on my best day. CVS, job applications, appraisals – we're taught to show our shiny side. But when it comes to establishing my disability, I'm supposed to base my assessment on the worst days. It goes totally against every grain. In the Spartan School of Unsung Heroes, the monumental effort you make to achieve something is your private challenge and success, not to be paraded. Alien territory.

10 DECEMBER—I had to go into town today to meet a guy who's thinking of joining our firm. Arkwright asked me if I could manage it. He wanted somebody who'd give a fair account of life 'at the sharp edge', who could impress him with long service, commitment, success – that kind of thing. Flattery got him what he wanted.

I should have realised that this close to Christmas, the city centre would be mobbed. Squirreled away in the suburbs, that kind of reality rarely impinges on my experience.

It's curious how little notice we take of other people's activities when we're part of that surge of humanity ourselves. But today I envied Moses: I wanted to be able to stretch out my hand and have the sea of pounding flesh part before me, the queues dissolve, the uneven pavements smooth out to ease my passage.

No miracles being on offer, I staggered haphazardly through the uncaring multitudes, fuming variously at the obstacles, the lack of consideration, the poor design, the wanton carelessness. Oh to be the undisputed centre of the universe!

It was a minor triumph to stagger into Brown's restaurant on time.

Colin Coleman was nothing like my mental picture. He was easily six foot five; not five nine. His thatch of black wire was much more striking than the slicked-down mouse I'd sketched in. The wide film-star smile oozed a confidence that belied the grovelling deference I'd anticipated.

A nice line in smart-casual showed he knew the ways of the world and my last advantage vanished as he declared himself pleased to meet me, with not so much as a flicker in the direction of my sticks. Maybe his assurance comes from a lifetime of taunting about the colour of his skin. Somehow, in his hands, black is dominant without being aggressive.

He is exactly what the place needs. There'll be no succumbing to Harry's bullying tactics in that quarter, I'll be bound. And the more he talked, the more I liked him.

I only wish I could be around to see him rise to fame and fortune over Harry's dead body!

The receptionist at Curtis's surgery left a message. The nurse is coming the day after tomorrow. Hmmmm. Childishly, I wish I hadn't rung back to arrange a date.

11 DECEMBER — Maybe it's foolish, maybe it's a reaction to yesterday, but today I booked an Easter break in Madeira. It's a place with fantastic memories for me. Naomi's never been. I want her to experience it with me. While I can still move.

It was a spur of the moment decision, triggered initially by an obituary, of all things. The name jumped out at me. There was a picture of a portly man with a chestful of medals standing to attention during some major national event, but it didn't ring any bells (not surprising, given that I've never met the man). But the name... ahh, that stirred something.

Grant-Hartwood. Lieutenant Colonel Gerald Ronald Stevenson Grant-Hartwood. Second son of the Duke of somewhere I've never heard of. Educated at Eton and Oxford. Trained at Sandhurst. Distinguished military career. Awarded the DSO in 1945, a CBE in 1968. Latterly Chairman of the local MND Association where he 'worked tirelessly until his sudden and unexpected death on Tuesday evening'. It's only Thursday now – this tribute must have been already prepared. They only do that for well-known figures. And these were the credentials of the man who wrote extolling my celebrity!... a nonenity from a newspaper. Whose invitation I turned down on the basis of my own speculation. Because I thought he had no right to involve me. He had every right.

'Diagnosed with a rapid form of Motor Neurone Disease in 2006' it seems he wasted no time in idle regret but used his contacts, his leadership skills, his assets, to raise the profile of the disease. He was an ardent campaigner for stem cell research and generated thousands of pounds for the cause from his innovative fund-raising activities, even abseiling down a rock-face himself weeks after he began using a wheelchair.

I was left staring at that rotund figure for an age. How did he die? Why was his death 'sudden and unexpected'? My churlishness in the face of his valour chastens me. He used none of his many levers to persuade me.

The memorial service/funeral is on Thursday week at 12 noon. It's to be a thanksgiving for his life.

He has left behind a wife, Lady Dorothy; two sons, two daughters and eleven grandchildren. Even on that level I am a pigmy by comparison.

Donations in lieu of flowers to MND research.

12 DECEMBER—I rang the local branch of the Scottish MND Association today. I explained about the letter from their late Director-Chairman. Would they still be interested in my visiting their group?

They were polite but cagey. Lieutenant Colonel Grant-Hartwood's sudden death had thrown everything into confusion, they said. Could they get back to me in the New Year? But if I wanted someone to come and talk about my MND... perhaps someone else with the disease? I repeated my sympathy and put the phone down quietly. They just don't give up. I feel insensitive for troubling them in their grief.

I was still feeling low when the nurse came. Toni Wagstaffe. Toni with an 'i'. Short for Antoinette apparently.

'So no relation to the ex-prime minister,' I said.

Pearls before swine.

Granted I was inwardly rebelling against the necessity to have this person in my home, assessing my needs, 'establishing my baseline'!... but I'm sure it wasn't just that causing me to switch off to this woman, Toni with an 'i'. If I had to write her appraisal after this one encounter I'd sum it up as: needs to lose that patronising manner; needs to develop a sense of humour; needs to thaw out. I do not want to be part of her community disability team, thank you very much. Wavelengths matter.

I postponed all her suggestions. Maybe some rich Arabian Sultan will entice her to go to warmer climes and condescend somewhere else before she remembers to contact me again.

14 DECEMBER—Sally and Matthew invited us to their house yesterday for a pre-Christmas celebration. Anabelle and Courtney put on a little play. They fluffed their words and had a minor disagreement backstage midway through a key scene, but everyone applauded vigorously and shouted, 'Encore!', as instructed. The encore consisted of a song about an angel visiting a child on Christmas Eve. Naomi wasn't the only one dabbing eyes when the lights were dimmed. I must talk to Curtis once things quieten down after New Year.

It was too much. She reached out and let her fingers touch the words lightly as if she could connect with his longing. Even then, when he was staggering around, unable to stand unsupported, his speech ravaged by the disease, even then he had clung to the hope of fatherhood. And she, unaware, had conspired to deny him that fulfilment, her only ambition to be strong for him until the end. What if she had known what he was thinking…? What if…?

17 DECEMBER—Aidan is struggling with his speech now, and after a full day of telling his story I'm completely drained. A real sense of urgency is propelling me. If Grant-Hartwood with all his advantages can die 'suddenly' then… Well, I'd like to be prepared as he seems to have been.

20 DECEMBER—For the first time I am brought face to face with the harshness of a death in December. The presents are probably already bought, the cards signed: Mum and Dad, Grandpa and Grandma, Gerald and Dorothy, Lieutenant Colonel and Lady. Festivity all around, sadness within.

When I arrive, by taxi to avoid unseemly delays and difficulties, there are only a handful of people already in their seats in the aisles. Wheelchair seats. By the time the service starts there are at least five hundred mourners packing the pews.

The cathedral is banked up with Christmas reds and greens, hundreds of tiny red nightlights illuminating the sacred gloom. The organ is playing variations on familiar carols, muted but recognisable. The family are wearing holly-red roses on their black lapels, dispensing quiet smiles. A single red rose relieves the dark mahogany of the coffin. Two simple wreaths, both in the Christmas theme, lie beside it, presumably representing the generations. In childish writing I can see 'For Granpops' on the card nearest to me, nestling inside the rich dark green holly leaves. I feel a sudden choking sensation.

The minister explains that 'our friend and brother', Gerald Ronald Stevenson Grant-Hartwood, asked that everyone who was 'kind enough' to attend should give thanks for the richness of the life he was given, for all the opportunities, all the love, all the happiness, he enjoyed. The family have added tributes to flesh out the character of the man but in the spirit of thankfulness, not boasting, as he specified.

It is an intensely moving experience – even for me who never knew him. This was the man I scorned. Whose courage in the face of a devastating disease touches me more deeply than he will ever know.

The burial is to be private and the rest of us watch with silent respect as the family follow the coffin to its last resting place with quiet dignity. The tiny splashes of red sing out a paean of praise. I send my apologies across the air in an unspoken tribute.

It is too late to make amends to Lieutenant Colonel GRS Grant-

Hartwood. But I vow to take stock and order my own priorities while the guilt still stings.

He'd been strangely withdrawn when he got home; she'd given him space. Not until they were in bed that night did he speak hesitatingly of his experience, his expression hidden in the darkness. He spoke of the dignity, the achievements, the tributes.

Listening, she wished she'd accompanied him. But her excuses had been genuine enough: she did have so much still to prepare for Christmas. What she hadn't divulged was her dread of seeing people in a more advanced stage of MND than Adam.

21 DECEMBER—After a couple of hours on the novel yesterday I was feeling pretty low. Aidan's in a bad way. So the sound of young voices giggling at our door impinged slowly.

They got off to an uncertain start, but by the time I'd staggered to the door with my zimmer, they were belting out 'Good King Wenceslas'. It crossed my mind that in all likelihood, not one of them knew Wenceslas was a real king; they'd probably never even heard of the Czech Republic, never mind its rich history. But they were loving the excitement of being out in the dark, singing with their mates, being thanked by their victims.

They were collecting for the local children's home. I must write a piece about this. The news always seems to feature the decline in standards of today's youth – the joy-riders, the muggers, the druggies, the teenage mums, the bullies. A spotlight on altruism might hit the spot at Christmas-time. I'll do it this week rather than commit it to my Ideas folder. Better still, I'll start it now. While the emotion is fresh.

Even Harry was grudgingly positive about my piece on those kids. It'll be in tomorrow's edition. I'm quite pleased with it myself.

22 DECEMBER—It occurred to me today that I've missed the opportunity to do something I've often thought of doing: dropping people off my Christmas list if they don't bother to say thank you. I read once of a woman who did that and I've secretly hankered to have that sort of courage but somehow never quite dared to. I guess a bit of me thinks I give for giving's sake, not for what I get in return. But I still resent those who take for taking's sake and don't even observe the common civilities. My mother was a stickler about letters of thanks when we were kids; it's ingrained in me. Maybe I secretly envy those who either were spared the childhood purgatory or abandoned the shackles as soon as they reached the age of discrimination.

Joel arrived tonight. With Paige. She seems lovely. Sort of peaceful.

And pretty. Green eyes, red curls, curvy in the right places. A good listener. And Joel himself seems different. Quieter. Gentler. I can't decide if it's Paige or me who's having this softening effect.

I caught him watching me closely a couple of times. It's understandable. I hadn't told him how much I've weakened since he last saw me. Well, I hadn't stopped to think about it. Seeing things through his eyes has served to underline for me the deterioration that has slunk in by the back door.

But the change in *him* is almost more unnerving. I realise that in this world that's spiralling out of control, I need him to be himself; my madcap little brother. Maybe when the clan gathers he'll revert to type.

Naomi sighed. For one so perspicacious, Adam had been remarkably blind to his brother's emotion.

'I can't bear to see him struggling like this, Nay!' Joel had ground out over the phone. 'If there was only something I could do!'

'You can. Your visits, your phone calls, they're a real tonic for him.'

'How does he bear it? I'd have jumped off the Forth Road Bridge long ago.'

'Please don't tell him that! He's thought about it but… please. Please, Joel.' She hadn't been able to suppress the tears.

Joel had been horrified by what he had unleashed, but the revelation opened the door to a new openness between them. Naomi found that sharing the worst moments with him eased and somehow legitimised her heartache. She came to trust in his capacity to maintain his jaunty image, and in his sensitivity to Adam's mood and needs.

23 DECEMBER—Naomi and I attended the Christmas Service in our local church this morning. It felt good, singing carols with so many other folk; making a joyful noise. I don't know if it was due to Thursday's experience in the cathedral, or my heightened awareness of the brevity of life, or just all the changes we've experienced this year, but somehow the words meant more to me than usual. My mother would rejoice to know her errant son was actually thinking about eternal things! Not that I could tell her. She'd be in there like a terrier, destroying this fragile thing. No, it's too private for public consumption.

A baby in the back row kept whimpering. I'd have expected some of the congregation to be irritated, but not a bit of it. He was as welcome as the infant Saviour! They turned, yes, but only to smile their pleasure. Glad you came, they seemed to say. Families especially welcome.

I saw Naomi glancing round. She smiled too. I reached across and took her hand. We both smiled. Maybe soon.

The sermon held my attention in a way I didn't expect. The minister, Reverend Tom Blackwell, talked about important people. If the queen is visiting a town, everywhere gets painted and cleaned up and hosed down. Even if a lesser dignitary is coming, everyone scurries around making the place look as good as they can. Everyone dresses up, provides the best food and drink, makes a big effort. But Jesus, the most important man who ever walked this earth, (he said), was born in exile, raised in simplicity, lived in borrowed premises, died amongst criminals and hecklers. He never went outside his own land, and yet his influence has been greater than any king or queen or potentate before or since.

Lieutenant Colonel Grant-Hartwood springs unbidden into my thoughts. I'm reminded of the old adage: Those that mind don't matter; those that matter don't mind.

I felt a sense of peace as the final blessing committed us all to God's love. He at least doesn't judge by the outward trappings. Rev. Blackwell spoke to everyone as they left, to us non-members as well as to the regulars whom he called by their name; wishing us well individually. I wonder what he'd say if I told him about my suicide ideas. Would he still smile with such warmth? Would he still welcome us into his church? Or would he gang up with my mother?

Not that she's raised the subject lately. Ever since my birthday she's been more subdued. She still comes once a week and wields a mean feather duster (with Naomi's blessing and our combined thanks). She and I have settled into a state of quiet equilibrium; we just don't raise difficult issues. Naomi is more generous in her sharing.

The suicide thing has returned to haunt me again, particularly since that service in the cathedral. I want to be remembered in technicolour. Strong red against the black. But the guilt still nags; my mother's teaching, her church's doctrine. Even some mighty intellects, unhampered by the myths and taboos of religion, regard suicide as unacceptable. I read about this guy called John Hale, a brilliant academic struck down by a stroke, who said it was as immoral as murder. Nobody owns their life, he argued, it belongs to all the people affected by that life. *(For Ideas Folder. See *The Man who Lost his Language* by Sheila Lane.)

But in my circumstances? Isn't it the lesser of two evils?

How macabre! – I've actually been reading a book about causes of death. It's designed as a source book for writers but I've found it fascinating in relation to my own end. I probably ought to read the Hemlock people's literature, and the Voluntary Euthanasia Society stuff too, but somehow this book keeps it impersonal. It isn't saying, if you want to do yourself in, use a four inch blade or a particular type of knot on the noose or… it just gives the facts. I can rationalise it as legitimate research for my novel, keep it at one step removed.

So, what have I learned?

DROWNING
Plus: it's nearly impossible to tell whether death by drowning was an accident or suicide – or murder! NB. Naomi needs a cast iron alibi.
Minus: Can be a pretty slow, agonising kind of death. People tend to struggle. Would I have the courage and resolve to see it through?

Later I got sidetracked by this marvellous account of inexplicable or so-called voodoo deaths. Apparently healthy men, convinced that they were the victims of evil sorcery, and totally certain that the time for their death had come, simply lay down and died! No cause for death found. Sounds ideal!

And in other cases, perfectly healthy people had unexplained experiences during the night, characterised by agonising groans and writhing, and then were found dead in the morning. Again, no cause of death found at autopsy. They're known as 'nightmare deaths'. I'm not so keen on the writhing in agony – even the fantasy variety! And it doesn't tell you how you procure one of these.

Okay, enough procrastination. What other options do I have?

HANGING
Minus: Requires dexterity – probably beyond me. Don't want Naomi's last memory to be of eyes popping and face all distorted and blue.
ACCIDENT
Plus: Always been a front-runner.
Minus: ??Beyond my capacity. Risk of waking up as strawberry jam with it all still to do. Beastly experience for any driver if go for traffic accident.
OVERDOSE
Plus: Easy. Clean.
Minus: Risk of vomit, wrong dose, unusually high tolerance level.
POLY BAG
Minus: Probably beyond my strength. Don't want Naomi to remember me like that.
SHOOTING
Plus: Clean and quick – for victim.
Minus: Don't have a gun. Maybe not strong enough or accurate enough.
SLASHED WRISTS
Minus: Messy. Could be painful and slow.
GASSING
Minus: No gas in the house. Knowledge of car mechanics unreliable.

All of the above, minuses:

1. Guilt. (?Consult man of the cloth who doesn't know me. Rev. Tom Blackwell maybe?)
2. Aftermath for Naomi and my mother.
3. ??Determination.

I have a vague memory of a programme about young people who harmed themselves or committed suicide. What struck me was their calm approach to the deed. Life was a kind of hell, one of the teenagers said, she just wanted to find a more peaceful place. And some of them tried everything – including setting themselves on fire. Imagine! Desperation of a different dimension.

Looking at this list I have a nasty suspicion I'm too much of a coward. I can't see myself even deliberately nicking my skin. Or am I just too much in love with life?

What did the Lieutenant Colonel do, I wonder? If anything.

24 DECEMBER—It was my job today to decorate the house, already scrubbed to within an inch of its life by my mother. The artistic touches have always been my domain. This year, however, Joel was dispatched to collect cones and holly – a big concession. I love tramping in the cold air, smelling the pines, searching for exactly the right fruits of the forest to create a different effect each year. It's all part of the anticipation, the preparation, for the big day.

In spite of the distraction Paige offered, Joel managed to bring back a creditable haul and I left them to weave the greenery and fairy lights through the banisters while I got on in the main rooms. Zimmers and stairs aren't compatible!

It took an unbelievably long time and my clumsiness was starting to rile me, when footsteps bounded down the staircase and the door was suddenly flung open. I was just on the point of threading loops of dark green velvet ribbon into the banks of holly on the mantelpiece without displacing strategically positioned crimson candles.

'I say, Adam.'

I turned too quickly, lost my balance, and crashed to the floor in a shower of Christmas baubles, berries and wax. One of my favourite dark red frosted balls splintered into fragments in the fireplace beside me. Joel hauled me up with more goodwill than skill, profusely apologetic. I was physically unharmed but all my Christmas spirit evaporated as Naomi swept up the mess. Joel took instructions on how to finish off decorating the mantelpiece and Paige glanced uncertainly from one of us to the other as she returned to festooning the banisters alone.

Memories of that day were etched on Naomi's own mind.

Steering a course through Adam's sensitivities and the pressure of having to cater for eleven on Christmas Day had been taxing from the outset. Joel's horror at causing the accident, her own anxiety, and Adam's palpable frustration had conspired to dampen everyone's spirits.

He'd looked so strained, it was a relief when Adam had cried off from attending the Watchnight service to conserve his energy for the following day and gone into his study 'to write'. She'd made her excuses too, unwilling to leave him alone. She'd brought him mulled wine, salted cashew nuts, and an affectionate hug. Strange. He must have been writing this very account of his accident. He'd smiled his thanks but she knew from his absent look that he needed to be alone.

She'd been glad to escape. The thought pierced her soul. Why had she not clung to every second? But it had been so hard to stop her mind dwelling on next Christmas. Her pact with Joel had helped: she would keep her side of their bargain. She would. But the struggle had been monumental.

28 DECEMBER—I owe Naomi and Joel a debt I can never repay. Thanks to them this has been a much better Christmas than I ever anticipated.

Naomi's mother and her sister as well as my mother contributed to the food – it must have been a major military exercise for Naomi to plan but it worked brilliantly. All four women shared the responsibilities at the table as well as behind the scenes, and since they're all good cooks we had a veritable feast. I'm staggered at Naomi's acceptance of their help. She always used to pride herself on doing everything independently, but from where I sat, they were all more relaxed because of their greater involvement. If there were tensions in the kitchen, they didn't spill over into the dining room.

Anabelle and Courtney kept things light with their excitement and artless chatter. Naomi had made little packages to keep them amused between courses and the whole company entered into the fun of unwrapping them, exclaiming over the tiny music boxes, the glow-in-the-dark pens, the noisy party poppers. It didn't take long to turn the elegant table into a bombsite of streamers and discarded paper. Their grandfather contributed to the mess by transforming napkins into ghosts and aliens. But the mounting debris symbolised the collapse of artificial restraint. We were once again a normal family.

Normal? Yes, it felt normal.

For us. Now.

I made no pretence at being the active host. Joel assumed the role without a word from me. And his crazy banter effectively took the sting out of his takeover bid. I think I may have underestimated my kid brother. Paige fitted in perfectly and I could see even my mother was impressed.

Present-time has sometimes been tricky in the past, with money spent on unwelcome choices, but this year Naomi and I had told everyone in the immediate family we didn't want gifts; contributions instead to the humanitarian crisis in the Sudan. It saved the family thinking, What do you give to a man who'll be dead by this time next year? It circumvented emotional moments. And the adults all took their cue from us and requested something similar for themselves. It was Naomi's idea that we exchange inexpensive joke gifts – no more than two pounds per person. I'd had a lot of fun searching through mail-order catalogues for the right thing for each of them. As a result, exchanging gifts was a riot of laughter. Just what we needed.

Highly excited children can be a strain for the older generation. Naomi, Joel and Paige had designed a competition for them to fill in the post-prandial slot. Each assisted by two adults, they had a list of items to find in the garden. The resultant collection of assorted feathers, leaves, handprints, petals, etc had all to be used to create something for the O'Neill Gallery of Modern Art. I was to be the judge and as such I was safely enthroned in a large, decorated chair in the bay window overlooking the back garden, to ensure there was no cheating.

The banishment of the girls from the house was designed to give their elders a chance to nap. In the event, they crowded around me, fully engaged with the hilarity outside, and when it came to the judging I had no shortage of advice.

Sally and Matthew provided a mini firework display once it grew dark and again the older guests could watch from the comfort of their chairs while the younger element huddled together outside in a steam of exhaled breath, their screams of delight muffled to a bearable level. My presence in the wrong generation was hidden behind my duties as nominal host.

A game of musical statues brought everyone together inside again and once more I was elected to watch for unwary movements when the music stopped. Joel contrived to be eliminated first and spent his time outside the competition, contorting his body into absurd positions to tempt the statues out of their own immobility.

It was with genuine regret that we said our farewells at 10 that night. For a last Christmas, it had been one of the best. I wished I could have expressed my gratitude to these special people who had masterminded each step to perfection, but any kind of speech would have undone all their efforts to avoid sadness or comparisons. Besides I could not have got through it myself.

Thank you cards will have to suffice. Tomorrow.

It had been good. Good for her too. She'd been so impressed by Joel. Early in

December he'd rung her, fearlessly addressing the issue of this being Adam's last Christmas. Hearing her distress, he'd quietly taken charge and devised a plan to make it a day of fun and enjoyment, even going to the trouble of checking out his ideas with various experts in MND to ensure he wasn't doing more harm than good.

'Thank you so much, Joel. What would I do without you?'

'It's the least I can do. Look what you're doing for my brother, day in, day out.'

'But it helps enormously, knowing you're there when I need you.'

'Remember then: it's a pact. No sentimentality; bags of hilarity. If you concentrate on the kitchen-side, I'll do the old MC bit. And if either of us smells a difficult moment coming up, it's a competition to see who can raise a laugh faster. Bet you a tenner I win!'

'I'd bet you a tenner you'd win too!'

'Spoilsport! Where's your competitive edge?'

In the event, the sheer busyness of the carefully choreographed day had effectively eliminated those dreaded moments when thoughts were in danger of slipping their leash. Adam had indeed sent them both cards – with extravagant bouquets. It was comforting to know that, though he'd been aware of their tactics, he'd been grateful rather than resentful.

She re-read his diary entry. Yes, Joel should see this section.

29 DECEMBER—I know I'm falling behind with my diary during these action-packed days. It's frustrating, because I'm conscious that my memory for the detail is not as accurate two days later, but nowadays I just can't deal with the battle of the day and then write all evening.

Boxing Day was in danger of being an anti-climax. We used to go for a long walk in the countryside to counteract the excesses of the 25th, but for obvious reasons that wasn't on the cards this year. Only Joel and Paige were left and I didn't want to limit their activities, so it was in my mind to pretend that I desperately needed to get the next instalment of my book down before I forgot what had come to me during the night, leaving them free to go out together or with Naomi.

But Joel had an ace up his sleeve. Soon after our embarrassingly late breakfast, the door of the sitting room suddenly flew open and my brother sprang in with a 'Dunn-de-da-da-daaaaaaaaaaaa!' and a state-of- the-art wheelchair. In the nick of time I grabbed the bar on my zimmer and stopped myself from falling sideways.

'Whoops! Sorry bro!'

We must have presented a comical picture; me stooping low over my frame, Joel complete with red wig, white coat and stethoscope gripping me round the waist and propelling me back towards my chair. I sank into it gratefully, glad there were no other witnesses to my weakness.

'What on earth are you up to *this* time?' I asked him, eying his clothing with some alarm.

'Apart from trying to destabilise you, you mean?'

'Apart from that, yes.'

'Ahhaaaa. Come in, handmaidens!'

I have to admit Paige and Naomi made comely figures dressed as Barbara-Windsor-type nurses, although under normal circumstances I would be the first to decry the stereotyping of professional women. Naomi advanced threateningly with a giant syringe. I cowered into my seat. Giggling helplessly Paige flourished a bedpan and a floating roll of toilet paper. I put up my hands to ward her off and whimpered piteously.

'Brilliant. We'll win hands-down,' Joel crowed.

'Win? Win what?' I demanded, instantly all suspicion.

'The Boxing Day race.'

'You aren't serious...'

'Indeed I am. Worthy cause. No excuses. Four adults with nothing better to do. We'll be there.'

'Hang on a minute. Slow down. I need more information.'

Nothing I could offer would dissuade Joel from his chosen path. By 1.55PM we were in that line-up waiting for the starter gun, the girls shivering in their skimpy dresses, me wedged into that wheelchair, sweltering, between them.

Joel had decreed that I should be permitted to wear three layers of woollies under the ancient but enormous stripy pyjamas he'd obtained from some second-hand shop. ('They've been washed, Mr Fusspot!' he assured me before I would even touch them.) But I still felt incredibly vulnerable perched in an unfamiliar form of locomotion with him at the controls, and horribly conspicuous surrounded by his sound effects: blaring horn, revving engine, squealing brakes. Even more astonishingly, Naomi and Paige showed no vestige of embarrassment as my fawning attendants, and there must be many a household who will drool over their charms if the flashing cameras were indicative of anything.

In a trial run down our drive I had been adamant on one point; I must be strapped in in some way if Joel was indeed bent on winning. Having anticipated some qualms on my part, he obligingly produced a hefty belt hung about with huge padlocks that meant I'd probably have to be sawn out of the blessed contraption in the event of an accident.

The competition looked formidable. Beds, wheelbarrows, trikes, prams – anything with wheels was permissible. There was even a cardboard car placed over two skateboards tied together. The costumes were sufficiently inventive and comical that I had actually forgotten my imminent danger when the starter struck up, '*On* your marks, get set...'

It's an annual event, in aid of a charity – this year, childhood leukaemia. We've watched it from the sidelines on previous occasions, we've financially supported it every year, but this was our first time as participants.

I don't recall ever being so petrified. Joel's 'It'll be a laugh,' only applied to himself. I spent every second of that reckless ride praying. Thanks to the belt (by now festooned with flashing fairy lights!) and my white-knuckle grip, I managed to remain physically in the chair but Joel gave no concessions to bumps or potholes or pavement edges. He had one goal in mind: winning! My disability was forgotten. Since I did, miraculously, survive, I lived to be grateful that he *could* forget it for that brief crazy time.

He insisted on wheeling me up to the improvised dais to collect second prize. I was mortified to find, when the local paper came out yesterday, that I'd had a soppy grin on my face. I can only continue to pray that Harry *et al* are a) above looking at the local rag or b) don't recognise me behind that gruesome wig, red nose and white face-paint.

What happened next took me by storm, but I am so exhausted by these past few days that I can't record it tonight.

30 DECEMBER—Joel's enthusiasm and drive got me through the rest of that day but by 7 I was aching all over. Just holding my head up required a monumental effort. In the end, there was nothing for it but to concede defeat. Joel joked his way through manoeuvring me into the bedroom but Naomi was pretty subdued getting me undressed and into bed.

It's a mercy that Joel was still here to lift her into a brighter mood again afterwards; I hate to be putting a dampener on her life. I told her twice I'd be fine after a good night's sleep. And I exaggerated the terror of that wheelchair ride to excuse my present state, putting all the blame at Joel's door. Unfair I know, but the least of all evils.

It was true, Adam had belittled the consequences but the gritted teeth, the tension around his eyes, the rigidity of his legs, his dead-weight, had told another story. Joel had been devastated, blaming himself. She reassured him, it had been exactly what Adam needed: a glorious few hours of normality, no concessions. To her chagrin, as she spoke, her composure crumpled and for the first time they clung to each other, appalled by the reality of what was happening to Adam. The bleakness obliterated any remaining pretence and together they faced what lay ahead and planned a strategy.

But how had Adam perceived it?

Joel really is incorrigible. A bright beacon in this gathering storm. He refuses to let this thing defeat us. And he's so completely unsentimental about it. Makes a joke about even the beastliest things.

What a tonic!

Naomi stopped reading again. Joel had been incredible. Maybe he deserved even greater credit than she'd given him. It had given her a warm glow to see the brothers together. Joel could take liberties not available to her. And his new-found maturity had made her see him in a completely different light.

She sat for a long time, just staring at the screen.

The good night's sleep didn't materialise, thanks in no small measure to the ghastly jolting, I suspect, and the strain of holding myself in that chair, but I kidded on that I was a new man next morning. And as long as I sat in the high-backed seat and kept my head supported I could just about concentrate on the conversation.

I'd understood both our guests were leaving on 30th but it transpired that only Paige was. She had to get back to work, having already taken a bonus day.

'Accountants! Her boss doesn't understand about hangovers,' Joel grumbled.

'*Somebody* needs to keep the wheels of society turning while you lay-abouts watch the world go by,' she retorted with an affectionate grin.

Joel, who has a propensity to work twenty-hour days keeping his computing business on its high-speed rails, pulled a face at her and turned the conversation back to which marmalade he was having this morning. Naomi is something of a preserver and keeps us supplied with jams and marmalades of varying degrees of exoticness, so the choice is rather more complicated and serious than he is used to.

I was sorry to see Paige go. She's great fun and good to talk to. And I'd say she's a good influence on my erstwhile lunatic brother. While Joel ran her to the station, Naomi ran the vacuum cleaner round the downstairs rooms. I had elected to sort through the piles of papers and magazines and post that had accumulated but I must have dozed off, because I didn't hear him return.

When I did surface I could hear murmurings from the kitchen and when I staggered through, Naomi and he were perched on the high stools having a coffee. They were instantly all concern when they saw me but I honestly did feel better for the nap. And by the time I'd raised my caffeine levels, I was much more myself again.

'So what's on the agenda today?' I asked. 'It's far too nice to be idle.' The winter sun was glinting on the frosted leaves and the last ribbons of mist were vanishing from the valley.

'Eeeh by gum, lad, tha's a glutton for punishment, is tha,' Joel said.

'Can't keep a good man down.'

'What d'you feel like doing? I'm at your disposal.'

'I feel like a good old tramp in the winter wonderland but the old legs have a different agenda.' I kept it light. I think.

'Nae probs!'

Joel was off the stool and bounding from the room. Naomi and I looked at each other and she shrugged her shoulders. 'Don't ask me!'

Next minute Joel was at the door.

'Your chariot awaits. Let's go, bro!'

'You have to be kidding! Subject myself to a repeat of yesterday? I'd have to be insane as well as disabled!'

'Scout's honour,' – he did the salute – 'No alarms. No breaking the speed limit. Granny-pace all the way. Detours around every speck of gravel. Rolls Royce of a ride. Promise.'

I looked from him to the wheelchair and back.

'Where did you get that thing from, anyway?'

'Friends in high places. Nothing that a little bribery and corruption won't obtain. And a smidgeon of the O'Neill charm.'

'Seriously, idiot. Is it stolen property?'

'Insulting as well as ungrateful, huh? I don't know why you put up with such a curmudgeon, Nay. Run away with *me*.'

She hopped into the chair and he was off, leaving me alone and instantly in a better mood.

By the time they returned, I'd managed to lean more comfortably against the work-surface and the change of weight-bearing relieved the pain in my back for a time.

'Okay, your turn, Adam. You can vouch for my expert handling of this contraption, can't you, Naomi?'

'Indeed I can.'

Still I hesitated.

'Go on! Where's your spirit of adventure? Naomi wants to go out. I want to go out. You want to go out. He, she and it want to go out. It's a beautiful day; just the kind you've always liked; deep and crisp and even. And I for one am raring to go.'

It took another thirty minutes to get me ready, and I was craven enough to insist on a solemn promise that he really would go carefully, before I let myself be eased into that chair. I also confessed to the problem with my neck. Between them they managed to hedge me about with pillows and sheepskins, and adjust the headrest to be an excellent support.

It was well worth the sunk pride. The stark trees were etched in white, the leaves crunched beneath my wheels, our breath threaded through the still air like chiffon scarves, and Joel manhandled my chariot with consummate care. We stopped at a little café for farmhouse soup and crusty bread and a legitimate excuse to attend to my personal needs.

The break gave me space to notice that Naomi had some colour back in her cheeks and a smile back in her eyes. I've been growing increasingly disturbed by her habitually drawn look. She needs Joel too.

She took over pushing my chair on one of the straight runs but I was instantly tense. In the intimate departments, if I *have* to accept help, she's my choice every time; but for the heavy-duty stuff, nope. I don't want her injuring herself. Or our unborn child.

Maybe I ought to take up Curtis's offer of that nurse. Maybe.

Noelani, curled up in her lap, stretched her legs out expansively and Naomi felt the sharp claws nick her skin. She stroked the warm fur back into a soporific purr, her own tension easing marginally in the process.

She'd done her best to be subtle about it, and as she put her hand on the wheelchair, Joel had launched into a monologue about a New Year resolution he intended to make. But Adam wasn't fooled. He'd turned immediately, in spite of the obvious pain involved, and given her a speaking look. When Joel eventually shut up, he'd questioned her strength, her stamina, her ability to bear his weight. It wasn't a strain but she heard his resistance.

Lydia might have a solution.

Thankfully Joel took over again as soon as we started to go uphill. It seemed to be a mutually agreed thing; no discussion.

My concern for Naomi notwithstanding, the walk was a vast improvement on being cooped up inside. The feel of the crisp air in my lungs, the constantly changing views, all without any effort on my part. It was a surprisingly smooth ride too – or was this only in contrast with yesterday's nightmare? Having Joel there to accompany me to the gents was a bonus. In an unguarded moment I told him so, and he was in there like a flash.

'I'll come up as often as I can.'

I instantly retracted and told him it was completely unnecessary, I'd manage.

'Even if you don't need it, Naomi does,' he said simply.

I stared at him.

'You know I'm right. So, no arguments. I'll be up.' I opened my mouth to protest further but he cut me dead. 'Besides, don't you think I want to do something. You're my one and only brother, for heaven's sake.'

Maybe I do need help to get around now, but I'm sure I could manage to steer myself if I had something motorised. And we could get these portable ramps (I'll even check them out in Ursula Major's wretched catalogues); then I can get in and out of the house myself. I needn't put demands on Naomi. I needn't disrupt Joel's life.

But this is a warning. I need to stay one jump ahead of them. They caught me on the back foot this time; I wasn't prepared for the wheelchair sneaking in under false pretences. I do not want other people to hurry me on to the next stage. This is the rest of my life we're talking about here. It's my fight.

It'll be like preparing for battle: getting inside the heads of the enemy; divining their next move, thwarting their plans. Deciding myself when I need what. I'll be the Lieutenant Colonel. Flamboyant red punctuating the black.

Naomi drew back from the screen.

'Oh, Adam. If you'd only known!'

It was one thing knowing how much he rebelled against Ursula Major's pressures, and the specialist nurse's take-over bid, quite another matter to see herself as 'the enemy'. It had been so hard not to go to his aid. Finding acceptable ways of helping taxed her ingenuity. It was Joel who had hit upon this particular master-stroke. The much-maligned Ursula and Lydia had acquired the wheelchair and arranged for its delivery to the surgery, storing it until Joel could collect it, take instruction in its use, secrete it away at the back of the garage over Christmas. Naomi had decorated it with balloons and lights for the race so that the first time Adam saw it, its true function was disguised.

She smiled ruefully, thinking of Lydia's horror had she seen Adam being jolted at breakneck speed over the race-course. But the very unsuitability of this initiation had been the camouflage to smuggle in serious assistance. And thanks to Joel's quick thinking, the transition had been achieved with all the appearance of respectable serendipity.

She closed her eyes, shutting out Adam's rebellion.

'Thank you, Joel. You're a star,' she whispered.

31 DECEMBER—The end of 2007. A day when I feel as if I'm saying goodbye, not to a year, but to my life.

A year ago I was relying on a snippet of lingerie and a quick wit to get me through the tricky moments as the year died; today I'm relying on Joel. I'm not sure if his extended stay is to support Naomi, or because he thinks he won't see me again, or what. I daren't ask. I hate seeing her so pale and tired, knowing I am the root cause. I hate seeing him changing from being my lunatic kid brother because of me. They are my links with the me I used to be, and for my sanity I need them to stay a step outside the life I know now. But there is no escape for Naomi while I live, and Joel's just reminded me that she needs him to be tuned into the trauma, to stand behind her, perhaps even alongside her, in the safety net.

Would it be easier to have the MND nurse…?

Maybe. No! She'll have me mutilating my beautiful house with ugly stair-lifts and double handrails. Turn me into a certified invalid. A wheelchair today; a hoist next month... where will it all end?

This is not good. I need to be robust for midnight.

Even Aidan is adding to my melancholy. His story used to be my salvation; no longer. I'm only a few chapters from the finale. The end is in sight – in both senses. But his death throes have become mine. I don't want to let go of him. I want to howl at the futility of it all. But I cannot – *must* not – inflict my grief for him onto Naomi; she has sorrow enough of her own.

Early evening I had to get out of the house.

Joel fell in with my plan with alacrity and managed to turn the whole thing into a dangerous undercover escapade. He drove us to the supermarket and we invested in some decent bubbly and some nibbles. And a vast bouquet of seasonal flowers and berries for Naomi. It was my first time there in a wheelchair but he loaded me up with the shopping so that I looked more like a trolley than a customer.

Julie from down the road was the only person we met whom I knew and she was polite enough not to comment.

'Well done for the Boxing Day race!' she said. 'We were over at the in-laws on the 26th but I saw your picture in the paper. Looked like a lot of fun.'

'Totally,' Joel said smugly. 'And did you hear what we raised? We, as in everybody, of course. Two thousand five hundred and twenty-three pounds and four pence! And if I discover who magnanimously contributed that four pence, I'll personally reimburse him!'

We all grinned and parted with good wishes for the New Year. Even that rang hollowly. Good wishes for... what? An easy death? A quick end? I know she wasn't even thinking of it. What else can people say?

Joel prattled on cheerfully all the way home. There was so much I wanted to say to him; nothing I could say. Not if I'm to get through this.

Now I've written it down I'm hoping I can let it rest and go out into this last evening of 2007 with a blank slate. I want the two people I love best in the world to remember the occasion with pride.

Naomi's precarious composure could take no more. She buried her face on her arms there in front of his diary and wept for all he had lost.

2 JANUARY 2008 — I was too raw to even enter my study yesterday. Today I need to cleanse my mind and regroup, ready for the rest of my life.

Naomi is out at the sales; the house is mine. If I scream and howl, there is no one to hear me.

Mother declined our invitation to see the New Year in with us.

Standard excuses: she can't cope with late nights – never could; she doesn't support heathen traditions like Hogmanay. I half-wondered whether she might make an exception this year, but no. Joel popped over to see her at around 8, but I couldn't face her.

Is there no end to my brother's ingenuity? With fifteen minutes left of the old year, he suddenly produced paper and pens.

'You'll have the advantage here, Adam, words being the tools of your trade. I guess I ought to handicap you, but since I'm in Santa-Claus-mode tonight, I'll be generous. At the top of your sheet you'll see 'NEW YEAR' written. When I say, 'Go,' you have to start writing down all the words, three letters or more, you can make out of those letters. I'll leave the TV on low to be sure we hear the bells at midnight and at that precise moment it's pens down. The person who has the most words by then is the winner. *Legitimate* words, mind you, Mr Clever Clogs, and you can bet your life, if I smell a rat, I'll look yours up in the Oxford Dictionary. On your marks, go!'

That fourteen minutes or so passed like so many seconds. As Big Ben struck, we all shrieked, 'Happy New Year!' and exchanged the obligatory embraces, but were then instantly catapulted into wrangling over spellings and the authenticity of the more outlandish offerings. It was perfect. Not because I won the competition, but because Joel beat the odds for us all.

Soon after that he went to bed leaving a strange silence behind him. Naomi broke it.

'It's a fabulous night. Look.'

With difficulty, I turned in my chair to face the garden. It was bathed in milky moonlight, not a breath of wind stirring the trees. The glow of the fairy-lights Joel had hung round our solitary outside Christmas tree was softened by a slight mistiness. As I looked, a lone fox stole out of the shadows and stood staring brazenly back at us. Both he and I seemed to hold our breath.

With his departure, I turned back without a word and held out my hand to Naomi. Though she responded instantly, kneeling beside my chair, her head against my side, she contrived to keep her eyes averted from mine.

'Thanks, Naomi... for everything.'

I couldn't continue. She couldn't reply.

Weeping together brought us closer together in that poignant moment at the start of my last year than any brave pretence could. We stayed awake talking well into the small hours.

After all the excitement of the past few days and the emotional trauma of the night, I was feeling pretty fragile when I eventually dragged myself through the shower this morning.

I was dreading saying goodbye to Joel.

He'd already breakfasted and was muffled in his coat and scarf when I appeared.

'What kind of an hour, d'you call this?' he asked, tapping his watch and glaring at me in mock reproach.

'Civilised?' I ventured.

'Positively countrified! No wonder we city slickers call this the backwoods.'

'Since when did you become a lark?' I retorted.

'Since the New Year!'

Under cover of the laughter, he advanced and took me in a bear hug, talking all the time.

'I leave it to you to coax my renegade brother into the middle lane of life in my absence, Naomi, and for goodness' sake get him into something more respectable before polite society gets a glimpse of him!'

I glanced down involuntarily at my loose trousers and polo-neck jumper. He had a point. But before I could form a reply, he had hugged Naomi and departed with a wave and a sepulchral, 'I'll be back'. It was on the tip of my tongue to respond, 'I may be gone some time', but the connotations hit me in time to bite it back.

A tyre track was all that was left by the time we got to the door.

It was impossible to fill the void alone.

Naomi coped by tackling the debris of celebration. I did my best to clear out the grate but succeeded only in getting ash all over the carpet, and was forced to abandon the attempt.

'Give me a sit-down job, Naomi,' I pleaded.

I got the sprouts, carrots and potatoes on a lap tray. Even the basics take forever these days.

Plenty of time to reflect. Too much.

'What d'you think of Paige?' I called through to her.

'I liked her.'

'She and Joel seem pretty close.'

'Yes. And she must be keen, coming up here for Christmas.'

I had my own ideas about that. Why do you ask a girl to see for herself your brother's got a crippling disease, to find out about the family history of depression, suicide, religious fervour? Not exactly a pretty backcloth to romance. Is it testing time before he lets himself get serious?

'Joel's changed.' I said.

'Mmmmmhhhm.'

'D'you think she's right for him?' I persisted.

'Who knows?'

I must write that card to him today. I owe him, big time.

Joel had assumed that she'd ordered the crate of vintage wine but she'd known nothing about it. The handwriting in the card that arrived two days later, though, that was unmistakably Adam's: 'For my favourite brother. Thanks for transforming the season.'

He'd choked over the words, repeating them on the phone.

'You know what kills me? Thinking... this is the last time... for everything.'

3 JANUARY—Is it time to relinquish ties with work?

Every year there's a bit of a bash to celebrate the end of another productive year; a chance for the riff-raff to hob-nob with the elite, a touch of mutual back-slapping, that kind of thing. This year's bonding was scheduled for a posh hotel in the centre of town. Ground-floor access. All on one level. Ideal. Naomi came with me, so no difficulties about getting there, and I used her as my support to avoid the problem of negotiating a crowded room. So far so good.

Naomi doesn't often accompany me to work functions – we're both so busy there isn't time to duplicate effort – so loads of people stopped to speak to her, which meant our progress was painfully slow, even for me. Standing, bearing my own weight – she knows it's a problem! Why couldn't she remember it? Even holding my head up is an effort these days. But have you ever tried walking into a party and saying, 'Mine's a double whisky and a neck brace'? I spent my time propping my chin on one hand or leaning against the wall.

At our table there was the customary banter you get with a gathering of wordsmiths, but I became increasingly aware that the conversation was carrying on around me not with me. When I did speak, they didn't seem to pick up what I was saying. I know my voice is weaker these days; I didn't realise how pathetic I must sound. I can't compete with the racket of a crowd any more. A sobering epiphany: the party – life – carrying on without me. Naomi reckons they were only trying to save me the effort of raising my voice. I say they were ignoring me. It's probably impossible for them to get it right but I haven't the space to make concessions on behalf of people for whom everything is so easy.

I sneaked a look at some old videos this morning. I needed to know I was once a normal bloke with a normal voice and a normal walk and a normal zest for life. Once upon a time.

I was. But it just made the reality of today even worse.

I've made an appointment to see Arkwright later this week.

Naomi slumped back in the chair. The tragedy of his deterioration had struck her forcibly that night. She too had seen the discomfort, the uncertainty, around him. It had been a turning point for them both. She hadn't forgotten his problem remaining upright. She hadn't. Intuition clamoured: whisk him away to the relative comfort of home, bolster his self-esteem by concentrating on what he can still do. Logic denied her: he must set his own pace. He's always wanted that.

Adam had been so quiet on the return journey. Only later had the flood-gates opened as he poured out his despair. She'd listened in appalled silence. Until he got to the subject of the deterioration in their sex life.

'Oh, come on!' she interrupted. 'You ought to be mighty thankful we don't need any outside help for that! I saw a film once where somebody had to wait at the door to go in at strategic moments to give a disabled couple a hand. We haven't come to that, at least.'

And how empty the nights were now, without him.

'Oh Adam! I miss you so much! The sound of your laughter... the twitch of your eyebrow just before some silly wisecrack ... the look in your eyes as you reach across to touch my face ... your fingers walking down the bones of my spine, slowly, one by one... the warmth of your body... Oh, how I miss you. The real you.'

4 JANUARY—Life stinks. I hate what's happening to me. Hate it, hate it, *HATE* it! I'm sorely tempted to hop on a plane to Switzerland tomorrow. But I know in myself that I haven't reached my own nadir yet. My novel isn't finished, I'm not ready to say goodbye to Naomi... or Joel. And yet objectively, I must meet the clinic's criteria: an incurable illness, a sustained desire to die, fully mentally competent. Some of their clients have had nothing more life-threatening than epilepsy or diabetes. But... if diabetes is an intolerable burden for you... Curtis, where are you?

These clinics apparently have hundreds registered, booked in way ahead of time. Should the patient always know best? I read somewhere they're thinking of making it obligatory for foreigners to have lived in their country for at least a year before they're eligible for assisted suicide. You can see the rationale, but what a hassle! I'd sooner park my car on a railway crossing here.

Maybe the powers that be in this country will take pity on people in my predicament soon. It may be a criminal act to assist someone to commit suicide at the moment – you risk fourteen years in prison – but the Assisted Dying Bill keeps coming up for debate. They won't give up on this one; the argument for it is too strong. It's no longer the tiptoe of the tiny minority. And much as I want to see it passed, I'm all in favour of caution. It has to be carefully regulated. We don't want some half-baked plan, botched jobs, general fear and mayhem all round – although I'm not about to concede that to Curtis just yet!

What makes life intolerable? At what point in my illness does my decision become fixed? I conceded a point to Curtis when he called in casually.

'I hate to admit this, Doc, but you were right.' I slurred.

'Goodness. Are you ill?' He grinned. 'On which subject exactly did I reach a pass mark?'

'The goalposts changing.'

'Ah, yes.'

'But I still think it has to be my decision.'

He simply waited; no chivvying, no filling in my sentences for me. That's worth a lot these days.

'Somebody else inside my disintegrating body might say, "I don't want to go on." Pretty much anybody thinking about my problems might say, "That's intolerable." But when will it be intolerable for me?'

'Time for me to say, "Only you can say," huh?'

'Steady now! Let's not start out-conceding each other! Where will it all end?'

He laughed, looking suddenly much younger.

'If I keep procrastinating, I'm in danger of losing that window of opportunity for being able to do it myself.'

He just nodded.

'I haven't the strength and courage to fight the medical and legal establishments. Nor the time.'

'Hopefully it won't come to that.'

There was a long pause – tolerable between old friends.

'You were right about the things I might want to live for. My book, Naomi, Joel, children.'

'Mmmmhmm.'

'Gee whiz, all this… and no argument? You sickening for something?'

'I'm just enjoying the peace and harmony while I may. Unless I'm much mistaken, we haven't finished yet.'

I sighed.

'Spot on. We come to the little matter of implementing that decision… when the time comes.'

'You can refuse treatment, remember.'

'But your mighty ethical consciences would still baulk at anything more than that.'

'Well, maybe not. Ahha! I thought that might take you by surprise! Let's say something happened and you needed emergency life-saving treatment. If they knew your expressed wishes – documented preferably – two doctors might agree that, given the prognosis and the effects of the disease itself, it's perhaps best not to initiate that treatment.'

'Would you be prepared to go along with that? Not treating, I mean.'

'In the right circumstances, yes, I would.'

'Strange that. I'd have thought that people like you would find it incredibly hard to just stand there, doing nothing, and watch someone you've taken care of just… die.'

'Oh, I didn't say we'd do nothing. We'd do something. We'd pull out all the stops to ensure your dignity and comfort.'

Curiously, I liked the way he didn't try to de-personalise this.

'I don't know how these nurses I see in hospitals and Homes do the things they do. There's no way I would ever want to clean up the backside of some doubly incontinent stranger, or mop up the vomit, or even trim their toe nails. These folk have to really care about people. And surely if they couldn't let them lie in excrement, they couldn't stand by and just let somebody die who might be saved… could they?'

'If there's a clear and sustained wish for non-intervention in the case of advanced and degenerative disease, yes. They can and do. That's not to say they wouldn't feel sad about it. Maybe even regret it.'

'Fair enough.'

'Can I put a different scenario to you?' Curtis said after a brief pause.

'Fire away.'

'Imagine you're lying there unable to communicate but you can hear what's happening around you. The doctors hover just outside the door of your room…'

'Good. You've given me a private room I see. Thanks, Doc.'

'No problem. I'll try to remember to pull a few strings, when the time comes.'

'I'll thank you now, then, in anticipation.'

He grinned broadly.

'Where was I before I was so rudely interrupted?'

'The doctors are hovering outside my palatial suite of rooms…' I said in my best story-telling voice.

'Yes, right. And you hear them say, "It's not worth doing anything for this guy. Just let him go. He's better off dead." How would you feel?'

'Vexed that my taxes had helped to train such an insensitive moron.'

'Indeed! But after that?'

I pondered the thought.

'Would I mind someone else agreeing that my life is worthless? I don't know. I'd feel a bit of a reject, maybe. So does this mean I secretly want people like you to refuse to let me die because you value me too highly? I'll need to think about that one.'

I have a sneaking feeling that there's a flaw in this thinking somewhere but I can't afford to be deflected too far from my principal question. No doubt Fuggins would have spotted it. He knew two and two didn't equal five in real life.

'Hold on a minute! I don't want to die from inactivity. By default. I want an active decision to be made. A logical, rational, thought-through decision.'

'I know. Hence the terrier instinct!'

'And suddenly you're not with me.' It was said entirely without rancour.

'Well... that would depend.'

I stared at him for a long moment.

'Don't tell me you're actually relenting.'

'Not relenting exactly. Exploring the possibilities, maybe.'

'Well, hallelujah!'

'Time changes the situation,' he said quietly. 'For me as well as for you.'

'Are we talking about helping me?'

'I am. And I presumed you were, yes?'

'Yes. So... I'm suspicious now. Are you saying that you might... help me?'

'I want to help, yes. That was always my intention. Now you're talking about a point much nearer a natural end, I'm qualifying my earlier response.'

'Ahhah. The careful obfuscation we know and love!'

He laughed aloud.

'So you're not agreeing to give me a generous gift of morphine to send me on my way rejoicing?'

'When I was a kid I liked surprise presents. My parents didn't ask me what I wanted. I was grateful for what I was given. And strangely enough they seemed to know what I'd like. I guess old habits die hard.'

Like I say, this man is good for my health.

Thinking in this focused way about death-bed scenarios led me to my mother. I can't see why she's so hell-bent on hanging on to this life when she believes there's something better to come. I tried asking her once but she just said, 'Adam! Don't be so irreverent. God wouldn't like to hear you questioning His judgment. He decides.' Maybe I'll ask the local man of the cloth, next time he comes, to pray for me to find a way through this. Nothing to lose.

'How could you... persist so?' Naomi said out loud.

Exhausted by the sheer effort of daily living, when it took him over two hours to shower and dress, when simply holding his head up required a monumental effort, he still had the capacity to engage with these issues, record his thinking so... so coherently. And yet he'd so seldom shared his preoccupation with her?

'Forgive me, Adam. Forgive me.'

5 JANUARY—Sigh. Yesterday I thought I'd got things sussed. Finally. Today a brief letter to one of our competition newspapers has made me slither sideways on that proverbial slippery slope. Damn it!

It's by some academic who's spent his life in a wheelchair. He's already in his seventies but he really, really wants to go on living. He's got some elaborate system in place which means no one else can say he'd be better off dead, let's not resuscitate him, or let's not give him food and drink; it'd be a kindness to let him go. If anybody manages to avoid all his documents and directives and his army of advocates, his relations are primed to hound them through the courts. However, if everyone agrees he's past saving, then death is to be swift and painless. The whole shebang signed and sealed by his own hand.

You have to admire his sheer... well, I don't know... grit? Bloody-minded determination? Here he is, a man who's obviously had his fair share of difficulties in life, but he reckons his quality of life is good and he doesn't want it ended a nanosecond sooner than it ought to be, and he doesn't want somebody who doesn't know the inside him to decide when that moment has come.

His bigger contention is that there is too much time and attention devoted to endlessly debating euthanasia and assisted suicide issues; efforts ought to be concentrated on providing robust support for folk like him, giving them as much control, as much say, as much independence, as possible. Hhhhmmmm. But he roundly denounces platitudes about the value of counselling and sensory rooms and Rich Tea biscuits. Amen to that!

I had my meeting with Arkwright yesterday. That man is a real gent. He went through the motions of trying to get me to change my mind about handing in my resignation, but then, when he saw I was resolute, he offered me open-house, basically. Write as often as you like as much as you like. We'll pay you handsomely; consultancy rates.

I came out of that meeting feeling like a winner. I'm going to be free of meetings and administrative slog. Free from Harry! And free from the pressure of deadlines. But free to write creatively, as and when. And what's more, Arkwright's going to talk to Harry himself. Oh to be the proverbial fly on the wall!

It was something of a dampener finding my mother in full war-cry when I got home from that meeting. I swear I smelt the tension the minute I opened the door.

Mother thinks decorating our house for the festive season is an affectation – especially the use of natural things like cones and fir that maliciously shed their component parts and leave a legacy to be found months later. Decorations – if you must have them – are for children, in her book, and should be one hundred per cent synthetic. She restricts herself to a solitary string of cards across one wall of her living room. That's the sum total of her extravagance. And the sum total of her friends.

So the big binge-clean yesterday and today has been a poultice on a fermenting carbuncle. Today was eruption day. In a curious way I'm grateful. It's a relief to know that she can still allow herself to be annoyed with me.

I sneaked into my study initially but my conscience eventually drove me out to join her in a coffee. It's our mess, not hers. After a few false starts I told her I was leaving work. She was slicing off the unused pieces of a4 white paper from my scrap tray when I said this and her scissors cut the paper – and the silence – viciously.

'Oh dear,' she said, not looking at me.

'I want to conserve my energy to finish off other things while I still can.'

'What kind of... things?' She seemed to be holding her breath.

'My novel.'

'Oh.'

'It makes sense to take the pressure off.'

'And when you've finished that book, what then?'

Ahhah. I see where she's going!

'Get it published. I hope. Make decisions – about the cover; about the blurb; about the marketing. Maybe even sign a few first editions. Who knows?'

She was gathering the scrap paper together, hitting the table with the edges as she sought in vain to tidy an ill-assorted bundle of hacked ends. This predilection for saving paper drives me insane but it suits her notion of economy and I hesitate to take away such an insignificant source of satisfaction.

'So you aren't still thinking of taking the law into your own hands then?' The words came out like hailstones.

Okay, I know she's angry with my father for dying, angry with his manner of dying anyway, and I do try to let that knowledge soften my own irritation with her but...

'Not at the moment. No.'

'You've got to think of Joel too. He looks up to you. He needs you to set a good example.' A new tack.

'I doubt it actually. He's all grown up now, got his own ideas.'

'Well, you boys always did gang up together.' I'm not sure what she means but I have to divert the incoming tide.

'I will say this, Mum: you should be proud of him. He was fantastic over Christmas, and a real help to Naomi.'

I made my excuses and hid in the study again, earphones blasting Debussy's best to shut out the concerto of angry steel and maternal frustration outside.

7 JANUARY—Curtis rang this morning after surgery and asked if he could pop in once he'd done his house calls; he had a book he'd value my opinion on.

He seemed in no hurry, lolling back in the chair, turning his enquiries as to my health into an exchange between friends rather than a medical inquisition. And as ever he listened intently to the answers. It crossed my mind that maybe he was needing to concentrate harder to understand what I was saying but not once did he ask me to repeat myself. I could almost see him going down his little checklist to reassure himself they were doing everything they could. Maybe assessing my mental state too. Who knows? He's more aware of my internal struggle than anyone else anyway.

After an excellent discussion on the literary merits of fiction as a vehicle for conveying serious opinion, he surprised me suddenly by saying he looked forward to using my book as a text with his students. I confess I didn't know he taught at the University – where does a busy GP find the time? But I'm flattered.

We've agreed a rough timetable for him to see the manuscript and give me his expert opinion.

8 JANUARY—My last few waltzes with Lydia have been rather subdued affairs. There's something missing. I can't forget she's grieving, and I'm so afraid I'll touch her wounds. Today however, she greeted me with a wide smile and a hearty, 'Happy New Year, Mister O!' and as soon as I was safely seated she was into expansive Jamaican mode.

'You sure did knock them for six with that jet-propelled wheelchair.'

I grinned back at her.

'You were there? You saw us?'

'In the flesh, honey. In the flesh.'

'But why didn't you come and speak to us? I could have introduced you to my brother.'

'And those nurses! Would I be right in thinking one of them was the little lady?'

'The dark haired one. That's Naomi.'

'Well! Well! Well!'

'But where were you?'

'Me? D'you recall number twelve? The giant-size frog and the floating lily pad?'

'You weren't...?'

'Indeed I was, honey. Ribbet! Ribbet!'

'I wish I'd known.'

'No, sir! I only said yes to my boys on the understanding nobody could see it was me.'

'Brilliant.'

'But, what I want to know, honestly now, is how did you cope with your bones being shaken out of your skin?' She was looking at me intently now, her verbal disguise forgotten in the professional concern. 'I've got a whole lot more padding than you and I know my teeth were rattling in my head!'

'I was terrified out of my skull and in agony. It took me days to recover from the aching. But I wouldn't have changed a thing!'

She listened without interruption as I outlined some of the ways in which Joel and Naomi had made it a memorable Christmas.

'You're impressive yourself,' she said quietly. 'It takes real courage to face this in the way you're doing.'

'No. Without them I'd have been a wreck this Christmas.'

She reached out to lay a warm hand over mine. There was a long pause and then she was briskly back into the safety of her craft. I needed every ounce of concentration to do the exercises she demanded of me.

What a huge debt they both owed this fantastic woman, Naomi thought. Would it be a violation of Adam's privacy to copy out some quotes from the diary to capture his admiration and affection? Could she herself bear to share anything of this personal legacy?

She resolved to consult Joel. He should certainly know how much Adam had seen his hand at work and what it had meant to him.

10 JANUARY — What a fiendish few days. What wouldn't I give to have my old strength and mobility back – just until this is over.

Mother has had a massive stroke. No warning. One minute she was there, driving me crazy with her obsessions; next minute she's lying in a hospital bed unconscious. Unable to decide even her own fate, never mind mine.

The worst thing about it is the loss of communication. We can talk to her, hold her hand, but even if she does feel or hear (as they say she might), she can't send a message back. Not by any route. I'm doing my best to reach her but there's a limit to how many hours you can natter on to someone who's lying there drooling, breathing like a steam train, oblivious.

Telling Joel over the phone made the actual happening real. Standing at her bedside, looking down at the wreckage, my brain is starting to take in the wider implications. But somehow my emotions aren't engaging with the facts – yet. I don't know if my personal illness and my own imminent departure have blunted my sensitivity, or whether it's because I've had to focus on all the practical things, or whether it's simply because even the simplest tasks take a huge effort of concentration. Joel has been more open in his reactions. He doesn't see much of her normally, but he was up here by the end of that day. And it was obvious he was distressed by the mere sight of her.

It has just struck me. It's not just Mother's present predicament that Joel's grappling with; he's facing the real prospect of losing his entire birth family in the near future.

The ward she's on is a designated Stroke Unit. If there's a chance she could recover, this is the place that'll get her through. Twelve beds. At one end, the 'catastrophic cerebro-vascular insults'; recumbent figures being turned and sucked out and talked at. Drawn curtains, empty beds. At the other end, lurching one-sided recoverees being cajoled to achieve their full potential. The frustration, the irritation, the outright aggression; you can't miss it. What would Mother be like if only half of her were to return to the land of the living? Or less. Or more.

Joel and I whisper together.

'If they ask us, what do we say? Don't resuscitate her? Don't feed her? Let her go?'

'All her life she's hammered it into us: life is not ours to take.'

'But what about the Golden Rule: do unto others what you would have them do to you? If I were in her shoes I'd say pull the plug.'

'Would you?'

I'm doing my best to really listen to what Joel thinks. He's back to being my kid brother again, looking for guidance. And I'm horribly aware that because of all the debate about my own life, I'm in a completely different place.

Sitting beside Mother the cogs of time grind oh so slowly. My attention wanders to irrelevancies, tiny details, and I make all sorts of value judgments. I assess from a walk or a look which staff are approachable and friendly. I can tell which ones really do care. I shrink from those still half-caught up in last night's party or tomorrow's date.

If she has to be in here, Mother is best to be unconscious. With her ridiculous standards she'd only rail against the stubborn dirt under the bed, the sloppy hand hygiene, the decaying flowers left to die of thirst, the cruelty of officiousness.

So do I wish her dead? I don't know. Do I wish her to recover even if it means the rest of her life lived with disability and frustration? I don't know. But one thing I do know: I do not want this incarceration for myself. Full stop.

I do not want to see staff rushing by my bed with eyes averted lest they see a cry for help. I do not want to overhear someone say of me: 'Oh let him wait. The world doesn't revolve around him.' I do not want to be relegated to the rank of a dumb animal because I can no longer plead my cause. I do not want to be pitied by the gentle ones, resented by the hard ones, tolerated by the indifferent ones.

A cauldron of anger seethes inside me for all the battles that should be fought for these people who lie alongside my mother. But I fear to raise my own head above the parapet lest she becomes the surrogate target when I am no longer sitting there as bodyguard. There are so many forms of ammunition, so many angles it might come from, some of them undetectable after the event.

I harbour an overwhelming urge to bundle her up in a blanket and convey her out of this impersonal place and surround her with love and tenderness until nature decides whether or not her time has come. Instead I hold my tongue and accept the second-rate shifts alongside the first-class oases, and try to convince myself that I serve her best by my silence, that these people really are better qualified than I to care for her, that none of them would actually do her harm. And maybe the weak links are not in this case deciding the strength of the chain.

It had been a strange time for her too, Naomi thought, re-reading this entry for the third time. Suddenly Adam was looking to Joel, not her, to share this experience. The common bond, the special relationship – it was theirs, not hers.

She'd wanted to cry. But if Mavis's sons were stoical, what right had she, a step removed, to weep?

12 JANUARY—Today the doctors laid their cards on my mother's table. The consultant surrounded by all the little Indians.

The scans show a massive infarct... the brain matter is like porridge... no possibility of recovery.

We'll continue with the iv fluids, but nothing more. It's just a matter of time. We'll move her into a side ward. You should feel free to come in any time, stay as long as you want to.

The entourage moves on.

They didn't ask us difficult questions. No need for agonising. Nature is to decide. Mother has got her way. For her, death was unexpected but instantaneous. The best way to go. For us, the questions remain. Why not a quick, dignified exit?

Despite the pathos of that moment, I found myself smiling. Behind the hunched backs of the medical fraternity a little biddy on the far side of the ward slithers down her bed, using the cot-sides as handrails until she reaches the foot, where she slips unevenly to the floor, then limps off down the ward and vanishes into the corridor, her shrivelled buttocks, her bruised iv sites, her yellow toenails, bare to the world. Two minutes later a care assistant steers her back to her bay.

'Where are you off to, Kitty?'

'I'll miss my train. Are you going to take me?'

'Take you where, sweetheart?'

'To the station. To Morecambe.'

'Morecambe? But it's January, Kitty. Too cold for the beach.'

'We always go to Morecambe on our holidays.'

'Okay. Let's go and find the train to Morecambe. There we are. Just in time. Up you go. Mind the gap. Now just you stay on the train until we come to get you at Morecambe, there's a good girl.'

Hoisted up onto the high bed, Kitty settles back against her pillows, scanning the countryside of her journey for familiar landmarks. The cotside clangs into place again. Three minutes later she begins the shuffle south all over again.

I dare not let my mind grapple with what this does to busy staff with timetables and outcomes and fluid balances and drugs and mealtimes and observations and bed occupancy and discharges and admissions and doctors and patients and relatives demanding their attention. Perhaps I'd be doing them a service if I took Kitty to Morecambe.

The care assistant appears at Kitty's side again. Same patience. Same gentleness. Same futile persuasion.

Suddenly I find I can forgive the lax standards of hygiene, the occasional sharp asides. In the face of dedication like this, the weaknesses fade. I can only pray that, *in extremis*, I too, and now my mother, will be cared for with such kindness. There it is again. It's kindness that makes the difference.

13 JANUARY—In the side ward, I feel freer to talk to my mother. Joel and I take turns, sharing our memories and plans, giving her jewels to bury with her, ready for the journey into the next life. Occasionally we converse together, always about superficial things, nothing unsuitable for her ears.

Joel brings us foul coffee in plastic cups. We whisper as we change shifts.

Concentration has gone. I abandon the book I brought with me today, and scribble onto my laptop. I'm acutely aware of each stertorous breath from the bed, rasping above the monotonous hum of the bed itself, rippling beneath her vulnerable pressure areas. Occasionally even the basic exchange of gases in her lungs is suspended, and I hold my own breath. But every time so far she has restarted her engines from force of habit. How long before her tired brain fails to send a message and silence fills this little room? It will all be over for her then. She will not have to stand at my grave and weep after all.

What had the staff made of this disabled man furiously typing beside his unconscious mother?

Did they respect his coping strategy?

Or did they perceive him as a hard-nosed business man just going through the motions of being a son?

Were they fearful of what he might record? Did they even know who he was professionally?

Probably not. It was never his way to flaunt his celebrity.

And in the hospital he was just a relative. Keeping vigil. Vulnerable. Afraid.

Later Naomi popped in for an hour. There's a whisper of her perfume lingering still but the smell of hospital soon overrides the impertinence. Bending closer to my mother, I detect the mustiness of a charity shop. Second-hand. Alien. Unbelonging. Bequeathed.

I have a sudden feeling of being smothered – by illness, by the imminence of death. Before my very eyes a light is being slowly extinguished in a malodorous, shrinking space. I want more than anything to escape from this place.

But I don't. I can't.

This is my mother.

After Naomi had returned home, a staff nurse came in to do my mother's 'observations'. Futile monitoring, but I don't voice my objection. She spoke in hushed tones and stroked my mother's hair back from her forehead. She's one of the ones I instinctively like.

'Don't these cases get to you after a while?' I asked.

'It's sad,' she nodded, 'but I like to think we make a difference.'

'And I'm sure you do. But why prolong it?'

'She doesn't know. We'll keep her comfortable. It'll be peaceful.'

I haven't the heart to challenge her inconsistency. She believes in what she does, why disturb her assurance? She's wired into curing and caring; she hasn't downloaded a programme for killing yet. Maybe she never will. Sitting here, I'm not sure that even I would want my mother's life to end ahead of schedule. There's something fitting in keeping vigil, waiting for her, or her Maker, to decide.

And the realisation dawns. I have known her all my life. I can understand the level of this catastrophe. I can *feel* it, not just see it. But I still couldn't bring myself to take the next logical step. I couldn't hold the pillow over her face. I couldn't inject the drug.

So what gives me the right to expect strangers to do it for me?

'Ooohhhhh. Thank you, Adam. Thank you. Thank you.' At last. He is seeing the impossibility.

14 JANUARY — Seven days, six nights. It feels like a lifetime. Every muscle in my body aches.

Joel and Naomi are both putting pressure on me to get some rest. 'She won't know.' 'It won't help anyone if you're ill too.' 'We'll call you if anything happens.' The infinitesimal space between that last breath and eternity is too short for any call. Instead I shall continue my vigil but immerse myself in editing the novel.

Evening At 9.15 this evening the pauses between breaths became elongated. It was as if Mother was trying death out for size. I asked the nurse to ring Joel and both he and Naomi came in, so we were all standing alongside her when she finally made up her mind to go.

What did I feel? Profound relief. This peace is so much better than that fearful noisy tenacity.

I was absolutely calm as I collected her belongings and staggered out of that ward for the last time, leaning on Joel's shoulder as if comforting my kid brother.

No other emotion. Only relief.

It's over.

For Naomi, the anxiety felt as acute today as it had on that freezing cold January evening, watching him staring down at the lifeless shell that had housed his mother. Was it natural to be that calm? When would the veneer shatter? Would she be able to hold him together?

It had been a struggle for her too, to force thoughts of his death from her mind, although for different reasons. Her own tears were for him and his loss, for all the pain he had locked away from her sight, much more than for Mavis's passing.

A vivid picture flashed into Naomi's mind. The cold windy churchyard. The stark simplicity of Mavis's stone. Dying chrysanthemums on the adjacent plot. How different from the glory of the trees surrounding Adam, the profusion of summer colours. Tended by her hands, watered by her tears...

The wheels on his chair squeaked under the ferocity of her sudden move away from his desk. Every time it was the same. The need to be close; the wrench of leaving; the anguish of picturing him there alone, cold, bereft.

She dragged herself upstairs and lay on the bed, dry-eyed, clutching the black jumper, until sleep claimed her.

15 JANUARY — I am so grateful for Joel's company. There is so much to do, so many decisions to make. He has divided up the phone calls to

relatives and friends. He has driven me everywhere, been my physical as well as my emotional prop, all through the trips to the undertaker, the minister, the church, the hotel where we shall sip sherry and, thanks to our combined forces, go through the motions of eating hot and tasty food rather than lukewarm pastries and dessicated sandwiches.

He has even brought humour to the experience. There are only three levels in the plot where our father is buried. She will lie above him, leaving one remaining space. Joel gave a ridiculous whispered performance, caricaturing the raging arguments they'd have about the manner of his leaving her, exaggerating his own reluctance to join them and be subjected to the eternal wrangling. We were still smiling as we left the cemetery.

Neither of us mentioned the imminence of my own death, but from the safe distance of his excellent health, Joel could shudder and say that we might have been thrown together in life, but surely we should have a choice about whom to lie with in death!

16 JANUARY — The Rev. Castlemaine is a sensible man with a comfortingly honest assessment of his recently deceased parishioner. He was matter-of-fact with us, no false sentimentality or absurd platitudes.

It crossed my mind to wonder if my mother had shared her disappointment about her sons' lack of commitment to the church with him. If so, he gave nothing away. He steered us through the service arrangements and by the time he left, the programme, the music, the flowers, were all taken care of.

It was reassuring to know that this funeral will be nothing like my own. I do not want a dress rehearsal. I want to preserve the element of surprise.

He had done that all right! As if his send-off could be anything like that subdued, polite event. The sheer size of the congregation, the presence of so many young people, ensured that. The tributes to a brilliant man cut down in his prime. The keenness of his loss to society was palpable.

Naomi clutched her arms around herself. It was too cruel.

17 JANUARY — Naomi is keeping on working now that Joel is here for me, but I was completely unaware of her leaving this morning. Joel too slept late. The exhaustion of that long vigil probably. Or maybe it's the body delaying the moment we have both dreaded: visiting the house Mother left suddenly without putting it in order.

I was unprepared for the huge sense of emptiness. It was all too quiet, too familiar, too suspended. Her presence was everywhere, yet nowhere. And where do we start? We wandered from room to room, gave the accumulated mail a cursory sort, checked the security, and left without touching anything personal. After the funeral. It can wait.

20 JANUARY — For some inexplicable reason I felt a real need to go to my mother's church before the funeral. The regular morning service today seemed like the right occasion. Normally I love the sound of the bells, especially in the echoing barrenness of the winter months. But today? Ask not for whom the bell tolls, it tolls for me!

Naomi came too, more to support me than because she wanted to, I'm pretty sure. Joel grinned wryly and said he had his limits and would cry off from this level of filial duty, if it was all the same to me.

It was a strange sensation being amongst these people who had worshipped with my mother, who knew her, but who didn't know who we were. It was right to go. I shall feel less of a usurper at the funeral now I've shared something of her environment beforehand.

The sermon was based on that famous passage in *Ecclesiastes*: 'To everything there is a season, and a time to every purpose under the heavens.' With my mother hovering too dangerously close for composure, it vexed me that my mind refused to steer clear of the parts that touched me most closely.

'...and a time to die... a time to kill, and a time to heal... a time to weep... a time to mourn... a time to get, and a time to lose...'

I agree: there *is* a time to die, and I wish the minister would stay with that topic. He doesn't. He's too busy decrying the violence of war and international conflict; calling for peace and understanding at a global level and nationally and in this little community where my mother prayed. What a missed opportunity.

There, in the coldness of that ancient church, I stopped listening to his exhortation to brotherly love and let my mind wander. This text – straight out of my mother's Bible – doesn't seem to prohibit killing. There's a time for it, it says. And after all, even in our own society, centuries after the author of *Ecclesiastes* was around, there are lots of people sympathetic to some forms of killing. This very church magnifies and lauds the work of the Armed Forces on Remembrance Day. Now there's killing! Innocent men, women and children. I don't condone war in any guise myself but the establishment figures who lead the nation's remembrance represent mainstream views.

And there are plenty of people today who support the death penalty for the more heinous crimes. I see their logic but I worry about the miscarriages of justice. Once you're dead, you're dead. Posthumous pardons don't magically breathe life back into executed corpses.

Against these scenarios the arguments for the kind of killing I have in mind are much more sustainable. The police, judges, juries, MPs; they all tend to be sympathetic to mercy killers. They recognise that Nature can be cruel.

Can't she just!

Look what she did to my mother.

Look what she has in mind for me!

I realise Nature also often provides a way out, but medicine has a nasty habit of thwarting her intentions. Pneumonia, infections, loss of appetite: nowadays all enemies to be fought, not friends to be embraced.

I glanced around at the congregation. Eighty per cent elderly, mostly women. Probably some with a stash of cash involving multiple noughts mouldering in their bank accounts. How many have relatives eager to see them in the cemetery? If doctors could help them on their way, how many would slip away too prematurely?

An ancient little soul in a fake-fur coat and hat, ramrod straight in the opposite pew, glared as she caught my eye and I turned swiftly to face the front, although my mind continued to wander laterally.

I guess there are always going to be potential loopholes with any rule or law. Maybe it's a question of semantics. Maybe by using terms like 'killing', we're fostering the notion that it's something unwelcome, something horrible being done to an unwilling person. A suggestion of violence. There's undoubtedly a sense that death is the ultimate evil to be resisted at all costs; most notably in medicine. That's something we need to change.

Maybe we'd be better to focus on the *helping* aspect; helping people to have a good death, something they really want. As far as I'm concerned, it's the last good thing someone can do for me – the ultimate demonstration of true caring and love.

So why didn't I want to do it for my mother? Why could I *not* do it? Hmmm.

I'll stick with the semantics!

Hey, Reverend Minister, up there in your safe pulpit, why can't the law allow doctors to be good neighbours, helping the needy to die with dignity? Why should they need explicit permission? Will they need to have every special circumstance spelled out in law before they'll feel able to contravene the centuries-old prohibition? Would they abuse such power? You must know how people tick – tell us what you think of this new proposal to change the law in my favour.

The announcement of another hymn caught me by surprise but Naomi shared her hymn book and held my arm tightly. Probably thought I was lost in grief.

On the way out, I thanked Rev. Castlemaine for his words. It would have been more honest to thank him for the peace and sanctity of his church – my mother's church. But he had no idea of the hidden agenda that had brought me here on this wintry January morning, and I saw no merit in rocking his sense of Sunday security.

'Oh Adam, why didn't you talk to *me* instead?' The words were wrenched from Naomi involuntarily.

He was right. She had assumed he was grieving for his mother. She hadn't wanted to trespass on hallowed ground.

And Joel had a prior claim.

21 JANUARY—No time to scribble. Too busy being polite to people. Paige arrived this afternoon. Sundry relatives have booked themselves in to local hostelries. A day of courtesy calls.

Next time these people gather will probably be for my funeral.

22 JANUARY—Today we buried my mother.

It was bitterly cold, with a snell east wind, ice making the paths of the cemetery treacherous.

I decided to dispense with my sticks for the walk up the aisle behind the coffin, not wanting to deflect attention away from Mother on her day. Joel and Naomi were my props and I was glad to have them close beside me. But I regretted the omission afterwards when people came to shake our hands. It was awkward to be so dependent. So I reverted to the sticks in the graveyard.

There was something rather lonely about the two of us receiving the mourners – the last of the line, two men, no progeny. I wonder if Joel felt the responsibility resting on him. Two green bottles... and one fell off... and then there was one...

But there was also something rather amusing about people's reactions to me sitting down for part of the proceedings. Joel felt it too and we exchanged a few grins, which probably seemed disrespectful, but got us through an extended and potentially emotional ordeal. In reality I was so focused on keeping Nemesis in check that there wasn't space for the reality of what we were doing to impinge at the time.

I had hoped to cleanse my spirit through this diary but I'm just too drained to write. Another day, another time.

23 JANUARY—It's been a weird kind of day – flat somehow, after all the busyness. I felt a strong compulsion to do something. The sooner we wrap things up the better as far as I'm concerned; I shan't be in any better shape weeks from hence, that's for sure. But, only the day after the funeral, it still felt too soon to go round to sort out Mother's house.

Reactions show today. Joel is subdued, Naomi is tearful, I'm... I don't know... withdrawn? confused? unavailable? I just want to be on my own. I don't want to analyse my feelings. I don't want to listen to how anybody else feels. However, I know that beneath the numbness there's a ferment of thought going on. Watching Mother die has dragged all sorts of issues out of the closet. Those tedious but precious hours sitting beside her gave me plenty of time to reflect on my own position as well as hers, and now she's gone, I need to follow that process to its conclusion. Maybe starting that will jerk me out of this catatonic uselessness.

1. I am resolved to avoid being in a state of being not quite dead.
2. I want the judgment of when it's time to go to be on my terms. Not the reference point of the nurse, be she warm-hearted or not, who pops in to change the bed or stroke back the hair or touch a hand and then goes about her other lawful business, forgetting the shell she leaves behind. Nor the reference point of the hospital doctor who lines up his scientific results and states the position and moves on to the next bed without a backward glance. Nor yet my community allies, for whom each patient is but one in an overwhelming number. None of them can truly identify with my perspective.
3. Curtis is my best hope. I just need to convince him that the burden of continued existence outweighs any expected benefit. Disproportionate burden, they call it.

So Hugo Curtis, friend, ally, very personal physician – I recognise your technical expertise, your clinical judgment, your ethical wisdom, and your own moral values. Could you be persuaded to take the risk of moving outside your normal boundaries in order to do what you know to be right and good and noble in my particular case? I'd trust your judgment more if you didn't just toe the party line, follow the rules laid down as your professional duty of care, shelve the big issues to stay out of trouble. You'd be engaging with the reality of my suffering.

I need to check. Would he feel obliged to document his actions? Least said. And will an autopsy be demanded? If so 'unbearable and hopeless suffering' is a legitimate reason to accede to the patient's request, and that's me all right! I rest my case.

I'm drained to the dregs.

Naomi closed the file and left his study with a heavy heart.

24 JANUARY—Joel has to go back tomorrow so we could delay packing up the ancestral home no longer.

My instability made it logical for me to decant things into the black polythene bags and brown cardboard boxes Naomi had acquired for the purpose, while Joel moved the heavy stuff and ferried Mother's belongings to the charity shops and the tip.

Naomi volunteered to deal with the women's stuff. We told her to take anything she liked but she said she didn't want anything – until she unearthed a studio portrait from underneath a pile of jumpers. Mother in her twenties; strikingly attractive. Before tragedy and bitterness etched the harder lines.

Was it taken for my father, in the early days? There's now no one to ask. It's a bizarre feeling that – knowing there's no access to the past, no living link with our ancestry. Even without my disease I would be in the frontline now, next in line for the Grim Reaper.

Seeing a young happy Mavis, a woman I never knew, I had to turn away, busy myself with packing books, before I could face going back to her bureau and siphoning the rest of her photos into a box marked 'Adam' – without looking at them. One day I shall examine them; then parcel them up for Joel. The box is sitting in the corner of the room as I write, sealed with brown tape. A compartmentalisation of life. A stepping stone to the emptiness of my own future.

Soon I must sort out my own possessions; this is no time to be inheriting anything.

Joel discovered a load of tablets in my mother's bedside cabinet. Given the price of drugs, they should go back to the chemist, but that can wait. I've just bundled the whole lot into a drawer of my desk and locked it in case Anabelle or Courtney go exploring.

It takes more than a day to pack away a life. We ended up stashing a lot of the personal stuff into boxes and ferrying it to our spare room.

I am dreading Joel's departure tomorrow.

It was a shock for Naomi to read about the thoughts and emotions these experiences had unleashed. Adam had kept them ruthlessly hidden. Another lonely struggle.

At the time she'd thought him incredibly unsentimental. She'd only held out for the portrait lest it be consigned to oblivion. There had been no mention of the other photos. Had he in fact passed them on?

She jotted down, Joel: photos?

Something made her go through to the dining room to look again at the photograph of the young Mavis. It was strangely comforting. She was nothing like the dreaded harridan of recent nightmares. Maybe if life had not treated her so harshly… Who knew what might have been?

25 JANUARY—It's still dark. Far too early for my orphaned brother to surface, but sleep eludes me and emotion threatens to overwhelm me. I must somehow take control. So I'm going to work on revising my novel.

But I must jot something down first. It occurred to me in the night that my mother has been a major stumbling block in my plans for my own end. Now she's gone, that leaves just Naomi and Joel to worry about.

Joel is leaving this morning and I want to send him away strong. He has just lost his last remaining parent; he doesn't need to lose his security. Not yet anyway. But what promises can I give him?

....

After five minutes I've written nothing.

And contrary to my earlier assumptions, Joel is already moving about upstairs, despite the hour.

Give me strength. I can do it. For his sake I will do it. I can promise to stay close, talk often, be there for him.

Later I decided on the spur of the moment to get Naomi to drop me off in town as soon as Joel had gone. No point in moping around here. Searching for information in the library would be an incentive to think of other things. I felt pretty pleased with myself that I was soon assembling a convincing piece about the changing face of the Government on privatisation in the nhs cleaning services.

The static and unchanging murk under my mother's bed gave me the idea.

It's often a shock to emerge from these absorbing searches into the outside world, into darkness or gales or sub-zero temperatures or noisy crowded streets. Today the surprise of steady drizzle brought me back to the present more rudely than I could have wished.

Were the roads safe for Joel? Had his visibility been impaired by the filthy wake of lorries on the A1?

Had he been trying to reach me?

Just as the tension began to grip my stomach, my attention was arrested by an unlikely couple approaching the library from the north. It was the shuffling gait of the woman that first impinged on my consciousness. (I'm finely tuned to awkward movements nowadays.) Her limp feet in their striped ankle socks and pink, unlaced trainers trailed through the puddles on the pavement without any effort on her part to lift them clear. A watermark crept up the long beaded skirt, faded now from black to tired grey. The buttons of her green cardigan were misaligned with the buttonholes, leaving at least six inches of wool hanging far too close to the wetness. A man's crumpled beige mackintosh seemed to have been slung haphazardly around her shoulders by some other hand, probably in an effort to counter her resistance. The woman was of indeterminate age, thin elderly hair hanging straight down both sides of her pale cratered face in a caricature of a schoolgirl bob. The total mishmash of colours seemed somehow symbolic of a complete malco-ordination of life. Her vacant (the Scottish word 'glaikit' is so much more expressive but feels too pejorative) gaze never left the pavement, as if she would not raise her eyes again in this life until she had found the tiny back of an earring underneath the trampling feet of an uncaring world, but after years of looking, the excitement of the search had faded to hopelessness.

Leading her silently was a pin-neat man, probably about fifty, with ninety years of desolation etched into his face, submission woven into the ghastly fair-isle pullover showing beneath his nylon anorak. He made no effort to steer her away from periodic drenchings. The inadequate umbrella he held over both of them dripped relentlessly, alternately onto her green cardigan or his synthetic navy trousers, without him seeming even to notice.

I stood in the doorway of the library, not wanting to lurch forward into the path of such a compromised pair. They stopped suddenly and she turned her head towards her companion, as if unsure whether or not she should allow herself to be propelled along by him.

'What time is it?'

Querulous voice.

'11 o'clock.'

Expressionless, no attempt to consult his watch.

Instinctively I checked. 11.50.

Three more shuffling steps.

Another halt.

'What time is it?'

'11 o'clock.'

The shuffling resumed.

'What time is it?'

'11 o'clock.'

I was aware of a spontaneous surge of gratitude. My beautiful wife. My active brain. My independence. My continuing opportunities. The sheer stimulation of life. My disease assumed a positive dimension in the face of something so much more grotesque.

How many times did that woman's... son?... brother?... husband?... carer?... have to answer that same question? Every three minutes since 11 o'clock? Every three minutes for her whole waking day? Day after day, month after month, year after year. And still he went through the motions of responding.

I stood there, motionless, transfixed by their trudging progress along the street. Appalled at my own selfishness, I nonetheless sent silent thanks to those beaten strangers for putting my life into perspective.

I was positively effusive with the taxi driver who took me home, and tipped him handsomely.

Toni with an 'i' has not been seduced by the rich Sultan. In spite of our obvious incompatibility, she actually wants to return. I'm glad she only got the answer-phone; I can delay getting back to her.

Joel arrived home safely, without incident.

Naomi understood Adam's reluctance to see his brother go this time.

They'd all been tearful. Goodbyes had a new poignancy so close to the final farewell.

'Never fear, I'll be yo-yoing in and out,' Joel had assured them as he wound down his window for a last wave. 'But for goodness' sake, get Mother's photo out of that room before I come back next time. It fair gives me the creeps having her watching over me in bed!'

She chuckled now remembering that moment. Trust Joel!

28 JANUARY—On Thursday there's to be a leaving party in my honour. The guys offered to postpone it (because of my mother), but I declined; postponing things is a luxury I can no longer afford.

Naomi insisted on accompanying me (her words), dragooning me (mine), to buy something new to wear. I *HATE* shopping for clothes and I was truculent, to put it mildly. So I'm going to use the rest of today to immerse myself in Aidan's life. Naomi will fare much better alone seeking the right thing for herself.

She had to smile. He'd always been impossible to shop with. By that stage his instability had made the expedition hazardous as well as protracted and he had settled for the first decent outfit he'd tried on.

It had been the last time they'd attempted to shop for his clothes together.

In spite of Aidan's imminent demise, the experience of bringing the story to its natural conclusion is so stimulating I resent every necessity to do anything but write.

Naomi understands my preoccupation and has been using the time to clean out the storage in our house. Seeing all the stuff my mother left behind has propelled her, she says. I agree in principle but can't bring myself to join in the ruthless purification – not right now at least. Perhaps it smacks too much of preparing for my departure. I don't want to analyse it. Nothing must be allowed to deflect me from my creative flow.

I'm postponing sorting out Mother's things, too. The financial and administrative kettles have to be kept on the boil but the dredging-of-memories stuff can wait for a less creative time.

30 JANUARY—I'm aware of a curious confusion in my emotional response to things. It's perplexing for me never mind others. I keep finding myself

tearful in mid-laughter. Or smiling at serious moments. And I don't know why. Is it a feature of the MND? Or bereavement? Or anxiety about Joel? Or my ambivalence about life and death? I don't know. Maybe all of the above. Maybe I'll make an appointment to see Curtis.

31 JANUARY—Everyone was there. The food was excellent, the drink copious. Arkwright said too many flattering things for my self-control in my present fragile state, but I think I saved face by managing a fairly pithy and humorous response. People must have heard because they laughed in the right places. Unless those near enough to my half-power voice laughed and the rest laughed in sympathy.

The gift was a stroke of genius; a laptop with a device that allows you to punch in letters with pressure from a finger or a chin or whatever parts of the anatomy are connected to it. Apparently you can hire these things but as Arkwright said, the gang knew I'd wear any such gadget to death, so they thought buying me one of my own would save some other needy person an interminable wait, and the technical support chaps endless journeys out to fix an overheated machine.

Naomi tells me there was a moment of suspended animation as I removed the last layer of paper and revealed the contraption, but I can honestly say my delight was sincere. The reality is, I'm fully aware that my days of normal typing are limited but with this equipment there's no reason why I must prematurely end my career. Arkwright quipped that both he and Harry would anticipate – nay, expect – a doubling of my output.

Tucked inside the gift tag envelope was an IOU for a couple of training sessions with an expert to master the unfamiliar techniques, and a generous cheque to pay for the electricity bills from 'running the machine day and night'! I was suddenly overwhelmed by the generosity and compassion of my colleagues. Mercifully the marketing crew created an instant diversion with a scurrilous sketch taking off the life of a busy journalist.

During the break for coffee I looked around at the assembled crowd and decided I've been a lucky devil. I've enjoyed the stimulation of a fulfilling career, the camaraderie of like-minded friends and the support of a beautiful wife. My thoughts at this moment flip unbidden to that sad character in the fair-isle jumper. Who is there to acknowledge his heroism?

It had been a weighty responsibility, advising on the best gift. In her efforts to give Adam a reason to go on living she'd been torn between the computer and a cruise dated for months hence. In the end Digby Arkwright had chosen on the basis that no one could predict Adam's physical state in the future; the cruise might become impossible but she had been all too conscious of the potential for Adam to interpret the computer as forcing the pace to invalidity. His delight had been such a relief. Digby had given her a conspiratorial thumbs-up from behind Adam's chair.

Her eyes flickered back to the machine which had kept Adam communicating until the end. Silent now. Idle. But the size of the file still to be read told its own story.

This was his legacy.

12 FEBRUARY—This gadget has given me a whole new challenge. Dave from technical support is a great guy: wacky sense of humour, fund of know-how, endless patience. He can say the most blunt things about using this bizarre computer but his very matter-of-factness seems to take out the sting. In two sessions he taught me all I need to know and inched me into modifying my techniques. He's bet against my achieving my target by the end of the month, reckons the novelty will soon wear off. I'll show him! I'm practising for half an hour a day minimum.

Later I'm down to the last container of Mother's possessions. So far all I've salvaged are two small shoe-boxes of bits and pieces, one for Joel, one for me – saved merely for old time's sake. Joel shrugged his shoulders when I asked him if there was anything in particular he wanted; he couldn't name a single thing. But somewhere just out of reach, he must be aware that he'll soon inherit the rest of the things I couldn't bring myself to part with anyway.

13 FEBRUARY—Toni with an 'i' rang again today. She seemed to believe my excuse for not having got in touch – my mother would turn in her grave knowing I'd used her death for such a purpose. But not even my new selfish self could deflect all the dates she offered.

My MND has just jumped up and hit me on the nose. I'm bloodied but not crushed. It was the unexpectedness of the attack that winded me.

I guess my mother's never far from my thoughts at the moment, so it probably wasn't surprising that the cascade of magazines and papers in one corner of the room reproached me in her tone of voice. One can't argue with the dead. I decided on a blitz, to be followed by an excursion to the recycling bin.

Mother was right: most of it hadn't been worth keeping. But one article grabbed me by the windpipe. An experimental treatment by a Chinese doctor, using fetal tissue. And one of his patients had ALS.

The reporter spoke of dramatic changes; the patient walking, talking, eating. Dancing even! The photos showed his happy face as he jived, arms raised above his head, no trace of support.

The breakfast marmalade is tangy on my tongue, the coffee fragrant to my nostrils, again.

But just as suddenly, the sceptical newshound robbed me of my appetite. The improvement after the transplant was short-lived – weeks only – before deterioration resumed with a vengeance. Imagine tasting a reprieve only to have it all cruelly snatched away, the accelerated pace of the degeneration collapsing months into hours. And on top of it all, the guilt for using aborted material.

The integrity of the experimentation is also in question. Why was the doctor unwilling to open his work to independent academic scrutiny? Was he really injecting fetal cells – or snake oil? I am disturbed by the idea of those illegitimate cells circulating in one's body. Of course, my journalistic mind leaps in with a caveat: why not? There's no shortage of such material in China. Their compulsory abortion programme ensures that. You wouldn't be altering the fate of those unborn Chinese children by so much as one iota with your conscientious objection.

But... in the privacy of my diary I can confess that emotion over-rules logic in this instance. Were I to allow myself to benefit from those lost lives, I would be condoning the destruction that made it possible. Morally suspect. Have I after all inherited something of Mother's illogical principles? That thought is as sobering as my revulsion at the antics of the renegade doctor.

I shared this depressing possibility with Naomi when she joined me but her reaction added another layer of confusion. For the first time I caught a glimpse of her suppressed mourning for my mother. I rushed away from the void left by my parent and into a diatribe against senseless abortion and the Chinese birth-control laws, but she was too upset to stay in the room. I let her go. We all need our space.

Adam had had no suspicion as to the real source of her distress. The desolation of her own double loss was so acute she switched off the machine. Would this rawness ever heal? Would it have been easier sharing the decision with him? Would it have been fairer?

Stella had tried to tell her that guilt was a woman's constant bed-fellow. The deed was done, and regret would still plague her even if she shared the knowledge with Adam. But the doubts lingered.

14 FEBRUARY — It took every ounce of my strength to be up and dressed before Naomi this morning. But my maternal inheritance of sheer bloody-minded determination stood me in good stead, and Naomi had the day off, so no pressure.

The art of carrying a tray of breakfast upstairs complete with the obligatory if unimaginative red rose has slithered into a distant memory, only mildly regretted. But, though I say it myself, the table looked creditable, the menu tempting, the small gift (impeccably wrapped, but by the jeweller's assistant, sad to say) tantalising.

Naomi oozed suspicion as she stuck her head around the door.

'What are you up to in there?'

'Courting the girl of my dreams on Valentine's Day. What else?'

I insisted she had to finish breakfast before she opened the parcel. She's too close to the edge these days to tolerate anything too sentimental. But she trumped my tactics by declaring that she had a surprise in store for me too – after breakfast.

The simple silver locket awaiting a tiny photograph spoke for itself. There was so much I wanted to say, so much I couldn't bring myself to put into words.

Naomi kept me dangling for her surprise through an ungainly scramble into warm clothes, and the whole of the car drive until we reached the canal. Not only had she booked us a trip up the water, but she'd arranged lunch on board. And best of all, Joel for company.

'A gooseberry at the party? Not my idea of romantic, let me hasten to reassure you!' he grinned. 'But she insisted.'

'Perfect,' was all I said, muffled by his enormous bear hug.

His presence lifted our spirits immeasurably. Even now, sitting here at night recording it, I can't help but smile at his irrepressible sense of the ridiculous. Nothing was outside his boundaries. In his hands even my disabilities were open to mockery. And gradually I felt my own caution melt in the warmth of his easy affection.

'Shouldn't you be with Paige, today of all days?' I ventured at one point.

'Trying to get rid of me already?' he countered. 'Cramping your style, huh?'

'Not at all. It's just – well, it *is* the 14th of February.'

'Of no significance whatever in the rarefied world of high finance.'

'Meaning?'

'The said Paige, lately a fully paid up awl-through-the-ear servant to the masters of the money-spinning fraternity has been dragged kicking and screaming to Paris for the weekend – by her extremely wealthy boss.' His face was turned away.

'Oh.'

'A whole weekend. In Paris. For Valentine's Day. No expense spared. I mean… How can one compete?'

'I'm sorry. I didn't know.'

'Of course, she *says* it's just some boring old financial conference. What kind of a sucker does she take me for?'

'Well, if she's that kind of a girl, maybe…'

I broke off at his affronted look.

'Adam Willoughby O'Neill! You were about to say, "You're better off without her", or some such pious claptrap. Will you listen to yourself? Shades of Mother and no mistake!'

I felt the colour rise. He was spot on.

'I was winding you up, idiot. Yes, she's in Paris. Yes, she's with her boss. But the guy's a happily-married grandfather of six. And I've seen the programme for what has to be the dullest day ever invented. She has to report on it at the next team briefing.'

'Okay. Okay. Okay. I retract every shred of sympathy.'

'Well, I think it's sweet of you to care about how Paige feels,' Naomi soothed.

I'm saving my reward till later.

Joel had indeed transformed the occasion. Not only had he brought new topics of conversation and a bright, uncluttered attitude, but he'd been a strong and safe pair of hands in manoeuvring Adam on and off the boat; hands to which his brother would take no exception.

In the weeks after Mavis's death and Adam's retirement, it had been sobering to realise how quickly things were moving beyond her strength. Joel had helped to gloss over the slippage. But later, once Adam was in bed, Joel had raged against the devastation of his illness. Naomi had been taken aback by the vehemence of his outburst. The ongoing strain was taking a heavy toll of them all.

15 FEBRUARY—Joel and I spent one last hour in Mother's house today. Together.

It still smells of new paint and carpet and our reminiscences felt curiously disembodied in the revamped modern emptiness stripped of the familiar. Our family ghosts had packed their bags and departed. Nevertheless it was a weird feeling locking that door for the last time, knowing memories of our childhood, our adolescence, our parents, would henceforth be homeless. I'm glad Joel was with me.

The 'For Sale' sign goes up tomorrow. Most of the proceeds will go to him. He should be able to upgrade quite substantially. In spite of our combined protestations, Naomi refuses categorically to gain considerably from her mother-in-law's death. She even said that people might suspect she'd got rid of me to capitalise on my assets. Naomi!

Joel met the MND nurse, Toni with an 'i', in the afternoon. It was comforting to do a wholesale assassination of the woman with him after thirty minutes of her condescending suggestions on how to improve my life. I wonder: does Curtis know what she's like? Dare I say I don't want her back? I rather suspect she is at this very moment compiling a sad report: 'still in denial', 'unaware of the implications of his disease', 'resisting assistance'.

I refuse to tick her damned boxes.

17 FEBRUARY—Joel's gone again. The house feels so silent without him. But their plotting and scheming behind the scenes to organise events bodes well. Joel will be there for Naomi – later. They'll help each other. It's some small consolation. Paradoxically, I already feel excluded. They share things, they need each other – because of me.

I must focus elsewhere.

Ahhah! A deadline to be met: a talk for the area MND meeting, as 'one of those who is dealing with it healthily' according to the branch president. Says who?

Later I've jotted down six points I want to cover, put in prompts for funny stories against myself, drawn up a positive take-home message. Bit like writing a sermon, huh?

Excellent therapy.

19 FEBRUARY—The president was embarrassingly fulsome in her introduction tonight. It gave me exactly the right opportunity to say, 'If my late father had been here, he'd have been so proud. If my mother had been here, she'd have believed it!' Straight out of the repertoire of *The Moral Maze*'s David Cook. Sorry, David, I didn't attribute it tonight.

They were kind. Nobody pushed me beyond my limits. I just wasn't prepared for the effect of facing so many fellow MND travellers – in every shade of ungainliness and immobility short of end-stage paralysis. Or the weariness and resignation in their carers short of end-stage despair.

Leaning on the adjustable podium, addressing them, was like gazing into a crystal ball at my own future. Lament, regret, self-pity – all superfluous. These people all knew. The wrestle for coherence, the determination to stay in control, the endless battle with hopelessness; they've all been there. I'm simply the new kid on the block.

Curiously, it was the relatives who cut through my defences more sharply. Their perceptive questions, their grit, their very presence given the burden of every day, caught at something deeply visceral. Naomi's lot, writ large. Can I allow this to happen to her life? More than once I had to consciously drag my thoughts into the present moment.

Suddenly I found myself sharing the story of my arrogant dismissal of Lieutenant Colonel Grant-Hartwood's request, and the humbling experience of attending his funeral. I knew his legacy was more eloquent than anything I might personally offer.

It was strangely healing to confess so publicly.

And it sealed my fate. I moved from being invited guest to part of the family.

All in all, I'm glad I finally went into that hall of mirrors. My so-called celebrity fades into insignificance alongside the unsung achievements of so many in the audience tonight, but I'm lucky; I have so many advantages. I couldn't endure regular meetings but tonight's encounter has been salutary.

Adam had returned home in the taxi the Association provided, a subdued and pensive man. He'd described the occasion in unusual detail but said little about his part in the evening, concentrating instead on the courage of the people he'd met. Two things on the following day gave Naomi some insight into his performance. The local paper ran a report on the meeting, paying tribute to his 'moving and eloquent' address, quoting him extensively. And a brief item on the local radio news next morning had included a couple of sentences of his actual talk. The shock of hearing his slurred speech and sharp intakes of breath, somehow exaggerated by the medium of the wireless, had made her sneak a look at Adam. He gave no indication of noticing at the time but a fortnight later he casually told her he'd decided to see the Speech and Language Therapist.

At last.

20 FEBRUARY—Lydia was in splendid form today. Almost back to her old self – on the outside anyway. She gives me hope that Naomi too, will find solace in work.

21 FEBRUARY—I'm still trying to persuade Naomi to have help.

'Me? No! I'm far too untidy to have a cleaning lady.' The old joke, misfiring now.

'But you could do with help, yes? Soonish anyway. Now Mum's gone. And things not getting any easier.'

'Could I? Are you casting nasturtiums on my standards again, Mr Pernickity?'

'No way. But there are more important things in life than cleaning lavatories and hoovering under beds.'

'Do people hoover under beds?' she asked with a look of absolute astonishment.

'Be serious, woman!'

'Well, that's rich, coming from you, I must say!'

'Touché.'

'Just you worry about the state of your desk and leave the domestic chaos to me.'

'But will you at least consider it?' I persisted.

'I like having my home to myself. I like not having to constantly tidy up because someone's coming in. I like being able to be slovenly when I feel like it.'

I stared at her in silence. She'd never by so much as a look betrayed the strain of my mother's invasion in all the months of her cleaning campaign.

27 FEBRUARY—I've had a fantastically productive week: galloped ahead with revisions to Aidan's story, written two features, and got up my speed on the new machine way beyond Dave's target.

1 MARCH—Dave was impressed. Reckons I'm a natural at this remote control lark. Not much more he can tell me. It's just a matter of practising.

4 MARCH—That'll teach me to count my blessings!

Naomi started the week with a catalogue of symptoms ranging from aching all over to a blinding headache. Typically, she declined medical assistance, but by last night she was so feverish, I called in Doc Curtis.

Cardinal sin number one.

'I *can't* be ill,' she croaked.

'Maybe you *can't*. But the fact remains that you *are*.'

Okay, I'd have been maddened too by the sheer insensitivity of the response.

It's a chest infection. Bed rest, fluids, antibiotics, Curtis decreed.

Then, was there anyone who could help out? Should he send in the nurse?

Help! Toni with an 'i' I do not need!

He got the message.

After Curtis had gone, and in spite of having no voice to speak of, Naomi left me in no doubt that I'd erred in the sight of God and herself, by nominating her sister, Sally.

Cardinal sin number two.

'She's got enough responsibilities of her own. I'll manage,' croaked my furious wife.

It's abundantly plain she couldn't, even if she tried. So here I am, lurching around on my zimmer, endeavouring to keep the bare essentials for existence ongoing just within the limits of health and safety, and doing my best to keep the invalid cool and supplied with fresh sheets and fruit juice. Anything beyond the essentials is an optional extra as far as I'm concerned.

6 MARCH—I swear I gave as impassive an account of the situation to her sister as was possible when she rang to speak to Naomi last night, and

I certainly didn't so much as mention my own difficulties, but at 10 this morning, there was Sally at the door. By lunchtime she had the place in order, Naomi bathed and sleeping like a baby, and a meal ready for her when she woke.

She whirled off again to collect the girls from their respective ballet and swimming groups, taking with her a pile of ironing and my sense of security; leaving behind an assurance of her return in the morning – with oven-ready food.

I was left to deal with Naomi's resentment alone.

'I don't try to take over *your* decisions!'

No amount of protestations as to my innocence had any effect on her annoyance.

12 MARCH — Sally has been wonderful this week. Preserving enough clutter to retain my ownership of my home, establishing enough order to make Naomi as well as me feel things are under control. I am hugely in her debt.

And she has confirmed to Naomi my version of events: I did not initiate her coming or even suggest it, but what kind of a sister would she be if she didn't help out in a crisis?

An uneasy truce has been established but the tension of the last few days has undermined my efforts to get Naomi to take things easy.

Naomi smiled ruefully. She had been a difficult patient.

'You need more help, Nay,' Sally had said bluntly.

'I'm coping.'

'But looking after Adam is hard work.'

'You don't need to tell me that! I live here, remember?'

'I know. I'm only saying, you ought to have more help now.'

'Which you're providing. And I'm terribly grateful, Sal.'

'Occch, this is nothing – merely fighting fire. I'm talking about long-term help.'

'It's just because you aren't used to it. We manage fine, normally.'

'You're exhausted. Look how much this infection has dragged you down.'

'This is just a temporary blip. We've got into a routine. I don't want any more people crowding us out of our own home.'

'It would free you up to do some of the things you want to do.'

'What I want is to be with Adam.'

And she'd remained adamant. Not yet. It would come – but not yet.

She'd been grateful for a second week of rest, thanks to Sally, though.

20 MARCH — We're on our own today. So far so good. Sally left us ahead of the game as far as housework, laundry, ironing, etc, goes. And food –

both the bought and the cooked variety. So between us we've just done the basics. No mishaps so far.

But in the confines of this confessional I can admit to a new problem ... well, maybe. I haven't forgotten Devlin's caveat. Three times now I've choked drinking plain water. I'm always careful about the amount of any fluid or food I take, but just a tiny quantity can catch me unawares. Is this the first sign of swallowing problems?

The books advise iced or fizzy drinks, sips before meals or between courses. I've tried that. And like they say, I fare better with sharp and spicy foods, rather than dry bland things. Presumably they stimulate the salivary flow.

I'm starting to dread mealtimes. I found it easier eating alone (when Naomi was ill), limiting the size of the meal, setting my own pace, quitting as and when I needed to. No temptation to talk and eat at the same time. But I can't start opting out of yet another sociable activity. Not yet. Not with her.

So it hadn't been her fevered imagination.

22 MARCH—Naomi insisted I kept my rendezvous with Devlin this afternoon.

In my effort to put on a good show and not feel pressured, I arrived far too early. Coffee seemed a good idea but I found myself eerily invisible to the harassed waitresses – but simultaneously too visible to other diners.

One hour and forty-five minutes I sat in the clinic. The longer I waited, the more reluctant I was to go to the loo in case I missed my turn. Discomfort compounded my agitation.

By the time my name was called I was sweating profusely and trying to summon up the courage to ask Devlin to excuse me for ten minutes. But... the big chief was not in attendance today. My hackles rose. I was on his list! My date has been fixed for three months!

The specialist registrar, Dr Rodney Stedeford, was most definitely not the man I needed. Pompous as well as patronising. A few platitudes, promises of 'excellent care' and it was over. Fifty minutes travelling, one hundred and five minutes waiting, for eleven minutes of garbage.

'We'll see you in three months' time.'

Not if I have anything to do with it!

But the taxi driver who brought me home reversed my bad mood. He made it seem as effortless to decipher my speech as to manhandle me into his cab. His genial conversation roamed over everything from concrete jungles to homosexual priests. Just as he pulled up outside our house, he turned to look directly at me and asked, 'What did you do for a livin' then, Guv?'

I told him I was still a writer. Only then did I get a glimpse of the Adam O'Neill he saw.

'Nah! You're kiddin'!'

I laughed with him. It was irresistible. Who cares about pompous asses like Stedeford?

Naomi found herself grinning too.

24 MARCH—I had an appointment with Curtis today, getting myself checked out for travel, although it's been on the cards lately that Naomi'd be the one whose fitness for flying hundreds of miles might be in question. She's looking tons better although I still catch glimpses of that haunted look she seems to have carried for months now, which makes me question her staying-power.

By some quirk I got the same taxi driver I'd had last time. Again he went beyond the call of duty and got me into the surgery as well as the cab with consummate ease – without recourse to the wheelchair too. I've noted his name for future reference: George Farmer. Nothing was too much trouble. George leaves my dignity intact. He instantly becomes a mate.

I had a few things on my list for Curtis. The emotional confusion was one: thinking one way, conveying something else altogether. He confirmed that it was par for the course. So that answers that. Nothing I can do about it, so no merit in wasting nervous energy trying to right that particular wrong.

On the matter of choking, he was less definite. Just monitor the situation. You're taking the right precautions. Let me know if it persists. No need to forgo the holiday on that score. He tentatively broached the subject of a Speech and Language Therapist – again! – this was her domain. He was mildly taken aback when I agreed to see her.

A rather more pressing issue on my agenda was the first draft of my novel, *Aidan's Story*, unfortunately currently minus the last two chapters. I want the security of a hard copy somewhere safe while we're away. I handed it to Curtis suddenly, mid-consultation.

'If I don't come back, I'd appreciate it if you'd get this thing published. There's an electronic copy on my machine, several back-ups on disc. Help yourself.'

He gave me a strange look.

'Is it likely?' he asked, perfectly calmly, as if asking about the possibility of missing the next bus.

'You never know. But somebody needs to know of its existence. In case.'

He riffled the edges of the paper.

'May I read it?'

I shrugged. 'It still needs a lot of tidying up.'

'Perfection always being a draft away, huh?'

'More than one draft in this case.'

'Is there something I should know?'

'As in?'

'A reason why you might not make it back?'

'Nothing specific.'

'I'm taking the fact that you haven't quite finished it as a good sign – yes?'

Enlightenment hit me foursquare.

'Ahhh. You think I might do the deed over there.'

He was watching me steadily.

'The thought crossed my mind.'

'Well, no, I wasn't actually thinking along those lines. I was thinking more of plane crashes.'

'Good. I'd like to see this book finished. And I doubt very much if I could find anyone to edit it to your exacting standards in your absence.' Curtis gave me a rueful smile.

'You'd have your ending though, wouldn't you?' I held his gaze.

'An ending, maybe. But would it suit your character in the book?'

'And would you have a problem writing suicide in – given your reservations, I mean?'

'If I'm honest... well, I've seen too many botched attempts.'

His fleeting expression conjured up sad messes he'd attempted to salvage. The ones who jumped. The ones who drowned. The ones who slashed. The ones who shot themselves. The ones who didn't get the dose right and ended up more damaged than before. What does the novice know of accurate doses or optimal times or distances or pressures?

'So why not put it all in the hands of the medical fraternity?' I said. 'Safer.'

'Even they don't always get it right.'

Is this a warning to me?

'I guess that's a feature of prohibition, huh? Driving the practice underground,' I offered lightly. 'Not enough experience, not enough accepted wisdom, no overt communication network.'

'It's all part of the picture.'

'But it doesn't explain why you doctors instinctively rush to save the life of someone who's attempted suicide. Maybe death is the wisest choice, for them. And there they are, dragged back into purgatory, without their consent.'

'Well, strictly off the record, I know exactly what you mean. I've done it myself and my conscience hasn't always been easy.'

There was a long silence.

'So, I guess I should be grateful you'll even talk about it, huh?'

He shrugged.

'For what it's worth, I do understand your reservations,' I said.

'And I understand your dilemma.'

We grinned at each other.

'But I really want to know how you end your story – in the book, I mean! And I want to have many more discussions about the ethics of medicine with you.'

It was my cue to leave.

The small hours It's never a good idea to have stimulating discussion late in the evening. Especially not nowadays, when sleep has become an elusive friend. And on top of that, I really needed to draft the outline for the end of the book while the ideas were still buzzing.

26 MARCH—I had to see Lydia before going away. She put me through my paces briskly and then said, 'Brilliant. Off you go and enjoy all that sun and scenery. A holiday's just what you need.'

28 MARCH—At 4.15PM today, the estate agent rang to say Mother's house has been sold. The sum realised was obscene, enough to build a couple of hospitals in the third world. Although Naomi still refuses any share, she has retrieved something else which belonged to her mother-in-law: an amethyst brooch. I gave it to Mother on her sixtieth birthday, but I suspect she never wore it. It was still in its original box.

Naomi lifted the brooch from the black velvet and turned it slowly, watching the light refracting on the facets of the stones. It was lovely. The only piece of Mavis's jewellery she had liked. For the first time, she pinned it on her jumper.

It was three days before she returned to Adam's diary; days spent sorting out a particularly messy adoption case, nights spent writing up reports. She felt robbed of energy.

1 APRIL—Digby Arkwright called in. He's better than any stimulant. He wants me to write something about holidays for the disabled. I watched him drive off without a backward glance.

2 APRIL—It's finally done. I know I've been stalling, revising instead of finishing, but it's been so painful to let Aidan die. He's been more real to me that anyone else I know. I not only see him, I feel and think with him. He is me. This morning, after surgery, I took the last chapters of his life in for Curtis.

'It's very much early draft. Needs lots of polishing. But I don't want it hanging over me while we're away.'

'I'll keep it safe.'

'And no peeking. It's not fit for your eyes yet. It would only show you how hard I have to work to produce anything passable.'

He smiled and then said, 'I hope Madeira is as good as you remember it. And please, if you need any advice... anything... either of you, just ring. Leave a message. I'll call back.'

'Thanks. Good to know.'

4 APRIL—Joel is due here tonight. Up for the weekend. Just what I need to help me forget Aidan.

6 APRIL—Joel has gone. We packed so much into the two days; quality quality-time.

We share a love of the sea so on Saturday he and I drove down the East Lothian coast. He tried to push my wheelchair along the shore at Gullane, but the softness of the ground and the obstacle of the dunes made it impossible. Instead we drove back to Joppa, where the sand was firm and smooth. I savoured the taste of salt on my lips, the glow of sun on my skin. I drank in the sight of my beloved brother skimming the water with flat stones and retrieving shells from the shoreline to present to Naomi.

She, having been out visiting one of her troubled families much of the day, gladly joined us for a meal in our favourite country restaurant. My treat. I watched anew, in a bitter-sweet kind of way, the light banter between the two people I love best in the world. I can see they are good for one another.

Joel set about beating me at chess before we went to bed, while Naomi sat under her spotlight sewing her sampler. We toasted his success in hot chocolate and laughed at how much we were starting to adopt the derided habits of our forebears.

Today we drove round past Mother's old house. The door has been painted sunflower yellow, a colour she always hated. There are slatted blinds at the windows, a whirligig clothes line and a startlingly blue trampoline in the back garden. The new owners have dispensed with her precise lawn and replaced it with low-maintenance plastic paving. The smell of barbecuing sausages and the amplified sound of a games show assaulted our senses. On a Sunday morning!

It was too much. We turned by mutual consent and left without a word.

We drove towards the woods behind our own house and Joel guided my chair with infinite care between the roots and stones littering the path. The sun filtered through the new leaves, birds sang their God-given harmonies, and peace entered our hearts again. A sanctified Sunday peace. Blessed by our mother. Or so I fancied.

Joel stopped at a place where the path opens into a clearing – to catch his breath he said; to give me a rest more likely. The clarity of the air after rain enabled us to see right across to the distant hills. We watched a lone farmer working his fields, a solo pilot practising his manoeuvres in the relative safety of this depopulated area, a foal frolicking around its mother.

We talked of inconsequential things.

He didn't finally leave until after seven.

I hid in here.

Naomi hardly noticed the tears sliding down her own cheeks, she was so lost in his emotion.

7 APRIL—Needing activity and purpose, missing Aidan as well as Joel, I began to edit this diary today but after thirty minutes I abandoned the attempt – for all sorts of reasons.

I'm acutely aware of Naomi's place in all of this, her critical importance not just in my diary, but in my life.

Naomi, you hold my world in your hands. You are the centre of my life; the colour, the music, the constant. No words are big enough to capture my love for you. Knowing I must soon leave you is the hardest thing I've ever endured. But I want you to be happy again, my dearest girl.

9 APRIL—Bearing in mind that planes crash I checked over my will and other papers. Seems to be in order.

10 APRIL Naomi reproached me for not cancelling the newspapers and starting to pack. Hmmmm. Am I secretly ambivalent about going, Mr Freud?

The sheer effort involved in gathering together the things I shall need in Madeira was colossal. I'm so slow. And clumsy.

11 APRIL—I'm ready.

There the file ended. Naomi stared at the blank screen, memories flooding into her mind. She'd been suspicious initially. Madeira had seemed such an improbable choice for a man with limited mobility.

'Why Madeira?' she wanted to know.

'I went there when I was a student and I fell in love with it.'

'I thought you didn't believe in revisiting places.'

'I don't usually. But Madeira's different. I want to show it to you.'

'But there are heaps of places nearer to home.' More suitable.

'Madeira's unique. The scenery is breathtaking.'

'And mountainous and dangerous.'

'You don't have to go into the really dangerous parts,' he said. 'You can get a real feel for it all from the roads and viewing points.'

'Is that what you're proposing – a coach holiday? For us? Adam O'Neill, you hypocrite! How many times have I heard you mock "silver sitters" stuck in a coach with a hi-de-hi guide?'

'I know. I know.'

'How are the mighty fallen!' she'd crowed. And there the matter had been dropped.

But she'd been intrigued. Should she deny him such an attainable wish?

It was breakfast time four days later when she opened the subject again.

'D'you know you can do fly-and-drive to Madeira?'

'Yeeeeees.'

'How about it?'

He'd put down his spoon in slow motion.

'Are you offering?'

'What's the matter? Afraid to trust yourself to my driving – on those roads?'

'Not in the least. I'd trust you. Besides what have I got to lose? But what about you? You'd be the one dealing with the sheer drops and no barriers! You up for that?'

'Pooooffff! If coaches of senior citizens can do it, I can do it in a scabby little runabout. No problem!'

At that point, of course, he'd been able to lever himself in and out of vehicles, move about on sticks. There'd been no premonition of his rapid decline. In spite of all Adam had told her, everything she'd seen and read about it, Naomi had been awed by the vastness of the cliffs and the precipitate drops at the edge of the winding roads. She was tense at first, driving on the right-hand side, with the controls back to front, all too conscious of Adam's intake of breath when she took sharp corners, or veered close to the edge to avoid oncoming traffic.

But as she had gained in confidence, he had relaxed, frequently requesting her to stop so that they could revel in the views. There were innumerable terraces carved into the hillsides, luxuriant vines and bananas so close to the roadside she could have picked them. Flamboyant bougainvillias cascading over doorways and walls. Strelitzias, lilies, multicoloured geraniums growing rampant in the warmth of the African sun. Mimosa, oleanders, a good twelve times the size of any she'd ever seen elsewhere. Great swathes of agapanthus and hydrangeas, banked up in a sea of blue and white, dwarfing the cars running through them. Sudden oases of colour at the side of the road where someone had painstakingly reclaimed waste ground and then tended the fruits of their labours.

He'd chosen their accommodation with care. A spacious, ground floor room, easily accessible to a wheelchair, marble-lined bathroom with wide corridors between the facilities, making it feasible for him to be as independent as possible.

The days were full but by the evening Adam was exhausted. She was content to read or sew on the verandah while he slept, she said, but twice he managed to persuade her to go out alone.

The first time she walked along the cliff road and sat on the retaining wall watching the breakers below, listening to the unique sound: a gigantic sea creature sucking gravel through its teeth. Mesmerising. In the evening light the white froth of the spent waves stood in sharp contrast to the blackness of the volcanic cliff. She must come back with a camera. Thoughts of past holidays where she'd been breathless keeping up with Adam's energy sent her back to him.

On the second occasion, she'd built up sufficient courage to drive around the coast to a little picnic spot they'd stopped at previously. She wanted to photograph the silhouette of rocky protuberances at right angles to the cliff edge, thrown into relief by the setting sun. The accumulated warmth of the day had brought a few lizards out to bask on the flagstones. She captured the evening sky through its many changes and it was with a start that she realised it was almost dark. She tossed her apple core and a tissue into the wastebin, only to recoil in horror. The inside of the bin was thrashing with lizards – black, grey, green, brown, large, small, dominant, crushed. Tails whipping, legs trampling, tongues forking. It was like some religious zealot's portrait of hell. She shivered and withdrew quickly, a premonition of disaster gripping her.

She returned to the hotel immediately. Adam was fast asleep. Outside, as she sat alone in the remnants of the day, the dread gradually receded.

Locals gathered in the village every evening, clustering under trees, in the gloom of doorways, in the shadows cast by their houses, as if the places that sheltered them from the fierce heat of noontide embraced them more intimately at night too. Animated conversations laced the streets; to her uninitiated ears they always sounded irritated, even angry. Many of the women wore scarves, shawls, or even twisted cardigans, over their heads. What did it denote? She couldn't tell and it seems too invasive to photograph them without permission. Such pictures cried out to her everywhere. She wanted to capture the old man limping barefoot up the steep road, his body bent double beneath some unnamed affliction; a teenager with obvious chromosomal anomalies trudging obediently behind her parents, staring vacantly at foreigners through her cracked glasses; a farm labourer staggering on the terraces, one atrophied leg clamped tightly in a supportive brace, as he struggled to balance a pile of canes on his back; a merry group of wheelchair-users jostling for position in a ragged queue, yelling their lunch-time orders for caldo verdi with crunchy half-risen bread. It was striking, this acceptance of disability and deformity here on Madeira. So different from the tourists' reactions: the sudden silence when she'd wheeled Adam into the dining room in his chair, sideways glances, whispers. She'd reached across the table to twine her fingers into his, giving the onlookers blatant messages about their relationship. She wouldn't let them think for a second that he was her brother or a friend she took pity on.

'Glad you came here?' he asked later, as they sat side by side on their verandah looking out at the ocean. The setting sun made her skin glow, deepening the tan she had acquired so easily during their stay on the island.

She smiled happily.

'Absolutely. I love it. I can see why you wanted to come back.'

'Thanks, Naomi.'

'What for? Agreeing to have a brilliant holiday?' she teased.

'For everything. Sticking by me. Caring enough.'

'Don't be daft. I love you – remember? In sickness and in health, for better or for worse. I meant it. Besides, you'd do the same for me.'

'I love you. Always remember that,' he said softly.

It was Thursday evening.

'Where would you most like to go for your last full day here?' he asked her suddenly.

'Porto Moniz,' she replied instantly. 'No competition. And you?'

'Just along from Quinta Grande. There's a flat ledge that gives a fantastic view of the coastline and the cliffs. I remember it from last time.'

'Okay. Let's do half a day at each place.'

'No. Would you mind? Just this once. I really want to be on my own.' There was a curious appeal in his voice. 'You look after me brilliantly but... you know how I need my own space.'

It had been a hard lesson to learn initially when she'd wanted to be with him every second of every day and every night. But it was ingrained, this deep need for solitude.

'Much as I love you – it'd be like a real holiday – just to be on my own for a few hours. With a book.'

She couldn't deny him that.

'You take the car up north to your favourite spot; I'll call a taxi and go to mine.'

'No, I can take you there before I go to Porto Moniz,' she said quickly.

'Please, Naomi. I want to do this by myself.' The smile had gone out of his eyes and his voice. 'I'll take my mobile. I can call a taxi when I've had enough.'

'But the taxi might not be able to take your chair and the driver might not...' she began.

Irritation simmered just below his control.

'I've spoken to the girl at Reception and it's easy to hire a taxi with special facilities for the disabled. I'll be fine. And I'll enjoy my solitude even more if I know you're happy doing what you want to do.'

'It won't feel right…'

'Naomi. Indulge me, please. Just give me my independence for part of one day.'

'Well, if that's what you really want. But if you're not up to it in the morning we can always change our plans.'

He'd been quiet but adamant next morning. She'd still been loath to go, spinning out her shower, extending breakfast.

'Come on, Naomi. Think of those breakers you're missing,' he said.

'Are you sure…?

'Sure I'm sure. Come here and give me a hug and then go and make the most of your last day here.'

She'd lingered over the embrace.

'Now, off you go,' he said briskly. 'Take loads of photos. And remember – don't hurry back! I'll be fine.'

The drive had been enjoyable but a strange restlessness stopped her from savouring the beauty of that far corner which had so captivated her three days earlier. Sitting with Adam watching the constant change of colour and pattern and direction, she had marvelled at the imagination of the people who had created exciting swimming pools out of natural rock pools. It had made her smile hearing the shrieks of the youngsters lined up with their backs to the wall when the ocean breakers had come crashing over the edge and deluged them.

Today the magic eluded her. Her mind was elsewhere. The frolicking of the swimmers, the sight of bronzed couples smoothing protective oil into each other's bare skin, lunching on her own; everything underlined Adam's absence. She forced herself to stay but when the skies darkened and the first heavy drops of rain fell it was all the excuse she needed to head for the car.

From Ponta do Sol onwards she drove slowly, her eyes scanning the sides of the road in search of Adam. He hadn't been specific about his destination, nor. how long he'd remain there. Would he be annoyed if she arrived to collect him earlier than he had intended leaving? She could always leave again, once she'd reassured herself.

There was no sign of him from the road. She drove on. Their hotel room was empty. But it was too early to panic.

Naomi went down to the swimming pool and did forty lengths, pushing herself hard, concentrating on her technique. She returned to their room. He was still not back.

She walked slowly up the hill to a supermarket to stock up on fruit and juice, pausing several times to look back at the ocean, still and sparkling.

Back at the hotel, the receptionist was sympathetic; she would ring the taxi firm, find out what time Mr O'Neill went out. After an animated exchange, she put the phone down, a smile on her face.

'Carlos, he will come. He took your husband. He can show you.'

Carlos drove like a maniac, presumably habitually. In every other respect he seemed to have no sense of emergency, stopping to gabble with a fellow cabbie, to buy cigarettes, to allow a herd of goats to change pastures in front of him.

'Here I drop him.'

She pressed money into his hand.

'I wait? Yes?'

'Yes, please.'

It was already getting dark. Carlos slouched against the bonnet, lit a cigarette, and watched her.

'Adam!' Her call sounded so puny in the vastness. Cupping her hands to her mouth she shouted his name more loudly, over and over, hearing it echoing through the valley.

'He want go high.' Carlos gesticulated vaguely.

She ran back to him.

'Show me! Where? Where exactly did you leave him?'

Carlos moved in slow motion, but with agility and confidence, up a steep incline, to a ledge about twenty feet from the road.

'But he couldn't have climbed up here,' Naomi stammered, suddenly afraid of this sullen man alone with her in the dimness.

He spat out some Portuguese expletive. 'I take.'

She stared at him uncomprehendingly.

'He want go. I take.'

'He wanted you to take him up here?'

Carlos nodded and stamped hard on the butt of his cigarette.

Her agitated gaze darted all around them. Nothing.

'Adam!' she shrieked.

Before she could repeat his name, Carlos suddenly swore and strode back down the slope, leaving her marooned on the ledge, with nothing between her and the ocean thundering onto the pebbles below.

'Please…'

But Carlos was already back on the road and vanishing into the denser shrubbery on the opposite side. Before she could move, his head re-emerged from the trees and he began shouting and waving to her. She crouched down, turning her back to the sheer drop, and began to climb gingerly back down the way they had come. She paused for a moment to steady herself on the security of the level road, but before she could begin the next descent, Carlos reappeared dragging something out of the bushes, his fierce language punctuated by gasping breaths.

Adam!

Fear paralysed her momentarily, then she flew towards him, falling on her knees beside his inert body. Her fingers went instinctively to his wrist. There was a pulse.

'Quick, quick, we must get him in the car,' she screamed.

But Carlos had vanished again.

Naomi crouched beside Adam, wrapping him in her jacket, crooning his name, darting glances into the gloom, wondering if she would ever see Carlos again.

After what seemed like an eternity, he reappeared, this time dragging the wheelchair, its wheels immobilised by broken branches and tangled roots. He tossed it into the boot, picked up Adam and laid him on the back seat. Gesturing to Naomi to get in, he jumped into the driving seat, and roared off, once again at maniacal speed.

The receptionist stared open-mouthed as Carlos strode into the foyer with Adam's limp body.

'Please, please, call a doctor!' Naomi shouted. 'Room 5!' she shot at Carlos, running past him to fling open the door.

By the time help arrived, she had covered Adam with blankets, and removed most of the leaves and twigs from his hair and clothes. The doctor's presence somehow filled the room. He was very tanned with silver hair and stooped shoulders but there was nothing of retirement in his brisk manner.

'Madison Wickham,' he said without preamble. The American drawl was like music to her ears. 'I'm staying in the hotel next door. What happened here?'

In a few short sentences she blurted out the history, all she knew of it. Dr Wickham worked silently, feeling Adam's pulse, peering into his eyes, palpating and tapping his chest and abdomen, carefully moving his limbs.

'Well, Ms O'Neill, ma'am, I'm no specialist in trauma but it looks to me...' He broke off abruptly, one hand feeling the pulse in Adam's neck again.

'Is anything... broken?' she whispered hoarsely. 'Is he...?'

'Not as far as I can see. But we'd need X-rays to be sure.'

'So why... isn't he... waking up?'

'Does he take medication, ma'am?'

'Yes... I don't know all the names. I could look in his bag...'

'If you wouldn't mind. It might help.'

He took the bottles from her, frowning at the labels, saying nothing.

'He's got Motor Neurone Disease,' she said.

'Any chance he took the dose wrong, ma'am?'

'I wouldn't know...'

He was pulling Adam's eyelids open again.

'I'm a surgeon not a neurologist. These drugs don't mean a whole lot to me.'

'Would it help to speak to his doctor?'

'Sure would. But...?'

'He said we could ring. Any time.'

'His neurologist said that?' He was staring at her in amazement.

'Oh no! Not his consultant. His GP. Family doctor?'

'You brought his number with you?'

She gestured towards the phone as she passed him the piece of paper. 'Please use this. We'll pay.'

As Dr Wickham sat waiting for the connection, he watched Adam steadily, occasionally feeling his pulse or his forehead or peering at his pupils. When he got through, the questions shot down the line like bullets on a firing range. Then abruptly Dr Wickham turned and, gesturing towards the door, said quietly, 'Ma'am, would you mind? Just for a few minutes.'

When he called her back into the room her glance went instantly to Adam. He was still breathing.

'Is he...?'

'No real change, ma'am. Probably won't be for some time, I guess.'

'And Dr Curtis? Could he help?'

'He was very helpful. He wants to talk to you himself so he's going to ring you back in five minutes or so.'

The doctor pulled up a chair beside the bed and sat down, checking Adam's vital signs yet again, but making no effort to leave the room.

The ring of the phone made her jump.

'Naomi?' It was immensely reassuring to hear the familiar Scottish voice. 'I'm so sorry to hear about Adam. How are you?'

'I'm fine but... what's happening? Why did Dr Wickham...? Is Adam...?'

'Naomi, I want you to sit down and listen carefully. I have something to tell you.'

She obeyed automatically.

'Okay?'

'Yes.'

'Naomi, this isn't going to be easy for you to hear but you have to know about Adam's wishes. Otherwise we could get this whole thing horribly wrong.'

There was a long silence.

'Naomi? Are you still there?'

'Yes.' It was a mere whisper.

'You know that Adam's been talking to me? About his MND; how he feels.'

'Yes.'

'Well, he's also talked about not wanting to be a burden on you.'

There was nothing she could say.

His voice was suddenly softened.

'Did you know that he's been looking into ways of ending his life? He wants to spare you both the worst effects of this illness.'

When she still didn't reply, he said her name again, it seemed to come from a very great distance.

'Naomi? Did you know he was thinking along those lines?'

'He mentioned… it… once or twice. I thought…'

'He's been thinking about it seriously, especially since things started to get so much worse. And I rather suspect – I don't know for sure – but he might have meant this to happen.'

'You mean… now…?'

'Possibly. I think he might have engineered this accident.'

The enormity of the idea temporarily robbed her of the power of speech.

'And if that was the case, I was just thinking… well, he wouldn't want you to pull out all the stops now. Would he?'

She was silent.

'How would you feel about just letting things take their natural course? Dr Wickham suspects Adam took something – extra medication, something different, maybe. Something to make him lose consciousness. And the taxi driver told him that Adam insisted on being taken up to some ledge or other. Perhaps he wanted to make sure… Look, I know this is hard for you to think about, but it makes sense. Before you left he gave me his book – in case he didn't come back, he said. He was pretty fed up with me because I wouldn't just promise to give him something, do it for him, when the time was right. And I'm wondering if, perhaps, he felt the time was now.'

'He didn't say anything to me…'

'He wanted to spare you. He didn't want you to feel responsible.'

'But now… you want me to…'

'No, Naomi. No. Listen carefully. I'm not asking you to do anything. Let Dr Wickham take the decisions. He's prepared to sit tight and watch Adam. If it looks as if he'll just sleep away… would that be such a bad thing?'

She couldn't answer; she was too numb.

'On the other hand, if he wakes up from this, then I think we must just get him back to Scotland. Either way, Dr Wickham will do what's necessary now. He tells me he speaks fluent Portuguese and he knows the law and how things work over there. He understands the situation. I've filled him in on Adam's wishes.'

'We're supposed to be coming home tomorrow,' Naomi croaked.

'I know. But Dr Wickham will get your tickets changed if necessary. Whatever. He sounds very on the ball to me. Or I could come out.'

'No! Please. There's no need… If Dr Wickham doesn't mind…'

'He volunteered to look after things. But what about you? Are you all right with sitting tight, seeing how things pan out?'

'D'you think… Adam's going to…?'

'I don't know. Dr Wickham thinks twelve hours or so will decide it – one way or the other. Adam's showing the classic signs of an overdose.'

'Twelve hours…'

Her voice petered out.

'Naomi, listen. Just think of it from Adam's point of view. What would we be bringing him back to?'

'He should have talked to me...'

'Like you talked to him about the baby?' The words were spoken gently, no hint of criticism, but they cut deep.

'You were both only trying to save each other more hurt. Try not to judge him too harshly. Just be there for him. He loves you very much.'

Through her tears she managed to choke out her thanks and to hear his assurances that he'd be there, she could ring any time, day or night. Keep him posted.

For a long moment she sat staring bleakly at her inert husband.

'Ms O'Neill?' The words came from miles away. 'Ma'am? Are you okay?'

'Just give me a minute... please.'

Throughout the next six hours, Madison Wickham listened, explained and encouraged, and Naomi drew comfort from his quiet assurance and practical skills. In between their subdued conversations, she assisted him in washing and changing and turning Adam.

She must have dosed off during the early hours of the morning because she awoke to a persistent voice.

'Ma'am. Ms O'Neill. Wake up.'

Even to her untrained eye there was a change. Adam's eyes remained closed but his head occasionally jerked to one side, and his breathing was harsh.

She shot a glance at Dr Wickham.

'I think he's waking up,' he said. 'I guess you need to prepare for that.'

How does one prepare to welcome someone back from death at his own hand? But when Adam eventually struggled through his medicated fog to consciousness, instinct took over. She held his hand, hushing any attempt at speech, assuring him over and over again of her love. He turned from her with vague, unfocused eyes. Not until he was more fully aware of his surroundings did Dr Wickham attempt any further physical examination. There were no obvious breakages although the bruising was by now lurid and Adam winced whenever his arms were moved.

'Ma'am, would you mind leaving us for a while? Go get a coffee maybe?'

Her eyes went to Adam. Surely... he would protest... he'd want her to stay. He did not.

She dragged herself from the room.

Unable to bear the claustrophobic hotel a moment longer, she let herself out into the garden. What had yesterday been part of a magical holiday was today sinister. Pale light cast a ghostly glow on the shapes of trees, the furled parasols above the tables, the stone pillars – all immobile, as if listening for the sound of her thoughts.

What was Adam telling this stranger? Why had the doctor requested to be left alone with his unregistered patient? What if Adam was still determined to end his life? What if he asked Madison Wickham to assist him? What was the legal position in America? What moral values did this particular American hold? What if... at this very moment...

She burst back into the room with such speed that the door banged loudly in the sleeping hotel.

Dr Wickham looked up with a frown. Adam dragged his heavy gaze round to where she stood, white-faced and shaking.

'Adam, please! Don't do it. Please, please, please, don't.'

In slow motion he held out a hand to her. In an instant she was on her knees beside the bed, clutching his hand to her cheek.

'I know... I know you want to go... but please, please, not yet. Not like this. Not here. Not now. Please. I'll help you. I will. When it's time. Please... let's go home... first.'

'I'm... sorry,' he whispered hoarsely. It was clearly a struggle for him even to hold his eyes open.

'Ms O'Neill, ma'am, I realise this has been a terrible shock for you. But your husband is exhausted. I think I've established his wishes and we can safely let him sleep for the next few hours.'

'What have you given him? Oh, what have you done?' Naomi wailed.

'No, I assure you, I haven't given him anything. He's just drowsy from the medication he's already taken. The best thing for him now is just to sleep it off.'

A strange sense of detachment clung to Naomi on the journey home.

Madison Wickham had insisted on accompanying them to the airport in Funchal. Hugo Curtis was waiting at the front of the queue in Edinburgh to take Adam's chair, while she reclaimed their baggage. He gave Adam a thorough check-over as soon as they reached home.

What Adam made of all this, she had no means of knowing. Throughout the transfers and the flights he had dozed. All her questions must wait.

* * *

It was a full week before Naomi could bring herself to return to his computer.

Where would he have recorded it? Would he have committed it to the written word at all? The cursor tracked down through the filenames.

Ahhh... This might be it... Filename: *'Why? Why not.'*

She clicked the mouse with a trembling finger.

26 APRIL—I think it was Winston Graham who wrote: 'I sometimes think that the most threadbare things in the world are yesterday's smart ideas...'

Why? Why? *Why?*

Timing, wherewithal, plan; it was all there. Worked out. It seemed every inch a 'smart idea'. After five unforgettable days in that majestic scenery. Solitude. A clean break. Perfect.

But I hadn't bargained for the intensity of my own enjoyment of life. Or for the altruism of a peasant.

Failure is a matter of split-second timing, it seems. I need to unravel this slowly, learn from my mistakes.

I was feeling good – a day to myself, and I was ready – just – when the driver arrived. Carlos, the receptionist called him. I used my map to show him the spot, cursing my shaking finger, but he seemed to understand and we were soon hurtling through the streets, me slung from side to side in the back thinking that any second now he was going to spare me the trouble of masterminding my own end.

The exact spot was easy to see from the road but it took a hefty bribe to get him to push me up to that ledge. He jabbered away and gesticulated expansively, but I just pointed to my notepad and my book, until he got the message that this was where I wanted to be.

Once the sound of his engine had died in the valley I sat for a long time savouring the sheer majesty and serenity all around me. Wonderful. A sense of eternity. The occasional lizard slithered in the leaves as it baked in the sun. A hawk swooped and hovered overhead. The ocean lulled me.

Then suddenly, vivid memories of almost twenty years ago. All that climbing, all that energy, all those years stretching ahead, full of promise. And now? Look at me! A dependent cripple with just months to go. I felt physically sick. I stared down at my useless legs, that damned chair. The fantastic panorama vanished. Everything else was reduced to shadow.

Swallowing the pills was harder than I anticipated. It takes a lot of coordination to open bottles, pick up a water-bottle, get my hand to my mouth, swallow – repeatedly, without choking.

Before the drowsiness hit I drank in the splendour all around me. I felt this huge urge to imprint something good on my mind, the peace as well as the sheer awesomeness of it all. First mistake: delaying.

From my vantage point I had a clear view of the road winding tortuously along both sides of the volcanic slope. I calculated there would be a good six minutes before a car rounding the corner now would pass me from either direction: time enough. Far below, the ocean rushed headlong into the narrow cove, out again, in, out, beckoning me. Only a precipitous bank, half-hidden boulders and jagged promontories between me and its embrace. Perfect.

I lingered.

Second mistake.

Quite where the workman came from I couldn't see; one minute I was entirely alone, next minute there he was running down the road, shouting, leaping up the path, wrenching me back from my escape into oblivion. How he managed to get me and my chair down from that ledge without sending us both into the ocean I shall never know, but manage he did. And despite all my protestations and entreaties, he dragged me all the way to the road, parked me on the safe side, and stomped back off to his vines, shaking his head and muttering.

Lethargy had already started to steal my senses and it was a monumental struggle to release the brake on my chair. Desperation drove me. Somehow I managed to throw myself against the back and destabilise it. By the time I eventually felt the wheels beginning to turn, there was no time to choose my direction, only a sense of relief. Third mistake.

I felt my body leave the chair. But instead of a free fall through space, there were sharp spikes piercing my skin and next moment I was slithering into humid vegetation and unconsciousness.

Naomi stared at what he had written. With absolute clarity she heard Adam's voice – perfect diction, young and carefree: 'It's the Uncertainty Principle: the act of observing alters the reality of what is being observed.'

How true.

I'm not really sure how long it took for the last vestiges of the drugs to leave me. Through a haze, I heard a jumble of sounds. American drawl, Naomi's soft Scots, Portuguese babble, American Portuguese, international weeping, American English. A bewildering polyglot... I sank back into oblivion gratefully.

I couldn't work out why Hugo Curtis was at the airport, but I felt reassured by his familiarity.

It was Sunday evening, I think, or maybe it was Monday, before I fully registered what had happened. The sense of failure was colossal. It was all still to do.

A week later, and I'm still reeling. I know I need to explain to Naomi; I just can't bring myself to start. Someone must have instructed her not to ask; it's the only explanation for her silence. At least my mother isn't here to harangue me! It wouldn't matter who told her to wait.

But he didn't get the chance to explain. Not then.

She'd made the chicken soup herself, packing in the nutrients, straining it, letting it cool, decanting it into a cup. She tried to joke; chicken soup for the soul. He didn't respond. Fair enough, he had to concentrate on the serious business of swallowing.

Instinct made her ring Curtis first. Then 999. The GP was quicker. Choking's always a hazard, he reminded her. She knew that. But...

'Was it... the soup?'

'No.' Unqualified. 'Anything can trigger it. Even water.'

'So… it wasn't the soup?'

'No. It definitely wasn't the soup.'

Behind the oxygen mask Adam's eyes looked frightened. What did he fear? Choking to death? Being saved from death?

'Don't try to talk. Just breathe deeply,' Curtis said.

She rang Joel from the hospital. Until he came she was completely alone with the weight of this responsibility. She had rung the doctor. She had called the ambulance. She was tacitly asking the combined skills of the hospital experts to be employed to save Adam. Instinctively. Would he ever forgive her?

Joel had driven up without a break, straight to the hospital. Seeing his tall figure striding across the car park, Naomi fled from Adam's room and ran to meet him.

He gathered her close and she burst into tears.

30 APRIL—They let me out today. Ostensibly no electronic tag, no minder on suicide watch, but I sense the vigilance on all sides.

It's a relief to have access to my therapist – my computer – again. I am bereft without that outlet.

The three days in hospital seemed more like thirty. Joel and Naomi spent hours at my bedside. Not a word about my suicide attempt escaped them. Trivial news, mindless chatter, no hint of the biggest thing in all our minds. And endless vigilance.

No one could get it right. I resented the team responsible for my medical treatment for not addressing my mental state. I resented the psychiatric consultant for not appreciating my physical frailty. But most of all, I resented their combined relegation of my autonomous right to decide.

One logical act and suddenly my wishes are ruled inadmissible in court. I am deemed mentally incompetent. The balance of my mind being disturbed (now beyond reasonable doubt), I am no longer even consulted as to my own perceived best interests. Naomi has become my proxy. Just what distortions are they filling her head with?

The more isolated I felt the more I scratched around for support. Bizarrely I felt a tremendous and frequent urge to present this diary as my proof. Incontrovertible… or was it? Would it too be consigned to the realm of inadmissible evidence, its authenticity and its competence questionable?

The medical retinue continued to huddle on the far side of my room, muttering just out of earshot, avoiding eye contact, beckoning silently to Naomi to accompany them outside.

The psychiatrist, Morton van de Veere, taxed my resolve most. Who asked him to get involved? I was taken into hospital simply because a quantity of food temporarily obstructed my trachea, threatening the oxygenation of my blood. It wasn't deliberate. Even a desperate man wouldn't seek to choke himself to death on chicken soup! It was scary having an expert probe my mind. Unnerving to think that in the space of forty-three minutes Dr van de Veere would form a written judgment as to my mental stability. I know I was defensive.

He was a big angular man with a gentle South African accent and an air of having heard it all before. He looked to me like a man who has spent ages searching through his wardrobe, studying himself in the mirror, to achieve the look that says he has just blindly selected the first thing that came to hand. But beneath that studiedly casual façade, his gaze was as sharp and quick as a predatory bird's. All the speed, all the power, were in his favour. Vulnerability was, I know, eroding my natural courtesy. There was a degree of impertinence in my challenges, a resentment edging my answers to his questions. It was probably undermining my defence but I neither knew not cared at this moment in the trajectory of my dying.

'What gives you people the right to try to stop me if I want to end my life?' I slurred out. 'I have to live it; you don't. My outlook is grim. I've had enough. It wasn't a cry for help. It was a mature decision; a solution to my problem.'

I could see the huge effort of concentration it took him to decipher my speech. He said all the predictable things about wanting to help me to help myself.

'Forget the psychobabble!' I shot out rudely. 'MND is enough justification.'

'Real life always transcends the rule books,' he said quietly. 'I'm more concerned with why you want to take this particular way out.'

If he couldn't see that, he didn't deserve any help doing his job.

I was gentler with the SHO, the most junior link in the medical chain. Poor bloke, the last thing he needed was a clever-clogs patient undermining his rote-learned tenets. He'd obviously had a hefty dose of training in bedside manners. He explained every single thing he was doing. Inside my head I screamed at him: stuff your potentially reversible apnoeic episodes where the sun don't shine; go hang your targets and your aims on the firing range; sling your fluid balance on the other side of the scales. I'd be far more grateful if you'd simply allow those little physiological imbalances to get way out of control. I was careful each time to thank him for his services.

But the hurt from these men was as nothing to the overheard comment from one agency night nurse, talking in a penetrating stage whisper at the nurses' station. Patient confidentiality had clearly been omitted from her curriculum. Apparently a teenager called Trixie had been admitted for the sixth time with slashed wrists.

'Me? I'd just leave her. I've no patience with these time-wasters. I didn't come into nursing to pander to people who just want attention. It's her choice. There are plenty of poor sods who are genuinely ill.'

I devoutly hope Trixie never comes within her personal ambit. On the other hand… she could be just the nurse for me.

Joel has been subdued. He's been here since the day I was admitted, and he seems unable to let Naomi out of his sight.

And where was Hugo Curtis in all of this? He did visit me; two days into my hospital stay – at least outwardly it was the shape of the Curtis I know – but he seemed ill at ease in the hospital environment. His polite doctor-questions probed my physical state, my comfort, my pain management, he reiterated the cause of my choking, he outlined steps I might take to avoid a repeat performance. Stilted, superficial. But as he left he dropped his voice and promised to come and see me when I got home – 'We'll talk some more then.' Is he fearful of his role in this? Afraid for his career?

All these people suddenly wary, not daring to name the dread. All because of my answer to an intolerable problem which none of them can (or will) solve.

Naomi had lived in moment-by-moment dread that she would be the one to say the wrong thing.

Without Joel she'd have broken down under the strain. But he'd been brilliant. He'd been there at the house when they returned from Madeira. He'd been there for her when the tears finally came. He'd sat with Adam through the long silent hours while they each grappled with what had happened. He'd dropped everything to fly to Adam's side when he'd ended up in hospital again this time. But even he couldn't rid her of the sense of failure.

'It must be my fault. I've let him down. I shouldn't have gone off that day,' she'd wailed.

'Now you're being daft. You're his world. You're his reason for hanging on this long, for goodness' sake.'

'But he isn't happy. He's still here, but he doesn't want to be.'

'Well, can you blame him? Good grief, Naomi! What does it do to a guy with a brain like his, to be trapped in a body that refuses to do what he wants it to do? How does he sleep at all, knowing what's ahead? The only wonder is that he's cheerful any of the time. I've got about a tenth of his talent and I'd have drowned myself on the day of diagnosis!'

'Would you? Would you really?'

'Too right I would! And if he didn't have you to think of, I'm pretty sure Adam would have gone long before this, too.'

'Is that what he said?'

'Not in so many words, no. But I have eyes and ears. And he's hinted as much.'

'So it is my fault.'

'Course it's not! But I'll tell you something for nothing: you're exhausted. You've got to get extra help. It's completely batty trying to do this on your own. I know you want to – Adam told me he wanted you to have help, but you refused. Far be it from me to come between a man and his wife, but he's right, Nay, you can't keep this up. It's far too much work physically. And it's going to put a strain on your relationship too, if you don't watch it. It'd be better for him to have professional people telling him what to do and how to do it. He'd take it from them – well, he might anyway. Although we both know what a cussed blighter he can be when he sets his mind to it!'

'Dr Curtis said something like that too.'

'About him being cussed?'

'No! About me needing help.'

'There you are then.'

'But you know how much he needs his privacy.'

'Yep. But the way I see it, he doesn't have much choice now.'

She dragged her eyes back to the screen.

Once they'd stabilised me, the hours between visiting times hung heavily. Nothing held my attention for long. Reading, radio, crosswords, even writing; everything felt remote or of no consequence. I managed to get to the common room on my third day, but a king-size TV ruled the space. Everlasting soaps and gameshows.

I had my fair share of visitors but, I don't think it was my imagination, most of them were glad when it was time to leave. It's hard work understanding me now. Naomi and Joel are used to deciphering my convoluted sounds but they had other reasons to dread coming. Being in the presence of someone who wants out of this life, who prefers death to their company. The knowledge lay between us all the time.

Sally and Matthew came once but didn't stay long. I had no idea how much they knew; I stuck to their agenda. They brought hand-made cards from the girls. Anabelle's depiction of my hospital ward was as nightmarish as my reality.

So no one who came to see me had it easy and I breathed a sigh of relief when the bell went each evening to signal an end to this forced, artificial conversation. I just needed to be left alone – to think.

It's doubly lowering, now I'm back at home, feeling their unspoken recrimination and dealing with my own disappointment.

4 MAY—Sunday. Church day. I felt a compulsion to go somewhere today. Not to my mother's church – I'm certainly not robust enough to deal with her disapproval!

Not yet.

Naomi agreed, after some persuasion, to take me to the local kirk. It's tiny and very old. Beautiful and very hallowed. And within a walkable distance. Joel insisted he would come too, 'to push my chair'. He could have waited outside, or gone home and returned at the end, but he didn't. Just what mischief does he think I can possibly get up to in a church on a Sunday morning with seventy people all around me?

The service, the ambience, didn't live up to my expectations. Other people's air of devotion jarred with my rebellious thoughts. The droning exhortation to rejoice in the bounty of the season was at odds with my passionate desire to turn my back on what this life holds for me. It was all too predictable.

I needed solitude; to be alone with my Maker: to take Him to task, to seek answers, to beg for His help.

But now no one trusts me to be alone.

Naomi re-read the last two paragraphs three times. It had been like living on a knife edge. She had searched every situation for any possible avenue to suicide. When he'd suggested church she had known a surge of hope. Perhaps finding God would give him the strength to go on. There were few enough straws blowing in the wind at that time.

5 MAY—Curtis kept his promise to return once I was back at home. Initially he stayed outside talking to Naomi and Joel for so long that by the time he sat down beside me I was not disposed to welcome him too warmly. He came to the point directly.

'Are you cross that we didn't let you choke to death?'

I was taken aback and had to think before answering.

'No, I don't think so.'

'If you swallow food the wrong way it could lead to a chest infection. Would you want us not to treat that?'

'No.'

'Why not?'

'Because it's not the death I want.'

'No, indeed. Nor is it the death we want for you.'

He sat waiting, letting this point sink in. Or perhaps he was rehearsing his next line of attack.

'You just wanted something more dramatic, huh?' he said with a hint of a smile. 'Throwing yourself into the ocean.'

'It would have been over in seconds. I wouldn't have known anything about it.'

'You wouldn't – maybe.'

Again, a long silence.

'And now?' he asked.

'Now what?'

'How do you feel about it going wrong?'

'Angry. Frustrated.'

'You still wish you'd been successful?'

'Yes.'

'So who are you angry with?'

'Myself. For not managing things better.'

'Mmmmhhmm.'

'And the man who insisted on dragging me off that ledge.'

'But he's not here.'

I didn't bother to grace this stupid remark with a response.

'Do you know that we did our best to respect your wishes in Madeira?'

'How?'

'Do you remember Dr Wickham, the American doctor who took care of you?'

'Vaguely.'

'Well, when he suspected you'd taken an overdose, he rang me – Naomi gave him my number. I told him about your wish to die before you lost the capacity to take things into your own hands and that I suspected it might have been deliberate.'

'You gave me the idea, actually,' I shot out – cruelly.

'I did?' His incredulity had to be genuine.

'Yep. When I gave you the manuscript. You thought it was because I planned not to come back. I hadn't actually considered doing it then.'

He shook his head slowly, struggling with that notion. Somewhere deep inside, my old self wanted to retract. I couldn't even bring my present pathetic self to apologise.

'Well, anyway, between us Dr Wickham and I put two and two together, and it felt counter-intuitive to both of us to pull out all the stops to save you. I was worried about Naomi though, because I didn't know if she had any idea of your intention. The news was probably marginally better coming from someone she knew, so I told her what we suspected. She was terribly shocked at first; she thought you'd just had an accident. But I must say she coped with it all remarkably well. And amazingly Dr Wickham was prepared not to intervene actively, just let things run their natural course. I take my hat off to him. Not an easy thing for a doctor – and an American one at that – to do. Especially on the say-so of a foreigner hundreds of miles away! But... well, you came out of it.'

I shrugged.

'Not because of what anyone else did,' he said quietly.

'Except that crazy little Madeiran guy!' I burst out jerkily. 'He just wouldn't take no for an answer.'

'Tell me about it, Adam.' Curtis was gentle now, reaching out to my pain. Like I've said before, the very man to have walking alongside you when the chips are down. Except I couldn't afford to have anyone too close right now.

I felt myself shrinking back into a dark space, no bigger than myself and my MND. All I ventured aloud was, 'Is there a DNR order in my notes?'

'There is. I'll let you see it for yourself next time you're in the surgery.'

'And you've seen my advance directive?'

'There's a copy in your file. On that subject, we agreed we should revisit it periodically. You've stated specifically today you don't want to die by choking or from a treatable chest infection. It would help to get a clearer picture of what you see as acceptable.'

A wave of weariness washed over me. The detail seems so trivial. I just want out of this. Why does it have to be so complicated?

By the time I re-engaged with Curtis he was talking about community support. I went through the motions of listening, but when he got around to Toni with an 'i', I was still sufficiently incensed to tell him in blunt terms that if I had to continue with this miserable life, there was no way I'd find space in it for that blasted woman. Writing this now, I'm quite appalled by my temerity. The poor creature's only doing her job; it's probably not her fault she's inadequate. But the fact remains, she's completely wrong for me. Curtis took it calmly. I wonder if he's sized her up too, and found her wanting.

I was instantly contrite and apologised for my outburst. What happened to my resolve to leave good memories? Curtis looked so taken aback I couldn't help smiling. Only then did I see the tension lines around his forehead and eyes relax a fraction. He's a saint for tolerating my ill humour.

Before I knew it we were discussing a target date for him to get his comments back to me on the novel, and the procedure by which a carer or a nurse can be brought in to relieve the strain on Naomi – amicably.

We were a team again.

Joel came in a few minutes after Curtis went away. Thinking about it, I suspect it was to give the doctor time to talk to Naomi.

'How come you've been able to take all this time off?' I asked him.

'You're my number one priority,' he said looking directly at me. 'You and Naomi.'

'I don't want you ruining your life on my account.'

'I won't.'

'That's why I…'

'I know.'

Neither of us spoke, for what felt like forever.

'You must get on with your own life. Don't worry about me. I'll cope.'

'But will Naomi?'

I stared at him. He held my gaze.

'She can't go on like this, Adam. She's knocked up.'

'Because of what I did?'

'No, just day-to-day living. She needs help. What you did makes it harder. She's afraid to leave you alone now, afraid of what you'll do. But she's just exhausted, trying to keep everything going. I can't leave her to cope with all that on her own. I feel responsible. You're my brother.'

'D'you think I don't know what it's doing to her?' I ground out, glaring at him. 'That's exactly why I wanted to quit now.'

'Well, it didn't work out that way and we've got to face the next phase of this thing. So I'm here for as long as it takes.'

'I can't have that. We're going to have to get help in whether Naomi likes it or not. Curtis is going to organise carers to do the heavy stuff and nights. Naomi can get back to a more normal life.'

Joel nodded.

'How d'you think it feels... being the cause of this?' The words slurred out raggedly.

'I can't begin to imagine,' he said, gripping my arm fiercely.

What a struggle it had been, giving way in inches.

At first she'd said she'd hand in her notice. He was much more important than work. He was adamant: she must not. She'd go part-time, then. He refused to countenance it. And he held the trump card. If she insisted on sacrificing herself, he'd find a way of cutting short her sentence.

A part-time carer had been the compromise, enabling Adam to retain something of his coveted solitude, Naomi her job. A personal alarm took care of potential emergencies. But guilt and anxiety remained her constant shadow, even though she still took every opportunity to do things with and for him.

If only she'd had access to his diary then. If only she had really understood.

9 MAY—We had dinner guests yesterday. It was a longstanding engagement, churlish to call it off.

Geraldine is a colleague of Naomi's; a social worker who specialises in fostering. She's a quiet, self-effacing person and in the past I've wondered whether families brutalised by life respect her at all, she seems so entirely lacking in authority.

Under other circumstances I'd have enjoyed the challenge of drawing her out on the problems of deciding what makes a good foster parent, or adoptive family. But now? I sensed her unease throughout the evening. Having to ask me to repeat myself so often only added to her reluctance to prolong any conversation directly with me. Naomi's interpretations seemed too blatant to me, but Geraldine turned back to her with obvious relief. I guess you need the cement of real personal friendship to persist in this game, not second-hand obligation.

Wilf had no such sensitivities. Difficult to see what possessed Geraldine to share even a week of her life with him, never mind eleven years. He's a prize prat, as puny in his intellectual capacity as he is unattractive in his person. I was reminded of John le Carré's pithy descriptor: he's someone who thinks ethics is a county east of London.

After that experience, I am resolved not even to attempt to eat in the presence of guests ever again. On my own, or with Naomi, I can just about cope. Ursula Major put me in touch with splades. More than one utensil is a recipe for disaster; one that combines knife, fork and spoon, offers my best chance to stave off the need for assistance.

Her other suggestions don't bear mentioning!

That meal had indeed been a distressing event, one that Naomi had been in no hurry to repeat. She hadn't missed the pitying looks Geraldine cast at Adam when his whole attention had been focused on skewering a broccoli spear or a piece of cheese. She too had resolved this would be their last invitation.

How painful, all the 'lasts'.

16 MAY—Digby Arkwright called on Monday.

Polly, my morning carer this week, had left me more than usually comfortable, packed around with cushions at my machine, and I said a special prayer of thanksgiving for Ursula Major's idea of an intercom at the front door. I didn't have to stir a muscle to let in this Father Christmas of a visitor, so I was at my physical best when he marched in, filling the room instantly with his good-humoured presence. He's always welcome but today he brought with him a special commission. He wanted me to do a retrospective, tracking some of the lighter moments in my life as a columnist over the years. No hurry – just when I can fit it in.

Was this his way of handcuffing me to life? I find it hard to believe he was being devious, but...

Reading my hesitation as modesty, he pitched into his own rendition of some of my journalistic anecdotes. We were soon wallowing together in newspaper nostalgia and he left me with enough material to fill seven columns and a promise to return if the well ran dry prematurely. I would cheerfully siphon every drop of creative energy out manually to have him return with this kind of medicine.

It was hard to drag myself away from the intensity of writing when

Curtis called in at lunch-time two days later, but he too brought an offering – in this case, my novel. Unprepared for judgment, I knew a moment of sheer panic.

'Tread gently, Doc. You tread on my dreams!'

He was kind, said all the right things.

'But...?' I invited.

'Well, I know you want me to be critical. There were a few places that didn't quite ring true psychologically for me. I just don't think Aidan would do or say certain things – see, where I've marked them.' He flicked about six protruding yellow stickers with his thumb.

His insight into the mind of Aidan was impressive. The thought flashed into my head, can I deal with that level of awareness probing my own personal words and actions? But Curtis was racing ahead of me, analysing, suggesting. I had to shelve the personal disquiet in order to concentrate on the fictional things he'd snagged on. Every query was constructive. I was totally persuaded of the necessity to re-write those sections and I wanted to get down to it then and there.

But first I must complete my retrospective.

So much stimulation in just a few hours!

28 MAY—I've drafted Arkwright's piece. But I'm not ready yet to let it go. It needs distance.

Much as I accept the need for carers, I'm finding their intrusion into my mental life even more disturbing than their invasion of my physical privacy. Short of greeting them with a barked, 'Don't speak to me. I'm in a different world', I don't see any polite way of getting around it. I'm using the wakeful but safely silent hours of night to let my imagination run unfettered, committing whatever I retain to my machine next day. Should I get a dictaphone? I've tried using one in the past, but hated it. And it would disturb Naomi.

It wouldn't be quite so irritating if it were the same carer all the time; we could at least dispense with the preliminaries then. But this business of getting-to-know-you is a colossal waste of precious time. Then, of course, I might be stuck with one of the carers I like least. Some just grate. Period. 'I am, therefore I irk', as someone famously once said.

On the other hand, it's easier to let trained people heave me around, than to be forever worrying about what the strain is doing to Naomi. And it has stopped Joel hovering round her all the time.

I've just finished jotting down all the sections of the novel I want to re-visit, with notes on Curtis's criticisms. As soon as I'm free tomorrow, I intend to get stuck into that. Get it finished.

After that I'll return to Arkwright's piece, give it one more polish. I want to go out with a bang not a fizzle.

It occurs to me that I'm reaping the rewards of all that practice with this machine early in the year. Writing is still definitely my main therapy, a principal reason to go on living.

29 MAY—I bargained without Joel. He didn't arrive until after I'd been put to bed last night. Spur of the moment decision, he said. Naomi said she didn't know he was coming either, but I saw the sparkle in her eyes. He reignites something in her.

He wouldn't hear of my finishing the article.

'No way. I haven't driven all up here to look at a closed door. Where shall we go?'

I am suspicious of everyone's motives these days. But I was grateful to him for making Naomi laugh again.

Naomi let out a quivering sigh. Noelani stretched expansively in her lap. Mechanically she smoothed the silky fur.

There had been precious little to smile about in those bleak days after Madeira. In spite of all the extra assistance with Adam's physical needs she lived in a state of permanent tension. Not, to her surprise, because of the intrusion into her home, but rather because those strangers went away – leaving Adam alone. There had been no warning of his intention last time…

Just knowing that he was seriously seeking an end to it all was hard enough. Not knowing when he might try again was a source of unrelieved anxiety.

'Please, Adam. Share what you're thinking.'

'I can't.'

'Pleeeease…'

'It's not that I won't; I can't. I don't know myself. But one thing's for sure I have no intention of continuing to ruin your life. And that's final.'

'You aren't ruining it. I can't bear to think of losing you. I don't want it to be a second sooner than it has to be.'

'Any idiot can see I'm nothing but a burden.'

'You are not! It's much more of a burden worrying all the time that you're going to do something silly.'

'Well, don't worry, then. It's my problem. I'll sort it. I don't want you getting dragged into this. '

She'd pleaded until he snapped.

'Okay. Help me, then. Put a pillow over my face. That'll put an end to all your worry. And mine.'

She'd left the room precipitately. The thought of him being alone in that kind of mood forced her back. But no amount of apologising could erase the damage. She reverted to tiptoeing around his silences. Only with Joel could she be brutally honest, pour out her frustration and share the sense of isolation. Only when he visited could she occasionally see a glimpse of the old Adam.

1 JUNE—Four days of Joel's company and I feel surprisingly reinvigorated. Somehow his very normality restores my equilibrium. His constant good humour is at once a reproach and a therapy. His humorous take on life sends me to bed with a mind free to let the subconscious do its work.

I now have pages of notes ready for revisions to my novel. Joel must get a large acknowledgement. And tonight I've finished Arkwright's piece. I'll email it to him tomorrow.

Only lost in the absorption of writing or sparring with Joel can I find peace from this endless turmoil.

2 JUNE—Mailed off the retrospective. Finished the revisions to the novel. Emailed them to Curtis.

Lydia was harassed today. Three times during our session someone came in to ask her to do something else. Without her inimitable banter, the exercises lacks sparkle.

I didn't linger.

3 JUNE—What now? What am I clinging on for?

I want to hear Curtis's comments.

Ideally I'd like the satisfaction of knowing my book has been accepted somewhere.

But I don't want to see Naomi getting more and more exhausted. I don't want to feel the distance between us increasing.

That was the evening... Naomi leaned back in Adam's chair, closing her eyes, remembering. She'd arrived home from work to find the table in the conservatory laid, a white rose in the centre, a bottle of wine cooling. There was no sign of Adam and a sick dread had stopped her in her tracks, her own pulse thudding in her ears.

A muffled sound sent her sprinting up the stairs. Adam – very much still alive – was struggling to get an arm into a clean white shirt. He'd been sheepish rather than angry, in a hurry to be ready for the delivery of a Chinese carry-out, glad of her assistance.

The whole evening had been a break from hostilities. She relaxed in the warmth, savouring something of the old Adam. He offered no explanation; she sought none.

4 JUNE—I'm stunned. Why didn't she tell me? Is it tit for tat?

It all started innocently enough, in my study. I was rummaging in the drawers of my desk for a letter I know I received from the Inland Revenue recently, when I came across my mother's pills. I'd forgotten all about them.

The bathroom cabinet seemed as safe a place as anywhere, high up and with a proper catch. It was, of course, virtually inaccessible for a man on a zimmer frame, but I was determined. When it eventually sprang open, my clumsiness sent a cascade of boxes and bottles crashing to the floor. I cursed under my breath. Since when did we keep so much stuff in there?

In amongst the vitamins and herbal potions, it was the neat row of names on the packaging that caught my attention. Days of the week? We've never been ones for prescriptions, never mind *daily* doses. Fortunately I was leaning on my frame while I read the packaging. The words burned themselves into my brain.

How long? How long has she been secretly thwarting my desire to become a father? And why hasn't she discussed it with me? Damn it, I've been contemplating going for fertility tests myself! Imagine the humiliation.

With no idea how the boxes and bottles had been stashed on the shelf, I couldn't even attempt to replace them without her knowing, even if my fingers had been capable of obeying my brain. I just picked them up, one by one, and put them on the windowsill. My mother's collection of pills I returned to my desk.

No point in them being inaccessible.

If I was looking for an effective way to prevent a single creative thought cluttering up my brain, I'd found it.

By the time Naomi came home from work I had withdrawn into a very deep defensive place. She was still in the slightly euphoric state of yesterday. I mumbled some sort of confession about being unable to fit Mother's tablets into the cabinet, having to leave things out for her to put away. She smiled – actually smiled! – said something like, 'No problem', and went off to do it.

I watched her face when she returned.

Nothing was said.

Nothing.

She just got on with making a cup of tea. She held the door open for me to stagger out to the garden, sat beside me on the seat outside the back door drinking her tea and just took her cue from last night.

She talked about the good showing of azaleas this year, the invasion of moss in the lawn, her plan to prune the escallonia harder next time. She told me about a difficult mother she'd been with that day. She talked about other families – anything, everything, except the one thing that blocked out every other thought from my brain: our own family – or rather, lack of it.

I didn't confront her there and then, only because I'd had time enough to realise that I was afraid of what I might unleash. Or maybe because I knew she had an unarguable case: I didn't tell her that I was going to take my life, why should she tell me she's taking steps to avoid creating a new one?

I was still awake when she came to bed. I lay artificially still. I couldn't bring myself to touch her. I was still awake at 3 o'clock. I still said nothing of my discovery.

What would she have said if he had confronted her? Because he said nothing, she'd assumed he hadn't paid any attention to the pills specifically, and forgotten about it. A far worse skeleton hung in her cupboard.

5 JUNE—I can't get my mother's drugs out of my head. There they are, within reach. The only wonder is I haven't considered them before.

Coproxamol. For arthritis and back pain. There's a warning against more than eight a day. Looks like it shouldn't be too much of a hassle to swallow enough. But I have to think this through carefully. What if I choke part way through? What if I vomit them back up? What if I'm so slow that I fall asleep before I've taken enough? Or worse still, what if I'm discovered in the attempt? I can't take that risk – not again.

Is it the novel holding me back? Naomi and Curtis between them could do what it takes to find a publisher. My death might even lend it a marketing edge.

How much they had lost. Trust, communication, sharing; they'd been the building blocks of their relationship. What had gone wrong?

His MND; that's what had gone wrong.

The discovery of her contraceptives had obviously been a severe enough blow to him. She had been right to protect him from the gravest decision of her life. She couldn't have coped with his reaction.

Only Dr Curtis and the staff at the hospital knew. Oh, and Joel – and only because he'd caught her at a moment of weakness.

She forced herself back from that bleak moment. She had to share Adam's own emotion in the light of what he knew then.

8 JUNE—I decided today to sort out my papers. I want to know everything is in order.

It was meant to distract me from all these questions that refuse to be stilled, but half-way through the morning I came across a photograph of Naomi and me on holiday in Cornwall five years ago. Wall-to-wall sunshine, I remember, days packed with activity, nights full of love. The pictures in my head are bolder, brighter, more painful. How confident we were, back then, in our mutual decision to defer parenthood. It was a shock seeing her youthfulness, realising how these last two years have robbed her of her radiance.

The sudden ring of the doorbell startled me. It was the new incumbent at the local manse, Rev. Ernest Kane, getting to know his potential parishioners. He's gangly, fiftyish, spectacles that went out of fashion ten years ago, suede shoes with toes scuffed to burnished leather. I liked his entire lack of ostentation. I liked the way he readily accepted a cup of coffee, and just accompanied me to the kitchen at my pace, making no attempt to take over.

I'd lay odds it's the first household he's visited where he's been drawn into a discussion about fatal diseases and euthanasia within half an hour of arriving, but he seemed completely unfazed. I was more at ease with this stranger after twenty minutes than with many of my acquaintances of years' standing. He radiates understanding and compassion. Don't ask me how, he just does. I've become something of a connoisseur on such matters.

My mother would have said his coming was 'meant to be'.

He asked directly about my MND and he really listened to the answers. Without a trace of superiority, he corrected my first misperception (as he saw it): No, not all churchmen are opposed to euthanasia. The religious spokesmen who are trotted out to make position statements, don't necessarily reflect mainstream religious opinion.

'Self-selected, then.'

'Something of that sort. And in fact, market research has shown that most church-goers actually favour compassion over rigid rules condemning merciful intervention.'

'They do?'

'Apparently so.'

'Not my mother! And she was as "religious" as they come.'

Somehow he coaxed me into talking about her particular straitjacket. It was like lifting anchor. A fresh wind blew in my sails; I gathered momentum.

'Ah yes.' He made me feel as if he'd met my mother personally. 'But you see, some people need rigid boundaries to feel safe, and I don't personally think we should rob such people of their security. It takes courage and a different order of understanding to accept shades of grey, to work out your own solution.'

'"Work out your own salvation with trembling and fear",' I quoted.

'Precisely.' He grinned back at me.

'My mother again. A verse for every situation.'

'Ah. She sounds to have been quite a character. It never really leaves you, that kind of upbringing, does it?'

'No, indeed. I can quote more of the King James' Bible than of any other book I've ever studied. Thanks entirely to her.'

He nodded – without judgment.

'I gather this is a personal issue for you?' he said, perfectly matter-of-factly.

'It is.' I hesitated, looking at him hard. 'Am I allowed to ask what you think?'

There was a long pause, but no sense of discomfort.

'Strictly within the safety of these four walls? I think doctors should be able to help people die with dignity – where the situation is intolerable. But please don't quote me on that. We humble servants of the church can't really divorce ourselves from our dog collars, much as some of us like to go around incognito.' He has a most engaging grin, this guy.

'But doctors aren't too keen on that idea. It's not just theoretical for them.'

He nodded.

'And for people like me their resistance is a live issue. It leaves me very little choice.'

He waited quietly, holding my gaze without embarrassment or fear.

'From where I stand, it's a form of cruelty. Nature is cruel. This disease is cruel. Doctors are cruel if they use every ingenuity at their disposal to prolong my suffering. It would be a true kindness if they'd listen to my request, recognise its sincerity, and help me.'

He nodded, still without speaking.

'All I'm asking for is help in dying when the burden of life outweighs the benefits of continuing. I don't want to foul up the job trying to do it myself.'

'You think you would?'

'I know I did.'

He didn't probe. I found myself respecting this unusual man more and more.

'Aside from their scruples, do you have good people taking care of you?'

'The best.'

I tried to tell him about Curtis and Lydia and… but emotion strangled the words.

'Keep talking to them,' he said gently. 'You're very persuasive. You have real life experience on your side. You'll find a way. Let me know if I can help. I'd like to be on your side.'

'Thanks. Thanks for listening.'

'A pleasure. Thanks for talking to me. And for the coffee. You've compensated for all the doors that are closed in my face.'

He drained his mug and then leaned forward with both hands on his knees as if he was about to rise – but didn't.

'When you wanted to remember names or numbers, what used you to do? As a journalist, I mean.'

'I made up associations. Or jotted them down on scraps of paper till I got back to the office – and prayed I wouldn't forget where I'd written them! Why?'

'I was in hospital visiting a few parishioners yesterday and I noticed nurses and doctors jotting things down – on paper towels, on the back of their hands. They used to scribble on the hems of their aprons in the old days when aprons were starched cotton and not these flimsy plastic affairs they wear today. Speaks volumes for the efficiency of their hygiene, eh?!'

He stood up creakily as he said this, smiling broadly at me as he did so. I watched him, uncertain where he was going with this.

'God has your name engraved on the palms of his hands. Did you know that? It says so in the Bible. Did your mother tell you that one? You can't be forgotten. You can't be washed away.'

I stared at him. If he'd offered to pray with me I'd have been less surprised.

'*Isaiah* 49. Hang onto that.'

It was my turn to nod mutely.

I tried to stand up but he pressed me back into my chair.

'Don't waste that precious energy on me, Adam. I'll see myself out.'

'Thanks. Thanks for coming.'

'I'd like to come again, if I may?'

'Please do.' I really meant it.

'We'll talk some more.'

The promise lingered long after he'd gone to rap on some other door. It's people like this guy that I want around me when I slip into whatever is next. If anyone has an umbilical connection to the Almighty, it's the Ernest Kanes of this world. Surely his compassion is closer to the divine view of human destiny than my mother's punitive exclusivity? I want to believe it, but all those texts of judgment and punishment are etched into my brain. It would take more than thirty minutes with Ernest Kane to eradicate them.

How hard it was for him to give himself permission to wipe the slate clean of Mavis's diktats. The tightness of the cords that tethered him to his past was woven throughout his diary.

9 JUNE—A sense of failure pervades my days. I've always been an achiever; it depresses me that, after all my careful planning, I got things so wrong. Why did I delay? Was I subconsciously less determined to end it all than I thought I was?

I can't seem to rise above this infernal watchfulness. They're all on suicide alert. I hate it! But how do I set this thing up?

Which reminds me, I read somewhere that the Suicide Act of 1961, which makes it a criminal offence to aid, abet, counsel or procure the suicide of another, doesn't apply in Scotland. I need to check that out. Maybe all I need is a kindly person who understands my plight and who isn't too emotionally attached.

I almost asked Naomi about the pills today, but something stopped me. I must. This thing is eating me up. I just have to choose my moment so I don't make a bad situation worse.

Naomi was finding more and more reason for guilt, in spite of Stella's reassurances. She, who should have understood him best, had denied him most.

'If you'd only known what it cost me!' she whispered, tears trickling unheeded down her cheeks.

On Madeira he'd chosen the perfect time, the perfect place, the perfect way – for him. What right had anyone else to force him to suffer more?

Blinded by tears, she closed down the computer and went out to hack at the brambles which were threatening to strangle the crocosmias and dahlias at the back of the herbaceous border.

10 JUNE—The physical act of writing is getting increasingly difficult. Every bone and muscle cries out, Stop! But having this release is the only thing that's keeping me sane. The physical aching I can compartmentalise; the mental anguish threatens to destroy everything I hold dear. I suppose taking a huge chunk of the day to record my thoughts does beat sitting idle, watching my pressure areas breaking down!

It's strange how relevant things leap out at you when you're preoccupied with a specific subject. Throughout my journalistic career I've been grateful for that phenomenon, even whilst not quite understanding how it happens.

I was sorting some old papers yesterday, and came across a story about a man with Chronic Fatigue Syndrome who took a fatal overdose of morphine. His wife found him shortly afterwards but she knew he wanted to end his life so she waited almost two hours after his death before she called the GP. Hmm. Chronic Fatigue Syndrome wouldn't be on my list of conditions warranting death. People get better from it. Lots of illnesses get to points which seem unbearable. But things improve. Reading the article raised the whole issue of patient autonomy.

Even though I know there's no return ticket for me, someone else might challenge my assessment of intolerable. Back in April on Madeira, was it really the right time? I've had all these weeks since when I've been able to do a, b and c. And even now I can still do x, y and z. I can make some sort of a contribution to society, gain a degree of enjoyment from life.

And now? This minute? If I hadn't botched my previous attempt, I think I'd have more confidence in taking Mother's Coproxamol right now. Well, of course I wouldn't, I'd be dead!! Okay, I can't bear the thought of being hauled back from another aborted attempt.

Later What a night! Sally called with the girls in the late afternoon, on their way back from some concert or other. Naomi seemed to know all about it, instantly asking all the right questions. The story told, Sally stayed talking to me while Naomi took the children out into the garden to play.

Lest I infect them with my mood?

Lest they ask awkward questions?

Who knows?

I could hear them, I could see them. I witnessed Naomi coming alive in their sunshiny presence. I daren't analyse my thoughts. They didn't stay long but when they'd gone Naomi didn't return to the sitting room.

Eventually I went to find her. She was in the kitchen, preparing food. She glanced up, her face betraying her before she turned away and gave her undivided attention to selecting onions, peppers, mushrooms.

'What's wrong?' I slurred out.

'Nothing.'

'Doesn't look like nothing.'

'Acch, I'm just being silly. Must be my hormones.'

'The hormones you've been taking?' It just came out.

She stopped chopping, the sharp knife poised above the onions.

'Why? Why didn't you tell me?'

I should have gone gently. I knew I should – too late.

She just stood there with the tears trickling down her face, scraping the onion shards together.

'Why?' I asked again, more softly. I hope.

She shook her head.

'We have to talk. But I can't stand here. Come and sit down.' It sounded more peremptory than I intended.

Once I was safely seated, I had space to think of her.

'Look, Naomi, I just need to understand. Why didn't you tell me?'

'Tell you... what?' I couldn't name the emotion in her expression.

'Why you decided to go on the pill without talking to me about it?'

The words seemed to be wrenched out of her... her distress watching me deteriorating... her wish to spare me more pain, not to take away hope.

'I'm not a kid!'

'I know. But everybody needs hope.'

'I thought it must be my fault. I was thinking of going for tests.'

Her eyes dilated. She half reached out to me, then her hand dropped back again.

'I didn't know... I'm so, so sorry.'

'Don't you want children any more?'

'It's not that...' A fresh paroxysm of silent sobs shook her.

'Tell me.'

'I... can't do it... it's just... too much. I couldn't...'

'Just not with me, huh?'

'We couldn't deal with that as well. We *couldn't*.' There was something final in her voice.

'Okay. I can understand that. Heaven knows, I feel badly enough inflicting all this on you.'

'I'm sorry,' she whispered. 'I wish I was stronger about this... but...'

I held out my hand. She came cautiously. I pulled her down into my arms. Holding her shaking body close, there was no resentment, only an overwhelming sense of sadness – for her loss, for my loss, for our loss.

When we eventually returned to the subject, it was my turn to apologise. She was right: I had been the one to say we shouldn't have children – early on in my disease. And she clearly had no memory of my change of heart. Perhaps it never found shape in words.

This time we agreed together: there would be no child.

The dream has died with my neurones.

Naomi slowly unclenched her hands and wiped the sweat from her palms. Her pulse was hammering. Reading this was like teetering on the brink of that abyss all over again. At the time she'd had no way of knowing just how far he would press her; now she faced finding out just how much he had discovered, how far speculation had taken him.

'Bear one another's burdens,' Mavis would have said. No, not on this occasion, she wouldn't. Had she known what Naomi was keeping from her son, she'd have condemned her without a hearing.

Her heart still pounding, Naomi let her eyes roam over the room. Adam was everywhere. In the discarded briefcase leaning against the side of his desk; in the Velcroed slippers still lying under the stool in the window; in the books, the papers, the pens his hands had held. Inanimate, but his. Would a baby have given her the solace she sought now? She would never know.

She flicked back to the April entry that had brought a ray of comfort into her bleak heart. Written just two months before.

'...you hold my world in your hands. You are the centre of my life; the colour, the music, the constant. No words are big enough to capture my love for you.'

This was the real Adam. Before frustration and disappointment clouded his world.

11 JUNE—Things are less fraught between Naomi and me (I think, anyway) but I just can't seem to shake this feeling of depression. Needing a purpose, I sent off four letters to publishers today, with synopses, first three chapters, biographies of the characters, CV, SAE. I felt a real need to do something I'm good at. I can feel my identity slipping away from me.

Later Curtis came unexpectedly. It didn't take him long to notice my spirits were low. I dismissed it: part of the illness. But he persisted. Goaded, I didn't wrap it up.

'Okay. Presumably you knew Naomi was on the pill?'

'I can't discuss confidential matters.'

'But you could tell people at the hospital about my suicide attempt.'

'On a need-to-know basis. It was relevant to your treatment.'

'To stop me hanging myself with the hospital sheets, you mean?'

He raised his eyebrows fleetingly.

'Why can't anyone accept that I've had enough? I don't want to go on like this. For goodness' sake, why shouldn't I feel depressed?'

'Nobody's blaming you for feeling low. We only want to help.'

'But you won't.'

He let that pass.

'This thing is changing my personality. I don't want Naomi to remember me like this.'

'I'm sure she knows it isn't the real you making you do and say these things.'

'This is just what I wanted to avoid,' I said through gritted teeth.

'I know.'

Another long silence. It's another thing I like about Curtis: he's comfortable with silence. In the end it was I who broke it.

'What gives suicide bombers their courage?'

'Passion for their cause? All sorts of promises of future bliss and reward?'

'So you just lack the passion, huh?' I had to smile as I said it.

'Well, can you promise me seventy-two nubile virgins in the afterlife?' he said lightly.

'You sure won't get them if you strive officiously to keep me alive!'

'Well, in that case...'

The tension had eased.

'Can I put something to you?'

'You can always try,' he ventured cautiously.

'According to the law, we have to stop at red traffic lights, yes?'

'Yeeeeees.'

'If we drive through them we're liable to be punished, right?'

'Yeees.'

'Indeed. It's the rule. But the emergency services can jump them.'

'In emergency situations. With due care and attention. Yes. But that's different.'

'Exactly. Certain people with particular responsibilities may be permitted to do what other ordinary mortals aren't allowed to do – provided they exercise due care. I rest my case.'

He grinned at me. 'You're persistent, I grant you that!'

'They're not crashing through the lights just to show how macho they are; they're doing it to save someone's life.'

'And that's where your analogy breaks down, methinks,' he said, eyes twinkling, though he kept a straight face. 'To save a life. I rest *my* case!'

In spite of the lost battle, I felt less oppressed when he'd gone. We had managed to move seamlessly from saving lives to saving books from oblivion. It seems he's wont to take books he's read to charity shops rather than hoard them. I'm the opposite. We were soon exchanging titles of books that had shaped our thinking over the years. I gave him four of my books to take away. He promised to bring me two he'd kept, about which he'd value my opinion.

Between three innocuous but worthy novels, I had slipped in a slim volume on euthanasia in the Netherlands. There's a lot of drivel talked about the subject but this booklet seems, to me at least, to be pretty balanced. It comes from a doctor who actually works over there. The dead can't change their minds.

Curtis might.

After he'd gone, I remembered something he said ages ago: since the mid-nineteenth century, the BMA has taken the position that doctors cannot be held to an invariable ethical rule applying to all patients in all circumstances, and that the exceptional case doesn't invalidate the general rule. At the time I took it to suggest he might, one day, consider my case as the exception. Maybe in a while I'll try him out on that again.

Oh dear. Why do people fear death so? Either it's the end, in which case I won't know anything about it. Or it's the start of something new, which is supposed to be idyllic. I see no point in lingering here enduring torment if I can escape to either of these alternatives.

Is that what my father thought?

Curiously, I find I can't bring myself to condone *his* decision, even though I know he was living in his own kind of hell. He had no business to do that to my mother and leave two fatherless boys behind. Except that... isn't that just what I was planning to do to my own child if I'd had my way on starting a family?

'Oh why did you have to analyse everything so?' Naomi wailed.

But in spite of the grillings, Dr Curtis had been incredibly patient throughout. He'd been both sounding board and friend. He'd encouraged her too.

'Be open with him. Tell him how you're hurting too. Share your fears with him. Listen to his.'

But the doctor wasn't the one who risked sharing one burden too many.

'With him', yes. Not dragging him into another slough of despond from which there was no exit.

I was saved from being sucked any lower by Digby Arkwright. That man should be awarded an OBE for services to the down-hearted. As soon as I heard his booming 'Room in there for a little 'un?' over the intercom, I felt a surge of excitement. What little strategy has he got up his smart white sleeves today, then? He'd called to talk about my piece on the experiences of a working journalist.

'Brilliant stuff, Adam. Loved it! Only one criticism.'

'Oh? And what's that?'

'I wanted more!'

I grinned at him. 'You did?'

'You're a born story-teller, lad. How many d'you think you could run to?'

'Sorry?'

'How many more could you rattle off?'

'Stories? Oh, I guess I could dredge up one or two more.'

'No, not stories! How many *columns* full of stories? You've got flair, boy, real talent. We can't let all that go to waste now, can we?'

I agreed to see what I could do.

He was suddenly guarded.

'There's something else I'd like you to think about.'

I watched him carefully. The words came out hesitantly, hedged about by qualifications, most unlike my incisive ex-boss. The gist of it was, would I consider writing something about life with a degenerative disease?

I told him about my book. No problem, he was looking for personal experience, not fiction.

I still demurred.

It would be compelling reading. It'd take courage, of course, he could appreciate that. Did I think I could do it? How long would I need?

I said I'd think about it; he said he'd be back!

As he left he shot me a laughing look. 'A couple of mugshots, before and after – that'd send you hotfoot to the barbers!'

I took a look in the mirror. He was right. What a wreck!

What is it that revives me from these occasional visits – from the Ernest

Kanes, the Joels, the Arkwrights, of this life?

I guess it's partly the pleasure of being with people I like and respect, who are good company. They give me a warm feeling about myself as being deemed worthy of their time and energy – despite the hard work it is to communicate with me now, and the difficulty for them of seeing a fellow human being disintegrating before their very eyes. They make me appreciate my own continuing ability to think, to interact, to challenge, to achieve. And they leave me with a sense that I still have a use... well, rather that I am still of value in some way. These special people temporarily halt the inexorable spiral downwards.

Not for the first time, I wish that I could titrate out these visits to give myself regular boosts of confidence. Curtis and Arkwright in one day give me emotional indigestion. Adrenaline overload. I need a magician to bottle their effects and release a little dose each day. The fall back into despondency is all the harder the more euphoric these visits make me.

Talk of gentle titrations and controlled doses leads me into the business of the medical assistance I crave – a subject never far from my thoughts these days. And especially relevant now Arkwright has commissioned x thousands of words on the subject of my illness. *If* I do it – and I am by no means sure I will – I'll need to record something of the evolution of my opinions about the solution. As Arkwright himself acknowledges, it'll take courage to deal with the hardest decisions. Can I – can Naomi – cope with seeing those private agonies exposed to public scrutiny? On the other hand, this project could be exactly what I need to focus my arguments and resolve my own dilemma.

I've wandered away from the kernel of what my visitors give me.

Hmmm. Why aren't Curtis and Lydia among the chosen few? I need to think about that one. I still respect, admire and like them both. But I am not always buoyed up after their visits. Sometimes I'm even more depressed than when they came. Why? I guess it's because I'm ambivalent about what they do. It no longer seems appropriate to be trying to improve my mobility or learn new ways of doing things. What fires me up is what my mind can still achieve; what depresses me is what my body can no longer do.

Curtis remains the biggest enigma. We've travelled a long way together, he and I, and I so much value the support he gives me, his enthusiasm for my novel, his personal involvement with me, not just as a patient. But there's an underlying resentment because he refuses to help me in the way I want. Although I respect his position, I suppose I see this as setting limits to our friendship. Unfair, I know.

After all, he stuck his neck out for me over the Madeira incident. And I rather suspect that now, if I needed pain relief, Curtis would consider increasing the dose, without imposing a ceiling. I used to think it was a form of medical hypocrisy to give drugs which shorten life under the guise of relieving pain or distress while at the same time rejecting the idea of euthanasia. I no longer see it that way – thanks to Hugo Curtis's careful explanations. So he's helped to educate me, as well as walk alongside me. I'm too exhausted to write more, but I know my subconscious will be filtering all this overnight.

For the first time in weeks, the nightmare returned. But for once Mavis was not amongst her accusers. In the wakeful hours that followed Naomi found herself itemising the arguments for and against her actions.

'You're starting to pick up some of Adam's bad habits, my girl,' she told herself sternly. 'It's done; it can't be undone. You did it for all the right reasons. Now let it go!'

If only it were that simple.

12 JUNE—Naomi still gets up early in the morning to scurry around getting the place ready for my carers. No amount of reassurance will rid her of this compulsion. So I seized the moment that presented today.

The agency rang yesterday to say they were short staffed, they wouldn't be able to send a carer until this afternoon. Naomi didn't need to get up at the crack of dawn; I had her all to myself without fear of interruption. Perfect. Except that things took a completely unexpected turn.

My intention was to tell her about my plan: Ask Curtis if he would specify accurate dosages and agree not to intervene. Ask her to agree to stay well away with a cast iron alibi in return for me giving her advance warning. I wrapped it all up in the story of the case I'd read about where the wife didn't alert anyone till it was too late.

I fully expected her to weep and beg. Instead she remained, outwardly at least, perfectly calm.

'I know you hate other people telling you what to do,' she said conversationally, 'but I've got an even better plan.' With that she turned onto her front so that we were suddenly looking at each other directly.

Though startled, I managed to hold her gaze – not so easy given her proximity and state of undress.

'I know you've had enough, I know you want to go sooner rather than later. But I can't bear the thought of losing you. So why don't we go together?'

I just stared at her.

'That way, I can help you but not be around to be prosecuted. They couldn't do a thing about it.'

I wanted to weep.

'Bless you, Nay,' I said thickly, 'but no, absolutely emphatically, no!'

'But why not? It's the perfect solution.'

'To rob you of life? I think not! I couldn't.'

'Better than going to prison and grieving in solitary confinement.'

'Maybe, but I don't want that either.'

'I've thought about it a lot.'

'Well, I haven't! And I can tell you now, I don't intend to give it another thought. It's outrageous. You have far too much to live for.'

'Are you still mad at me – about going on the pill?' she whispered.

'No, I'm not. And I never had any right to be. You were only trying to do what was best. What I'm really mad about is this disease. That's what's to blame for everything wrong between us.'

'I want so much to help you.'

'And you do, especially putting up with my moods. I wouldn't blame you if you just walked out.'

'Don't be silly. Where would I go?'

'To Joel?'

'He'd cart me straight back here!'

We laughed together, her innocent response soothing my green-eyed thoughts.

'Hey,' I said, deliberately lifting the tone back up into my comfort zone, 'Did you read that piece about the guy who had his ashes scattered by his shooting buddies?'

She shook her head. 'Some of us have better things to do with our time than read the gutter press.'

'Oh, it wasn't gutter stuff. No, I think it was in our rag.'

'As I said…' she crowed.

'Okay, okay.'

'So what happened?' I knew curiosity would get the better of her in the end.

'Apparently the deceased was an expert in vintage shotguns. So his widow had his ashes mixed with traditional shot and loaded into cartridges. Then she invited a bunch of his closest friends to the last shoot of the season. So between them they scattered his ashes in a way he would have approved of.'

'That's really going out with a bang!'

We laughed together.

'She even had the cartridges blessed by a minister.'

'Your mother would turn in her grave!'

We spent the next twenty minutes devising ever more outlandish ways of disposing of my ashes and in that way I stopped all talk of a suicide pact. The thought still appals me.

Later Much as I'd welcomed a leisurely start to the day, it can be annoying having to wait in until the carer eventually comes. Naomi insisted she could manage pretty much everything I needed, so we rang to cancel the visit and took off up the Fife coast. I was craving sea air, but I wanted to protect Naomi from heavy pushing; the straight stretch of road beside the sea at Leven was a smooth and easy ride for both of us.

Watching the rhythmic waves, I found myself contemplating death by drowning. Would I be able to think peaceful thoughts and just let the water fill my lungs, or would I instinctively thrash and struggle? Maybe I'll experiment in the bath – always supposing I am ever allowed to have a bath on my own again. And if I am, whether I have the strength to pull myself back up out of the water if I am only experimenting.

Naomi looked so relaxed basking in the sun, eating her ice-cream – she has this taste for Mr Whippys! – I didn't share these thoughts with her. It is such a relief to be at ease with her again, I want to savour every moment we have together. But privately I'm considering my options. Insulin's another possibility. Apparently you can't detect that after thirty-six hours.

But where would I get insulin? And who would inject it?

Maybe a hefty bolus of air into a vein, then? Air is at least freely available. Could I manage to find a vein, inject it, tie/untie the tourniquet, all by myself? Not a chance. But if I could, all I'd need would be a syringe. I should have thought of this option while I still had some manual dexterity and strength. So all I really need is a syringe and someone sympathetic to my cause...

If an injection of something is a viable option, just to make sure, I/we could do it in the bath so that when the deed was done, they could slip away and I could just slip down into the water and it would look like a simple accident.

Would the authorities feel compelled to do a post mortem? Surely not... although in detective stories there's always some eagle-eyed sleuth who notices the puncture mark and gets suspicious. I suppose they'd ask how did I get in the bath in the first place, and who had left me there alone?

It's all so fraught. And I have a nasty feeling that I might be overlooking the obvious. I'm struggling to write fast enough to keep pace with my thinking nowadays and there's an anxiety that I've missed chunks out and there's a walloping great hole in my argument which I can't for the life of me see.

Fuggins, are you listening? *HELP!*

15 JUNE—The carer was early today and I was ready in good time for the morning service. I wanted to hear Ernest Kane in professional mode. Naomi was sufficiently intrigued to want to come too.

The church looked splendid. There was a wedding there yesterday and the whole place was bedecked in flowers, white with the most delicate shades of pink – perfect against the old stone pillars and rich maroon drapes. The scent of freesias, jasmine and stephanotis disguised the faint mustiness I've detected on previous, unadorned visits.

Ernest Kane wore no ornamentation, just his everyday black, and looked somehow much smaller in that setting. And yet his very simplicity spoke to me powerfully and provided the perfect foil for the message he wanted to convey.

'About ten years ago,' he began in a conversational way that made you feel he was speaking to you personally, 'I met a man who lived in a windmill. His name was Josiah Dreghorn. Perhaps it still is.'

He had us all in the palm of his hand.

The sermon was about the ephemeral nature of worldly fame and riches, and I know it comes from the heart. All this is vanity and vexation of spirit (as my mother used to say). Just as I heard her voice, he too took his text from *Ecclesiastes*! Weird. The same book as last time. In January. Just after her death.

But in a curious way the choice of text initially felt discordant coming from him. My mother carried a renunciation of the rest of the world with her throughout her life – at least the life she shared with my brother and me. But Ernest Kane has a sort of inner peace and contentment, a sincere love of, and hope for, his fellow man. His cheerful optimism doesn't square with the depressing conclusions of the preacher in *Ecclesiastes*.

In spite of that, it was no effort at all to listen to him. He's a born orator. By the end of the eighteen minutes he'd painted a startlingly vivid picture of divine riches. And that does square with the man I met! He positively exudes such wealth.

Furthermore the whole vanity thing gels with my own experience. The closer I get to my end, the more I see that my small celebrity, my worldly wealth, count for nothing in the great balance of life. What sort of a person I am is of much more consequence. Who better to remind me of such a truth than this humble man?

At the door afterwards, he seemed genuinely pleased to see me, instantly remembering my name. (I'm not sure if this speaks of his excellent memory or the paucity of houses where he gets a welcome.) Given that I was glued to my walking frame, he sensibly gripped my arm rather than my hand. I was sincere in my thanks to him.

When we got home, as soon as I'd set the table, I went straight to my study and started to read the book of *Ecclesiastes* while Naomi cooked the vegetables for our roast. Mother would have cherished hope for my eternal welfare had she seen me poring over her much-thumbed Bible, nodding at the pertinence of certain truths that seem to me undeniable at this stage in my disintegration.

'That which is crooked cannot be made straight...'

'And I gave my heart to know wisdom, and to know madness and folly: I perceived that this also is vexation of spirit. For in much wisdom is much grief: and he that increaseth knowledge increaseth sorrow.'

'For there is no remembrance of the wise more than of the fool for ever; seeing that which now is in the days to come shall all be forgotten. And how dieth the wise man? As the fool.'

By the time I'd got to the end of the second chapter, I was exulting in the sheer poetry of the language, and I'd got the message.

Roast pork and Naomi's famous herb stuffing – even mashed to a pulp – further heightened my good humour!

Naomi had a report to write up in the afternoon so I staggered out to the conservatory and buried myself in the papers. More weeping and wailing and gnashing of teeth! Another GP under investigation, suspected of having murdered a patient or two. Maybe Curtis has a point.

I hadn't got beyond the general pages (and a few multiples of forty winks) when in breezed my brother. He'd been up in Aberdeen for a meeting yesterday and decided on the spur of the moment to call in on his way back down south. We had a nostalgic couple of hours before he needed to get back on the road. This time I insisted on seeing him off. If he was irritated by an extra ten minutes delay in his departure, he gave no sign of it. I'm increasingly impressed by the character of this man who used to be so casual about other people's sensitivities.

As ever he left me with a joke on his lips, a triumphant punch of the air from his open window. Today is the first time it occurs to me that maybe the last minute levity is for him as much as me. What must it be like for him each time he has to say goodbye?

Naomi sighed. She knew what it cost Joel to remain so outwardly cheerful, how he lived in daily fear of hearing Adam had taken his own life and that history was repeating itself. Perhaps not even she really understood.

His visit had taken her by surprise too. Finding Adam asleep, he'd gone in search of her, only to discover her in tears over the report she was supposed to be writing. The harrowing details of the family she was dealing with, coming so soon after the reflections prompted by Ernest Kane's sermon, had brought her own sadness to the surface.

She explained it away, but he hadn't been fooled. Somehow he managed to undermine her resolve. She hovered on the very edge of confession, and then held back.

'You'll despise me!'

'Course I won't. You're being melodramatic now.'

'You don't know what I've done.'

'Try me, then.'

In the end it had simply tumbled out, the agony in her heart finding release after so many months of being repressed. Since that awful day, almost a year ago now. 25 July – a date forever imprinted on her brain. A day that could never be changed.

At first he hadn't understood, the facts of the story lost in her distress. But when he did finally piece together the fragments, Joel's reaction had surprised her.

'How you managed to keep all this from Adam I can't begin to imagine.'

'I had to. Don't you see? I *had* to.'

'Even so.'

'Can you…?' She kept her eyes averted.

He'd moved to face her directly.

'Look here, Naomi, this is none of my business, but for what it's worth, I think you did exactly the right thing.'

'You do?'

'Most definitely. Good grief! You couldn't possibly have managed a baby as well as Adam – as he is. And especially not a baby… like that.'

'It kills me to think…' She couldn't say it.

'I can't imagine what it took for you to make that decision – on your own. Especially doing what you do all day at work. Seeing all these other families.'

'We would have loved it… so much… if…'

'Of course you would. You'd make a fantastic mum. The best. Adam too, he'd have been a great parent… before all this anyway. But you couldn't have coped with that. You couldn't. Not now. It would have been the last straw.'

'And it wouldn't have been right… for the baby… either.'

'No. It wouldn't.'

'I was so afraid… your mother would find out.' It was a mere whisper.

'Well, she's the last person you should have been worrying about. No question about that!' he said abrasively. 'Her and her convictions! Most of them not founded on anything sensible.'

'She'd never have forgiven me.'

'Whether she would or not, we'll never know. Anyway, her opinions are totally irrelevant. You were the one who'd have had to juggle responsibility for two disabled people.'

'If the baby had lived.'

'That bad, huh?'

'Severely malformed they said. Physically and mentally.' A profound coldness enveloped her, just repeating those awful words.

'Life stinks sometimes. What a bloody cruel deal.'

'The worst. I just couldn't let our baby suffer. I couldn't. Not to spare myself.'

'Would it have been easier… for you, I mean?'

He asked the question reflectively.

She stopped to think again.

'Nothing was going to be easy. Whichever way I went. But if I hadn't decided on a termination, I wouldn't have had the guilt.'

'Not this particular guilt maybe. But knowing you, you'd have felt guilty about bringing the baby into the world, and seeing it suffer, for however long it did live, wouldn't you?'

She nodded mutely.

'You are far too nice a person for your own good,' Joel said, a break in his voice.

There was a long silence.

'How on earth did you keep the termination itself from Adam?'

'I told him I had appointments at the hospital all day.'

'And he bought that? Even when you came home? I mean, you must have been...'

'Well, a colleague of mine from work brought me home, afterwards. Adam didn't say anything. I don't think he noticed anything out of the ordinary. But then I do get emotional sometimes. He's used to it. Goes with the territory in my job.'

'Even so... You must be a damn good actress!'

She shot him a wintry smile. It faded instantly and she searched his face.

'It was right... wasn't it?... not telling him?'

'Who knows?' He shrugged. 'I can see why you didn't, of course. But it must have been a hell of a burden for you all these months.'

'I've coped. I just thought, with all the things that he was having to deal with, Adam didn't need to know the baby he wanted was... so deformed too.' She crumbled under a fresh wave of misery.

'He wanted kids?'

'Oh yes. Very much so.'

'Poor bugger,' Joel muttered, half under his breath. 'That, on top of everything else.'

'I just couldn't have given him that burden too. It was one thing I could do to help him.'

Joel had given her a swift hug.

'Naomi O'Neill, you are a very special woman.'

'I did have some counselling, so don't worry, I'll be okay. Sorry to dump this on you.'

'No problem. And for what it's worth, I don't think you should waste another second feeling guilty. You made the best choice you could. It's done. You can't change it. And you've got enough else to worry about!'

He'd made them both a strong coffee and by the time they'd drunk it, Adam had woken. Strange really, they'd never returned to the subject but it hadn't hung between them. A degree of closure had come with that exchange. Joel's approval had given Naomi permission to move on, not forgetting, but forgiving herself.

Mavis's ghost receded.

'Thank you, Joel. Bless you,' Naomi whispered.

16 JUNE — I'm positively skeletal these days. Easier for carers and Naomi lifting me, not so good from the point of view of my personal comfort. Cushions and sheepskins help, but sitting in one position is becoming a disincentive when it comes to writing for any length of time. I rail against this particular restriction to myself but it's too much effort to grumble aloud.

An increasingly inadequate intake of nourishment is also, I suspect, contributing to the sore throats, the headaches, the general feeling of malaise, I'm plagued by these days. People nag me to eat more – *they* don't have to fight for every swallow.

Today I was feeling pretty sorry for myself when I woke up after a bad night with muscle spasms and nightmares, and much in need of some healthy distraction, so I got the carer to pile extra padding under me and settle me in for a longish haul at the computer. I set myself a target of twelve letters to publishers about *Aidan's Story*.

Reminding myself that it was for Naomi, I managed to persist beyond my comfort point. I no longer harbour any hope of seeing the novel in print myself, but I warm to the idea of her getting something tangible out of this horrific experience. I don't know why I didn't start this part of the process a long time ago. Was I subconsciously delaying the date of my death by procrastinating? I'm suspicious of even my own motives.

The letters completed, I started on my second piece about journalistic experiences and was soon well into my flow and a healthy distance away from my bodily discomforts. It's an immeasurable bonus to have this best of therapies within my control and at my fingertips – literally! Dave, I salute you!

I haven't decided yet whether I'll do the MND article. I suspect the trauma would outweigh the benefits. Would I gain anything from such an altruistic endeavour? I don't know. I have a nasty feeling that I might plummet into irreversible depression. *Not* the state of mind I need to make wise choices about my life and death.

Later It's another door closing. A lifeline weakening. I had to give up this morning. It is so frustrating. My mind surges ahead but I get to a point where I simply can't tolerate remaining in that position any longer. If I can get the bare ideas down it helps; I can lick them into shape later.

Maybe I need an amanuensis as well as a physical carer! Do they come on the National Health? Now there's an original angle! Of course, I know it wouldn't work. Headings maybe, notes possibly, but not the flow that in my case requires absolute solitude. Could I record the ideas onto tape? They'd be there then ready for me to write when I feel able. With my speech problems? Hellloooo!

This is all exactly what I wanted to avoid. Damn that Madeiran peasant!

Later again Curtis rang this evening after surgery. Was I up to a visit? He'd finished reading the corrected manuscript and would like to discuss it with me, if I wasn't too exhausted.

My thoughts fragmented.

That was quick!... he's only skimmed it... he knows it'll never see the light of day, no point in wasting time over a lost cause.

He's hurried through it... he knows I haven't got long left... doesn't want to leave unfinished business.

Why hadn't he procrastinated, delaying my suicide? He knows something I don't know.

He didn't like it... he could have told me over the phone if it was an improvement on the last draft.

Do I keep re-writing to suit his preferences? If I do, will it ever be done? Why do I so much want his approval? This is a work of fiction, not a medical treatise.

His eventual arrival came as something of an anti-climax. He was wreathed in smiles and gave his verdict before he'd even sat down.

'Tons better! Totally consistent now. I like it.'

'Really? You really mean it?'

'Don't sound so surprised. It's a masterpiece.'

'But I need it to be authentic.'

'It is. Definitely. It's a terrific read. And I'll certainly be promoting it in medical circles.'

I tried to thank him but it all sounded so trite and hackneyed, so I reached for the acknowledgements I'd printed out just before he arrived and I handed it to him without a word.

He read in silence:

'A particular debt of gratitude goes to my friend and doctor, Hugo Curtis. Not only did he give me the benefit of his medical wisdom but he endlessly rehearsed the philosophical niceties of assisted death and kept me sane. He helped to shape my thinking on many things and I could have asked for no better companion along the path to my own death.'

When he eventually looked up, he was shaking his head.

'Far too generous. And quite undeserved. But thank you.'

'Sincerely meant,' was all I managed.

In his controlled and measured way, he steered me safely into neutral territory: where I was with getting the book published. And, as so often, he surprised me with his understanding of the publishing process. Just as he was leaving I remembered the question of Digby Arkwright's request. Curtis, the only person to have read the whole novel, was just the man to advise me on one point. Was there a conflict of interest? He saw none. One was fiction, one was fact. Different style, different perspective, different language, different audience.

'In fact, it'd be a great opportunity to use the newspaper to promote the book, wouldn't it? If I read that an author had your credentials, I'd be doubly keen to get hold of the novel. Go for it!'

First get the book accepted then! A great big incentive to get cracking on both fronts.

Like I say, this friendly neighbourhood GP can be positively inspirational at times. He has shot several places up the pecking order of my visitors. When he left today I was already seeing the dollar signs of a bestseller!

By the time Naomi had gone in to see Adam after this visit, he'd been engrossed in drafting an outline for the feature on his illness. It had been good to see the glint back in his eyes.

A sparkling dribble down his shirt-front stopped her in her tracks. It was no longer just a question of co-ordinating breathing and drinking; by this stage, simply swallowing – even his own saliva – had become a huge effort. She could only hope he was so absorbed he hadn't noticed.

Eating was already something of a battle ground. Staying well nourished helped to counter the effects of the MND; he knew it, she knew it. But at what cost! The evidence of untouched food-flasks and picked-at meals despite her own or the carers' best efforts three or four times a day, told their own story. She'd been prepared to accept his eating what he felt like – until Dr Curtis had taken her aside and painted a picture of the consequences: emaciation, pressure sores, constipation... She'd redoubled her efforts to make food appetising. But just knowing the facts didn't make swallowing any easier. There was only so much you could pack into a smoothie!

That night, as he stood at the door talking to her, the doctor had looked so grave. Light-hearted and unconcerned he might have appeared to Adam, but his watchful eyes had missed nothing. For the third time he suggested getting a dietician involved.

He was sympathetic; he understood why these offers had been declined before, but Adam was still here, and there seemed no point in his refusing what little effective help there was available.

17 JUNE The first rejection letter came today. Polite – the novel didn't fit their lists. I've had very little training in dealing with failure. Naomi commiserated but she had more pressing news to convey: advice from a dietician. She took a day off work to see this woman, such is her concern.

I am now to be on the receiving end of lumps of various hues and guises: apparently having everything liquidised is counter-productive since it doesn't help to keep my jaws working. My fortified drinks are henceforth to be girded about with steel reinforcements. My mashes and slops are to be laced with a huge new range of additional extras to support those said chunks of highly chewable food. Gravy, sauces, melted butter, these are to be my staple diet.

Naomi did her best, bless her, to sanitise the advice and make a joke of it, saying how she envied me being able to have as much cream and chocolate and sticky puddings as I wanted. I tried to respond in kind: what wouldn't I give for a massive heart attack right now! Hardened arteries might offer more rigidity to my stick-like legs!

This damned disease has got me by the scruff of the neck.

The words that had been too much for her self-control had actually been: 'This is the lump that makes the jaws act that make the tongue work that deals with the saliva that gathers in floods in the mouth of the man with the bib on.'

A vivid picture of Adam before the disease struck flashed before her eyes, rushing through the kitchen in the morning, an uncut wedge of toast in one hand, a mug of coffee in the other, gathering papers together, flinging out his expected timetable for her information, perfectly co-ordinated.

Perhaps that merciful cliff fall would have been a better way.

19 JUNE—Joel's here again. I tremble to think what all this travelling is doing to his own schedules. He makes light of it but… Paige is no longer in the equation. I don't know why and I don't like to ask. He'd tell me if he wanted me to know. Or is it that I don't want to find out that it's down to me?

Joel had fallen into the habit of ringing most evenings. Naomi had done her best to give him unvarnished reports but despite her warning, he had been shocked by his brother's gaunt appearance on that occasion.

There had been no mention of Paige.

Curtis called after morning surgery. Was it of his own volition? Did Lydia clype? Worse still, did Naomi summon him without reference to me?

He was concerned about my weight loss, he said, and wondering about a PEG tube. Percutaneous Endoscopic Gastrostomy. Apparently it involves a minor op to insert a feeding tube through the abdominal wall into the stomach. Food can be given as a bolus or be drip-fed or by electric pump, bypassing the mouth altogether.

My first reaction was fury.

Have all our discussions meant nothing?

He understood.

He wasn't seeking to prolong my suffering, he said mildly, but to relieve my present difficulties.

The answer was still no... unless... could he arrange an anaesthetic catastrophe in the process or a massive dose of a killer hospital bug?

He shrugged. 'You never know.'

Once we'd moved out of danger, we talked more about possible escape routes.

He had no magical solution. But at least I feel he has now recognised things have gone far enough, even for his conscience.

If a way could be found... I think he won't stand in my path.

'At the risk of alienating you completely, can I just clarify – you still want to decline the PEG tube?'

'I do. End of discussion.'

Naomi had felt real concern for Dr Curtis that day. His own powerlessness was clearly troubling him enough, he didn't need Adam's constant challenges.

The wonder of it was that he persisted in going out of his way to support such a complicated patient. She'd tried to apologise; Curtis had stopped her.

'It's perfectly normal to lash out. Don't deny him that. I don't take it personally.'

But she did, on his behalf!

21 JUNE—Lydia was briskly British today. Curtis must have told her.

In amongst her manipulations and massages, while she pummelled my chest and supervised my breathing exercises, she probed for details. When she heard the Speech and Language Therapist still hadn't been in touch she pounded my rib cage like a jungle drum in time to a denunciation of a system that permitted such deficiencies. She promised to rectify the situation without delay or her name wasn't Lydia Grace Lovelock. I have no doubt her indignation will already be reverberating in the corridors of the guilty.

Much as I love her staunch advocacy, I so miss her glorious Jamaican metaphors and her uninhibited conversation. It seems my disintegration has compounded the sorrows of her widowhood and we can't seem to recover our old camaraderie.

I feel impoverished as well as very alone.

Dull apathy, that's what he needed, just not noticing, not caring.

23 JUNE—Two more rejections from publishers today. I don't need this.

One did say graciously that they'd considered my submission carefully, but I know it's a standard letter, so I can't find solace in that assurance.

The other one looked as if someone had at least bothered to read the stuff – probably some lowly minion! They commented on my 'strong writing style' and the 'powerful material', but regretted that 'misery memoirs' fell outside the genres they handled. They wished me well elsewhere, 'sure it will eventually find a publisher and do well'… huh!

It was Devilish Devlin day today. Three months since my last check up with that prat, Stedeford. Is it really half a year since I saw the big white chief himself? I hadn't planned ever to see him again.

He has lost none of his clothes sense in that time out of my view. Green is today's choice, the colour of a dark forest, soothing on the eye – my eye anyway; both of his are as wayward as ever.

He watched me in silence as I staggered into his room on my frame. And he seemed to spend an inordinate amount of time flicking through my notes, reading letters, checking reports. In the silence I imagined what van de Veere and co. were telling him.

Eventually he leaned forward to face me directly.

'So, how have things been?'

'Increasingly intolerable,' I slurred out.

He wanted more specifics; he got them.

He gave nothing away as he examined me. But what was there to say?

'So, where do we go from here?' he mused, more to himself than me.

'Have me put down,' I suggested.

He half smiled. You think I'm joking?

'Dr Curtis tells me you don't want PEG feeding.'

I shook my head.

He leaned back in his chair, lacing his fingers.

'I had a patient in here, earlier today as it happens, who felt the same way as you initially. She's since had a tube and been surprised at how much stress it relieved. Getting enough food into her was becoming an ordeal for all her family, and the act of swallowing was a constant source of anxiety for her. And she's had a couple of chest infections from inhaled food. The PEG tube has improved the quality of life for all of them. Her own energy levels have risen because of the better nutrition and because she isn't now expending a great deal of effort on trying to eat. She tells me she sucks chocolate and has a taste of things she really likes – curry and Chinese food and chilli-flavoured crisps. And apparently one of her grandchildren has asked if he could borrow her PEG tube on spinach days!'

I rewarded him with a smile. I can only admire his tactics but my mind is made up. I can still lick my Stilton cheese and sip a glass of port. Besides, I have no grandchildren.

He made no attempt to put pressure on me, just checked that I knew

I had the whole team on board if I wanted them.

'Dr Curtis seems to be on top of everything. I don't need to see you myself for...' – long pause – 'shall we say, two months this time? August? Or are you going away for the summer?'

I hope to be going away for good, never mind the summer. I simply shook my head.

'Just ring and make an appointment if you feel you should see me before then.'

I thanked him without specifying that this was my comprehensive acknowledgement of his support. He accompanied me in slow motion to the door of the consulting room, missing nothing of my ungainly exit. I wanted him to penetrate through to my desperation, but he didn't relent; he didn't come after me and offer the help I really wanted.

I willed the hospital car driver to be involved in a fatal car crash. He didn't oblige me either.

Later I've just watched the video of my fellow-sufferer, Phil Such, for a second time.

Could his choice – starving to death – be the choice for me? I think not. I just know I'd fail. Even cameras and a publicly-avowed intention didn't stop Phil eventually succumbing to the urge to eat and drink.

Naomi shivered, remembering that night.

She'd walked in just as Phil Such's carer/girlfriend had been describing what it was doing to her being with someone who didn't want to go on living. Naomi had slipped away, shaken. Did she have the stamina to see this through to the end?

30 JUNE—Arkwright rang tonight. Naomi fielded the call. I wasn't up to a visitor right now, not even Arkwright. I sent a second-hand message: I'm well on the way with the journalistic reminiscences, still undecided about the more personal reflections. He chatted to Naomi for a while and accepted my apologies for today without delving into my reasons.

I can still see the value of that newspaper feature as a promotional vehicle for *Aidan's Story*, but in reality, I'm finding it too emotionally as well as physically exhausting. It'd be at the expense of this diary, and this diary is my principal coping strategy. Brutal honesty, that's what I need; it's of no positive benefit to me to write a sanitised version for public consumption at this stage. And I certainly don't need to concern myself with royalties; Naomi won't be in want of a pound or two.

1 JULY—Lydia popped in again today. She'd been to some sort of exhibition and seen a gadget and thought of me, she said.

'Does it involve criminal activities in the company of maverick physios?' I asked her.

The sudden Caribbean metamorphosis lifted my spirits instantly.

'Why bless you, Mister O, you sure are suspicious of your oldest friend these days!'

'Go on then, reassure me.'

'Weeeell, you've been getting tired legs, yeeees? A mite uncomfy round the rear end, yeeeees?' The sequence of rolled out vowels emphasised her point eloquently.

'A mite, yeeeees.'

'You need something gentle, yeeees? To get those luuuuuvely legs I've had my eye on for all these years moving like oiled pistons.'

'And?'

'Well, since I'm your Number One fan, I've been thinking. And I think I've found the exact right object, Mister O. Yes, sir!'

She vanished into the hall and then reappeared with a cross between a footstool and a body massager.

Next minute I was treated to the extraordinary sight of Lydia squeezing her ample frame into the chair opposite mine and hoisting her legs up onto this rolling contraption. She pressed a button and her feet began to move back and forth on the rows of polished wooden balls. Once a steady rhythm was established, she leaned back with her eyes closed, a beatific smile playing on her lips, as if she was experiencing something wonderfully satisfying.

'Lydia,' I said, 'You give every appearance of once again exceeding your brief!'

She opened one twinkling eye.

'Now Mister O, after all we've been to each other, over the years, I hope I can depend on your discretion. I'll leave this little beauty free for you in exchange for your silence about my irregular manner of working, yeeees?'

I had to laugh.

She sprang out of the chair and next minute she'd manoeuvred the contraption under my feet and her powerful hands were 'walking' my legs in mimicry of her actions. Once the footstool started to move rhythmically she withdrew and beamed at the effect of this effortless exercise.

'You're a genius,' I said. 'I owe you.'

'Neat, huh?'

'Fantastic. Where did you find this little gem? Or did you invent it?'

She may not have invented this gadget but I have a strong suspicion that she it was who patented her particular brand of getting truculent patients on board.

She rocketed back up my list of favourite people.

Later It really is bizarre how often my visitors come in twos. Like buses. Only tonight I feel as if a whole depot full of buses have driven through my day.

Not long after Lydia had gone, Curtis rang to see if it would be a convenient time to come round; he wanted to see both of us, there were things we ought to discuss. Intrigued, I agreed – I happened to know Naomi was home tonight because we'd made a tentative arrangement to be in together to watch a travel programme that included Madeira. I'd observed her carefully when I made the suggestion and hadn't detected any reluctance, but now when I came to think about it, recording it might be safer.

Curtis doesn't shirk the grotty tasks, I'll give him that! He was quite shockingly direct and eloquent – maybe shock tactics were part of his strategy. A summary of his points must suffice. And my reactions.

a) It's time to talk about how we'll manage my death. (At last!!)
b) An emergency might present and we all need to have agreed a course of action.
c) Madeira was a turning point for him. (And me!)
d) He needed what's been called 'a pause'. Not a pause to reflect; a pause, a break, from reflection. (This gave me something of a jolt. Maybe that's what I need too, rather than this relentless thinking.)
e) The break has clarified his thinking and now he believes the three of us, together, need to try to grasp something rather elusive – partly a matter of careful reasoning, but also something more subtle... more reflective, more comprehensive, more sensitive, more aware. And painful.
f) He'd start with something concrete: my advance directive. We can safely trust that everyone who knows of its existence will do their best to respect it, given the circumstances. Does it still represent my current wishes? (It does.)
g) It states, among other things, that I don't want to be resuscitated in an emergency. But families can't always envisage what those emergencies will feel like, so it's best to talk about the possibilities and anticipate just how much we're both prepared to tolerate.

At this point Naomi suddenly said in the lightest of tones, 'If they end up treating you against your wishes, Adam, I could always sue the Trust for trespass to your person and end up a rich woman!'

I turned to stare at her.

'Where did that come from?'

'Trespass against the person, you mean?'

'Yes.'

'Bertie. He told me.' Albert Finnegan, a lawyer we know. But when did she discuss all this with him? This woman is a darker horse than I ever knew.

Curtis interrupted, also in a mildly humorous vein. 'Unfortunately these cases don't exactly carry much financial weight. You might still be doomed to penury.'

'Well, please don't trouble to leave me with an inflated view of my own worth, will you?' I said sarcastically.

h) Curtis stated solemnly, when I asked him outright, he wouldn't himself initiate any heroics to prolong my life if we were both at ease with that. (We are. Hallelujah!)

i) He would sedate me if I was distressed. (We both agreed with that.)

j) He outlined some scenarios where I was at the centre of a medical drama that might end in my imminent death. This bit was tough on Naomi – and weird for me too, but now we know and have agreed (in theory at least) what would be best for us all. Curtis alone, I think, has inner confidence in what he would or would not do even in a crisis, but he is the only one of us who has any experience of these things. And he is the only one who isn't losing the person he loves most in the world. At least now Naomi and I are aiming for the same goals and he knows what they are.

It's something of a comfort to have his hand on the reins, to know that he has heard our promises and would, I think, have the strength to help us hold to our resolve. Maybe this was part of his agenda, this reassurance. I pressed him to share a glass of port with us afterwards. The three of us talked of bestsellers and weedkillers, of pedigree cats and damp-proof courses, and by the time he left, I felt composed enough to grip his hand for a long moment to convey what my tongue could not.

In the privacy of our bedroom that night, I could finally tell Naomi what it meant to me knowing that I had her support for the rest of my life.

So often at night the doctor's graphic scenarios had swirled against Naomi's closed eyelids. She could only pray for the strength to hold firm when it actually happened. Having Dr Curtis so emphatically on her side had been some consolation.

3 JULY—My fourth rejection letter. I know even bestselling authors

have drawers full of rejection slips but stupidly, I thought I'd be the exception.

The timing is all wrong. I should have done all this when I was powerful enough to thumb my nose at poxy editors who can't write a decent paragraph themselves but who get off on crushing those who can. Today's letter had two typographical mistakes in eight lines of text! Some bumptious upstart dismissing my perfectly constructed manuscript – it's an insult.

I'm mad at myself for letting this get to me. I thought I was big enough to let it wash over me. Another myth exploded. But it makes Arkwright's offer all the more tempting. At least I know that what I write for him would be published; he's commissioned it. That way I can be confident something of my experience lives on; all my effort to live creatively with my disease won't die with me.

Another duty-visit from Jerry. I found myself blanking out his newspaper gossip. All that politicking leaves me cold. Was I really once part of it? I like to think I forged my own path and remained detached from the back-stabbing. It doesn't matter now anyway.

I was much more pleased to see IT Dave, even though he did overlap with Jerry. I think he was impressed by my speed with the machine, but he tutted over the state of my desktop, calling me a 'slovenly worker'! Hey, you're talking to a dying man here! Apparently the hard drive was 'obscenely fragmented' so he pressed keys and created wonderful kaleidoscopes of colour until everything formed into even-coloured bars and he pronounced himself satisfied. He unscrewed things and took the base apart, tinkered around with sprays and brushes and peered knowledgably at a whole board of electronic wizardry.

'You should call me if you need things tidied up,' he said with a hint of criticism. 'It's all part of the service.'

'I would if I knew I had a problem,' I retorted.

He shook his head at me. 'You arty types! Haven't a clue about how to handle machinery, have you? Doesn't the reduced speed drive you crazy?'

I shrugged. 'It's just a tool to me. As long as it works. How would I know it was slow? I'm reduced to snail speed myself nowadays.'

'Philistine!'

It was good to have an opportunity to thank him for giving me such a lifeline. He asked what I was writing at the moment but I got a distinct impression that he wasn't paying much attention to the answer. Even so, he was a welcome link with the real world, and a decreasing number of people fall into that category these days.

Apparently he's a cat lover and Noelani really took his fancy. I thought he'd condemn her long hair in the vicinity of the computer but no; he even stroked the traitor as she curled up in his lap during the long waits while the belly of the machine grumbled a way out of its indigestion.

Dave's a big muscular bloke, so I risked asking him to help haul me out of my chair enabling me to stand to relieve the pressure on my backside for ten minutes. The trouble with peripatetic carers is that they aren't always there when you need them.

4 JULY—It's abominably hot and sticky. Sheepskins and cushions aren't what you need in July!

After another disastrous night, I was exhausted by the time the carer had got me bathed and dressed this morning, so I slept for two hours. But at least I can; Naomi had unavoidable meetings all day. I'm putting pressure on her to sleep in the spare bedroom; so far without effect.

My joints are stiffening up. The discomfort is definitely getting worse. Curtis is considering muscle relaxants to ease the muscle cramps and spasms, the only trouble is they may increase my weakness and hence limit my mobility still further. Talk about the devil and the deep blue sea!

Naomi has finally conceded we need more frequent help. It's a mixed blessing, of course, having all these unselected strangers coming in and out of my world. I'm the first to accept that I'm a harsh critic of my fellow man, but they do seem to invite judgment. In my present captive and dependent state, I can't avoid their foibles, so I'm quickly irritated by them. If I wasn't indebted to them I'd find a useful outlet in using their mannerisms and habits as an endless source of rich detail for my fictional characters, but it would be too cruel to throw their help back in their faces. You wouldn't catch me doing their job!

Maybe a little secret exploitation…?

Cathy talked about herself constantly – every minute detail of her mundane life – all in this affected nasal twang that gets right up my nose!

Dorothy's conversation revolved around me rather than herself, but her personal remarks about my 'smooth shoulder blades' or my 'long thighs' seemed somehow faintly indecent.

Louise gave every appearance of being breastfed on misery. She couldn't seem to complete more than an hour of tasks without going out for a cigarette. Foul breath in my face I don't need.

Shamus brought a wonderful Irish humour to the business of caring but I found his personal habits left a lot to be desired. I couldn't quite bring myself to request that he washed his hands at strategic moments, but my very cowardice compounded my tension.

Findlay was the best of the bunch when it came to manhandling me from A to B. Nobody has got the supporting framework in my chair as exactly right as he did. But I found myself cringing when he said, 'Yeeeeeeah, right!' in response to everything I said.

Kristel's variation on that theme, 'Absolutely' when she meant 'Yes', was almost as annoying. And she has a laugh like a mechanical digger.

Some of my carers have had such strong local accents that I've been at a loss to engage in any meaningful conversation with them, but they actually served a useful function: they reminded me forcefully, and rather painfully, of what it was like for everyone else struggling to decipher my own grunts and slurs. Normally I'd have persevered but it's such an effort to keep asking for a repeat performance, with every attempt feeling the heightened pressure to pick up what they're saying this time. I just don't have the space for it now.

Chas snorted; Hilary kept picking her face... does all this constitute libel, I wonder?

Of course, these minor irritations are as nothing against the positive things these dedicated people do to keep me mobile, clean, decent and functioning. I am indebted to them.

Phew! What a relief to get that off my chest! I take comfort from the fact that I've kept all these nerve-jangling foibles sternly to myself. I do not want to turn into a Victor Meldrew!

Naomi stared at the list.

Her own irritation had been of a different order. She had baulked at the need to be constantly polite to these people who were invading her home. She didn't want to be pleasant to the nurse who arrived at 11.45PM to put Adam to bed, because it suited her schedule. She didn't want to be understanding to the helper who appeared an hour and a half ahead of expectation, because the person before Adam on the list died last night.

She didn't want everything to revolve around other people's timetables and priorities.

But there was more...

Not long ago I felt that the days were flying by too quickly, rushing me towards my death. That feeling is receding. Some days crawl by and I find myself wishing I could wind the mechanism up tighter and whiz through the indignities faster. It gives me no pleasure to watch every step, in minute detail.

I must be terrible to live with.

7 JULY — Another rejection letter today. I found it depressing contemplating the pettiness of my present world last night. Seeing my swollen ankles today, my feet encased in Velcroed slippers, I feel like a social leper. The

only marvel is that Naomi still wants to be close to me. I don't want to be anywhere near myself. I hate the disfigurement on top of the distortion. But her kindness is a constant reproach as well as a consolation. I do not know if I could have been so generous, were our positions reversed.

Should I try the diuretics Curtis wondered about? But diuretics mean more trips to the loo. More trips to the loo mean more exertion, more help needed, more exposure of my ravaged limbs. Maybe I should just burrow inside a huge quilted bag to hide the whole of my offending body. And never come out.

This thing is spreading inside me like ink on blotting paper. Soon I will be entirely soaked in MND.

Words like 'future', 'hope', 'joy', have vanished from my lexicon.

Later I'm quite pleased with myself. In spite of my low mood I made a concerted effort to drag myself back from that dark place. I started Arkwright's piece on my experience with this accursed disease. And having finished his other column last night, I checked it once more by the cold light of day and emailed it to him before I scrapped the lot as an exercise in vanity.

8 JULY—Curious. It's only Wednesday, not a weekend, but Joel is up again. He says he just decided to take the day off.

I wanted to be bright for him; I couldn't do it.

He said he wanted to help; his presence helps. But I worry about him getting so involved. He dragged out of me the fact that I'm hating the physical changes. He reckons he doesn't notice them nearly as much as changes in my mental state.

I told him about Curtis and our big chat, so he knows where we all stand. No point in him worrying unnecessarily about how bad things will get.

That visit was still sharp in Naomi's memory. Joel had fallen into the habit of ringing Adam several times a week; a regular therapy of jokes and light-hearted banter. On this occasion, sensing the despair, he'd dropped everything to come in person to rally his brother's spirits. The potential for suicide was still preying on his mind.

'Don't get me wrong, Nay, I wouldn't blame him. How he copes with all this, I just don't know. But... ending it all... himself... well, it screws me up somewhere inside. To think of him *having* to do *that*!'

'Oh, I know! I know. It feels so... selfish, but I feel physically sick walking up the path, putting my key in the door, in case I find him...' It didn't bear putting into words.

'I know it's what he wants and I wish I had the courage to do it for him, but... I'm a wimp. I'm a lily-livered coward. I'm useless. I just couldn't. I couldn't.'

'Don't beat yourself up on that score. Neither could I.'

'We'll be cowards together, huh?' The words trembled in spite of his attempt at levity. He turned abruptly and left the room.

10 JULY — Another letter from a publisher. I like its logo. I chose it for its name: Omega Press.

'I am Alpha and Omega, the beginning and the end, the first and the last.' Apposite.

I sat for several minutes not wanting to even slit the envelope open. How much more rejection can I take before I go under? I put it down and waited until I'd had a strong mug of coffee.

'Thank you for sending us'... 'intrigued by the synopsis'... 'the first three chapters hold promise'... I stopped and started from the beginning again.

No, I had understood correctly the first time. They want the whole manuscript! Yes!

Slow down, O'Neill. This is by no means acceptance. But someone likes the beginning enough to give it a whirl. I think I may be permitted a modicum of satisfaction.

Joel ran me off four full copies a few weeks ago – in readiness for the fierce competition for film as well as publishing rights! So all I had to do was write the specific reply to Anthony Frobisher (Editorial Director, Omega Press), and get Naomi to package it up and post it off tomorrow – well no, perhaps in about three days' time. Don't want them to think I'm desperate.

It's like walking out of a dark cave into brilliant sunshine.

I must keep a check on unrealistic expectations.

Seeing myself through Joel's eyes this week, I've suddenly become much more aware of the deterioration in my swallowing. I'm dribbling like a baby cutting four incisors at once. And regurgitation is a real problem. Apparently my diaphragm is weakening.

'Picture a steel band around your body holding all your organs in place,' Curtis said. 'As it slackens, things start to migrate.'

The acid and food reflux is an offshoot of this migration, it seems. It helps marginally if I stay upright after meals. I'm still waiting for the Speech and Language Therapist to advise me on this. It's been nearly four months since Curtis and I agreed the time had come to see one; three weeks since Lydia blew her gasket – not that I'm pathetic enough to be counting the days; I just checked back, using the search facility. It probably means that the managers don't hold out much hope of her being much use in my case, better to spend her valuable time where she can make a difference.

Hey ho! Joel already jokes about my 'retinue of servants'.

12 JULY—Talk about coincidence! A young lady answering the S&LT description actually made contact today – rang in the morning, came in the afternoon.

Chloe. Friendly but brisk. She overrode all my petty reservations. I expected a posh elocution teacher, instead I got a thoroughbred Scottish lassie who is three parts common sense to one part private education. (As soon as I knew she was Edinburgh born and bred, I asked the ritual second question, that's how I know she wandered the converted hotel corridors of St Margaret's School for Girls.)

Today's shared wisdom included making a conscious effort to swallow more frequently, having my head better supported (she's gone off to find a proper headrest for my chair), and sleeping on my side so that the saliva doesn't pool in my throat. The simplicity of her measures appealed to me. While she was rummaging in her bag, she muttered something about a suction machine but I didn't understand the words frilling round the edges even on a second repeat. It can wait.

Naomi said she felt reassured too. Like Devlin, Chloe said in reality choking is relatively common but rarely fatal. If and when I choke, she said, Naomi should resist the temptation to slap me on the back; that would just make me breathe in and exacerbate the situation. She's to keep calm, try to retrieve whatever's causing the choking (yuck!), and get me to lean forward with my head above my knees.

I had to laugh. They both looked at me as if I'd flipped my lid. But the thought of me being able to bend into a preordained position at this stage in my paralysis was irresistible. They eventually saw the point but the smiles were faint. Apparently the Heimlich manoeuvre is rarely necessary. Just as well given the impossibility of Naomi getting us both into position to carry it out.

Chloe also explained another phenomenon that's been more annoying than painful. My eyes sometimes feel like balls of grit, and yet I seem to have an overflow of tears. It can be embarrassing; must look as if I'm weeping when I'm not. Chloe says it's another feature of the loss of muscle tone; as the facial muscles slacken, even normal quantities of lubrication overflow. Marginally easier to accept once you know.

This new therapist has wafted into our disorderly lives like a breath of spring. I now regret my past stubbornness.

Later Digby Arkwright came this evening. It crossed my mind to wonder if Harry knows about these visits, and if so, what he thinks. He, of course, sends no messages. As far as I know, he has forgotten I ever existed.

Anyway, Arkwright liked my piece in principle but had a few minor amendments to suggest. And he was spot on every time. I've sometimes wondered if his comprehensive approval lately has been merely a kindness to a dying man, but when I showed my appreciation for today's critical comment he reassured me on that score: even if he felt inclined to go gently in my case, nothing I write goes out with a footnote about my condition, so it goes into the race with the able-bodied scribblings.

My kind of language.

14 JULY—In my dippings into this diary for Arkwright's piece about my disease, I've become aware of a change in my intentions *vis-à-vis* these reflections. I need to make them explicit.

At the outset they were for my own release, my eyes alone. I have become increasingly aware that Naomi needs an explanation. I want her to understand more completely why I've been as I've been. So today I wrote a note to her and labelled the envelope: 'To be opened in the event of my death'. It gives her the names of the appropriate files and express permission to access them.

While I was tidying things up, I checked my living will again. It still represents my considered wishes.

I hope my death can be engineered within the law and the boundaries of medical permissibility but I haven't ruled out something on the grey side of that line. Oh, and on that subject, I need to record my latest musing. I might write a piece on the distinction to be made between legal and legitimate. *(Ideas folder: *legal v legit*)

Legal = what the law allows or dictates.
Legitimate = what we believe to be right and proper, a kind of
intuitive morality, a sense of natural justice.

It seems to me, it's this intuitive sense of right and wrong that underpins a civilised society. It's about according universal respect and dignity to one's fellow man, not because the law tells us we must, but because our innate sense of right tells us to. It's about those things that aren't enshrined in law, but a strong moral imperative exists to do them nonetheless. Legal imposition feels more restrictive. Doing things because they feel right is more a matter of personal choice, a freedom to do it this way because of inherent values and legitimate standards set in a context of communal good.

Wow! Where did all that come from?

Ergo doctors ought to respect my wishes because of the essential rightness of them. If it's known you've discussed the advance directive with a doctor, it has extra clout, improving your chances of having your wishes followed. Brownie points there, then. Curtis has documented our agreements. And signed my directive. And promised me that he'll do his level best to protect Naomi from any compromising situations.

If only the guy would agree to be active about this himself we could all feel more secure. Medical consciences!

Later The Reverend Ernest Kane called again today. I think he more than merits the title of Very Reverend, although I don't actually understand the real distinction in church terms. I couldn't help but notice he had a hole in his sock, because he's wearing... Jesus sandals!! With socks. Holey socks. Holy socks!

He came right out with it: he was shocked to see the state I was in. I surprised myself by my instant response. 'Blessing in disguise. The faster the end-stage, the better for my sanity.' That from me! – utterly and implacably opposed to the Pollyanna principle!

He raised an eyebrow but let it pass without comment.

As before, he instinctively adapted his pace to mine. He enquired about my novel's progress and said something kind about the contribution I can still make.

'I see a lot of lonely people who get precious little reinforcement in life,' he said quietly. 'If you don't feel valued by others, it's a lot harder to appreciate your own self-worth.'

Is that why he goes about making everyone feel valuable, I wonder?

'You evidently have a lot of reinforcement. From your writing. From your friends and family. From colleagues and people whose lives are the richer for having known you.'

'But it makes for complications,' I said slowly, my brain galloping ahead of me.

'Yes?'

'When I first found out I had this disease, I wanted to die while I still had most of my faculties. Now look at me! I've drifted into exactly the situation I was so desperate to avoid.' Did I sound bitter? The thoughts were tinged with sourness as they formulated. 'If I could have just suited myself, if I'd been one of your loners, I could have ended this exactly when I wanted to.'

'So what made you keep going?'

'My wife. My brother. My writing. My GP.'

He tilted his head questioningly, not making the connection.

'He refuses to help me die.'

'Ahhhhh. I see.'

'So I've sunk into the depressed and morose freak you see today!'

He smiled gently. 'Oh, Adam, "wad some Power the giftie gie us..."'

296

'Oh, I'm quite sure "ithers" see me in just the same way,' I flashed back. 'I don't like what I've become either. I never used to get depressed.' It somehow blurted itself out without my permission.

He sat in silence. Waiting.

'It's a particularly hard thing to deal with,' I ground out.

'I can feel that.'

Again he simply waited.

'My father committed suicide. He suffered from depression.'

'Ahhhh.' A long pause. 'But in your case depression is perfectly understandable.'

'I tried to end it all back in the spring. Someone intervened.'

'D'you wish you'd been successful?'

'Yes.'

'Has anything good happened since? Or has it all been bad?'

'Well... there've been some good times, I suppose, but there are certainly bad times I regret having survived for.'

'Do you still have goals you'd like to reach? Seeing your book published, perhaps?'

A baby. It just flashed into my head, unbidden.

'Not now,' I said. 'And I know I shan't see the book published, so I'm not pinning any hopes on that.'

'I'm sorry. Is there any way I can help you with living this out?'

'Thanks, but no – unless you can find me a shortcut.'

I instantly regretted it. I wanted to send him away feeling he had done some good.

'I really do appreciate your coming,' I said lamely through a sudden rush of saliva. He stood beside me as I coughed and spluttered my way back out of the paroxysm. 'Sorry about that.'

'You have nothing to apologise for,' he said, gripping my shoulder. 'I'm just sorry life has dealt you such a raw deal.'

'This is where I say, "Whom the Lord loveth he chasteneth," isn't it?'

'Your mother again?'

I nodded. 'It took care of a lot of punishment!'

'There's chastening and there's chastening,' he said gently. 'Remember the tower of Siloam.'

'Those unfortunates weren't in her Bible!'

He half-smiled.

'I was weaned on the idea of unworthiness,' I said.

'Not one of us is worthy – not even your mother! The only chance is through grace.' He turned as if to leave and then threw his punchline. 'And there's enough of that for all of us.'

He knew exactly when to make an exit.

I wish I could be convinced, but throughout my formative years, I had this impossible target held up to me. Every day I went to bed knowing I'd failed. My mother saw to that.

It's in my bones.

Maybe I can fail and still feel Rev. Kane's confidence. I'll need to think about that.

15 JULY—The more stiff and immobile I get, the more impressed I am by these professionals. They make it look effortless to haul me up and frog-march me around. Everything takes forever but they never seem to share my impatience.

I've just discovered that it was Lydia who taught Naomi, and I confess I like to think of these two women in this together, Lydia including my wife in her enormous motherly embrace. Véronique, for all her efficiency, just wouldn't have been the same.

I've noticed this in life generally, you either warm to someone or you don't. It's not so much what they do, as the kind of people they are. I used to have a favourite uncle and aunt. They were spasmodic in their present-giving on birthdays, they didn't visit often, but when I saw them I just loved them – so much more than the worthy ones who kept calendars and sent cards without fail and wrote me letters when I left home. Unfair, I know, but just life.

Much as their habits jar, it's a relief having these paid professionals taking the strain. Naomi may have been well taught but I can see she finds it hard going sometimes – emotionally as well as physically.

She was right to decide against having a baby.

I must let her know that.

This buried jewel brought sudden tears to Naomi's eyes.

She still paid a heavy price for deciding to abort the one child they had created together.

His acceptance of her other choice, not to become pregnant, was some consolation.

She picked up Noelani and buried her cheek in the thick fur, feeling the warm vibration of the feline heart, imagining the softness of a baby's breath.

More intervention! I mentioned to Naomi that there's a specialist 'village' in Aberdeen, a residential facility offering twenty-four hour care to residents with wasting or degenerative illnesses, but with the emphasis on maximising independence and being part of a community. Tailored care. I read out the advertised strong points.

She heard me out and then said, 'And you *want* to move to Aberdeen, and live in a community of disabled people, away from me, do you?'

'No. But I do need to reduce the strain on you.'

'Then let's get more help,' she said.

Today, a mere forty-eight hours later, Lydia called to ask if we'd consider hiring a friend of one of her colleagues, somebody called Brendan Buchanan. Very experienced, including several years working as a specialist nurse in a spinal unit, but currently unemployed while he goes through the emigration hoops for working overseas. He's been filling in time working as a personal carer, that is until his last patient died, twelve days ago. Sounds perfect – his qualifications, his availability, I mean, not the fate of his last victim! A recommendation from Lydia is worth a fist-full of references (although we're to get those too).

I've decided he'll be known as my 'personal assistant'. Ever since hearing about him, my mind has been racing. What if he's someone who recognises futility when he sees it? What if he's big and brave and would hold the syringe or pillow for me? Do the deed; leave the country. Ideal. I have new hope. I am resolved to get him on my side.

Naomi wanted to make up the room next to ours for him – 'so he's within easy hailing distance.' I have personal reservations about anyone being that close to our bedroom; I want him to be at the other end of the landing, on call by means of a bell. Keeping assistance on our terms.

21 JULY—Enter Brendan as the next stage of my descent into invalidity. We had a pseudo interview on Friday but the result was a foregone conclusion – after all, none of my other carers was selected.

He moved his meagre belongings in at the weekend ready to start this morning – not that it's a nine-to-five job; it just felt right, starting on a Monday.

I'm not sure quite what I expected. It certainly wasn't this! Brendan's six feet tall, solid muscle. Moving me seems like child's play.

In spite of an instinctive resentment, I have to admire his physique, but everything else seems curiously incongruous in a man of his stature. His skin is luminously fair and freckled. His hair is blond, so fine you can see the pinkness of his scalp through it, like the brave perm on an octogenarian. When he stands underneath the light it gives him an ethereal look. His eyelashes and eyebrows are fair too, but sufficiently coloured to be seen, unlike that albino fairness that makes a face look as if the outline has been rubbed out by the Creator's eraser. And he has what I can only describe as perfectly etched lips. It's that sort of sculptured mouth a film star might draw for a plastic surgeon: 'the exact shape I'm looking for'. He keeps his moustache trimmed straight, well above the lip, not like Harry, whose straggly ends get caught in his yoghurt.

But this Adonis has one maddening trait: he closes his eyes when he's talking.

How I hate that!

Over the years I've been amazed at the number of people who do it. Though I can hardly use it as a reason not to take him on, not when he comes with Lydia's blessing. Oh, and he's a tad too liberal with his aftershave for my taste. Well, nobody's perfect. I daresay he'll find things about me annoying too – although, of course, he can escape.

I'm horribly conscious of the fact that if I don't get this live-in minder on my side, he represents another chain locking me to this life.

It was curious to see Adam's first impressions of this man who soon became his shadow. Naomi herself hadn't been bothered by his closed eyes, only by his invasion of her territory.

20 JULY—Brendan has already drawn up a list of the key people involved in my care. He says he wants to talk to them all and build up a care package that maximises my potential – and I quote.

He assures us he's happy just to take so many hours off here or there, so as to be available for the heavy stuff each day, but I want to keep this properly professional. He's entitled to days off. Naomi wants to fill in the gaps. Hhhmmm. I do not want her knocking herself up again.

I like the idea of one full-time person paid to get the job done, who won't panic in a crisis, and who can switch off the minute he leaves me.

À *propos* of nothing: I'm worth more to Naomi dead than alive.

It was more than a physical relief for her. There was someone available if he got into difficulties. There was someone to stop him attempting anything silly.

23 JULY—It was a perfect opportunity – presented to me on a plate.

What are my own goals and hopes? Brendan wanted to know. Given his intimate involvement in my life, there seemed no point in prevaricating. And to his credit he was completely unfazed by my honesty.

I was impressed. He agreed that death by euthanasia can be less traumatic than death from natural causes (he read the same BMJ article!) and that there are distinct advantages in families having time to prepare, to talk openly about death, and a chance to say goodbye. So far, so good.

Having heard me out, he didn't offer an opinion either way but simply said he would be talking to Naomi too, to ascertain her wishes. I suddenly felt less secure. My honesty might backfire on me. But it's therapeutic, anyway, just to be in the company of someone who can bear to listen to dark thoughts without feeling the need to say something comforting or to knock down my arguments. A fair hearing counts for a lot round here.

I sneaked in a few choice snippets about Naomi: her selflessness, her stoicism, how this whole business has changed her. How she's my biggest concern these days. And it's true, not just a ploy to strengthen my case for him. I still see that look sometimes; as if she's keeping her own feelings suppressed and in an unguarded moment they bubble up and I see... I can't quite put a finger on it... but I know I'm not meant to.

I have to make Brendan see she's the one who'll be left to pick up the pieces. The further down I drag her now, the steeper the climb back up to normal life again afterwards. I have to get him on my side, for her sake as well as my own.

The early hours I just couldn't bear to lie there. Whatever I tried, or Naomi tried, I just could not get comfortable. She grew more tense; I became more morose. She wept; I snapped.

'This is silly,' I hissed. 'We hired Brendan so you wouldn't have to do any of this.'

Brendan made nothing of being woken. He took over without a qualm. I was carted off to my study and Naomi despatched back to bed with a cup of hot chocolate (also made by Brendan). He massaged my joints and pressure points, piled things round me to hold me upright but cushioned, and handed me a fortified drink – I didn't ask what he'd laced it with. But my brain raced with the possibilities. It was too soon to suggest a lethal combination.

I've dispatched him back to bed and I'm going to write myself into sleepfulness.

In spite of the fact that this is what he's paid for, I feel irrationally guilty for disturbing Brendan's sleep. I guess it'll take me a while to adjust. I should feel more guilty for having disturbed Naomi's sleep all these weeks and months.

Her tears tonight are a salutary reminder of what this is doing to her. Exhaustion is making us both irritable and upset. Being together for long periods is getting harder to deal with. It's exquisite torture.

Now Brendan is in residence I hold a trump card. A bad night for me is a bad night for her. She must move into the other bedroom, she must get out and have a fuller life, she must start to conserve her resources.

Should I invest in a special bed to facilitate changes of position (as Brendan has suggested)? Or sleeping tablets? Or something more lethal?

Eternal sleep sounds like bliss. Is Brendan the key? A pillow over my face? An injection of air into my veins?

I think it was Victor Hugo who said, 'The supreme happiness of life is the conviction that we are loved.' I have been loved; I am still loved. I do not want to get to a point where that is in question.

'You were, you were! So very, very much.'

Through a blur Naomi felt the sudden rush of fur as Noelani leapt into her lap. She turned in circles for a moment, her nose scenting, her tail erect, before she wrapped everything in concentric circles and buried her face out of sight. It took only seconds to produce a contented purr.

If only Naomi's own needs could be as easily met. There was no one now to smooth away her cares. How she missed the touch of Adam's hands, mussing her hair, caressing her skin. The sheer Adam-ness of the man.

24 JULY—Having one constant carer is great; having him on site is a terrific boon. I no longer have to hang around half the morning waiting for a shower. I don't have to wait for Naomi to pop in at lunchtime for a drink. I can eat, go to the loo, take a nap, just when I feel like it. I am no longer obliged to go to bed when someone else can fit it in.

Better still, Brendan doesn't impose his schedule, or his methods on me. He listens, he fits everything around my requests. Maximum efficiency, minimum fuss. He doesn't stand gossiping. We don't have to keep working at getting to know each other and I find I can accept what he offers without breaking my concentration.

Writing is again a tremendous outlet. My piece for Arkwright is taking shape very nicely. I'm eager to get to work each morning. My inner spark – that third original aim – is burning more brightly again.

That's not to say I've given up on my quest for a way out – once I've finished Arkwright's feature, that is. I'm looking for the perfect escape into oblivion: 'immaculate anonymity' (the reverse of immaculate conception). Pity it has to involve doing something premeditated. I wish I could cast an invisibility cloak over myself and simply just not be there any more.

When I did eventually nod off in my chair last night, I dreamed of my mother. Not surprising really, given my current preoccupations. In this case I guess it was more of a nightmare than a dream, because she was in full punitive mode, with just enough sorrow in her voice to make me feel guilty rather than rebellious. And her presence seemed so real. In the cold light of day I rather suspect I was only half-asleep and it was my subconscious playing tricks.

'Life is a sacred trust.'

'We're only stewards, we don't have absolute dominion.'

'Suffering is part of God's plan for mankind. Don't fight it. Embrace it.'

'Share in Christ's redemptive suffering.'

The sentiments were hers. The voice was hers. The language was not. I must have read this stuff somewhere and stored it in some corner of my brain.

I woke unrefreshed. And feeling a keen desire to talk to Ernest Kane. Maybe Brendan can factor him too into our timetable.

25 JULY—I've lost track of the number of times Joel has 'popped up'. He commented on my fatigue. I told him about the bad nights, then gave him an account of the nightmare of Mother's visit. He shrugged.

'It's your life. You don't have to answer to her.'

'Would you... would it trouble you... if I ended it... deliberately?' I felt my palms sweating. His opinion matters hugely.

'I'd miss you.'

'But you wouldn't... would it be like Dad's death?'

'Well, as you know, I don't have your hang-ups about that. It happened. I guess he had his reasons.'

'And me?'

'I understand your reasons.'

'And you'd... forgive me?'

'Nothing to forgive. Like I say, it's your life.'

'What if I asked you... to help me?'

'Do what?'

'Hold a pillow over my face?'

'Bloody hell, Adam.' He stepped back from me. 'You aren't seriously...?'

'No.' I waited until my voice steadied. 'I just wondered. That's all.'

'Bloody hell,' he said again, staring at me.

'I know. I couldn't either.'

He frowned slightly.

'With Mum.' I waited for the picture to formulate. 'Even if she'd wanted it, I couldn't have done it. I wouldn't ask you.'

'You're... my *brother*!'

'Yeah. Don't worry. I'll find a way.'

The silence hung between us.

'For what it's worth, I think you've been a hero. I wouldn't have stuck it like you have,' he said unevenly.

I shook my head, buying time. 'Nice of you to say so, but it's all a show. There's a great big coward inside struggling to get out.'

'I wish...' He broke off abruptly.

I stretched out one hand and he gripped it hard in both his own.

'Thanks, Jo, for everything.'

After a long moment, he let go of my hand and slapped the back of my chair. 'Hey, big bro! Where shall we go today then?'

Reflecting on that brief exchange now, safely away from his perceptive eyes, I'm content.

I have his permission.

Naomi resolved to share this with Joel that evening.

The conversation had shaken him to the core – more than Adam ever knew. He'd been strangely silent with her that weekend, endlessly mulling over the request, and his answer.

'I never thought he'd ask. Not actually ask!' he blurted out late that night.

'He's only testing the water. He needs to know how we all feel about it,' she soothed.

'But... I couldn't.'

'He'll understand. He knows why.'

'But I feel as if I'm letting him down – just when he needs me to be strong for him.'

'No, you're not.'

'And you; I'm letting you down too. I said I wanted to help you too.'

'And d'you think it would help me knowing you'd killed your own brother? Come on!'

'But somebody needs to help him.'

'I honestly believe it will all work out in the end – without either of us doing... that.' In reality it was more a wish than a conviction.

27 JULY—Joel is certainly not Brendan when it comes to the mechanics of personal care but what he lacks in dexterity he makes up for in humour. It was too good an opportunity to miss. I could in one stroke give Brendan a day off and keep my brother to myself.

I told Joel about Ernest Kane. We went together to his morning service. On my own I think I would have enjoyed the feel-good factor of worship; with Joel I was too conscious of his scepticism to really lose myself in the feeling. But Mr Kane's welcome was as warm as ever and I found myself suggesting we meet... soon? He promised to ring and arrange a date. I left with a spring in my heart, if not my step.

But there was nothing springy in my heart at 8 tonight. It was harder than ever to watch my scamp of a brother leave. His hug was too eloquent, the complete absence of humour in word or act was too final for my composure. His presence is still here now, like a watermark against my eyes.

28 JULY—Monday again. Brendan is back in control.

Lydia came at 10 on the dot. I have an unspoken dread that she is relinquishing her role to him.

I don't ask – I might not like the answer.

We were never alone; Brendan watched her every move; watched and learned.

There was no hint of the Caribbean, not even with me.

Curtis arrived after morning surgery. He had a consultation with

Brendan first but when he came to see me, mercifully Brendan didn't follow. I don't know who set this up, I'm just grateful.

'Buchanan working out?' he asked me.

'Brilliantly.'

'I'm glad. How're things otherwise?'

We darted through the gathering storm clouds and possible lightning conductors at our disposal, which led seamlessly into the subject of my death.

'There's one thing that's still bugging me,' I said.

'Oh? What's that?'

'Well, I just can't see... Tell me, Doc, the difference between forseeing that a patient will die if you give him extra drugs to keep him comfortable, and intending the drug to kill him; is it just different legally?'

'No, it's different experientially. The *intention* makes it different. It *feels* different. And morally it's different, too.'

'Morally? How so?'

'I'm under a *prima facie* moral obligation to care for my patients within the law. Killing them is morally wrong.'

I nodded. 'Thanks.'

Still churned up about Joel, I have no heart for battle.

He leaned forwards suddenly. 'Can I ask you something? – just out of interest. It's not a criticism.'

'Fire away.'

'What made you so opposed to going to a self-help group?'

'I don't want my identity to be defined by my MND.'

'An interesting perspective. I'll remember that.'

'And I haven't got the space to bear other people's emotions.'

'Fair enough.'

'And I don't want my nose rubbed in what comes next.'

It wasn't the full story, of course. But it served the purpose.

'So how do you want to be identified?' he asked conversationally, leaning back in his chair.

'As a writer...'

We were well into literary criticism when Brendan appeared with the coffee and an offer of lunch. I was suddenly completely exhausted. Like a deflated balloon four days after a party.

It was weird seeing Adam's account of this conversation, which made it seem so fluid, so coherent. In reality, his fractured speech and tortured respirations, had made all exchanges slow and laboured by this stage. How appallingly frustrating to have his brain continuing to grapple with complex issues like these, but to be trapped in a body that refused to keep up with his thinking.

No wonder Dr Curtis had marvelled.

He'd emerged from this conversation looking bemused.

'He's amazing. I don't know how he does it.'

She'd smiled ruefully, and when he'd left, berated herself for her own impatience with Adam's endless analysis of his situation. Dr Curtis seemed so much more calm about listening, over and over again, until he understood.

A sigh escaped her now. Sharing secrets, when it was too late to respond, was so draining.

30 JULY—I'm still flabbergasted by that discussion with Curtis on Monday.

I've been denying it, but I know my concentration is poor these days. Attention span of an autistic gnat! I can still write (at the speed of a snail with a ball and chain) but talking and really listening are getting harder every day. Words elude me; which is an incredibly painful development, but probably good for my pride, and maybe part of the continuing punishment that Mother predicted for me when I was five and cheeky to her. Maybe the 'outer darkness' into which I was to be cast, where there would be 'weeping and wailing and gnashing of teeth', is not being able to articulate words.

This latest deterioration has forced me to contemplate the immediate future. It's not a pretty picture: me pointing at pictures to make my wishes known, uttering nothing more illuminating than offensive grunts. Brendan, Curtis, Lydia, Chloe, humouring me like a child. Naomi looking at me with pity in her eyes.

In desperation I told Naomi what this latest development was like. She made a joke of it, told me she can't remember things nearly as well as she did ten years ago either. It was the last straw.

I cannot bear this. *I CAN NOT.*

I WILL NOT!

She could take no more. Scalding tears fell while she scrubbed the dining room carpet, heedless of the shampoo spraying onto the furniture.

10 AUGUST—Another weekend with Joel. I noticed for the first time the lines around his eyes, the drawn look on his face in repose. He reminds me of Father. I'm afraid I'm to blame.

All through today I had to distance myself from him, switch off my heart, just to get through the hours. Now he's gone I want to hold his bright image in my head without letting go.

I need the diary again. It's taken a back seat of late. I've been concentrating all my diminishing reserves on finishing Arkwright's feature. First draft is done. But it's so exhausting even typing now, I can't do both. Maybe the diary's day is nearly done.

Where am I with all this?

Both resolve and plan are getting stronger by the hour. Brendan has been here three weeks now. I still haven't asked him outright if he'll help me. I nearly did last night but I heard him out in the kitchen laughing with Naomi. They were together; I was alone.

17 AUGUST—Another week has dragged by. Nothing gets better, some things get worse.

My wrists are so weak now. Curtis has asked Lydia to do what she can. Her presence may be magical but she can't turn water into wine.

I still haven't asked Brendan. But on Friday, my door was open, I could see the hall mirror: he was hugging Naomi.

She's always saying, 'Brendan thinks... Brendan says...'

Naomi smiled for the first time in days. This pain at least was short lived.

18 AUGUST—Naomi came out with it in a rush this evening.

'Brendan wants to know if he's offended you in some way.'

'Can't he ask me himself?'

'Would you tell him?'

'I saw you.'

'Saw me what?'

'Hugging Brendan. Last night.'

'What? I never... Ahhhhhhh!' and she actually grinned at this point. 'Actually *he* was hugging *me*!'

I waited.

'And for your information, Mr Green Eyes, he was just being sympathetic.'

'About what? Being saddled to a cripple?'

'No, being saddled to a jealous grump!'

I looked at her hard.

'Idiot! Of course not. I had a bad day in court on Friday; my family didn't get to keep the kid they'd been fostering for ages. I was upset. He was just being comforting.'

My conscience smote me – *I* should be the one to comfort her. I didn't even notice she was upset.

She shot me an arch look.

'Besides, didn't you know?'

'Know what?'

'Brendan. He bats for the other side!'

It never entered my head. But now I know, I'm suddenly squeamish. All that physical care, the intimate personal things. Idiotic, I know. I didn't attribute ulterior motives to all those female carers.

It had been such a depressing time for them all, seeing Adam withdrawing into an irrational, self-centred place.

Joel was her lifeline. With him she could be honest and acknowledge the changes without feeling disloyal. He'd tried to cheer her with his light banter: 'Good thing to know the old boy's still sparky enough to feel jealous!'

But there'd been nothing good about Adam's slow loss of contact with everything he'd held dear. As his own world shrank, it was one thing she could do for him; protect him from her work problems, spare him the reminders that the world went on out there, heedless of his private battle; the knowledge that there were other real families in trouble, sometimes even of their own making, and that she was part of the solution.

No. She'd been right to use other shoulders to cry on.

25 AUGUST—It was an exhausting weekend. Joel's energy is hard to take now. But Naomi needs him, I see that. And I dare say he needs to see me for himself.

As for me, I spent the whole time dreading that moment of parting – again. As soon as he'd gone I went to bed, too worn out even to cry. It was my worst night so far; difficult even to breathe. Brendan stayed in the easy chair beside my bed from 1 o'clock on. I tried between breaths to find out what he thinks. He values all life. Quality of life doesn't matter. Contribution to society (or lack of it) doesn't matter. Drain on resources doesn't matter. I tried to tell him it matters to me.

Today he took me out in the wheelchair. 'Fresh air might help.' The wind was spiteful. Nevertheless, we did a circuit of the area. 'In the teeth of the wind' felt literal. Maybe it's just my lack of adipose tissue. Brendan was in short sleeves.

A young woman jogged past us. 'Money over Morals' her t-shirt proclaimed. I'd need to think about that.

Naomi pushed back her chair and left the room without even stopping to switch off the computer. The abbreviated entries as well as the staccato sentences were so eloquent.

Every time now Joel faced an agonising decision – to stay or to leave. Every night she tossed and turned herself, listening to the sounds of Adam's battle, fighting the impulse to go in and take over from this stranger, this paid helper. But Adam had insisted. She couldn't deny him what little control he retained.

It still hurt. She still wanted to be the one he needed.

27 AUGUST—I'm screaming on the inside. I've descended into a does-he-take-sugar world. I am not a moron. I have two degrees. I have lost count of the things I've had published. I am – or at least I was until recently – a wordsmith *par excellence*. It is an insult, an offence to slowly over-

pronounce your puny vocabulary, to offer me closed sentences.

I do not want to be coaxed into accepting an alphabet board or a Dalek-like pre-programmed voice.

I do not want this grotesque parody of life.

I do not.

Later Well, I may be past the stage of changing the path I'm on, but I can at least select the company I keep along that way.

In no particular order...

1. Arkwright. He's brilliant at working on my text with me; reckons in places I've assumed too much knowledge of MND. Not surprising. My whole world is written in its language these days; I can't think myself back into a position of ignorance.
2. Lydia. Her monologues are wonderfully soothing and vibrant with pictures. And even in her British guise, I still love to see her eyes vanish inside her bass chuckles, and feel her massive ebony fingers ironing the wrinkles out of my muscles.
3. Brendan. He's been gradually but not unwillingly re-shaped in my image. And he's admirably receptive to suggestions and advice on how to improve my care.
4. Curtis... I don't know. He's playing a waiting game. But I *think* when the moment arrives he'll come through for me.
5. Ernest Kane. There are things I want to hear from him.

I can relax with all of them, just be myself. Surely a man in my advanced state of decrepitude ought to be allowed to choose his companions without the burden of other people's sensitivities weighing with him. Or is this as utterly selfish as my embryonic plan for my own end?

1 SEPTEMBER—All visitors are exhausting – even the most welcome.

Chloe suggests adapting the phone so that I can stay in touch with people – hands-free. But she has no magic bullet to fire the neurones that used to activate my speech and breathing. The phone would be one hundred per cent frustration.

Inside my head my diction is perfectly clear. I can see from the faces around me that once the sounds escape into the outside world, they develop impediments and shyness and fall over themselves in their haste to hide.

Joel's fantastic at understanding me. Of course, he can trade on a lifetime of practice; he's known me longer than anyone else I know. But he can't be here all the time. I hate to think Paige scarpered because of me. He said not, but I'm not sure if that's the truth; he didn't elaborate.

Understanding me is part of Brendan's job, of course, but I hate it when he translates for other people. He doesn't stand in that relationship to me. It's not his right, even though I know his motives are good. I've told him, but it's instinctive with him; I need help, he supplies it.

The purge of redundant visitors began today. I said my last goodbye to Jerry. I can't handle his unease with my situation. My disintegration hangs between us. Now I can no longer fill the breaches, the silences are not the kind friends can tolerate. Perhaps I make him face his own mortality.

2 SEPTEMBER — My first major outing for weeks. Devlin day. Naomi took the day off to accompany me, but Brendan drove and he pushed my chair.

Once I was safely in the consulting room, they both withdrew.

It was a blue day in Devlin's wardrobe. Sky blue. So bright even when I closed my eyes during his examination, the sheer vibrance of it stayed imprinted on my retinas.

I told him about my lack of concentration.

'Is it… the start of… dementia?'

(I've been resisting the impulse to record my speech with all the rasping breaths, but it seems relevant here.)

'I presume you've read that somewhere. In the region of three to ten per cent of people with ALS develop dementia,' he said calmly. 'From what I've seen, you're not in that percentage.'

'Yet!'

He smiled. His asymmetry is somehow less daunting warmed by humour. And that brilliant blue.

'If I exhibited… socially unacceptable… behaviour… would you… knock… me out… with some… thing?' I wheezed.

'It would depend.'

'On?'

'How antisocial that behaviour was.'

I tried to shrug my shoulders.

'Difficult to fake,' he said wryly.

Nothing for it but to take him down a different track then.

'I have… a DN…R… order.'

'I see that.'

'It's… futile… to per… sist… with this.'

He nodded with pursed lips for a long moment.

'Is there anything you're looking forward to in the next few weeks?'

The question took me unawares. I took my time thinking.

'Sorry?' I was completely mystified.

'Any big event? Anything that you really do want to see or experience?

A wedding perhaps? A book coming out? An anniversary? Something like that.'

'Not... in... my life... time.'

I raised my eyebrows. I still couldn't see where he was coming from.

'Futility. It's a strange concept,' he said quietly. 'Sometimes even a couple of extra days can be of supreme value to a person who is otherwise set on dying.'

'Mending... fences?... Seeing a... relative?'

'That sort of thing.'

'Nothing left... in... my... case.'

'No unfinished business.' It was a statement. 'Fair enough.' Then he suddenly lifted his head and said quite briskly, 'I'll just call your wife in.'

He was kind but honest. It was just a question of keeping me comfortable, dealing with the symptoms as they presented. Nothing heroic; he promised that. He was satisfied that Dr Curtis had things well in control.

There was no mention of a next appointment.

Naomi recalled that day with perfect clarity. Dr Devlin radiated authority. She felt compelled to listen to the words she did not want to hear articulated. The deterioration was gathering pace now.

Even with all his experience as a neurologist, he could offer no promises – about how long, about how bad things would get, about a solution. Only that Adam could be admitted to hospital if they felt unable to continue caring for him at home.

Adam's powerlessness – intolerable didn't come near it.

Joel too railed against the cruelty when she reported back to him that night, and together they inched closer to Adam's abyss, his answer.

She'd clung to him across the miles, not wanting to be alone with her thoughts.

7 SEPTEMBER—It's uncanny. Just when I've declared I have nothing left to live for, I get a letter from Anthony Frobisher (Editorial Director, Omega Press). He liked the 'unusual angle' of *Aidan's Story* (but not its title!). 'Some editing' will be necessary. But they're prepared to negotiate a contract... if I'm interested. If... ? I have to keep going for long enough to sign that piece of paper. Yes, Devlin, you're right. Even a couple of days can be of supreme value. Today I understand that.

I shan't see it in covers, of course. No publisher works that fast and these guys don't even know I'm dying. But Naomi and Curtis have agreed to nurse it through the birthing process. I just need to ensure that my little embryo is safely embedded in Omega's womb. And I like to think even a hard-nosed editor will respect a freshly dug grave and go lightly with the red pen.

So, how far to go?

Okay, Doc Curtis, I'll accept I could do with more help – just to keep me functioning until that contract's signed. I confess I'm knackered just taking in enough oxygen. Now that my intercostals and diaphragm are throwing teenage tantrums, I have to use the muscles in my neck and shoulders to breathe, which means I ache everywhere. And coughing's a killer, inasmuch as it's exhausting, not in the sense of finishing me off, more's the pity.

So yes, I'm ready to accept painkillers now, thank you. As strong as you like. The time for keeping a clear head is past. It was so bad last night that I got Brendan to fetch Mother's Coproxamol from my desk drawer. Two can't hurt, I coaxed. I couldn't wait. I needed it now. I sent him out of the room so he could say, hand on heart, he had no part in the unorthodox action. There were no watching eyes – well, only my mother's ghost! – but I limited myself to just two.

Night-time is worst. It seems my shallow breathing is partly responsible for my disturbed sleep. The effort, the nightmares, the sweats and panic attacks, mean I wake up completely done in, 'hung-over' and headachy. So Doc, if you're offering...

A koala would be in paradise in my room right now! Brendan swears by eucalyptus oil, to ease breathing – it's on my pillow, tucked into my shirt collar, on my hanky. I've no idea whether or not it's helping me, but it's helping Brendan, and I need him on-side – especially in crises. It's illogical to panic, I know, but it's outside my control. Breathing is such a fundamental, instinctive need.

Curtis asked me about assisted ventilation last week. I didn't need to think.

'No! We agreed. No heroics.'

'It needn't be invasive... just a mask, to provide extra air as you breathe... perhaps just at night?'

I held out.

Now... since Omega's letter... should I reconsider? Just until the contract's in the bag. But there again... the longer I extend my life, the worse the other disabilities become. I'm in a sort of limbo. Medical technology offers me an illusion of choice.

Ernest Kane is coming on Wednesday. He's the chap I need. Three days to go.

10 SEPTEMBER—Ernest Kane came. Early. I feel a sense of peace. I have his unspoken blessing. I think.

'His grace is sufficient.'

Brendan understood too. And agreed.

I'm ready. Only one thing left: the contract.

Joel's coming up again this weekend. He's the one who unnerves me most.

I will be strong. I will.

Naomi held her breath.

15 SEPTEMBER—Omega's publishing contract arrived. Scrawled something. Joel posted it straight away.

That's it.

Jigsaw finished.

Naomi stared at the last entry. Then she backtracked five pages and read it all again, more slowly.

The cues were there.

But even knowing what she knew, suspecting what she suspected, there was nothing to incriminate, nothing to use in evidence.

* * *

That afternoon Adam had asked her to call Dr Curtis. His breathing was shallow and with every breath his shoulders heaved.

'D'you need some oxygen?'

'No... I'm... exhausted... I just need... something... make me... sleep.'

Dr Curtis looked concerned when he eventually emerged from Adam's room.

'He's struggling. I've given him something now to ease his breathing. And I've left him some night sedation. It should help. I've told Brendan, give it to him just before he settles for the night. There's a second dose if he needs it in the middle of the night. He's just exhausted – the effort of breathing, the lack of sleep. It should be enough to help him get over. I'll pop in again tomorrow. We might need to think again about assisted ventilation.'

Naomi had sucked in her breath sharply at that. He smiled ruefully.

'Oh, don't worry! I didn't mention it to Adam. Let's see what a good night's sleep does.'

'He was adamant. No ventilation.'

'I know. But circumstances sometimes alter cases. Goodness, how he'd slate me for such a hackneyed statement.'

The smile faded before it even took shape. He moved closer.

'What about you, Naomi? You look all in yourself.'

'I'll be all right. Especially if you can give Adam a better night.'

'I can give you something, if you like?'

She shook her head. She was tired enough to sleep. If only Adam did.

'Joel's here. He's staying on. Thanks for coming.'

'No problem. Don't hesitate to call me if you need me.'

She peeped around the edge of Adam's door without making a sound. He half smiled.

'Can I get you anything?'

'Couple of... tablets. Headache.' His eyes closed as he said it, a frown creasing his forehead.

She tipped them out onto his hand.

'Another... one... It's thumping.' But he hadn't taken them immediately. 'In... a minute... on... my own... Don't... want to... choke.'

She moved the beaker closer, turning the straw towards him, dropped a kiss on his forehead, noting the damp heat of exhaustion, and left as quietly as she'd entered. They tiptoed around his room whenever anything needed to be done but most of the time he lay with his eyes shut, not moving, his breathing steadied for the time being.

Joel elected to sit with Adam for the evening while Brendan got some sleep in case it was another difficult night, but for most of the time, with nothing to do but read, in the gathering gloom of evening he found himself nodding off.

An early night appealed to everyone.

It was Brendan who roused her.

8.15. What...?

'I think he's unconscious,' he whispered.

Adam was certainly unrousable.

'When did you...?'

'I checked at 6 – when I woke myself. I thought he was just sleeping. I didn't want to disturb him.'

'Could it just be... Dr Curtis's medicine?'

'It's possible. Presumably Joel gave him the second dose some time last night.'

Joel!

He woke with a start.

'No. I didn't get up last night. I thought you were doing the night shift, Brendan.'

'Yes. But he didn't ring for me.'

They all stared at the row of empty medicine glasses.

'He asked me for another dose of his painkillers with his night-time drink,' Brendan said slowly. 'I gave him two. He asked for another one.'

'He had three after Dr Curtis left too,' Naomi whispered. 'Said he had a thumping head.'

'I left two more in case he needed more in the night,' Brendan spoke slowly, a watchful look on his face. 'He asked me to.'

'And they aren't there now?'

He shook his head.

'That makes eight, plus Curtis's stuff times two,' Joel said, staring down at his brother.

'On top of whatever the doctor gave him for his breathing,' Naomi added.

Joel suddenly opened the drawer of the bedside cabinet. His breath seemed suspended.

'What were those tablets in the drawer?'

'Your mother's Coproxamol.'

'He asked me to press tablets into those coffee creams Sally brought him – said they were more palatable that way.' Joel's voice sounded tight.

Two pairs of eyes gimletted into him, waiting.

'He said I might as well make myself useful, not sit there just nodding off. They'd be ready when he needed them. I did them all. Like he said. All six of them.'

'Six more tablets – Coproxamol.' Brendan tallied them up.

'No, twelve. Two tablets in each.'

'And have they... all gone?' Naomi hardly dared voice the question.

Joel checked the dish where he'd laid the chocolates, and nodded.

'And the rest of the tablets – where are they?'

The question hung suspended in the air as they stared at each other.

'Well, he won't have eaten the container! They must be somewhere.'

Their eyes scanned the vicinity, nobody daring to move.

It was Brendan who turned back the sheet, he who took the bottle from Adam's hand and placed it back in the drawer. In silence. Without even the rattle of pills against the glass.

'Should we call Dr Curtis?' Naomi whispered hesitantly, not looking at either of the men.

Fifteen minutes later she rang. He came immediately.

'May I have a moment alone with my patient?'

He closed the door firmly behind him.

It felt like an eternity before he reappeared and beckoned them in. Three pairs of eyes flew to the bed.

Adam now lay semi-recumbent, the sheet over him hardly moving as he breathed. His hair was newly brushed, the saliva that had previously speckled his chin had been carefully wiped away. The faint sweet scent of baby cleansing wipes hung around the bed. A neat pile of washed medicine glasses stood on the bedside cabinet, back in their usual place.

'Naomi, would you like to sit at this side, facing Adam?' Dr Curtis said quietly, gesturing to his right.

She moved like a robot. A gesture sent Joel to the seat close beside her.

Dr Curtis stood on the other side, watching his patient for a long moment before beckoning to Brendan. The two professionals withdrew without a word, leaving only the light sound of air gasping in the silence.

Naomi felt her own breathing synchronising with Adam's, shallow and hesitant. The long pauses made her light-headed. Her will-power alone seemed to drive each new intake of air.

Dr Curtis slipped in and out of the room twice, each time pausing to check pulse and respirations, to touch Naomi lightly on the shoulder and nod slightly to Joel. Saying nothing. On his third visit, he took longer checking, double checking. Waiting.

When he eventually spoke, the words sounded fragmented.

'He's gone. Peacefully. As he would have wished.'

There was only silence. No laboured breathing. No challenges.

Naomi stared at the still face, smooth now, free from the exertion of living.

She felt Joel's arm around her shoulders and reached up to cover his hand with her own. It was he who steered her out of the room while Dr Curtis and Brendan did what needed to be done. But he shook his head when she made to take him back into the room.

'This is your time.'

She heard the break in his voice and walked in alone. Joel closed the door quietly behind her.

The silence was unnerving. Naomi found herself glancing nervously around, fearful of what she might see. Dr Curtis's confidence... how could he have been so sure this time – unless he had...? The neatly stacked medicine glasses reproached her. It was the doctor who had tidied away the rest of the evidence; he would not have been careless with his own.

Adam lay on his back now, the clean sheet smooth over his still frame. For a long moment she stood unmoving beside him. Slowly, slowly, slowly she stooped until her lips touched his skin. There was no hurry for this farewell.

By the time she eventually emerged, Dr Curtis had completed the paperwork. It was written in his usual bold, perfectly legible hand. Date of death: 16 September 2008. Time of death: 09.45 hours. Cause of death: Respiratory complications secondary to Motor Neurone Disease. Signature of certifying officer: Hugo McHendrick Curtis, MB ChB FRCGP.

Naomi could only marvel at the compassion of this busy man, who could sit with them for another hour, talking quietly, reminiscing, grieving with them.

'Dying with dignity, it's something inherently within the domain of the patient. And over this last couple of years Adam died with a dignity we don't often see.'

'I'd have opted out long before this,' Joel muttered fiercely.

'He's taught me such a lot,' Dr Curtis went on as if there had been no interruption. 'I've had the enormous privilege of reading his book. I haven't seen the newspaper article about his lived experience, but I suspect it too, will go a long way towards changing attitudes. Our laws will change eventually. You can't base laws on individual cases but there can be nothing as powerful as the patient's own story, what it's like from the inside. That's Adam's legacy.'

The words settled around them like a benediction.

For more information

If you have been affected by any of the issues in this book, or related subjects, you may be interested in the author's website. It provides discussion questions and notes for reading groups; more information about the author, her books and the ethical topics covered in them; links to websites relating to the laws on medical ethics and the issues in the books, and much more.

www.hazelmchaffie.com

The Bower Bird

Ann Kelley

ISBN 1 906307 32 6 (children's fiction)
PBK £6.99
ISBN 1 906307 45 8 (adult fiction) PBK
£6.99

I had open-heart surgery last year, when I was eleven, and the healing process hasn't finished yet. I now have an amazing scar that cuts me in half almost, as if I have survived a shark attack.

Gussie is twelve years old, loves animals and wants to be a photographer when she grows up. The only problem is that she's unlikely to ever grow up.

Gussie needs a heart and lung transplant, but the donor list is as long as her arm and she can't wait around that long. Gussie has things to do; finding her ancestors, coping with her parents' divorce, and keeping an eye out for the wildlife in her garden.

Winner of the 2007 Costa Children's Book Award

It's a lovely book – lyrical, funny, full of wisdom. Gussie is such a dear – such a delight and a wonderful character, bright and sharp and strong, never to be pitied for an instant.
HELEN DUNMORE

The Burying Beetle

Ann Kelley

ISBN 1 84282 099 0 PBK £9.99
ISBN 1 905222 08 4 PBK £6.99

The countryside is so much scarier than the city. It's all life or death here.

Meet Gussie. 12 years old and settling into her new ramshackle home on a cliff top above St Ives, she has an irrepressible zest for life. She also has a life-threatening heart condition. But it's not in her nature to give up. Perhaps because she knows her time might be short, she values every passing moment, experiencing each day with humour and extraordinary courage.

Spirited and imaginative, Gussie has a passionate interest in everything around her and her vivid stream of thoughts and observations will draw you into a renewed sense of wonder.

Gussie's story of inspiration and hope is both heartwarming and heartrending. Once you've met her, you'll not forget her. And you'll never take life for granted again.

Gussie fairly fizzles with vitality, radiating fun and enjoyment into everything that comes her way. Her life may be predestined to be short but not short on wonder, glee, the love of things as they really are. It is rare to find such tragic circumstances written about without an ounce of self-pity. Rarer still to have the story of a circumscribed existence escaping its confines by sheer force of personality, zest for life.
MICHAEL BAYLEY

Atmospheric and beguiling
HELEN DUNMORE

The Blue Moon Book
Anne MacLeod
ISBN 1 84282 061 3 PBK £9.99

Love can leave you breathless, lost for words.

Jess Kavanagh knows. Doesn't know. 24 hours after meeting and falling for archaeologist and Pictish expert Michael Hurt she suffers a horrific accident that leaves her with aphasia and amnesia. No words. No memory of love.

Michael travels south, unknowing. It is her estranged partner sports journalist Dan McKie who is at the bedside when Jess finally regains consciousness. Dan, forced to review their shared past, is disconcerted by Jess's fear of him, by her loss of memory, loss of words.

Will their relationship survive this test? Should it survive? Will Michael find Jess again? In this absorbing contemporary novel, Anne MacLeod interweaves themes of language, love and loss in patterns as intricate, as haunting as the Pictish Stones.

High on drama and pathos, woven through with fine detail.
THE HERALD

As a challenge to romantic fiction, the novel is a success; and as far as men and women's failure to communicate is concerned, it hits the mark.
SCOTLAND ON SUNDAY

Driftnet
Lin Anderson
ISBN 1 84282 034 6 PBK £9.99

Introducing forensic scientist Dr Rhona MacLeod...

A teenager is found strangled and mutilated in a Glasgow flat.

Leaving her warm bed and lover in the middle of the night to take forensic samples from the body, Rhona MacLeod immediately perceives a likeness between herself and the dead boy and is tortured by the thought that he might be the son she gave up for adoption seventeen years before.

Amidst the turmoil of her own love life and consumed by guilt from her past, Rhona sets out to find the boy's killer and her own son. But the powerful men who use the Internet to trawl for vulnerable boys have nothing to lose and everything to gain by Rhona MacLeod's death.

A strong player on the crime novel scene, Lin Anderson skilfully interweaves themes of betrayal, violence and guilt. In forensic scientist Rhona Macleod she has created a complex character who will have readers coming back for more.

Lin Anderson has a rare gift. She is one of the few able to convey urban and rural Scotland with equal truth... Compelling, vivid stuff. I couldn't put it down.
ANNE MACLEOD, author of *The Dark Ship*.

Last of the Line

John MacKay

ISBN 1 905222 90 4 PBK £6.99

The call came from a place far away where the dark was deep and the only sound was the fading breath of a woman on the edge of eternity.

A summons to the bedside of his dying aunt drags Cal MacCarl away from the blur of city life to the islands where time turns slowly and tradition endures. He is striving for the urban dream of the luxury apartment and the prestige car and has shed his past to get there.

Aunt Mary is his only remaining blood link. She comes from that past. She still knows him as Calum. When she passes he will be the last of the family line. But for Cal, family and history are just bonds to tie him down.

Reluctantly embarking on a journey of duty, Cal finds himself drawn into the role of genealogy detective and discovers some secrets which are buried deep. He begins to understand that Mary is not the woman he thought he knew and the secret she kept buried for so long means he might not be who he thought he was.

The Road Dance

John MacKay

ISBN 1 84282 024 9 PBK £6.99

Why would a young woman, dreaming of a new life in America, sacrifice all and commit an act so terrible that she severs all hope of happiness again?

Life in the Scottish Hebrides can be harsh – 'The Edge of the World' some call it. For the beautiful Kirsty MacLeod, the love of Murdo and their dreams of America promise an escape from the scrape of the land, the repression of the church and the inevitability of the path their lives would take.

But as the Great War looms Murdo is conscripted. The villages hold a grand Road Dance to send their young men off to battle. As the dancers swirl and sup the wheels of tragedy are set in motion.

This is a writer able to pace a story, with believable characters and a telling sense of time, place and culture. The Road Dance is a very good debut and (...) I can see MacKay producing even more memorable books in the future.
SUNDAY HERALD

A sombre and immensely moving book, it is not to be recommended to those who like their fiction light and cheery in tone. However, with a gripping plot that subtly twist and turns, vivid characterisation, and a real sense of time and tradition, this is an absorbing, powerful first novel.
SCOTS MAGAZINE

Heartland

John MacKay
ISBN 1 905222 11 4 PBK £6.99

A man tries to build for his future by reconnecting with his past, leaving behind the ruins of the life he has lived. Iain Martin hopes that by returning to his Hebridean roots and embarking on a quest to reconstruct the ancient family home, he might find new purpose. But as Iain begins working on the old blackhouse, he uncovers a secret from the past, which forces him to question everything he ever thought to be true.

Who can he turn to without betraying those to whom he is closest? His ailing mother, his childhood friend and his former love are both the building – and stumbling – blocks to his new life. Where do you seek sanctuary when home has changed and will never be the same again?

A fine, rewarding read.
Ottakar's Scottish Book of the Month Review, THE SUNDAY HERALD

…broody, atmospheric little gem set in the Hebrides. THE HERALD

Letters from the Great Wall

Jenni Daiches
ISBN 1 905222 51 3 PBK £9.99

You can't run away from things here in China, there's too much confronting you.

Eleanor Dickinson needs to see things differently. To most her life would seem ideal; 33 years old, a professional university lecturer in a respectable relationship with a man who is keen to start a family. But Eleanor is dissatisfied: she's suffocated by her family and frustrated by the man she has no desire to marry. She has to escape.

In the summer of 1989, she cuts all ties and leaves behind the safe familiarity of Edinburgh to lecture in the eastern strangeness of China, a country on the brink of crisis. Basing herself in Beijing, she sets off on an intense voyage of self-discovery. But as the young democracy movement flexes its muscles, Eleanor is soon drawn into the unfolding drama of an event that captured the world's attention.

What freedoms will be asserted in this ancient nation, shaped both by tradition and revolution? And will Eleanor discover what really matters in her life before the tanks roll into Tiananmen Square?

Uncomfortably Numb:
A Prison Requiem

Maureen Maguire

ISBN 1 84282 001 X PBK £8.99

People may think I've taken the easy way out but please believe me this is the hardest thing I've ever had to do.

It was Christmas Eve, the atmosphere in Cornton Vale prison was festive, the girls in high spirits as they were locked up for the night. One of their favourite songs, Pink Floyd's 'Comfortably Numb', played loudly from a nearby cell as Yvonne Gilmour wrote her suicide note. She was the sixth of eight inmates to take their own lives in Cornton Vale prison over a short period of time.

Uncomfortably Numb follows Yvonne through a difficult childhood, a chaotic adolescence and drug addiction to life and death behind bars. Her story is representative of many women in our prisons today. They are not criminals (only 1% are convicted for violent crimes) and two-thirds are between the ages of fifteen and thirty. Suicide rates among them are rising dramatically. Do these vulnerable young girls really belong in prison?

This is a powerful and moving story told in the words of those involved: Yvonne and her family, fellow prisoners, prison officers, social workers, drug workers. It challenges us with questions that demand answers if more deaths are to be avoided.

The English Spy

Donald Smith

ISBN 1 905222 82 3 PBK £8.99

He was a spy among us, but not known as such, otherwise the mob of Edinburgh would pull him to pieces.
JOHN CLERK OF PENICUIK

Union between England and Scotland hangs in the balance.

Propagandist, spy and novelist-to-be Daniel Defoe is caught up in the murky essence of eighteenth-century Edinburgh – cobblestones, courtesans and kirkyards. Expecting a godly society in the capital of Presbyterianism, Defoe engages with a beautiful Jacobite agent, and uncovers a nest of vipers.

Subtly crafted... and a rattling good yarn.
STEWART CONN

Delves into the City of Literature, and comes out dark side up. MARC LAMBERT

Smith's version of Defoe picks his way through it all, arguing, wheedling, scribbling, bribing and cajoling the cast of nicely-drawn characters. Anyone interested in the months that saw the birth of modern Britain should enjoy this book. THE SUNDAY HERALD

Excellent... a brisk narrative and a vivid sense of time and place. THE HERALD

My Epileptic Lurcher

Des Dillon

ISBN 1 906307 22 9 HBK £12.99

That's when I saw them. The paw prints. Halfway along the ceiling they went. Evidence of a dog that could defy gravity.

The incredible story of Bailey, the dog who walked on the ceiling; and Manny, the guy who got kicked out of Alcoholics Anonymous for swearing.

Manny Riley is newly married, with a puppy and a wee flat by the sea, and the BBC are on the verge of greenlighting one of his projects. Everything sounds perfect. But Manny has always been an anger management casualty, and the idyllic village life is turning out to be more *League of Gentlemen* than *The Good Life*. The BBC have decided his script needs totally rewritten, the locals are conducting a campaign against his dog, and the village policeman is on the side of the neds. As his marriage suffers under the strain of his constant rages, a strange connection begins to emerge between Manny's temper and the health of his beloved Lurcher.

Raw, immediate and affecting.
THE BIG ISSUE

A tale about the wonder of all those things that only at first glance appear to be small, this novel is a valuable and welcome reminder of the importance of that second look.
STIRLING OBSERVER

Bodywork

Dilys Rose

ISBN 1 905222 93 9 PBK £8.99

How do we feel about the flesh that surrounds us and how do we deal with the knowledge that it will eventually do so no more? How do our bodies affect our emotional, physical and spiritual lives?

Winner of the 2006 McCash prize, Dilys Rose's third collection of poetry focuses on the human body in all its glory, comedy and frailty; on the quirks, hazards and conundrums of physiology; on intimations of mortality – and immortality. Rose draws fully-grown characters in a few vivid strokes; from a body double to a cannibal queen, their souls are personified in a limb, affliction or skill. These poems get under your skin and into your bones – you'll never look at the human body in the same way again!

Dilys Rose exposes and illuminates humanity with scalpel sharpness... ingeniously exciting, quirky and perceptive.
JANET PAISLEY, THE SCOTSMAN

It's an extraordinary book, brave and unusual, full of unexpected insights and delights – and a consistent compassion, respect and reverence for the human body, in all its oddity and complexity.
CATHERINE SMITH

The Fatal Sleep

Peter Kennedy

ISBN 1 905222 67 X HBK £20.00

The bite of the tsetse fly – a burning sting into the skin – causes a descent into violent fever and aching pains. Severe bouts of insomnia are followed by mental deterioration, disruption of the nervous system, coma and ultimately death.

Sleeping sickness, also known as human African trypanosomiasis, is one of Africa's major killers. It puts 60 million people at risk of infection, occurs in 36 countries in sub-Saharan Africa, and claims the lives of many thousands of people every year.

Transmitted by the tsetse fly, trypanoso-miasis affects both humans and cattle. The animal form of the disease severely limits livestock production and farming, and in people the toxic effects of the treatment can be as painful and dangerous as the disease itself.

Existing in the shadow of malaria and aids, it is an overlooked disease, largely ignored by pharmaceutical companies and neglected by the western world.

This is a remarkable book. It is filled in equal measure with passion for science and compassion for the people afflicted with this cruel disease.
SIR ROGER BANNISTER

Napiers History of Herbal Healing

Tom Atkinson

ISBN 1 905222 01 7 PBK £8.99

What are black spleenwort, figwort and toadflax and how are they traditionally used?

How did Scottish herbalism develop from its crude Celtic roots into widely-used alternative medicine?

In what ways has the practice of herbalism changed in modern times from the Victorian world in which Duncan Napier founded Napiers?

Herbalism is the oldest form of medicine in the world. It has been practised for thousands of years, and is still the most widely-used method of healing in existence. This concise history reveals the development of herbalism through the ages, a unique journey from Neolithic Kurdistan to present-day Edinburgh.

It also contains the casebook and autobiography of Duncan Napier, a Victorian practitioner of herbal medicine, with notes from a modern herbalist. From the creation of Lobelia Syrup for coughing to the 48 foot tapeworm, the history of Napiers makes for fascinating reading.

Luath Press Limited
committed to publishing well written books worth reading

LUATH PRESS takes its name from Robert Burns, whose little collie Luath (*Gael.*, swift or nimble) tripped up Jean Armour at a wedding and gave him the chance to speak to the woman who was to be his wife and the abiding love of his life. Burns called one of 'The Twa Dogs' Luath after Cuchullin's hunting dog in Ossian's *Fingal*. Luath Press was established in 1981 in the heart of Burns country, and now resides a few steps up the road from Burns' first lodgings on Edinburgh's Royal Mile.
Luath offers you distinctive writing with a hint of unexpected pleasures.

Most bookshops in the UK, the US, Canada, Australia, New Zealand and parts of Europe either carry our books in stock or can order them for you. To order direct from us, please send a £sterling cheque, postal order, international money order or your credit card details (number, address of cardholder and expiry date) to us at the address below. Please add post and packing as follows: UK – £1.00 per delivery address; overseas surface mail – £2.50 per delivery address; overseas airmail – £3.50 for the first book to each delivery address, plus £1.00 for each additional book by airmail to the same address. If your order is a gift, we will happily enclose your card or message at no extra charge.

Luath Press Limited
543/2 Castlehill
The Royal Mile
Edinburgh EH1 2ND
Scotland
Telephone: 0131 225 4326 (24 hours)
Fax: 0131 225 4324
email: sales@luath.co.uk
Website: www.luath.co.uk